Colossus

by
Craig Thompson

Published by Thompson Publishers

Thompson Publishers
https://thompsonpublishers.com

Colossus

Edited by David Thompson.

Requests for information should be addressed to:
Thompson Publishers, PO Box 2605, Cleveland TN 37320-2605

ISBN: 978-1-64407-012-3 [print]
ISBN: 978-1-64407-013-0 [ebook]

Cover design Craig Thompson © 2020.

Image of statue by Goran Horvat from Pixabay. Image of millstone by skeeze from Pixabay. Binary code image by Carsten Mueller from FreeImages.

Printed in the USA.
First printing.

Contents

"Do not attack a poor man with family or friends. Though he may have not material wealth, his greatest strength lies in the breadth and depth of his relationships. You may find that the cup of tea you are drinking was poisoned by a fifth cousin who bears the offense as deeply as if it were his own."

Donald, Steward at the Lion's Head

At that time, there were some who were reporting to him about the Galileans whose blood Pilate had mixed with their sacrifices. He responded to them by saying, "Do you think that these Galileans were greater sinners than all other Galileans because they suffered this way? Not at all. I tell you that if you do not change your ways, all of you will be destroyed, too."

Jesus of Nazareth (Luke 13:1-3)

Prologue

The Don sat in his leather club chair calmly enjoying the view out the window of his villa overlooking the sea. In one hand he held a hand-rolled cigar. In the other he held the fate of two men.

The door to his study opened just wide enough for Antonio to peer around the iron-banded wooden frame. "They're here, sir," he announced..

The Don glanced across the room to Antonio's face. "Show them in," he said.

The door closed. The Don listened to Antonio's footsteps echo across the black and white marble floor. Not for the first time, the Don was reminded that the acoustics of the villa made it very difficult, if not impossible, to approach his study without being detected. A maze of cameras and sensors in the villa and around the grounds also aided the security.

Not that anyone would attempt such a feat. The villa itself was at the end of a long road through gradually rising hills which led to the highest point for many kilometers. The surrounding farmland was owned and worked by men who understood clearly that it was in their best interests both to observe boundaries as well as to notify the Don's staff of anyone seen to be approaching either out of ignorance, curiosity or less-than-pure motives. Then there were the three rings of hedges, the nasty, impenetrable kind of pyracantha which were interwoven and whose Creator had chosen to endow them with a particularly abusive thorn. Other than a handful of trusted men, the only other occupants besides the Don who were allowed to roam the grounds freely were the dogs, a cluster of bull mastiffs (for sheer terror value) and Dobermans (for speed and efficiency). Unlike human guards, the dogs were much more random in their movements, and even if they slept, their noses and ears were still on high alert.

For all practical purposes, the Don was untouchable. He was the head of one of the most powerful crime syndicates with tentacles running through every major city and fingers in every crime pie which either generated significant profit or served as a support system for the ones which did. His few public appearances were usually in the company of heads of state or

1

entertainment icons whose enormous influence in the public square had been funded by none other than the Don through his intermediaries.

There was a knock on the door. Antonio was returning with his guests. "Enter," the Don said firmly. The broad wooden door opened wide, and Antonio gestured to a couch placed opposite the Don's chair. The two men, dressed casually in tailored suits, seated themselves across from the Don. The taller of the two, Aldo, leaned back comfortably, while Liberto sat on the edge of his chair with his arms crossed over his knees. Antonio motioned through the doorway to someone outside the room and then seated himself on a stool against the rough-hewn bar in the corner. From where he sat, he had a clear view of each of the participants.

"Gentlemen," said the Don, "I presume you know why we're having this little gathering today?"

Liberto's eyes darted to Aldo and then focused on the Don. "Yes, sir."

Aldo nodded in affirmation.

"Good," said the Don, addressing Liberto directly. "Perhaps you can begin by explaining how three shipments out of our Gioia Tauro operations were raided by Interpol."

"I don't know. I swear to you that it came as a complete shock to me," said Liberto.

"Three shipments in a row were raided and over €20,000,000 worth of our product was seized, and you have no ideas about how this happened?" the Don asked in a fatherly tone. "Really, Liberto, I would have expected you to at least have some theories. You do have at least some theories, don't you?"

Liberto swallowed. His eyes darted to Aldo again. "I—I don't want to make baseless accusations without proof," he started.

"But you have some theories," the Don repeated.

"Yes. After the first raid, I gave orders that the next shipment two weeks later would be relocated to one of our secondary warehouses in a different district. When that warehouse was raided, I took drastic measures. I informed our supplier that we could not accept anything coming through Suez directly. He must deliver all the way to Port Said. He was very resistant due to the extra risk it placed upon him, but I told him that we would pay a bonus of twenty percent for this arrangement. We agreed on a ship and a date. The delivery was to be made to a third warehouse in a completely separate area of Gioia Tauro. No sooner had our men placed the shipping containers into the warehouse than they were accosted by the police. It's as if..." Here he paused.

"Go on," nudged the Don.

"It's as if they had all the information handed to them on a platter," said Liberto.

"But who was privy to the details for each of the three shipments?" asked the Don.

Liberto swallowed hard. "Only I was. And the supplier. The crews were informed only when the ships had arrived. Each crew was different. I made sure of that."

"How did you communicate with the supplier and the crews?" asked the Don.

"I created new email accounts for each contact with the supplier based on our prearranged system of addresses. Once I logged into the account, I created a draft message and left it for him to read. He responded. The same as always. Then the draft was deleted and the account closed."

The Don nodded.

"For the crews, I used separate burner phones to make the call to each crew chief. I even made the calls from different locations the second and third times in case my office or home were bugged."

Aldo squinted and looked sideways at Liberto. "It sounds as if you are digging a deeper hole for yourself, Libi."

"I'm not the one who compromised the shipments!" Liberto turned to face Aldo. "I've followed all of our precautions to the letter. Every time I connected to the email accounts, I always used our Internet security to protect my identity, just as I was instructed. I have the same protections on all of my phones, even the burner ones, as well as my office and home computers."

Had either of the men been looking at the Don, they would have seen a flicker of recognition pass through his eyes for a brief moment.

"But if your security precautions are to the letter, then either the supplier is compromised or you are," said Aldo. "We've built a relationship with this supplier for over twenty years. He knows his business as well as his life would be worthless if he gave up his customers."

Liberto looked around desperately. This meeting was going far from the direction he hoped it would. He focused his eyes on the Don. "I did everything just as I was supposed to," he said.

The Don remained impassive, his eyes studying Liberto. Here was a man who had been in his organization since his coming of age. His father before him had been an enforcer before rising to become a mid-level lieutenant. He knew the consequences of betrayal. Why would a man even contemplate such a thing knowing the results if caught? And few ever got away with medium-sized graft from the organization, much less this level of behavior.

"Are you sure you have always followed our security protocols to the letter?" he asked Liberto.

Liberto nodded.

"Every single time with no exceptions?"

Liberto swallowed and nodded again.

The Don looked down at his left hand. "Then it appears that you really have sold us out."

The two men sat in silence. Liberto knew that protesting his innocence would bring no change once the Don had made a decision. In the other chair, Aldo's features relaxed slightly. This was very unfortunate for Liberto, but it could mean many big opportunities for himself. He knew it. The Don certainly knew it.

The Don opened his left hand, which had been closed during the entire interview. With his right he began to unfold a small piece of note paper. As he looked at it, he began to speak. "It was almost foolproof. The fact that the police raided only the three largest shipments out of Gioia Tauro put the focus clearly on you, Liberto. No small shipments were interrupted. Only the large, ripe plums were plucked. The security protocols seemed to be followed to the letter. We even investigated the supplier and his pipeline thoroughly. They all checked out. Both of you know what this type of betrayal would mean for you, Liberto, and the opportunities for you, Aldo. But you made one mistake, a grave one." The inflection upon that word was slight but unmistakable.

"You used the Internet security program to connect to the email accounts every time except for one. That single time was from a different Internet address. We traced it to a phone." Here, the Don looked directly at Liberto.

"But I know that I followed protocol every single time," he protested.

"Yes," said the Don. "I'm sure that you believe that to be very true. The phone was not yours."

Confusion covered Liberto's face. "Then who..." he started to say.

The Don continued. "It was good. Our boys with the computer skills tell me it was really, really good. We had to use not one but two of our higher-up assets in the police to get to the bottom of this. But they tell me that every one of your personal and business computers and your phone are all compromised. It's apparently some type of program which can be bought from hackers for a pretty large sum. It's been going on for a few months. The person was able to know what email accounts you set up for the supplier and even record the passwords to the accounts. The person could even copy your Internet security settings in order to access the email accounts so that it would appear to only be you. All except for one time."

He switched his gaze to Aldo. "The phone was yours, Aldo."

A look of complete horror fell across Aldo's face. His mouth went dry. He jerked his gaze from the Don to Liberto to the empty seat where Antonio was no longer seated. Suddenly he became very aware of someone standing directly behind him. He turned slowly and saw Antonio, a pistol in his hand calmly leveled at him.

He turned again. "Don, you have to believe me. I would never betray you, our organization, my oath. I swear on my mother's grave…"

"Aldo, it's not your mother's grave of which you should be thinking. All of the control pieces of the software are right there on your own computer. The boys have already checked. I only want to know who else was involved. I don't want to waste good men if they are not part of this."

Aldo was sweating profusely now. "Don, I don't know anything about this. I have never paid anyone for such software. I wouldn't even know where to look or how to use it!"

The Don gave a small smile. "Aldo, like I said. This was very, very good. The boys could not find any large payments coming out of your operating accounts or even your personal accounts. What they did find, however, were a series of cash withdrawals you had marked down for entertainment purposes, such as food and drink and other things. When they added those up, they came up to the amount necessary to buy such software. When we put the word out, we located a group in Bulgaria who admitted to selling the software. Their contact, a lady in Sophia, confirmed your identity when we showed her your photo. Apparently, you traveled there in person to pick up the goods directly in order to avoid having any electronic traces of the purchase."

Aldo was trembling now. "Don, please, I traveled to Sophia for personal pleasure. I met no lady to purchase hacking software. I would never betray you!"

"Or Liberto?" the Don asked. "What about him? You knew coming in here today that his life hung by a small thread. Again, I ask you: was this your own idea? Were you working with someone else? Were you trying to set up your own operation, or were you trying to split the organization? Or maybe you were just greedy? Were you not happy with your cut of the doll shipments?"

"I know nothing of this!" Aldo looked at Liberto. "I would never set you up like this!"

The Don looked back down at the paper. "It was your phone, Aldo. Your phone which connected to the email server. It was you who had the access to the details of the shipments. It was you who leaked the details to Interpol."

Aldo began sobbing. "It wasn't me. It wasn't me. How can I get you to believe me?"

The Don spoke in a fatherly tone. "I knew your father and your mother, Aldo. They were good people. For their sake, I'm glad they're not alive to know about this. Do their memory a favor and go quietly with Antonio."

The squeeze of a hand on Aldo's shaking shoulder signified that the interview was over. He looked at Liberto, whose eyes had now changed from fear to contempt. Then he looked at the Don one last time, his gaze imploring more time, forgiveness, a belief that he was not the culprit. The Don dismissed his gaze by looking down at the paper in his hand and crushing it into a ball.

Aldo rose and walked quietly out of the room with Antonio.

Liberto exhaled a deep sigh of relief and placed his head in his hands. He realized that the roles could have been reversed. After a few moments of silence and collecting his thoughts, he looked up at the Don. "Sir, all of the evidence pointed toward me. Why did you not believe the evidence? Why did you choose to look deeper to verify my innocence?"

The Don looked at Liberto for a full minute, his eyes searching, evaluating, then lost in thought somewhere else while still looking at Liberto.

"I was given a tip," he said. "A tip that we had a Brutus in our midst. And that it wasn't you."

The Don retreated into his thoughts. With Aldo gone, who would take over the doll shipments? How long would it take to find someone who could be trusted with that level of responsibility? And more importantly, had Aldo conspired with anyone else, or was he simply greedy?

Chapter 1

Italy
Present Day

Dona Martinez was out of sorts. The cafe would be opening for business soon, and her busboy was unable to come to work because of what sounded like a bad case of slightly old shellfish. She brushed a wisp of hair back and looked around. Tables had to be set outside with cloths to cover them, place settings arranged and the sidewalk had to be swept for cigarette butts and the detritus the nighttime wind had deposited in every nook and cranny.

Well, there was nothing for it. After sweeping the sidewalk, Dona began lifting a table in order to move it outside. She tried flinging the door open and putting the table ahead of her. After catching a table leg on the doorjamb and abruptly stopping her progress mid-abdomen, she decided to walk backwards dragging the table behind her. This led her to the swift conclusion that the table was most certainly wider than the doorway.

As her mind was calculating her next move, a voice behind her interrupted her thoughts.

"Would you like some assistance?" The question was measured in its words, if not peasant in its delivery.

Dona turned and saw a man with tanned skin and muscular forearms looking at her inquisitively with the most striking pale grey eyes she had ever seen. The whole effect of this genetic anomaly caught her off guard such that she could only stare at the man until she realized that she was doing so. "I, uh, yes. Yes, I certainly could use some help. My hired boy is sick, and I'm running late to get the cafe open."

"Then I will be happy to assist you," said the man with a pleasant smile.

"I can pay you for your time," said Dona.

The man smiled again. "I did not ask for a job. I just offered to help."

Dona relaxed. "Thank you so much then…"

"Pietro," said the man.

"I'm Dona. And we need ten tables out here with chairs, cloths and place settings. And the umbrellas need to be opened and put into position." She paused and looked at him again. "I'm sorry. I'm very pressed for time. I don't mean to be rude."

"You do what you need to do inside, and I will take care of this for you," said Pietro.

Dona needed no more prompting. The morning crowd would be arriving soon for their coffees and pastries. And shortly after that, Giacobbe Manco had arranged to have a meeting in the private room. It would be a short half hour before the serving staff arrived to begin their tasks, and food needed to be prepared before then. She turned and strode inside briskly.

While she was preparing, she heard a pattern of chairs and tables being lifted, the door opening and closing and the occasional "whump" of a sidewalk umbrella being opened. Once, she glanced up from her work to see Pietro with four chairs in one hand and in the other a table being lifted by a single leg. It was startling enough that she watched to see how he would make it outside. When he reached the door, he placed the table on its side so gently that she could not hear it touch the tile floor. Then he opened the door and flicked it with just enough energy that it angled toward the wall but didn't slam against it like it did with her hired help—or even some of her customers. While this was in progress, the hand with the chairs went out the door while the other hand picked up the table angled such that two legs went out first, followed by the other two. All without touching the doorjamb. This visual ensemble was completed by the door slowly swinging shut while the table and chairs were already being put into position.

Dona shook her head to herself. He may speak like a farmer, but he had the grace of a ballerina.

An hour and a half later, the morning rush had begun to slow down. Dona remembered Pietro and asked one of the waitresses, "What happened to the man who was helping me?"

"He's outside doing something to the sidewalk," she said.

Perplexed, Dona walked outside to see Pietro lying prostrate on the ground near one of the tables. One hand held a small hammer, and in the other was an odd-looking chisel. Beside him was a growing pile of chips. Pietro caught sight of Dona and said, "There was a big bump in the sidewalk here. It looked dangerous, especially for an older person or someone with limited sight."

Dona nodded. "I've called the public works department many times, and they assure me they will send someone out to take care of it. But they never come." She walked closer and inspected the spot. What had been a protrusion of concrete and paving stone in the shape of a small mountain range was now as smooth as river rock.

8

She looked again at Pietro. He was sweeping up the stone chips into a dustpan, which he had apparently borrowed from one of the staff. He walked over to a public waste bin and poured the chips into it. After returning, he looked down at his work and said, "I think that is safer now."

Dona nodded again as she looked at the smooth sidewalk. One of the city workers with a grinding tool would have left a mess and probably several divots. "Yes. Thank you, Pietro." She looked at him and said, "How much do I owe you for this?"

"I told you. I did not ask you for a job. I offered to assist you."

"Yes, but this is more than just moving tables and chairs. I have had customers trip over this more than once. I need to pay you something."

"You need not trouble yourself over it," said Pietro.

"Have you eaten?" asked Dona.

"No, not yet," he answered.

"Then come. Let me fix you a proper meal."

"Only if you let me pay for it properly," Pietro said.

Dona fixed him with her gaze. She was pleasant enough in her public persona, but her staff and not a few of her unruly customers had learned that she was no pushover. "There will be no paying for this meal," she said firmly.

Pietro smiled the biggest she had seen yet. "You win," he said and followed her into the cafe.

After she had prepared a dish of hot sausage and eggs with a platter of fruit and some of her best pastries, she brought it to his table. Pietro had already washed up and, other than a bit of dust on his pants, appeared no different than he had when he showed up three hours earlier.

"Thank you," he said as she placed the array of food on the cafe table. He had chosen to sit inside, although only half of the outside tables were occupied at this point. She would have sat down and visited with him, but one of the waitresses announced, "Dona, he's here."

Dona looked up and saw the shiny form of a Lamborghini Murciélago as it pulled along the sidewalk and stopped. Although not technically a parking zone, the car would not be ticketed. As the gull-wing door opened, and a handsome man in casual attire stepped out, Dona spoke to the staff. "Is everything ready?"

"Yes," one of them answered.

"Excuse me," Dona said to Pietro. "I have a customer who has an appointment for our private room."

Pietro glanced outside. "Please, do what you must. I have plenty of food to keep me occupied."

With that, Dona was away to the door. Giacobbe had not reached it before Dona was there opening it and greeting him. "Welcome, Mr. Manco," she said in her cheerful and gracious tone.

"Thank you, Dona. And every time I ask you to call me Giacobbe." He entered the shop and took in the whole picture with a quick glance, his eyes lingering for a moment on Pietro, who was busy with a piece of fruit. "Who is he?" he asked.

"His name is Pietro. I haven't seen him before. He offered to help me this morning when Samel was unable to work."

"What else do you know of him?"

"He speaks like a farmer, and he is very strong like one. But he is strange. He fixed that nasty bulge in the sidewalk out front using a chisel and hammer which he apparently carries with him."

Giacobbe's eyebrow raised. "Did he now? How well did he fix it?"

"It's smooth, not the hack job the city workers would have done."

"Interesting." Giacobbe glanced back at Pietro, who was still cutting slices of fruit and eating them, and then turned to Dona. "The priest will be here soon. After you take his order and deliver it, I'll ring the bell if we require further service."

Giacobbe walked through the cafe to the rear. As he passed by Pietro's table, he glanced down at him. Pietro was now head down devouring a pastry. The man wasn't overly curious. Typical of farmers, he thought as he entered the private dining room.

Fifteen minutes later a man in business attire walked through the front door. He was clothed in a modest-looking tailored suit. He could have passed for any number of mid-level business owners in any Italian city were it not for the glimpse of a clerical collar peeking from under his ample chin. His face was set with the look of a man who had heard many secrets and had borne them in privacy. There was a kindly and worried smile which was affixed to his features, and the casual observer would have accounted to him a level of piety which would be counted proper for one in his religious station. Only on a more careful examination of the face and especially the deeper consideration of his eyes would one be left with a sense of discord. Upon entering a room, he had long practiced the habit of setting his face to bestow a custodial blessing upon those who might look at him while his eyes were steadily scanning the room in order to assess its occupants. At this moment, his eyes had quickly moved past the routine occupants and were studying

Pietro. Two seconds, then they flickered to Dona, who was approaching him with her smile.

"Father Donati, welcome!" She offered him her cheek and received the appropriate peck of greeting.

"Dona, how are you, my daughter?"

"It has been very busy this morning."

"Ah, well, you seem to have kept things in order in spite of it." He looked to the rear of the cafe. "I saw his car out front. He is here already?"

"Yes, waiting patiently. Do you want to give me your order now, or would you like to think about it?"

"No, I want your wonderful veal. Go light on the pasta."

"I will."

Dona smiled. They both knew that she would fix the priest an ample portion, and they both knew that he would eat it and enjoy it. She returned to the kitchen, leaving him to walk slowly through the restaurant greeting the patrons, pausing to acknowledge a welcome or to offer a word of consolation to those expressing a need. When he arrived at the rear of the cafe, he paused at Pietro's table and affixed him with his benevolent smile.

"Blessings, my son. I do not believe I have met you before. I'm Father Donati."

Pietro looked up from his table at the priest. His relaxed features were a blank slate, and with his eyelids slightly drooped, he manifested the provincial appearance the priest had been obliged to serve these many years.

"Hello, Father. I'm Pietro," he said simply.

He glanced at the priest's face and briefly held his gaze before lowering his eyes. They both had seen exactly what they expected—although on Father Donati's part, not exactly what was reality.

"What brings you to our area, Pietro?"

"I am looking for work." The answer was repeated weekly if not daily by the transients.

"Perhaps I can help you. What type of work do you seek?"

"I am strong and can do many types of labor," said Pietro.

"Yes," said Father Donati. "Many strong young men have come through looking for work. Do you have any particular skills which would set you apart from others?"

"I have been told that I am skilled in carving," Pietro said.

11

The priest was pleased with this answer. Here was a man who did not assume enough to assert his own talents. "How skilled are you, Pietro? What type of carving have you done?"

"I have made many walls…"

"Brick?" the priest interrupted.

"Stone. Chiseled," continued Pietro.

"Any other types of carving besides walls?"

"I like to do sculptures," said Pietro.

"Really? Do you have any pictures of your sculptures, Pietro?"

Pietro fumbled in his pockets and produced an older model phone. He stared at it for a few moments as if struggling to remember its intricacies and then located his photo gallery. After poking at it and staring, he offered the phone to the priest.

Father Donati had long practiced the ability to maintain his composure in the face of any revelation, but Pietro caught a glimpse of something more than stoic impassiveness as the priest studied the photo. "May I?" he asked, motioning as if to swipe to other photos.

"Please, help yourself," said Pietro.

After swiping through the photos to the left and right for about ten selections each direction with a look of some intensity, the priest returned the phone to Pietro. "It seems you have understated your abilities, my son. I may be able to locate some work for you sooner than if you were just a common laborer." The benevolent smile had returned.

"Thank you, father," Pietro said, accepting the phone and returning it to his pocket.

"I'm always available to help anyone who is in the boundaries of my flock." He turned to leave and then turned back. "Here is my card," he said as he offered it to Pietro. "Would you please call me or text me so I can contact you with any job opportunities I find?"

"I will call you," said Pietro. "Text, not so much." He shrugged.

"I understand. I look forward to it."

And with that, the priest turned from the table and strode into the private dining room. Pietro watched his back for a full three seconds before speaking under his breath, "Sì. I am certain that you do." He rose from the table and walked to the front of the shop where Dona was speaking with an elderly couple at a table. She turned and met him halfway. "Did you enjoy the meal?" she asked.

"I was just coming to tell you thank you for it," said Pietro.

"No. It is I who am thankful to you for making my day start with a smile rather than stress to my neck. Did you have a good talk with our priest?"

"It seems that I may have found work not once but twice today," said Pietro. "He offered to find me a job doing what I love best—sculpting."

"Father Donati is a good man," Dona said.

Pietro held her gaze. "All priests are supposed to be good." Then, changing the subject, he said, "Do you need anything else before I go?"

"No. You have done more than I ever expected." She reached up and patted him gently on the cheek. "I do thank you for fixing that terrible bump in the sidewalk. I have been cursing it for years—and the public works department."

"I was glad to help," said Pietro as he made to leave. "Perhaps I will see you again soon. Your food is very good."

Dona laughed. "Flattery! But I will believe you and enjoy the compliment. Goodbye."

Pietro nodded and walked out the door. It was not yet noon, and the day was already a success.

Chapter 2

"I'm telling you that the man is gifted like no one I have seen in my lifetime," said Father Donati. He looked up from his veal, the pasta already gone. "The man has the touch of someone like Michelangelo."

"That's high praise, Prete," said Giacobbe. He used the term both as a jest and as a sign of their long and deep friendship. "So far, we have found no one in all our searching who can fulfill the job, and here is the man deposited on our doorstep. Does that not trouble you in the least?"

"I will look into him. Who knows the people of a region more than the priests?"

"The prostitutes, pimps and drug dealers, for a start," said Giacobbe. "But I'm being redundant." He chuckled.

Father Donati scowled. "The church has done much good throughout the ages," he said.

"You have no argument from me that its founder was a good man," said Giacobbe. "But we both grew up knowing that business is what matters to our leaders." He fixed Father Donati with a firm look. "And that is why we have been searching for the right person to complete the tasks necessary for this job. We can wait long enough to ensure that we find that right person and not just accept a skilled hand who may blow the whole plan."

"That's no longer true," said the priest as he wiped his face with a cloth napkin. "The project has gone from being a simple investment to being one of the top priorities." He looked straight at Giacobbe. "From the highest authority."

Giacobbe sat back in his chair. "The Holy Father knows about this?"

Father Donati nodded. "Knows, and not only approves but has stated that it be given a higher status. Of course, there are a few modifications to the plan, but I was told that with the correct exposure, along with some well-timed leaks, this could net well over two hundred million euro. Net, not gross."

Now Giacobbe was fully attentive. "What happened to this being a low-level project to introduce to the medium-sized museums and collectors?"

"The economy," said the priest. "That, and some poor timing on the part of the lawsuits surrounding the scandals of the American priesthood." He shook his head in disgust. "The Americans always were sloppy about how they handled those children. Now they are costing us more than anyone realized."

They sat in silence for a few minutes, the priest savoring Dona's veal and Giacobbe sipping from his glass.

"Okay," he said finally. "But I still want to use a cutout for the initial evaluation of this peasant while you do your research on him."

Father Donati nodded. "Agreed. I will make calls today. If he has a name, he has to have a place and a history. He has agreed to call me. Where should I send him?"

"Send him to the clothier on the square," said Giacobbe. "He will tell him that he wants to surprise his wife with a gift for their anniversary. Something small but detailed enough to test his work."

"It has to be stone," said Father Donati. "And it has to be quick."

"It will," said Giacobbe. "I will check in after one or two days to look at his work myself. If it shows promise, then the owner will complain that his work is unsatisfactory and chase him out of his shop. That will free him up for our work."

Father Donati rose from his seat. He stared down at the empty plate. He wished there had been more pasta. "The Holy Father is concerned that whoever is involved in this be trustworthy, loyal and able to be controlled. If this project goes well, there is a desire to expand the project here as well as beyond Italy. There is a belief that with proper handling, this could serve the needs of the church very well."

"I don't like working in haste, but I do appreciate a good challenge," said Giacobbe. "Let's see what the next two days bring us, shall we?" He also rose from his chair. Leaving a generous amount of money on the table, he walked with Father Donati out of the café, pausing only to thank Dona for her excellent food.

Two men, lost in their thoughts, returned to their domains. The priest began making calls as he walked back to his office. Giacobbe made a call to the clothier. Patience was now the key.

Chapter 3

It took Father Donati longer to find what he was looking for than he thought. First, he had to deal with the troublesome fact that he had not, in fact, asked Pietro his last name or exactly where he was from. But the clerical grapevine has deep roots. On no less than the twelfth call, he hit pay dirt. The priest was someone he knew—and despised—from his college days. He was one of the radicals who believed that the vows were to be truly embraced by the heart. To Father Donati, people like him put a whole new spin on the phrase "one-percenters."

The priest, one Father Darien, served in a parish deep in the farming country, right where Father Donati suspected he would find Pietro's history. His work there included one of the orphanages which dotted the country. At first, the priest had been hesitant to respond to Father Donati's inquiry, but when Father Donati told him that he was looking to help Pietro secure work with a wealthy patron who required the most exacting references, he relented.

Pietro, he explained, had been orphaned at an early age. What had happened to his parents was shrouded in mystery, but the loss had been catastrophic to the young child. When he arrived at the orphanage, he did not speak at all for years. The nuns had at first considered him to be a deaf mute and likely mentally deficient. But that had proven not to be the case.

Over time, the boy had shown not just a knack but a complete gifting for art, specifically working with stone of all kinds. The first time this was noticed, he was found by one of the nuns with the groundskeeper's hammer and a screwdriver tapping on a foundation stone. Horrified, the nun had rushed to reprimand the boy, but as she approached, she saw that he had almost completed an engraving of a bird, unmistakably a dove, in the stone. So lifelike was the appearance that the nun was left speechless. Rather than scold him, she wisely and quietly spoke to him to finish what he had begun.

Being one of the kinder-hearted nuns, this stroke of fortune (or providence, the priest had said) resulted in her taking Pietro under her wing. She began to provide him such meager tools as her own ability allowed. A hammer and a few chisels were slowly collected, and with each addition, Pietro's work began to blossom from engravings to rudimentary sculptures.

When asked why he was able to engrave so well but not sculpt with equal skill, a local craftsman responded that they were providing him with the wrong stone. In retrospect, that should have been obvious, but to those uninitiated in production of the finer arts, it was a simple mistake. The nun began to seek out cast-offs from the surrounding craftsmen and merchants, and almost immediately the sculptures began to match the quality of Pietro's engravings.

The priest would have gushed on about his prodigy, but Father Donati asked him to abbreviate the story with more recent and pertinent details. Pietro, he was told, had begun to talk one day out of the blue as if he had always done so. Although greatly shocked, the nun responded as if they had been conversing for years. Since that time, their insight into the young man grew slightly. He was brilliant in his artistic ability. He was more of a peasant in his mind, at least from what the priest could discern. Still, there was always a sense of mystery about him, as if down deep there was an untapped reservoir of greatness waiting to be discovered.

This was all very exciting news to Father Donati, and had it been true, it would have exactly the confirmation that he had been seeking in his recommendation for what was now the Vatican's project. The skill with which the parish priest set forth the story spoke less about the facts of Pietro's past and more about Father Darien's own understanding of what was considered permissible in the building of God's holy kingdom here on earth. That Pietro had never set foot in his orphanage, at least as a child, was matched only in truth by the priest's equal contempt for Father Donati. It was less about the man himself, although there was much he despised about him, but mostly it was what the parish priest recognized to be the sickness which Father Donati represented under the guise of Christendom.

The phone call concluded with mutual well-wishes in their respective works, neither of which was anywhere as sincere as the goals which each hoped would be accomplished by the call. Father Donati was satisfied that someone whom he knew to be at odds with him personally would vouch for the background of Pietro, for though he cared not for the parish priest's piety, he acknowledged that it bound him to tell the truth. And with that, he was content to push forward with the story he had heard, even though the retelling might result in embellishments of his own.

On the parish priest's part, he was happy to play a small role in a play which he did not fully understand but that he hoped would accomplish at least some level of cleansing in the ranks of those who called themselves the representatives of God but whose entanglements with the world system blotted out any semblance of reality of that. He would make confession of and penance for his untruths soon enough. He rather wondered if any were actually deserved, given the nature of Father Donati and all that he knew of him from the past and had heard of him since.

Father Donati's next decision was whether to wait patiently for Pietro to phone him or to seek to locate him by some measure of searching. While he was weighing alternately the urgency with which he had been pressed by the Vatican's representative and the need to maintain the appearance of appearing too eager to help someone of low station, his thoughts were interrupted by the sound of his own phone ringing. He checked the number: unknown. He stared at it wondering if he could be so fortunate to have his quandary solved. He cleared his throat and answered it.

"Father Donati speaking."

It was Pietro.

"Father Donati. This is Pietro. We met this morning at the cafe."

"Yes, Pietro. How are you, my son?"

"Well, I have just spent the past two hours at the local employment office filling out papers and looking for work. They say it will take some time to process my file. While I wait, I wanted to see if there is anything I can do for you at the church as a way of saying thank you for showing interest in my needs this morning."

"Pietro, bless you. I have no need of any work at the moment..."

"Oh. In that case..."

"But I do have what I believe is some good news—for you."

There was a pause. "You have news for me? What news is that?"

"It appears that Providence has smiled upon you, my son. I was speaking with someone earlier, and it seems that a certain merchant here in town is looking for an anniversary gift for his wife. He wants it to be very special, and he is particularly interested in a small work of art, a sculpture. After seeing your work this morning, I recommended you wholeheartedly. I hope you are interested, yes?"

"I...Of course, yes. Yes, I would. Thank you so much!"

"Excellent. Are you familiar with the central district with all of the merchant shops?"

"Yes, I am a little."

"On the square, there is one large merchant who sells some of the finest clothing for men and women. The name is Giovanni's. It is in gold lettering on a black field."

"I have seen it."

"Good. You are to go there at once. Ask for the owner and tell him that you are the man Father Donati recommended for the gift."

"Father Donati, I don't know what to say."

"No need to thank me, my son. It is one of my greatest joys to be able to help those in need. And when an answer to our needs comes so suddenly, we can all thank Providence. Perhaps if you do a good job, more opportunities will arise. Signor Giovanni is a well-respected man in the community. His good word could mean a great deal."

"Yes. I will do my very best for him. Thank you again, Father."

After ending the phone call with Pietro, Father Donati placed two more. The first was to Alberto Giovanni to notify him that Pietro would be coming perhaps a bit sooner than anyone would have expected and to be ready. After that, he called Giacobbe to inform him of the details on Pietro's background. Giacobbe listened quietly as Father Donati recounted the information given to him by the parish priest. When he was finished, Giacobbe asked only if Father Donati was satisfied with the accuracy of the information.

"I am," he said. "Father Darien was known for nothing if not his piety. Heaven knows he was good for little else in seminary. He made few friends among the movers and shakers in our class."

"Then it is settled. Now we wait to see how good our new sculptor really is. I will let you know when I have heard from Giovanni on his progress and what I find."

Chapter 4

As it turned out, their carefully constructed plan was unnecessary. Pietro met Signor Giovanni at his shop and conferred with him on what he desired for his anniversary gift to his wife. It was determined that Signora Giovanni was particularly fond of the classical depiction of the cherub angel (it had previously been decided by Father Donati and Giacobbe that, for their purposes, animals and inanimate objects were to be avoided). In order to prevent any leaking of the gift to Signora Giovanni, Pietro was to work in a semi-secluded storeroom on the upper floors of the clothing shop if that were acceptable to him. After reviewing the room in question, Pietro assured Signor Giovanni that the room was sufficient, especially if he could provide one or more powerful window fans to serve as a bit of a vacuum for the dust which invariably filled the room of a stone craftsman. The fans were ordered at once by an assistant, and the only thing which remained was for the arrangement of the purchase and delivery of stone suitable for the piece itself.

Pietro asked for a certain marble with rose hue available from a regional quarry. The calls were made, the rush order was placed, and the stone block was set to be delivered along with sufficient heavy lifters as early the next day as could reasonably be done. In the meantime, Pietro was turned over to an assistant who handled the details he requested for a table adequate in strength for the weight of the stone, a second smaller table to hold his tools, three powerful floor lamps, and a comfortable chair and side table. When these were all in place, Pietro dismissed the assistant and spent careful time studying the room from all angles. Then he turned out the lights and left for the day after confirming with Signor Giovanni that he would arrive in the morning prior to the delivery.

The next morning, Pietro arrived with a bag in each hand, one noticeably heavier than the other. He greeted Signor Giovanni and then showed himself up to the workroom. He found two powerful fans, which he placed near the windows, and then opened the windows. The sounds of the square drifted through the open frames at once and provided a low hum of background noise. He arranged the table and chair to his liking so that he could face the table from a short distance. He then opened his first bag, removed a long felt cloth and arranged his hand tools in order. From the second bag he withdrew an older model radio complete with collapsible antenna, which he placed along the side wall and plugged into an outlet. He switched on the radio and found a station with classical music and little else, set the volume medium low and returned to the bag. Next he pulled out a thermos, a well-used mug and a brown paper bag bearing the logo of one of the local food merchants. Pietro would not be leaving for an extended lunch.

A knock on the door announced the presence of the assistant who informed the guest that the quarry truck had phoned to say that they were fifteen minutes away from the store and that Signor Giovanni had informed the assistant that anything Pietro needed was to be provided without delay. The assistant himself was astute enough to take in the spartan surroundings and determine that the craftsman was surely on a budget. He informed Pietro that fresh coffee and condiments would be available to him whenever he asked and that he himself would find it a privilege to ensure that his guest would not have to trouble himself by attending to his own culinary needs. Pietro stated that when he worked, he preferred to be undisturbed generally, but that he would come downstairs for coffee and that a dinner would be very much appreciated in order to give him extra time to devote to the task at hand. Most anything other than fried foods would be acceptable.

The assistant thought of offering to upgrade Pietro's sound system to something more powerful but then decided that the radio bore the looks of having been part of a comfortable arrangement to which Pietro had probably grown accustomed. With that thought, the assistant disappeared until the quarry truck arrived. It took two healthy men no small effort to carry the crate by its handles into the rear of the building and up the stairs to the workroom. There could be no mistaking that they were delivering the stone, what with the creaking of the wood underneath their combined weight and the occasional grunts which escaped their lips.

Pietro met them at the door and helped to ease their burden by lifting the case with them. The workers stayed long enough to uncrate the block in order to verify that it arrived unscathed. Pietro assured them that he would handle its placement on the table himself, thanked them for their service, and dismissed them. Then he lifted the marble block and placed it on the heavy wooden table. He turned it around completely, taking his time as he went. He studied the surface and features of the stone, his eyes pausing on a few spots in particular. Then he retreated to his chair and sat down.

When Signor Giovanni knocked on the door a little over an hour later to check on him, he heard the words, "Come in," and entered only to find Pietro still lounging back in his chair, eyes transfixed on the block of marble.

"Signor Pietro, good morning," he said.

Pietro glanced his way as if lost in thought. "Good morning, Signor Giovanni."

"I see the marble has arrived and is intact."

No answer.

"Signor, do you not think that it would be best to start carving? My anniversary is coming up very soon."

Still silence.

Giovanni bristled. He was accustomed to giving orders to his staff and having them respond immediately. Who was this workman who thought he could brush him off as unimportant?

"Signor Pietro, if you are unable to do this job, I shall be forced to find someone else!" he said crisply. This was all bluff. This was entirely a test of one man's abilities, and Giovanni had allowed his emotions to get the better of him. He wondered if he had gone too far, and he immediately regretted the possibility of having to explain to Giacobbe why his sculptor had left without even beginning.

Without looking at him, Pietro stated in a calm voice, "They sold you a defective block of marble, Signor."

"Defective? What do you mean? Is it cracked?"

"No. There are no visible cracks in it."

"Then how do you know it is defective?" Giovanni approached closer.

Pietro lifted his frame out of the chair and walked to the table, never taking his eyes off the marble. "Here," he pointed at a spot on the marble, "and here," he said, placing his finger on the rear of the block. This is a vein which passes through at an angle in this block. It looks like a slightly darker shade to the untrained eye. I must work around that vein, or the block will split, usually at a very bad time."

Giovanni looked at the block. He could not see the danger, of course, but he respected the fact that Pietro could. "What will you do? Should we order another block? That would put us behind schedule."

"No, no," Pietro assured him. "I can work around the problem. I have been thinking and listening. The stone will speak to me and tell me how to shape it in spite of the imperfection."

"How long will this take?" asked Giovanni. He knew his part in this test, but he was still nervous to ensure everything was done on his part. He knew that Giacobbe would not balk at ordering another block of marble if that were required to ensure a good test of Pietro's abilities.

"I had seen two possibilities and was thinking through a third when you came," said Pietro. "I believe there may be up to five." He looked at Giovanni. "It should take no longer than another hour before I begin with the stone." He looked at the stone for a few moments and then turned back to Giovanni.

"Your very able assistant offered me a dinner. I would appreciate that. Also, do you have a night watchman who can let me out after hours?"

"Yes, we do. I will notify him to not disturb you but to expect you sometime after the store closes. What time would you like your dinner?"

"Seven," said Pietro. Then he walked to the chair and sat down again with his gaze locked on the marble.

Signor Glovanni retreated to his commerce feeling a little less miffed. It was apparent that the workman knew something about his craft. How much skill he possessed remained to be seen.

Pietro made two appearances after lunch to fill up his thermos with coffee. When the assistant delivered his dinner in the evening at seven, his approach to the workroom door was greeted with the clink of metal on stone. This he took as a positive sign, and he would have been delighted to report on the progress he observed, but when he knocked on the door, Pietro answered from inside with the words, "One minute, please."

After a pause, the door opened with Pietro blocking the frame. It was clear that he did not intend to have the meal spread and prepared for him. The assistant proffered the bag which Pietro accepted with a smile and a "Thank you." With that, Pietro closed the door. The assistant listened briefly, but there was no more activity. Seven o'clock dinner apparently meant stopping in the middle of whatever was in progress.

Chapter 5

When Signor Giovanni arrived very early the next morning at 6 a.m. before his assistant (and only because his curiosity had eaten at him that night), he glanced at the note from the night watchman. He had left orders not only to expect Pietro to ask to be let out at some point but also to note the time. The guard had recorded 3:15 a.m. as the departure time. Reading that, Giovanni alighted the stairs and knocked lightly on the door of the workroom. No answer. He opened the door and peered in. No one was inside.

The lights had been arranged around the block and had been left on. Giovanni was careful not to touch anything as he approached through the dust and rubble. Work had certainly commenced, but when he saw the marble block, Giovanni snorted aloud. What he saw on the table was the work of a child. It had a shape, and one could squint and imagine a cherub. But the overall appearance was grotesque. The figure was blocky, square on many of the edges. The figure appeared to be stooped, which lent an air of deformity. Signor Giovanni was not impressed.

Still, he was a man under orders. He took out his phone and snapped several photos, again being careful not to touch or disturb any surfaces. He sent the photos immediately to the number Giacobbe had requested and waited. Two minutes later, his phone buzzed with an unlisted number.

"Hello?" said Giovanni.

"So that is the work of one day?" It was Giacobbe.

"Yes. I fear that you have found the wrong person for your test."

"Never mind that. He has at least another day. Make sure that he has everything he needs and that he is not disturbed."

Giovanni sighed inwardly. "As you say." The phone clicked as Giacobbe ended the call. He looked back at the block of marble again. It emanated a certain sadness. He shook his head and walked downstairs to begin the morning.

Pietro arrived at 7 a.m. He greeted the assistant, who happened to be near the stairwell. He was offered and accepted the promise of another dinner. Then he mounted the stairs to the workroom.

Upon entering the room, he looked around at the floor, walked carefully to the table and then pulled his phone from his pocket. He opened an app and located a video file. After pressing the start button, he watched and listened as Giovanni observed his work, took photos of it and then received a phone call. The audio was not high definition, but in the relative quietness of the empty store, it was clear enough. Pietro smiled, walked to the old radio against the wall and switched it on. Music filled the background. His next step was to open the windows and switch on the two fans so that the day's dust would be mitigated. Then he returned to the table, picked up his hammer and a select chisel and began the steady tapping which would continue throughout the day.

For Giovanni, the day was a repetition of the previous one. He was told that Pietro made two appearances for coffee after lunch. He received the dinner from the assistant at 7 p.m. at the door to the workroom. When the noise of the day's sales had subsided, from the bottom of the stairs could be heard the sound of metal striking metal.

The plan called for Giovanni to continue to pass along photos and assessments of the progress of the work for Giacobbe to review. If it was determined that Pietro possessed the requisite skill to be invited as a part of the Vatican's project, rather than waste his time on the test sculpture, Giovanni was to play the part of the enraged client. He was still smarting from the relative dismissal by someone of Pietro's station from the previous day. In truth, he rather looked forward to storming in, waving his hands and expressing his anger at the slow pace and unimpressive work by the hired craftsman.

Giovanni had left express instructions to the night watchman to record the time of Pietro's departure. So, when he arrived the next morning, again at 6 a.m., and spoke with the night watchman before he departed his shift, he learned that Pietro had only just left thirty minutes prior. Once again, he walked up the stairs, knocked softly on the door to verify the room's emptiness and then opened it. He turned to the table and stopped in his tracks.

Giovanni was a seller of fine clothing, was well to do and had seen his share of art in his country. What he saw from a distance stunned him. He did not realize that his mouth had opened wide or that his eyes were actually bulging as he hastened to the table.

There before him was one of the most exquisite pieces of art he had laid eyes on at close range. The figure was that of a cherub, slightly stooped, after having just plucked a flower from the ground. The right hand with the flower was returning toward the face, the left to the side and behind in counterbalance. The neck had a look of tautness to it as if the cherub were stretching forward toward the flower. But what was astounding to Glovanni was the expression on the face of the cherub. It had at once the look of divine wisdom and sheer delight at the prospect of enjoying something so simple. The lips were parted slightly as if about to break into a smile.

The more he looked at the sculpture, the less Giovanni could believe his own eyes. There were nuanced folds in the clothing which were revealed by the careful placement of the work lights. The hair was not an amorphic mass upon the head. Rather, it had texture and detail that lent a sense of youthfulness and playfulness to the figure. Instead of blowing air out of his nose as he did the previous day, this morning Signor Giovanni was sucking air in through his teeth as he imagined the credits he would gain on his wife's balance sheet when she received this as a gift out of the blue from her husband; their real anniversary date was a full five months away.

The mere thought of snapping photos of the figure seemed almost profane. He opened his phone, dialed the number and then hung up. Less than a minute later, the phone rang with an unlisted number.

"Hello," said Giovanni.

"You have news?"

"Yes. The sculpture—it's finished."

"Then why did you not send photos?"

"You really must see this for yourself. I called because I knew you would want to come yourself."

There was a pause, then Giacobbe said, "Are you sure I won't be interrupted?"

"Quite sure. He only left in the past half hour."

"Then I will see you within the hour."

Chapter 6

In just under an hour, three people ascended the stairs to the workroom. They were Signor Giovanni, who spoke in animated tones as he described his previous entrance to the room, Giacobbe and Father Donati, both of whom listened patiently but whose excitement began to grow the more Giovanni spoke. When they arrived at the workroom, Giovanni dismissed the assistant whom he had left to remain at the entrance as a verification that Pietro had not returned prematurely. Then the three men entered the room.

When he saw the expressions on the other men's faces, Giovanni felt relieved that he had not overreacted. The priest broke into a wide smile, and even Giacobbe smiled and nodded repeatedly.

"Did I not tell you?" asked Giovanni as he led the men to the table. "Is it not exquisite?"

"Exquisite indeed," said Giacobbe quietly. He walked around the table, observing the sculpture.

"It is magnificent!" exclaimed the priest. "I have seen nothing like it since the masters of old!"

Yet it was Giacobbe who discovered the true genius Pietro had displayed in the piece. At his request, the other two men stepped back from the table. Giacobbe turned off two of the lights. Instantly, the piece took on a different feeling. Then he turned that light off and turned on one of the others. The same thing happened. With each of the combinations of lighting, the sculpture took on another aura, and different features of the piece were highlighted.

He looked Father Donati in the eye. "It seems we have found our sculptor," he said.

When Pietro returned later that day at noon, he inquired for Signor Giovanni and asked him if he had time to review the sculpture. Signor Giovanni feigned business which needed to be shuffled off to an employee and then smoothed his lapels and joined Pietro for the trip up the stairs. When they arrived at the workroom, Pietro opened the door and allowed Signor Giovanni to enter first. He expressed the right amount of surprise—it wasn't difficult. Even though he had seen the piece twice already that morning, it still took his breath away to look at it again. Having appreciated its beauty, he was secretly pleased that he had not had to play the part of the angry patron and end up losing this opportunity to secure such a piece.

"So, you like it?" asked Pietro.

"Yes! Yes, I most definitely do," said Giovanni.

"And your wife, will she like it?"

"My wife will be beyond overjoyed to receive this gift."

Pietro seemed pleased. He looked around the room. "I need to pack up my tools and clean up," he said.

"The cleanup will be done by my workers. I insist. You need only concern yourself with your tools and personal items."

"Thank you," Pietro said. "With whom should I leave my bill?"

"You can tell me now how much I owe you, and I will pay it," said Signor Giovanni.

"One thousand euros," Pietro replied.

Signor Giovanni hoped his face did not express what he felt inside. The price was akin to highway robbery. A piece of this quality could easily fetch five to ten times the price at auction. He reached for his wallet inside his jacket and counted out ten one hundred-euro notes. He paused before putting it back in, reached inside and pulled out two more. He knew his wife would love the piece, and his generosity was genuinely motivated by its beauty.

"Here, please accept a bonus."

"Thank you, sir!" said Pietro heartily. He placed the money in one of his cavernous pockets. "I shall be on my way as soon as I'm packed up."

"You are most welcome. Please be assured that I will give a very positive review of your abilities to Father Donati." He turned to leave and then looked back at Pietro. "Perhaps he will be able to find more work for you soon." Giovanni was remembering again his role in the drama. With that, he left to resume his job as a shopkeeper.

Pietro waited until he had departed and then pulled his phone from his pocket. He opened up the app and pulled up the video and audio from earlier in the morning. There they were, all three of them together discussing his work. He saw Father Donati almost salivating at the work. There also was Giacobbe Manco discovering the function of the lighting on the piece. The man knew his art.

He picked up the radio player with the tiny hidden camera and microphone, placed it in his bag and began the methodical task of repacking his tools.

"Perhaps he will have some more work for me very soon," he repeated to himself.

Chapter 7

Philadelphia

Margot couldn't wait to get off work. It wasn't that she hated her job. As her first job out of college, working as an intern at a pharmacy while she saved money for her next level of schooling was really a reasonable opportunity. The pay was above average. The hours were consistent. She even liked most of her coworkers.

But her phone had erupted with a burst of messages on social media three hours earlier. Something was afoot, and in fairness to her employer, there was no time at work to devote to updating herself on the latest information.

When quitting time arrived, she quickly cleaned her work area, said a hurried goodbye to the staff and left by the employee entrance. Glancing at her phone, she quickened her pace. If she hurried, she could catch the next bus on the route to her neighborhood.

While waiting, she scrolled through numerous messages. Her heart leaped when she saw one near the bottom.

`Godfather. Ports. Shell game. Why?`

"Yes!" she exclaimed under her breath. This was going to be a fun evening.

She wanted to jump right in, but her caution overrode her curiosity. She waited until she got home, skimmed her mail, started some coffee and sat down at her desk. After opening her laptop, she logged into her VPN, opened up her Tor browser and clicked on the bookmark to the message board. It was a pattern she had repeated for many months.

While other single young women her age were out with their friends going to restaurants or bars and making the most of the social scene, Margot was on the other end of the spectrum. Back when she was in college, other students were protesting anything that moved, but she began to question the views she kept hearing repeated over and over. The fact that the same themes were being repeated over and over bothered her. As she changed from one TV channel to the next, it seemed that the anchors all were reading from a script. Whether "the walls were closing in" on some politician or "climate change will destroy us all," it sounded more like one large echo than a bunch of independent journalists seeking truth.

So Margot stopped listening and watching. Instead, she began to look for the facts herself. Her journey led her through a plethora of newspapers and magazines (both printed and online), startup news organizations, blogs written by wild-eyed fanatics, and social media commentators. In the year after graduation, she found a set of message boards where serious researchers hung out. These were communication channels inhabited by numerous people who pretty much all stayed cloaked in anonymity while posting some of the most eclectic and, at times, unbelievable information she had ever read.

At first, Margot was skeptical. However, one of the biggest challenges to her skepticism was the degree to which the members of these message boards challenged each other. "Prove it" was a mantra that was repeated in various ways over and over. If someone made an absurd claim without any basis in fact, they were roundly excoriated, and their trustworthiness was knocked down in the community. If someone made an equally absurd claim but provided numerous links to journals, news articles, and other forms of information to back the idea, their trustworthiness grew. It seemed like journalism in its own right, or at least how journalism should be.

Margot read for weeks on end. She explored one thread after another (and it seemed that so many of the issues in the world were somehow interconnected). One actor was involved in dark dealings and was married to the sister of a politician who was tied to this global foundation which had ties yet again to a modeling agency which served as a recruitment tool for human traffickers who supplied gratification to yet another group of world leaders. On and on it went.

There were times when Margot became angry. At times she was depressed and didn't want to wake up another day. If just one tenth of what she was reading were true—no, just one percent—it was enough corruption to last a lifetime for the average person. Twice she became physically ill to the point of heaving over her sink when she read accounts of what one of her favorite movie actors had been involved in with children.

One day she awoke knowing that she had to do more than read. It wasn't enough to be awakened to the sinister plots around her. She had to become involved in the fight against it. This was a bit of a conundrum for her, since she really had had no moral training. Her parents never went to church. Many of her friends throughout school lived similar lives. Certainly, in college she had been insulated from mostly anything except moral relativism. Good and bad were terms defined by the talking heads on the TVs. She had believed that her whole life in her mind. Yet, here in front of a computer screen, she realized that something inside of her so rebelled against the idea that the rich and famous could exploit the weakest in society for their own pleasure and get away with it. This made her question why she felt that way. Was it because she herself was not one of the so-called elites? Or was there really a gold standard somewhere which defined a basic level of right and wrong?

Coincidentally, this was when multiple paths converged for her. She decided to post for the first time to ask a few questions, not really to offer thoughts but to try and gain some clarity on one of the topics. When she did post, one of the first people to respond to her was one of the anonymous users who posted frequently and who had a higher-than-average level of trustworthiness. This user sent her a private message. In it, the person welcomed her to the board and then proceeded to ask her what security measures she was using to protect her identity.

Margot was shocked. She had never thought about any of that. She wrote back that she was using nothing. The reply came to her that many people from all over the world accessed the boards. Some of them could be involved in the intelligence services of nation states, which meant that their ability to surveil traffic to and from various servers around the globe could allow for "doxing" users in order to harass, intimidate or (in the worst-case scenarios) physically attack them.

Margot panicked. She realized that she was treading in water which was not just over her head but could be filled with actual predators. In all her reading, she had not thought of the fact that "the bad guys" were reading or even actively participating on the message boards right along with the good guys.

She wrote back a message.

`What can I do? I'm scared.`

The reply that was sent to her included a list of things she could do to help to protect her identity. The first was to sign up for a VPN account with one of the reputable providers. This would allow her to connect to one of many servers around the globe and funnel all of her traffic through an aggregation point with other people's traffic. What this did, the person explained, was to help encrypt her traffic from her computer to the VPN server in order to prevent her Internet provider from being able to easily monitor her traffic.

`Even if you are only visiting websites using a secure protocol, your provider can still see WHERE you are going.`

The person explained that by connecting first over an encrypted tunnel to a VPN server, all of that traffic would be obfuscated to the Internet provider.

Then, the person recommended getting a separate email address from one of a handful of secure email providers.

31

You may eventually want to communicate with other people here on a one-to-one basis while still protecting your anonymity. And if you want to segregate your communications, you can set up more than one email account on multiple services. But don't use the big, free email providers.

The next thing the person recommended was that Margot download and use a browser called "Tor." He explained that this browser used a random server list in order to further obfuscate traffic into and out of the Internet.

There are good arguments that while the Tor network itself could be compromised by intelligence services with enough resources, using it does add another layer of complexity and protection. At worst, it's way better than simply firing up a standard web browser.

Another recommendation popped up:

Purchase a handful of cheap cell phones based on different carriers from different stores—preferably in different cities if you travel much—in order to have the ability to make calls or text people you love in the event of an emergency.

Did she read that right? How serious were these people? Margot decided to forego that one for now, although later she wished that she had acted on it immediately.

It was the last recommendation which completely caught her off guard. The last line of the message was one word:

Pray.

Pray? To whom? About what? Why? It seemed so odd given the context of most of what she had read for the past few months. Sure, people were agreeing that they were trying to expose and, by virtue of exposure, fight "evil." But pray?

Margot wrote back:

I'll try to act on some of your recommendations right away.

She paused at her keyboard and then typed in another note:

Why should I pray?

It was not so much a sarcastic retort as it was a genuine question. Margot had never prayed in her life, and she really had no idea why people did it at all.

And although words get transmitted at times across the Internet without the context of an emotion, the person on the other end did not assume the worst about her reply. Instead, Margot received a message back which she read with interest:

> If, as your post states, you really believe that what these people are doing is evil, then on what basis do you call it evil? For evil to exist, good also must exist. For good to exist, there must be a basis to call it good. This is deeper than you think. If you want to discuss it more, contact me when you have acted on my recommendations. Your security really depends upon it.

Margot finished reading the message and then looked up from her computer monitor. Her walls seemed quiet and observant. She shivered. Impulsively, she pushed the power button and held it until the entire machine shut down. For the next thirty minutes, she sat in her bed with a pillow clutched to her chest. She had never felt so uneasy in her life, but she didn't pray.

Chapter 8

Three days later, after working each day and then going to the gym for a workout in the evening, she no longer felt that her world was coming to an end. Cautiously, she turned on her computer. The first thing she did was to sign up for a VPN account. After installing the software, she looked at all the server addresses available. She picked one in the Netherlands if for no other reason than it seemed a world away. Then she downloaded the Tor browser and installed it. She then went to two of the secure email providers and signed up for different accounts. The first she signed up for as "polkadotpanda" because she couldn't think of much other than the animal when she was creating that account. On the next server, she decided to be a bit more cryptic and created that one as "1a2s3d4f" because it was easy to look at a keyboard and remember while also being a bit less female.

She figured she would read a bit more about VPNs and the Tor browser, so she searched some sites online that had good graphics and tutorials which talked about how they worked and the strengths and weaknesses of each. After she felt reasonably comfortable with what she had learned, she typed in the Tor address of the message board.

She read some of the posts from the past three days. Much had transpired, but that always seemed to be the case. A foundation was being researched for its ties to money laundering. More progress on that front was provided by way of a document dump from someone who had located it in a trove of hacked files which had been posted online a couple of years ago. The information had been there the whole time, but when there were tens of thousands of pages to go through, one had to know what to look for or be willing to spend days and weeks reading through it all.

Margot decided to write her new acquaintance and at least thank the person for the security recommendations. She sent a private message and was about to return to the various threads when her inbox notified her of a new message. It was a reply. "Did these people never take a break?" she wondered.

```
Welcome back. I began to wonder if I scared you off.
If you have any questions, please feel free to ask
me.  Please do not include your real name.  You may
call me Serious.
```

M: Thank you. Yes, I was pretty scared after the last exchange we had. I took some time off, and that helped a lot.

S: I understand. This can be a heavy load to try to bear alone. If I didn't pray every single day, I'm sure I wouldn't be able to make it mentally or emotionally.

There it was again. Margot ignored it for now.

M: How can I help? I don't want to sit on the sidelines and watch. I want to do something.

S: Out of all the topics you have read about, what would you like to help with the most?

That caused her to stop and think. There were several. But drugs were always at the top of everyone's list for societal ills.

M: Maybe the drug trade.

S: OK. A group of us are working together on something in Europe. Would you like to be part of that?

M: Sure. I don't know what to do. I'll need some help on where to start.

S: Don't worry. We will start you out with specific tasks. If you like it, you can do more. And once you get into it, you will begin to learn to look for your own clues.

M: Sounds great! When can I start?

S: Right now. We need someone who can do some digging on public arrest records in Europe. Make a list of people by country and city in a spreadsheet. Do that for Spain, France, Italy, Greece and Romania.

Serious listed several links that contained public arrest records and then continued.

S: You will have to look for more yourself. Remember, the more you dig, the more you will uncover.

S: What do you want me to call you?

Margot thought. One of her favorite books and movies was *The Lord of the Rings*.

M: Gandalf.

S: We have a Gandalf in this community already. You'll have to choose something different or be more specific.

Margot smirked and then wrote back.

M: Gandalf the White.

S: OK, Gandalf the White. Welcome to the team.

And with that, Margot began her official entry into what some people called a digital army. It was more like a covert operation. Every day she would go to work and learn more about prescriptions and customer service. After work, she would eat dinner while sitting at her computer, clicking on link after link and searching database after database of arrest records for criminals in five European nations. Serious had not told her how far back to go, but she thought five years was probably sufficient, at least for starters. She learned quite a bit about spreadsheets, copying and pasting data from websites and even some quirky things about making sure the fonts stayed the same so that the spreadsheet didn't look like a jumbled mess. Eventually, she settled on the inspiration of having one worksheet for each country and for sorting arrests alphabetically.

It was after a few weeks of doing this that a pattern began to emerge. She noticed it at first when some of the names began to be repeated. Excited, she worked with more energy until she had several thousand names, dates and cities in her lists. She also had a column for the crime with which the person was charged. She messaged Serious about her discovery.

M: Noticed several names that appear multiple times in these arrest records. I thought if a person were arrested, he would be put away for at least a few months if not years. Some of these arrests are for more than just pickpocketing.

S: Congratulations. Now take a few of those names and dig deeper. Find any news articles you can and see what they have to say about the arrests or the crimes. Oh, and maybe you should make some notes about the arresting officer(s) or judges if they are mentioned.

That sounded weird. But Margot liked the challenge. She selected three of the most frequent names who had been arrested in multiple countries and began to search the websites of the newspapers and TV stations in those cities. It took a few days, but it began to click.

She messaged Serious again.

M: Are you kidding me? Over half of these arrests for five people are Interpol. And at least half of those are by just three Interpol officers.

S: Congratulations again, Gandalf the White! What do you make of it?

Margot hadn't thought that far.

M: These officers really know their stuff and are on the trail of these criminals.

Serious sent back a perplexed emoji.

S: Length of sentence. Judges. Recommendations. Dig.

Margot sighed. Well, it wasn't going to be a walk in the park, but if there were more, she was determined to find it. She started searching again. Some of the databases actually contained the transcripts of the courtroom proceedings. As she began to research these, she had to use online translator tools, since they were typically recorded in the local language of each country. Although it was a bit stilted to read the computer-generated grammar, it was clear enough. In many cases, the criminals were arrested by one of a handful of Interpol officials. The officials made recommendations to the court for leniency based on "important information" divulged by the criminal, and the judges rubber-stamped the recommendation as the sentence. In case after case, criminals involved in serious offenses were given light sentences. The longest she saw was six months for "simple possession" when the news article had reported a haul of multiple kilos of narcotics. The lightest sentence was three days "due to overcrowded conditions" at the local jail. That one was for aggravated robbery against a shop owner in Romania.

Margot was stunned. Could it be that Europe was that soft on crime across the board? She logged into the board again and sent a message to Serious. It was a half hour later before she received a response.

M: Sort by arresting officer. Look at the judges and sentences. Dig.

She was beginning to be annoyed at that word. But she quickly sorted her spreadsheet by the arresting officer where she had it noted. She squinted through her eyes. Looking at just one of the Interpol officers she had been learning about, she realized he had been involved in the arrest of multiple criminals. Nothing out of the ordinary there. That was his job. Then she started looking at the details of the arrests. As she searched for the next few hours, it became apparent that there were some serious incongruities. One criminal had been arrested for possession with intent to distribute for two small bags of heroin. Another had been charged with felonious assault. Both of those had resulted in stiff sentences of between five to ten years in prison. She pulled up the courtroom transcripts and began to work through them. There it was, the recommendation was for the full extent of the law to be brought to bear upon these men. The judges seemed to wholeheartedly agree. And off they went to serve time behind bars.

Her head was spinning, and not just because of the information. It was 4 a.m. Margot closed her browser, logged off the VPN and shut off the computer. Then she collapsed on her tiny sofa. She was glad it was a weekend.

Chapter 9

When Margot awoke Sunday morning, she decided that getting out of her apartment for a bit would be good for her mind as well as her body. She packed her gym bag and then made her way out to a local coffee shop. After she placed her order, she walked over to the table with the magazines and newspapers. She looked around. Everyone in the entire shop was on their phones. Margot couldn't bear the thought of looking at a screen for several more hours after her marathon session last night. She sighed, reached for one of the local newspapers and looked for a small table to claim. There were none. She picked a larger table for four and sat down.

While waiting on the barista to call her name, she began perusing the paper. The main headlines were about a trade agreement discussion which was surely going to change the world, at least according to the subtext. She scanned the page for anything of interest. The words jumped off the page at her: "Drug Bust Nabs Twelve." Margot wasn't sure why it seemed so important. It seemed like several times per week there were articles about drug arrests. But something was stirring in the back of her brain.

Scanning through the article, the gist of the news was the local detectives had engaged in a months-long sting with the help of undercover officers. They had managed to infiltrate one of the local narcotic suppliers with potential ties to a Mexican syndicate. After managing to arrange for at least seven transactions, all of which had been caught on remote mics, surveillance cameras or hidden recording devices, the task force had closed in with pre-dawn raids and had arrested the network of local suppliers they had been able to identify.

"Is this seat taken?"

Margot was startled. She looked up to see an athletic, medium-build man with a faded buzz cut and a coffee-colored complexion looking at her with an inquisitive smile.

"No. It's free. All the small tables were taken."

"Do you mind if…"

"Not at all. Have a seat."

The man settled into a chair and placed his phone and a small leather binder on the table next to him. Margot felt a bit awkward with the idea of placing the newspaper back in front of her face. She had followed the story to the inside pages of the main section of the newspaper. She fumbled to fold it together so that she could continue reading on the table without taking up all the space. The man glanced across the table out of curiosity.

"So you're reading about the big bust?" he said.

"Yes. For some reason, it caught my attention."

The man took a deep breath and sighed. "They'll probably all be let out on some semblance of being first offenders or low-risk criminals or allowed to post, at most, a nominal bond. Then they'll be in the wind or back to their old tricks blanketing our city with drugs."

"You sound pretty jaded, Mister..."

"Carson," he said, extending his hand toward Margot. "Detective Deshawn Carson. And you are, Miss..."

Margot hesitated. She wasn't sure about this man. "Norwood. Elaine Norwood," she said, borrowing one of her coworkers' names. His eyes probed hers for a second.

"Nice to meet you, Elaine. And to answer your question, I try not to be jaded, but I have to deal with the realities of my job. Too much of my career has been spent catching bad guys only to see many of them not get locked up, or at least locked up long enough for what they have done. How would you feel?"

Margot's mind was in a whirl. This was what she had just been reading about in Europe. Now it was...here? She had never thought about the local application of her research. "Before I answer that, Detective Carson..."

"Please, call me Deshawn. I get enough of the Detective bit during work hours."

"Okay, Deshawn. Before I answer that, I'd like to ask you a couple of questions if I may."

"Sure. Go ahead." He leaned back in his chair with one hand resting on the table, a relaxed look on his face.

"What were the recommendations by the prosecutor in those cases where the criminals got off so easily? And did you have any say in the recommendations?"

His expression tightened noticeably. "Well, well, Miss Norwood..."

"Elaine, please," Margot said. She could play the informal game as well as he could.

"Elaine. Those are some very insightful questions." He paused as he searched her face. "Very insightful."

"What would the answers to those questions be, Deshawn?" she probed gently.

"Jackson!" the barista shouted over the din of the coffee shop.

Margot flinched. She got up and walked to the counter, where she picked up her order of a steaming French press of coffee and a couple of napkins. After returning to the table, she sat down and busied herself with pouring out her first cup of coffee. Had he noticed?

"To answer your questions, Elaine, in most of the cases where the criminals got off lightly or scot-free, the prosecutor recommended lenient sentences. Sometimes the reasoning was that the person was a young offender. At other times, it was because the jails were overcrowded and the type of crime did not warrant incarceration—which is complete hogwash because across the city, county and state, we have plenty of room. Some of the time the recommendation for leniency was issued in private conference with the prosecutor and the defense attorney in the judge's chambers away from the public."

"Wait. You mean to tell me that for some of these crimes there was no record of why the criminal got a reduced sentence or no jail time?"

Deshawn nodded. "That's right. And to answer your other question, most of the time, I haven't been asked for my opinion on sentencing recommendations. The few times I have been asked, I have always recommended that the prosecution seek the maximum sentence available. Well, except for a couple of times." He looked down at the table.

"And what were those times?" Margot asked.

"There are three different young men I know who have been caught up in wider busts. I know their families, their home life. All of them come from families where the mother or parents really are trying to raise their kids right. A couple of them were raised in church. They weren't the ringleaders or even anywhere near the top of the gangs who were busted. I thought that leniency and some type of structured parole would be the scare they needed to help them stay on the straight and narrow."

"What happened with those young men?"

Deshawn looked up at Margot. "They all got the maximum sentence and are serving time in lockup."

"Carson!" the barista yelled.

Deshawn got up from the table and walked to the counter. Margot watched him as he walked. He had a confident stride, but it wasn't quite energetic. He engaged the barista for several moments. The barista's eyes flickered over

41

to the table and back to Deshawn. Then Deshawn picked up the items he needed for his table and returned.

His phone vibrated on the table. He picked it up and looked at it. "Well, it seems that my weekend has been interrupted. Good thing I got mine in a to-go cup." He stood as he put his phone back in his pocket. He glanced at the newspaper again and then looked at Margot. "It was nice to meet you, Miss 'Norwood.'" There was a little smile at the edges of his lips.

The inflection was slight, but it was there.

Margot felt her face flush slightly. "You too, Detective Carson."

"Maybe I'll see you again," he said. Then he turned and strode out the door, all business. Whatever the text was, it wasn't social.

Margot felt foolish. Why had she lied about her name? She didn't really know. Her stomach was in knots. Why? Again, she didn't know. She looked at the paper and her coffee. No way was she going to be able to relax and finish drinking it here in peace. She took it up to the counter and asked the barista for a paper cup and lid.

After he brought it, Margot asked him, "Is the man I was sitting with a regular customer?"

The barista looked at her sideways as he was pouring the coffee into the cup. "You got some interest there? 'Cause he was asking the same thing about you."

"Uh, no, not that kind of interest. Just wondering."

"Yeah. He comes in several times a week. He's a cop of some kind. Laid back kind of guy, mostly. He's actually kind of funny when he wants to be. You could do worse."

Margot flushed again. "Like I said, I'm not interested in that way. Just curious."

Margot grabbed her gym bag and headed out. She decided that some exercise would still do her some good, so she made her way to the gym. Twice during the walk, the back of her neck tingled, and she had the sensation that someone was watching her. Both times, she whirled around. The street had the normal Sunday morning light traffic of cars and pedestrians. Nothing seemed out of place, and there was no one she recognized. No one was staring at her or seemed to be keeping pace with her.

She exhaled. She was getting paranoid. Again, she didn't know why, and that didn't ease any of her feelings. After an hour-long workout, she retreated to the sauna. After leaning back in the searing heat, she actually started to relax. Listening to music on her headphones helped to block out the surroundings and allowed her to focus her thoughts on work and other parts of her rather simple life. As she reflected, she realized that during the past year, her life had taken a turn. All the research and digging had given her a sense of purpose, some goals. But did they matter? And were her goals something she wanted to pursue for a lifetime? She really didn't have any social relations to speak of. In the middle of her musing, Serious' email popped in her mind. "Pray." There it was again. Why was that echoing in her mind now, in the unlikeliest of times? She laid back and closed her eyes. There was too much to think about right now.

Chapter 10

Italy

Dona was focused on planning for the noon lunch crowd when the door opened. It was Father Donati, wearing his ever-gracious smile.

"Hello, my daughter."

"Father, good to see you."

"I would have called, but urgent matters kept me from having the time. Is the private room available for a meeting?"

"It is." Dona liked to be notified in advance, but she could hardly say no. "How many will be joining you today?"

"Two. Giacobbe will arrive shortly, and our new friend Pietro will be arriving within the half hour, I expect."

"Please give me a moment to make sure everything is prepared, Father. I wasn't expecting anyone today." Dona didn't say it in anger, but it was clear that she was trying to be gracious to cover the surprise.

"Take your time, dear," said Father Donati. He gestured toward a pitcher on the end of the counter. "May I help myself to some of your lemon water?"

"Of course." Dona reached below the counter and handed him a stout mug. She strode to the private room and set about making sure the table and chairs were straight and laying the appropriate number of place settings. She looked around. Flowers. The room needed a new bouquet. Quickly, she called her shop boy and handed him some money to run down to the local florist and return with a bundle of fresh girasoli or peonies, whatever they had available.

Ten minutes later, the room freshly prepared, Giacobbe arrived, parking in his usual spot. He entered and greeted Father Donati and Dona, who showed them both to the entrance of the room.

"Would you like your usual?" asked Dona.

"I'll wait to order until our guest arrives. I want him to be comfortable. In the meantime, I believe I would like a glass of the lemon water our good Father is enjoying so much."

"I'll bring a pitcher for you," said Dona.

44

After she left, Giacobbe turned to Father Donati. "Well, Prete, how much shall we tell our new friend?"

Father Donati frowned. That had been the question even before they had found Pietro. How much information could a person be trusted with in order to make the project successful without arousing suspicion or causing a potential recruit to say no for fear of failure?

"I believe that Pietro's unique background represents an opportunity to call upon his loyalty to the Church which provided him a haven throughout his youth. If we couch the project in terms of need to His Holiness, I believe that Pietro will not only agree to it; I also think that he will throw himself into the project with everything he has."

"Those were among some of my thoughts," said Giacobbe. "But I wanted to hear from you first to see if your perception matched mine. And if he really does give himself to the project, there's no telling where this may lead."

"He certainly is gifted. Giovanni continues to rave over his creation. Apparently, it was such a wonderful gift that his wife has overlooked all past indiscretions and fallouts between them. He claims that they are currently living in a second honeymoon."

Giacobbe laughed. "Giovanni is an old fool who allows his wife to rule with an iron hand. But it would be hard not to appreciate such a piece."

Their small talk was interrupted by Dona at the door to the room. "Your guest has arrived," she said. She stepped aside to show Pietro into the room.

Pietro looked around meekly as he entered the room. Father Donati rose and greeted him with a hearty handshake.

"Pietro, my son. Welcome!" He gestured to the table. "Come have a seat." As Pietro approached, Father Donati pointed across the table and said, "This is Signor Manco, one of our Church's finest patrons and an important man in the community."

Giacobbe nodded and extended his hand. Pietro took it firmly and smiled. "I'm Pietro," he said.

"I'm pleased to meet you," said Giacobbe. "I'm glad you could join us. Have a seat. Order anything you like today. This is my invitation, and I treat my guests well."

Pietro smiled as he sat. "Thank you," he said. He looked at Dona. "I would like your wonderful lamb grilled with herbs and vegetables."

Dona took the other men's orders and then departed.

Father Donati looked at Pietro. "I have been telling Signor Manco about the excellent job you did on the piece for Signor Giovanni at the clothing store. He was eager to meet you because of his unique position in regard to our Church and special projects related to His Holiness."

Pietro looked at Giacobbe. "You work for the Holy Father?"

"Not directly as a cardinal or such, I assure you," said Giacobbe. "But I have acted on the behalf of the Holy See in a number of business transactions which were to the benefit of the Church. One such project has arisen which may have brought us together, Pietro."

Pietro seemed to noticeably relax. "Please, if there is some way that I can help the Church, I would be most thankful."

Father Donati shot a glance at Giacobbe, which did not go unnoticed by either of the other two men.

Giacobbe smiled at Pietro. "Of course. I'm glad to hear that. You understand that many of these projects with which I am involved are of a... sensitive nature."

Pietro stared at Giacobbe with a blank look for a few seconds. "You mean that I must keep a secret?"

"Yes, very secret. If you agree to be part of this project, no one is allowed to know of the details of your participation. Your needs will be taken care of—very well, I can assure you—for the entire time you are on the project. If your experience is satisfactory to you and your work is satisfactory to the Holy See, you may very well be asked to participate in future projects." Giacobbe was already thinking ahead to ways he could use a man with skills such as those Pietro possessed.

Father Donati nodded. "Of course, we understand that this is all very sudden and could be much to ask to someone new to the area. If you need time to think things over..."

"No," said Pietro with a shrug. "What do I have to do? I have no other jobs lined up currently." He looked at Giacobbe and asked, "Will I be paid also for my work? Please understand, I wish to help the Church more than anything else. I also want to be able to support myself and not be dependent on the state for my needs when this project is done."

"Yes. You will be paid a fair wage for your talents. How does 1,000 euro per day sound?"

Pietro's eyes bulged and his mouth parted slightly. "I couldn't possibly charge the Church that much for my services."

"Nonsense," said Giacobbe. "From all that I have heard, you are a premium craftsman, and as the good book says, 'The worker is worthy of his wage.'"

"Then I am very interested, Signor Manco," said Pietro. "What do you need me to do?"

Giacobbe pulled out his phone and opened it to a set of notes. "Let me explain to you the details."

Chapter 11

South China Sea

Hijan Datmari was a good sailor. Tanned, weathered skin, and the glint of the water in his eye, he had been at sea most of his life. More than that, he was mostly an honest man. True, he had had a few wild adventures at some of his ports of call during his earlier years. And he drank things which were forbidden by the Quran. But through the stern beatings of his father and the patient advice of his mother, his parents had instilled in him a sense of fairness and decency which had stayed with him the rest of his life.

So when Captain Andar of the freighter ship *Ahil* told him that they would be bringing on two more last-minute shipping containers, Hijan knew that his job was to run the boom that would lift the containers, place them in the hold and ensure that none of the cargo, whatever it was, was damaged because of him. But when the Captain stood on the deck and personally supervised the onboarding of the containers, Hijan was a bit surprised. The captain trusted his crew to take care of the loading and unloading in port after port. And when the captain shouted at him to be careful almost a dozen times, Hijan was downright perplexed.

There were no markings on the containers. He had not been given a bill of lading to tell him whether the containers were filled with Asian electronics or German glassware or even boxes of alcohol. Not that it mattered. Hijan could place a shipping container on top of a balloon and let it press down lightly without bursting it.

When he was about to place the first container in its logical place on top of a group that had space, the captain shouted up, "No! Put it in the empty space at the far end by itself. And put the other one beside it, a few meters apart."

That made Hijan's eyebrows go up in the cab of the crane. It wasn't that the order was dangerous to the safety of the ship. It was big enough to handle another forty or more containers before it would be nearing capacity. But never in his time with Captain Andar had he ever been asked to separate any freight at such a distance from the main cargo area. It wasn't efficient, for one, and it required extra strapping to keep containers separated from the rest of the cargo.

Hijan made the adjustments to the crane's mechanism and slowly began extending the boom further into the recesses of the hold. It took more concentration than he was used to, but he gently placed the first container down. He called down to the captain, "There, sir?"

"Yes. Now the next one. And be careful!"

Hijan shook his head and repeated the process with the second container. He called down, "How close do you want them to be, Captain?"

"About ten meters."

Hijan's brows furrowed. This was highly unusual. The most efficient way to store these containers would be to put them beside one another and then lash them together as a unit with cables to the deck. Nevertheless, he complied with the captain's wishes. The second container was placed just as lightly on the cargo deck as the first and, Hijan noted with satisfaction, in near symmetry with the first.

"That will be all, Datmari. Prepare the crane for departure."

Hijan set about retracting the boom and setting it into its locking guides as the crew in the hold was busy at work lashing down the last two containers securely. Within twenty minutes, the *Ahil* was moving away from its moorings and was beginning the process of navigating the harbor with the help of the guide pilot. Once the local harbor pilot had departed onto his shuttle, the ship entered the sea and began its voyage toward the next port.

The last straw for Hijan came when the captain called all the crew together for a meeting. In the meeting, Captain Andar informed the crew that they had been asked to carry a particularly valuable cargo of some importance to a foreign government. No, it was not radioactive. No, it was not a weapon of any kind and their lives were not in danger by its presence. However, the cargo containers were off limits to all crew. He would see to the cargo on a routine basis to ensure that nothing about its safety was disturbed. All other crew were forbidden to have contact with the containers or to wander into that area of the hold.

With that, the meeting was over. For most of the crew, life went on as normal. Day in and day out, the routines and chores were the same. But curiosity had gotten the better of Hijan. It nagged at him like a schoolchild in the days before a birthday. When it was his time to sleep, he actually tossed and turned in his bunk. When he had reason to pass through the hold, and he found more and more reasons to do so, he could not help as his gaze wandered to the two remote containers.

"What was in them?" he wondered. "Why would the captain make them off limits? And what was so important about the cargo that the captain had to check their safety on a routine basis?"

After just a few days at sea, Hijan made what turned out to be one of the best decisions of his life. When he had time alone during his time off duty, he sat down at one of the ship's public workstations and connected to the Internet via the ship's satellite link. Logging into his free email account, he typed a letter to his brother and carbon copied his first cousin.

Something strange is going on with Captain Andar. We took on two containers at the last minute in Qinzhou. That is not unusual. What is really weird is that the Captain has forbidden any of the crew from going near these containers. Also, he said that he would check on the safety of the containers and their cargo personally. What could be so important for a captain to do this? Some of the crew are wondering if the containers contain a weapon even though the Captain has assured us that they do not. It is driving me mad. I must find out what is in those containers." Then, after a few moments of reflection, he wrote, "If anything happens to me, know that the containers must be something very dangerous or very illegal.

He reread the message and pressed the send button. The die was cast. He would find out at his first available opportunity.

Over the next three days, Hijan made a conscious effort to acquaint himself with Captain Andar's schedule. When he was pretty sure that he knew the times he would be on duty, dining, spending time in his quarters and sleeping, he made his plans.

On the fourth night, he dressed in his darkest clothes and slipped quietly through the corridors of the ship. Making his way into the hold by one of the several entrances, he crept quietly along the outer walls of the hold in the shadows. He looked furtively in every direction. He knew that the hold had its share of rats, but he was determined that if one even ran up his leg he would not scream. Once he reached the rear of the hold, he edged back into the darkness and stared at the containers for several minutes. The ship was too big to rock back and forth the way smaller boats did at sea, but every sailor could sense the motion of the waves and the movement of a ship no matter the size.

The hold was quiet. The cargo containers themselves were not well lit. Hijan already knew that and had brought along a flashlight in case he needed it. It was now or never. He steeled his nerves and scurried low across the deck like a crab. He looked at the first container up close for the first time. It was no different than most other containers other than the lack of markings and the fact that it looked newer. He examined the door and found that not only was it bolted from the outside, but there was also a hefty padlock. This wasn't unusual in and of itself, although most cargo containers did not commonly have them. He crept quietly to the second container and looked. It was the same.

Undeterred, Hijan slipped down between the two containers to the rear. Sometimes containers opened on both ends. As it turned out, these containers did. But they were locked just the same on this end as they were on the other. Hijab kicked himself mentally. He should have anticipated this. Would he be missed? Had he aroused any suspicion? Should he return now?

Then he remembered something he had seen while loading these containers. He hadn't paid much attention to it at the time, but each of the containers had a slot on the top which looked like it might be an auxiliary hatch of some kind. That was unusual, since most containers were built to withstand the salt air and moisture which invariably found their way into every hold during a sea voyage.

Hijan looked around for a ladder. No, that would make too much noise. He looked at the container in front of him. It had enough hinges and bars on the door that he thought he could climb it directly. Going up would be probably quieter and easier than getting down, but Hijan was committed.

His years at sea had kept his muscles reasonably toned, and Hijan soon found himself on top of the container. He peered over the edge of the container and listened in the quietness. Nothing. Slowly, he crawled across the top of the container to the hatch he had seen. It was a little over a meter square. In the dim light, it looked a bit like a mushroom shape. He felt it with his hand. It wasn't smooth metal. It was some kind of foam or insulation, almost like a gigantic air filter.

Hijan saw the hinges on his side of the container, so he moved to the other side. He found the latch but couldn't figure out how to trigger it. He covered the lens of the flashlight with one hand and flicked it on with the other. A few rays of light played over the latch, and Hijan knew how to open it. Unlocking the hatch with a soft but decidedly audible "click," Hijan paused and listened again. Still nothing.

He slowly eased up the hatch. The first thing that surprised him was the faint glow emanating from inside the cargo container. The second surprise was the lack of boxes stacked to the ceiling. Seeing nothing yet, he raised the hatch just enough to lean his head forward and peer inside.

Hijan's heart stopped for a moment. Fear gripped him with icy fingers, and the hair on the back of his neck stood up. He jerked his head back, and his hand involuntarily slammed down the hatch. The clank echoed through the hold like the sound of the loudspeaker in his village at the call to prayers. Hurriedly, Hijan slid the latch shut. He would have to alert someone. He did not know who or how, but now Hijan knew why Captain Andar had kept the cargo such a secret.

With his heart racing, Hijan peered over the edge of the container again. He saw nothing. He let himself down as quickly and as quietly as he could, landing on now-trembling legs. As he turned the corner of the container to make his way back to his cabin, a vicious blow struck him in the temple. He was knocked sideways into the container. Stars burst in a field of blackness in his eyes, and in the eclipse which was occurring within his brain he saw the face of Captain Andar, distorted with rage.

Before he blacked out completely, he managed to slur out the words, "Why, Captain? Why?" Then, as more blows rained down, he fell into unconsciousness as his body slid completely to the ground.

"Because, you fool, it is 200,000 euros, tax-free," Captain Andar muttered. He wasn't the strongest of captains, but he was still robust. He hoisted Hijan's body over his shoulder and walked slowly to the freight elevator, which opened onto the top deck. He knew that at this time of night and with the sea calm, there would be no watch on hand.

As he dragged Hijan's limp body to the railing and hoisted it over the side, he felt a twinge of regret. Datmari was the best crane operator he had ever known and would be difficult to replace. Too bad he would have to report to his next of kin that he had been lost at sea after being seen leaving the ship's bar. For the right amount of money, two or three long-time hands would agree that they had seen him in this condition. "In for a penny, in for a pound," he muttered as he made his way back to his cabin. It was a good thing he had installed the motion sensors at the rear of the cargo bay.

Chapter 12

Philadelphia

Margot was staring at the computer screen intently. When she had arrived home from the gym, she had fixed a quick lunch to eat as she began more research. She had been happy to find that Serious was online, but it wasn't very surprising. Some of these people seemed to live in cyberspace more than they did the real world. She had typed out a message summarizing her findings about criminals, arresting officers, judges and the lengths of sentences. She had been pretty excited about her findings, and she had included her own supposition that the disparity in sentences handed down to the criminals was possible evidence of bribery or some other type of underhanded dealings with the arresting officers or perhaps even the attorneys involved.

Now she was reading Serious' reply to her message. Like most, it was brief:

`Bigger. Think turf wars. Links between short sentences and long sentences.`

Margot was asking herself how deep this rabbit hole really went. She thought long and hard. What did Serious mean by "turf wars"? That sounded like a fight between rival gangs. Okay, maybe there were rival criminal gangs fighting over a particular town or section of a city. Maybe they had much to gain or lose depending on who controlled the flow of drugs or the ability to move stolen goods. She could even grasp that there could be an occasional dirty cop or lawyer who would be taking bribes in order to look the other way. But that didn't explain the exact pattern to which some of these sentences seemed to fit. What if...? No, she pushed the thought from her mind at first. But one of the lessons she had heard over and over in her initial research was the need to "Expand your thinking."

She allowed the thought to enter her mind and began to turn it over for inspection. What if the police were involved with a larger gang: no, an enterprise? What if defense attorneys and prosecutors were also part of the picture? And what if the judges themselves were bought and paid for? Could it be that the turf war was between huge criminal organizations which controlled not just the underbelly of society but also the prestigious leaders and those who were charged with upholding law and order?

Margot felt sick to her stomach. If she told this to anyone in her circle of acquaintances, they would look at her like she was a certified mental patient and call her a conspiracy theorist. She smiled wryly to herself. She could hear herself replying, "Did you know that the term 'conspiracy theory' was popularized by the CIA in 1967 to discredit anyone who questioned the official narrative of the Warren Commission on the assassination of JFK?" So maybe she wouldn't bring this up with her coworkers.

And maybe it was just that: a theory. There was only one way to find out. She typed a message back to Serious.

M: Yes, I know: dig. Right?

The reply came back.

S: You catch on quickly. :-)

Before she could open up more browser tabs, another message came through.

S: How are you doing?

At work, that would have elicited a polite, "Fine, thank you." But somehow, here in cyberspace, the question bore more weight. Serious didn't have to adhere to standard social norms, yet he—or she—was asking her about her well-being.

M: To be honest, the last twenty-four hours have been tough to process. I didn't expect all of this. I don't like the thoughts I'm having, and I definitely don't like where this road is leading me with regards to the justice systems in these countries.

S: I understand. It was like that for me at the beginning.

M: How long have you been doing this?

S: About seven years.

Seven years! Margot could hardly believe what she was reading. In less than a year, she had learned way more about the darker things going on in the world around her than she ever knew existed. How could someone stand the knowledge of what they were learning about for that long? And Serious must know much more than she herself was privy to yet.

M: That's incredible. I don't know how anyone could handle as much information as you possess about all of this by now.

S: Read this: Ecclesiastes 1:18.

It was a hyperlink. She clicked on it and read, "For in much wisdom is much grief: and he that increases knowledge increases sorrow."

Whoever wrote that stated the truth. Wait, was this the Bible he was linking to? Margot looked at the headers around the page. Serious had linked her to a Bible passage to read? Margot always expected the Bible to be filled with dos and don'ts. But this was something she actually could relate to.

M: That makes sense. But it doesn't help me feel any better.

S: Sure. It's a warning and a guideline to remember. The normies never worry about any of the things you are learning about. Once your eyes are opened, you can't go back.

M: Yeah, now I'm really not feeling better.

S: Sorry. A couple of years after I started this, I had become so depressed that I was suicidal—I mean really suicidal. Two failed attempts with a combo of alcohol and medication for depression.

M: Wow. That's heavy. How did you beat that?

S: Believe it or not, when I was in the hospital, a young chaplain intern came by. I thought he was just doing his rounds to get his degree. But he spent time with me and really listened.

S: He threw up a couple of times when I told him some of the details of what I had found in my research. I don't think they teach much about those things in seminary.

Margot found herself chuckling at that.

S: Anyway, he mainly listened to me. Then he asked me if I had any concept of where God fit into the big picture.

S: Honestly, I had never thought much about God. When people would mention God, I would get angry. I thought that if a God existed, He would have to be pretty twisted to let this mess go on like it does.

Margot felt a bit uncomfortable. She realized that part of the stress she had been feeling was due to some of the same conflicted thoughts about how good could even exist, whether it was called "God" or anything else.

Serious continued the messages.

S: So, this chaplain told me that in the big picture, God really is 100% good, that there really is a 100% wicked devil, and that if I was really trying to fight what was wrong, it only made sense for me to get to know the One whose side I was trying to be on.

Margot had never thought of it that way. It sounded pretty simple, and she could have tried to think up a dozen objections, but at the base level, it made sense.

S: This guy pointed to my bedside table and told me that there were a lot of people just like me in the Bible in the drawer, people who hated the evil that they saw and who fought it with everything within them. He also told me that the guy who wrote most of the New Testament, Paul, got so stressed out that he thought he was going to die.

S: It got me interested enough to try it. I asked him where to start. He suggested that I read through that book I linked to earlier, Ecclesiastes. He told me that it describes the kind of life I was seeing and that the message of that book is how messed up life can be without God in the picture.

M: So, he didn't try to preach at you or tell you that you were going to hell?

Margot felt half-ashamed to write it because she never had actually met anyone like that, but it was the stereotype she had heard most of her life about church people and preachers.

S: No. I started reading that book after he left that day. He apparently had some emergency in his family in another state and had to leave town. I never saw him again after that last meeting.

M: But how did all of that help you to deal with the knowledge you gained about all the awful things people are doing in the shadows?

S: I could tell you. Or you could dig. :-)

Margot laughed at that.

M: You just sucker-punched me, and you know it.

S: Maybe I did. But you would rather find out for yourself, I think.

M: OK. I'll maybe give it a try. Right now, I need to figure out how these gang arrests are connected to the different judges.

After she sent that, a thought occurred to her.

M: Oh. I saw an article about a drug bust in the city I live in. Something about the details made me think of all of this.

M: Anyway, I met a local cop, a detective, who claims he has always asked for stiff sentences but keeps seeing the criminals set free by the prosecutors and judges—well, some of them. He said that some of the least hardened ended up getting the maximum sentences. It made me think about doing some digging locally, you know?

S: Be careful.

M: Why?

S: One of the reasons that we dig around other parts of the globe is because of the actual geographical distance.

M: OK. But what would it hurt to do some digging in my own backyard?

S: Gandalf the White, you are still new to much of this. Never forget: this is not a game.

A slight chill ran over Margot.

M: I would be careful, of course.

S: This detective, did you tell him who you are? Can he find you? How do you know which side he is on?

Another cool breeze seemed to blow over her. He had definitely heard the last name "Jackson" at the coffee shop. That was it. But was it too much? Maybe Serious was right. It might be best to stick to Europe for now.

M: Thanks for the good advice. I think I'm ready to do some more digging on Europe.

S: If you need any help, or when you find something, let me know.

Margot closed her message panel, clicked open several tabs in her browser and began to dig.

Chapter 13

Italy

Pietro looked at the mammoth block of white marble before him in the secluded warehouse. It measured 120 centimeters square by three meters tall. Its weight was unimaginable. At Pietro's insistence, it had been placed on a base of wood consisting of oak timbers joined together by the kind of bolts which usually see service in quarries or shipping yards. There were cutouts at the bottom of the timbers for one or more forklifts, which was how it had been put into place in the warehouse.

The warehouse itself was nondescript on the outside in a commercial district. There was routine traffic outside, but most of it was muffled by the insulation in the walls. About thirty meters in depth and about twenty meters in width at the street, the warehouse had the capacity to hold a decent amount of commercial goods. Now it stood empty save for the marble, ten high lumen lamps (six of which were on stands and four of which were on mobile booms like those typically found in a television studio), two sturdy wooden tables loaded with hand tools and electric implements, respectively, a comfortable chair, a stool and a couple of smaller side tables. On one of these tables, Pietro had placed his radio. He had, of course, been offered his choice of current sound systems, but Pietro had explained that of the few possessions he had, the radio had been one of his first and oldest purchases other than tools. As long as he could access one or more classical music stations, he was content to use it.

Next to the bathroom, Giacobbe's men had outfitted one of the walls with a refrigerator stocked with juice and water, a microwave, a shelf with an assortment of fruits and snacks and a coffeemaker with a selection of gourmet coffees. Giacobbe wasn't kidding when he said he took good care of his guests. Pietro was given a telephone number which he was assured would be answered within two rings if he had need of anything.

Above the marble block were two ventilator pipes for vacuuming out dust and a gantry with an air hose hooked to a commercial-grade compressor on an opposite wall. The gantry also held a high-pressure water hose with interchangeable nozzles. It was quite the setup. As an artist, Pietro could not help but be pleased and impressed with the speed and efficiency with which all of it had been assembled.

During the lunch meeting, Giacobbe had explained the project. The Pope's birthday was coming up, and it was to coincide with an anniversary of key dates within the Holy See. For such a special occasion, a magnificent gift would be commissioned at the behest of the leading cardinals. The head of the Vatican treasury was agreeable and was underwriting most of the costs along with key benefactors which included, it was inferred, men such as Giacobbe himself.

This was, of course, a lie. It was all very carefully crafted to appeal to Pietro's sense of duty and a response to a higher calling, one worthy of service to God's representative upon earth. In truth, powers within the Vatican were seeking alternate means of cash flow which could be laundered due to the overwhelming financial strain which had been placed upon the church by the worldwide litany of sexual abuse scandals which continued to surface. Further, the global economy had been rocked by a series of disasters. And, of course, church donations were not what they used to be.

If the right artisan could be located, one of such magnificent talent and the right background—which meant the inability to ask questions—then the sculptor would be commissioned to create a piece which would be relocated, aged, and "discovered" by archaeologists of impeccable pedigree. Such a discovery would take the art world by storm and could be potentially auctioned off for numbers in the nine-figure range. After accounting for overhead, everyone stood to make an incredible amount of money. And, if it were handled with the highest of care, the same thing could be repeated a handful of times over the ensuing years. The artist could make a very decent income and have the assurance of His Holiness' blessings and that he had been pleased with the gifts and additions to the Vatican's collection. Most artists would give their secular career to know that just one piece was enshrined in the Vatican museum or in the private collection of the Pope's personal apartment complex.

Pietro had expressed the appropriate incredulity at the opportunity and had assured both Giacobbe and Father Donati that he would commit himself heart and soul to the task. Both were sufficiently blinded by their own greed and the pressing demand of meeting the Vatican's schedule that they forewent any other consideration and gave Pietro the job on the spot. The only thing that remained at the lunch meeting was to cover a myriad of details for the project. This consisted of Pietro's explaining what he would need by way of the setup previously described. (It had been met to the letter—and then some.)

Giacobbe assured him that his team would assemble everything within three days. Pietro suggested that he use the time to visit Rome and Vatican City "for inspiration" and to put himself into the proper mood. This was acceptable to both of the others, and Giacobbe insisted that he provide a car and driver for Pietro to get him there as quickly as possible. He also insisted that he stay in one of his properties located at the heart of Rome. This property was, of course, outfitted with a few discreet surveillance measures which could be used to check in on the artist, as it had been used numerous times to record secret dalliances between heads of state who had been offered the use of the property and their numerous paramours.

True to his word, Pietro had spent much of his time walking through museums, staring for hours at works of art. The driver and one other person assigned to generally keep tabs on Pietro had quickly grown bored with the task, given the sheer length of time Pietro would spend on any given sculpture he was observing. His only breaks were for food, which consisted of walking to nearby restaurants and eating a meal alternately inside or outside the restaurants. By the middle of the second day, they had agreed that the artist could look after himself and had found other entertainment which involved less-than-reputable parts of the old city. It was during this break in discipline that Pietro had purchased three burner cell phones and had used one of them to text an international number. Less than five minutes went by before the reply came. A rendezvous was scheduled for the following afternoon during the lunch hour at three different locations. The first would be used if Pietro's minders were still keeping their distance. If any surveillance was detected, Pietro would use basic evasive tactics to lose them and test the second location. The third would only be used as a last resort.

Thus it was that, on the third day at lunch, Pietro walked into a restaurant with darkened glass windows, confident that he had not been followed. He actually had taken the time earlier to send a text message from his personal phone for the driver that he was going to take public transport that day just to relieve him of having to always drive him everywhere. The driver, who was quite hungover, had only just begun to get ready for his morning chauffeuring duties when he received the text. He gratefully acknowledged the message, notified his counterpart in the next room of the apartment they were sharing and immediately went back to sleep. They would sleep well until noon and would have no idea where Pietro was until he contacted them in the evening for the trip back home.

After requesting a seat at the rear of the restaurant in one of the high-backed booths, Pietro ordered his drink. Five minutes later, the door to the restaurant opened, and the maître d' greeted a woman in a flowing white dress. Although not particularly beautiful in a standout sort of way, her posture, auburn hair and sunglasses gave her the appearance of someone who belonged in the class of women who are used to being sought after but rarely conquered. After a few words, she was shown to the rear of the restaurant, where she sat opposite Pietro. After her drink and both meals had been ordered, they were left alone.

"So glad you could make it on such short notice," Pietro said after the waiter had departed.

"I've been close enough, but you were correct about your assumptions. The Vatican did assign one person to observe you loosely the first two days. She also was apparently satisfied that you were nothing more than the sculptor here to immerse yourself in art and has not been seen today. Nor have we detected anyone else on you."

Pietro raised an eyebrow. "She? Was she good-looking?"

The woman frowned at him. "She was as ugly as the perfect nun. Actually, yes. Short-cut blond hair. She was dressed to look like an American tourist."

"Oh, her!" Pietro feigned interest. He was having fun.

The woman's brow furrowed more. "Do you have more to talk about than the observation of living sculptures?"

Pietro laughed out loud. "The masters used to study the human body for years in order to perfect their techniques. Surely you wouldn't deny me a bit of on-the-job training, would you?"

An icy stare was all that greeted him.

Pietro laughed again and then settled down to business. The drinks and meals had arrived during their banter. Over mouthfuls of veal, he told her the details of what had been discussed at the lunch meeting with the two men. From his pocket, he pulled out several sketches he had made while observing the statues in the museums. A casual observer would have assumed he was sketching what was in front of him rather than what was in his own mind.

"There have been just a couple of changes. I've noted them here with detailed descriptions. If they follow my notes and what was agreed upon earlier, then we should be fine. If anything else changes which is urgent, I will send a message to you only."

"And you are sure that you are being surveilled in the warehouse itself?"

"Three cameras, all with audio, discreetly hidden along the gantry, the beam above the door and one opposite by the air compressor. I was told that I had access to WIFI, so they are no doubt using the same network for the access to the cameras from outside. The only certain location that has no camera or microphone is the toilet. I plan to make a point of leaving my phone on the table when I am not actively using it and establishing that as its place. I'll use the burner phones when I'm in the toilet if I need to communicate."

"What about long-term?"

"Eventually, as the piece progresses, I will discover one of the cameras and then go on a mad-artist rant the next time I meet with Manco or Donati or Manco's assistants. I'll declare that I cannot work with the thought that someone is watching over my shoulder the entire time. Then I'll threaten to abandon the project entirely. By that time, I believe that they will be on the hook and will acquiesce to my demands. Either way, I'll let you know what happens."

"You'll need to have yourself free of surveillance by the halfway point or just beyond," she said.

"I know. I don't think it will be a problem. What about the other sites?"

"They are all prepared. Because of the complexities of the logistics of handling the pieces, we have a warehouse in each of the three locations as close as possible to the discovery sites."

"And the equipment?"

"All three of them are on site and have been thoroughly tested after installation." She looked straight at him. "Marble CNC machines which can work on pieces this size are extremely expensive to build."

Pietro smiled. "You could have me do it instead."

She smiled back at him. "No thank you. That would present a greater logistical nightmare than even I could handle. You stick with your piece, and I'll stick with the rest."

Pietro closed his eyes as he savored the last of his veal. He leaned his head back against the padded booth and let out a deep sigh.

"If only..." he began to say.

She cut him off immediately. "Don't even start your philosophizing. You know I don't agree with you and never will. They're all crooks. The only difference between any of them is the direction they wear their collars."

Pietro opened one eye in a squint and studied her. Tina Colletti was a strong woman. That was clear to anyone. But she was a woman with deep wounds, wounds which had locked the doors of her very soul against that which was most beautiful and worthy of consideration in life.

"If one acknowledges the existence of sheep, must not there also be shepherds, true shepherds?" He knew the question seemed futile to pose. But Pietro could not look at the granite encasing her heart without attempting to touch it with the occasional chisel of kindness in the hopes of revealing true beauty once all of the bitterness had been chipped away.

"All I see are wolves," she said in a tone of bitterness tinged with a hint of sadness. "I've never met a real shepherd in my life."

Pietro leaned forward and reached across the table with both hands. He encased her hands crossed on the table in front of her with his own.

"Then let us expose the wolves and see if the true shepherds will arise."

Now, a day later and after a mostly silent road trip back with his chauffeur, Pietro contemplated the stone in front of him. The weight of the stone rested just as squarely upon the wooden beams as did the enormity of the project with which he was faced. So much depended on getting this done in the right time and with the right nuances. Pietro picked up a massive hammer and a broad chisel and approached the stone before him.

Chapter 14

Philadelphia

Alex Ingram was coasting, and he knew it. So did his editors. The grizzled veteran of the investigative crime reports and political intrigue had not had a really good investigative journalistic piece in at least five years. The salary continued along with most of the perks mainly because of the stature his presence commanded in the daily newspaper. For years, his career had been a string of unparalleled successes. Junior reporters, editors and not a few colleagues lived in a constant state of envy at the depth of his reporting.

"If I only had just one of his sources!" was a comment he had overheard or had repeated to him by bootlickers attempting to curry favor with him. And he did have sources. Whether it was a report about a foreign conflict, a multi-national corporation caught with its hand too deep in the investors' pot or even a local politician who needed to be exposed for graft, Alex always seemed to have rock-solid sources who were capable of repeating the words whispered in a bed chamber.

Now, though, Alex was in a funk. At least that's the way everyone had chosen to explain it. "Everyone hits a dry spell," his editors would tell him with a pat on the shoulder, hoping that it would snap him out of it. True, he had brought such renown and prestige to their media parent that he could sit in a corner office and never write another piece and still draw a paycheck. But after five years of a dry spell, even the most jealous among them secretly were rooting for the old man to pull a rabbit out of a hat and get back on track.

He opened the door to his office, turned on the lights which were supposed to indicate the beginning of hard work and inspiration and shuffled to his plush chair behind the desk. He squinted at the huge dual monitors on his desk through red eyes and swore for the thousandth time that he would never stay up late drinking again. He knew his resolve would fade as quickly as had his success. He doubted he would ever see it again.

While everyone else looked at his fall and questioned the psychological complexities and the frailty of genius, Alex sank deeper into a realization of hopelessness. He knew why his career had tanked. Alex had transgressed.

It wasn't the venial sins of alcohol, drugs, adultery, felony or any other minor moral debauchery. It was the gravest of mortal sins: he had disobeyed his masters.

It wasn't the people who ran the newspaper or even the board of directors or CEO of the parent media company. No, Alex had disobeyed his handlers. Not for the first time, he sat at his desk and relived his career with wistful regret.

Alex knew that he had been a bright-enough and aspiring journalism major at Georgetown University. When one of his professors recommended that he attend a conference over his second summer break, Alex told him he would consider it. A couple of weeks later, another professor recommended it and explained that it would help his career to show attendance at such a conference. "Besides," he had explained, "the conference is run by a foundation that looks to help the cream of the crop advance in their careers. Your travel, food, lodging and conference fees are all underwritten by the foundation. And," he added in a conspiratorial undertone, "they actually supply a stipend for attendees to offset the money they would lose by giving up a couple of weeks of work over the summer."

When Alex heard the amount of the stipend, he almost choked. It was more than he would earn in a month bussing tables at even the best restaurants in town. He expressed his definite interest. The application was filled out, duly approved, and Alex had found himself attending a conference among some of his generation's finest. The speakers were all big names. The food was prepared by the kind of chefs who typically served congressmen. With all that he saw and experienced, Alex had forgotten to ask two of the six questions every journalist learns to live and die by: "who" and "why" never once crossed his mind.

After the conference, Alex got more face time with his professors. His status among his classmates grew with public comments in class about the quality of his assignments by the faculty. Alex and a handful of others seemed destined to be bright stars as the best of the upperclassmen.

Near the beginning of his senior year and after his second conference, Alex was approached by a man who introduced himself as a member of the US Department of State. He had been encouraged to seek out Alex, he said, as a potential intern to imbed in the Department and to potentially accompany ambassadors, State Department employees and the occasional congressman on trips in order to "see the world firsthand." What did Alex think about it? Would he give it some thought?

Alex was giddy. First of all, the question of where to land an internship was settled for him rather than having to compete for spots in local media organizations. The unlucky would have to travel outside the DC area and work in a small town for companies whose viewership would be local or regional at best. Also, he couldn't think of anything better than to be at the heart of one of the most powerful organizations on earth and see how decisions are made. He jumped at the chance, and at the beginning of his last semester, he reported for duty as a green intern with the US Department of State.

What began as a three-month stint continued after graduation for an additional twelve months. Looking back, Alex likened his experience to that of an eager prepubescent schoolgirl being groomed by a school counselor. He had been so eager, and they had been so good.

There were "suggestions" and "talking points" which each reporter traveling on each trip was given. At first, Alex tried to bring a creative outsider's approach to his articles, which he submitted to his boss at State. But after a few furrowed brows, frowns or shakes of the head, Alex began to tailor his articles to more closely align with the talking points. So, after almost a year and a half, Alex had progressed to the point that his boss was approving his work with scarcely a glance. About that time, he had called Alex in for a meeting and asked him where he was thinking about working full time. Alex expressed an interest in Philadelphia. It was close enough to be connected to that area of the country while also having its own appeal. His boss said that he knew someone at one of the major newspapers there and could put in a good word for him. "Why don't you give them a call and see if they'll do an interview with you after looking at your resume?"

Looking back, it had gone so smoothly: too smoothly. After a few weeks on the job, moving in was complete, his routine was beginning to form, and people's faces and names were clicking. The phone call was from one of the people he had met at State. The man had a tip on a hot story and couldn't think of anyone else who would do it justice. Would he be interested in the details? Alex was happy to oblige. He was glad that he hadn't been forgotten (he had not) and was eager for a chance to prove his mettle to his new employer.

The story involved a treaty between the US and a previously hostile regime. The details had been worked on in secret for almost two years and were culminating at Camp David under a shroud of secrecy. An official announcement would be made through State the following week. But, the man noted, it would throw things into an uproar in a good way if a few details of the talks were released ahead of time. "For one," he said in answer to Alex's question, "it would give the administration a much-needed few days of rest from the talk about the economy" (which was lagging). "It would also shift the focus onto that part of the world for upcoming negotiations between the Democrats and the Republicans on budgets for operations in that area."

Alex had the first real pause of his young career. Should he go forward on unsubstantiated data? It could spell the end of it before he really got started if the talks fell through. The upside was tremendous. Why else would he be getting the call if the man at State wasn't sure about the tip? Alex made his decision. "Okay. I'm in. Give me all the details you can."

Before the phone call was ended, the man reminded Alex that he couldn't use his name. Thus began Alex's official introduction to "a person familiar with the matter who wishes to remain anonymous." His editors were leery, very leery, of running the piece, especially for someone so new and for a story with such potential to turn around and bite them. But the man who was somehow connected to his boss at the State Department said, "What have we got to lose, really? If he's wrong, we run a retraction and blame it on an overzealous rookie. And if he's right..."

With those sage words, it was decided to run the story on page one but somewhere on the bottom half and not as the main headline. That took a bit of the credence off the story in case Alex's source proved to be incorrect. It was the last time for many years that Alex's stories did not command the top half of the page, if not the main headline itself.

The story itself did create a stir. It caught the majority party whose leader had lost the last presidential election with their pants down. They had been advancing their own agenda steadily against someone they had deemed a lame duck. Now their enemy was being hailed as one of the great peacemakers of the generation. The President himself was invited to more talk shows than he had been on in months. And when State Department stated that they could neither confirm nor deny the story, the rest of the media knew what that meant. The actual announcement put out by the State Department by the following week was almost an afterthought. Alex's star was set.

Alex's stories kept coming because the tips kept coming. He didn't have time to be asked to cover a local beat and work his way up the ladder. His brand of investigative journalism was too broad to stick down in a local trench. Not that his stories never had a local impact. More than one Philadelphia politician felt the sting of his pen. His first source introduced him to several other sources over the course of the years. All of them proved to have a solid set of facts and gave him plenty of leads he could easily follow up on his own to add his own touch to each story. But the stories were always consistent in one regard: they never strayed from the talking points he was given.

Chapter 15

Alex crossed a threshold ten years into his career. There was, it seemed, a particular Gospel mission in the heart of Philadelphia that was being run by a minister who was not all that he seemed to be. The mission itself stood on a piece of prime real estate which had been donated by a wealthy patron whose conscience had gotten the better of his fiscal sense in the late 1800s, and it had been run continually by one do-gooder or another for the last century.

"What if," the source said in a hushed voice over the phone, "it turned out that the mission itself was nothing more than a front for the distribution of drugs and sex trafficking of young women who were vulnerable and abused by someone they trusted the most?" It was suggested that Alex begin by doing a gloss piece on the mission by way of introduction to all the good it had done in the community the past century. Build it up so that the readers became engaged. Put a spotlight on it. Then bring out the truth. "I'll be in touch later," was the promise.

Alex had enough real journalistic skills to pursue the first two parts of the story. Everyone was delighted to recall the good which had been accomplished at the old Gospel mission. City leaders from the previous generation were interviewed with interspersed snippets of testimonials from men and women who had been set on the right path. All in all, the mission itself was brought back to the forefront of the community which knew it existed but had largely forgotten it.

Unmarked packets arrived in the mail with photos. Names of local women were given, along with the best numbers to call to reach them. A policeman or two were willing to speak off the record about concerns they had based on tips they had been receiving from their street contacts. It was enough to give Alex the skeleton of a story to which his own interviews and research added the meat.

When the next installment hit the stands, the right Reverend Billy "Happy" Lewis was himself in the glare of the public spotlight in a way that did much to turn his nickname into a much-lampooned source of derision. It seemed, the story informed the reader, that the good preacher, an African American with a "hard-luck-turned-out-good story" had pulled the wool over the eyes of the community, the mission's board of directors and, worse yet, the very people he was supposed to be helping. No fewer than three women were willing to speak directly on the record that "Happy" seemed happiest when he was forcing them back into the very lifestyle from which they were so desperately trying to extricate themselves. The photos themselves were grainy enough to not be definitive. The editors agreed only to permit the captions to read things to the effect of, "Is this Reverend Lewis with a known drug dealer making a transaction?" and, "Who is the man in the photo with his arms around two women in a local nightclub?"

The police raided the mission in the middle of the night. Heroin, some weed and packets of unused condoms were found in a supply closet. Happy wasn't looking so happy in his arrest photo, where he was charged with running a drug den and a house of ill repute. The board members came forward for the sake of the mission to say they had no idea what had been going on under their very noses. Charitable donations nosedived understandably. A public defender was appointed who made a strong statement of support in Happy's defense (that was, everyone understood, his job). The last Alex heard after all the hubbub, the mission itself had been sold due to being unable to pay its bills. It seemed the cost of doing good was rather high in a place like downtown Philadelphia. And Happy? Well, he never would admit to the crime. He maintained his innocence. When the public defender managed to get the case thrown out on a technicality, Happy had his freedom, but he would no longer be welcome in any pulpit which cared an ounce about respectability.

It wasn't until five years later that Alex received an anonymous call from a woman whose voice sounded only vaguely familiar. Where had he heard it before? He couldn't place it. But the voice only told him to meet her at a dive in one of the seedier parts of town. Alex wasn't really afraid. His face was recognized by most of the bar owners, if not the bartenders themselves, because of his prominence for the past fifteen years in the local newspaper. He arrived at the appointed time and was directed to a table by the bartender with an accompanying, "She said you'd be coming."

Alex walked to the table and said, "Your voice sounded familiar on the phone. Do I know you?"

The woman certainly looked the worse for the wear. One thing Alex hated was to see people who had let life run over them. Maybe it reminded him of just how fragile life was. Maybe it was because his successes only highlighted just how terrible failure was. Regardless, here before him sat a prime example.

"Well, if it isn't ace reporter Ingram, in the flesh. That's Mister Ingram to you and me," she said as she looked sideways at an imaginary companion. Alex tried not to grimace. Her breath could stop a bull mid-charge and was probably dangerous around open flames. "Have a seat, Mister Ingram, and let me tell you a story."

Alex didn't want to sit anywhere near her mouth or, as he bent to pull out the chair, her body. She smelled of cheap whisky and a body that had come into contact with everything except clean water for some weeks. Alex sat down. "Do I know you from somewhere?" he repeated.

"Yeah, you know me. Or at least you know who I said I was at the time. Rita. Rita Steinbrenner was the name for your story."

That was it. She was one of the three ladies he had written about in the exposé of the Gospel mission. "Now I remember. Rita, I would ask how you are doing, but I can guess that you've seen better times. How can I help you?" Alex was all business and doing his best to get ahead of the conversation.

"I said I was Rita, not am," she slurred. "Not Steinbrenner at all. The name's Torie Spalding. And I'm going to die."

Alex didn't find that hard to believe. Her liver could probably be put straight into a jar for a medical school without any formaldehyde. Still, he played his part. "Torie, I'm a bit confused. If you weren't Rita Steinbrenner five years ago, why did you say you were?"

"Because they paid me to. They paid all of us. Me, Goldie and Sammie. We used to all hang together down at Phil's club. Two men in nice suits came down and hung out with us. One of them had a big head of red hair, parted straight down the middle. He made me nervous. Goldie called him Mr. Creep when we were alone. Well, they got to talking to us and asked us how we'd like to score some big money. It didn't take much convincing. Goldie asked what we had to do. They spun us a story about how they were with the state attorney's office and that they had been investigating old Happy. They said that he was in deep but that they were willing to go lighter on him because they didn't want to see the mission destroyed. They said it had done a lot of good in the city. So they were looking for some women who would testify that he had gotten them back into their old lifestyles. They would present him with the evidence they had and confront him with our testimony and then force him to step down real quiet like.

"Well, we hated to hear it, but we all knew people who had been through the mission. With some of 'em, it stuck, and some of 'em it didn't. But we were all pulling for the mission, so we said yes. They gave us the names to use and the details. They told us to add whatever we need to make the stories believable but to not stray too much from the details they gave us."

Alex started to get cold when she said that. He listened a bit more attentively.

"They told us you would be calling us soon. They also got a guy that kind of looked like Happy to pose for some pictures with us. I saw one of the pictures later in the paper with me and Goldie and the guy. The way they did it, you would never know it wasn't Happy himself."

Torie stopped talking and looked straight into Alex's eyes. For a moment she seemed stone sober. "God is my witness; I would take it all back if I knew what they were going to do." She stared through Alex and retreated back into herself.

Alex waited for at least five minutes for her to speak. "Why did you want to see me now?" he finally asked.

Torie focused her eyes again on his face. "Because I'm going to die."

"We all are going to die, Torie."

"No. They're dead, and now I'm going to die."

"Who's dead?"

"Goldie. And Sammie. They got 'em two weeks ago."

"Who got them? What are you talking about?"

"Goldie never could get over what happened with Happy. His religion never took with her, but Happy had helped her little sister. She was hooked on heroin bad, and she took an overdose to try and end it all. Happy found her lying in the gutter a few blocks from the mission and called an ambulance for her. Old Happy wouldn't leave her bedside in the hospital. He prayed and read his Bible over her for three straight days. When Lisa woke up from her coma, she said she saw Happy looking down at her, and she swears that Jesus was standing behind Happy with his nail-scarred hand on Happy's shoulder. He looked straight at Lisa and said, 'This man will tell you how to live with me forever. Listen to him.'"

Torie broke down in tears. They formed deep crevices in her thick makeup. Alex found himself struggling to keep back his own tears. Something was going on here that he couldn't understand.

Torie's nose began to run, but she didn't seem to notice. She began to gasp out the words. "Don't you see? You and me, we ruined a good man's life. We stole his name. We sold our souls to the devil, and now we have to pay him for what we've done."

She was getting frantic. Alex was afraid she would hyperventilate. He pulled out a handful of napkins from the holder and handed them to Torie. He grabbed her shoulder and said, "Torie, get a hold of yourself. Tell me what's going on. What's got you so shook?"

"I told you. When Goldie realized what had really happened to Happy, she kind of went off the deep end. She was always spouting off about what she was gonna do to those jerks who lied to us. We just told her to keep quiet.

There was nothing we could do against people like that.

"Then about a month ago, she shows up and says that she saw Mr. Creep, the one with the red hair. We thought she had just had a bad run-in with a customer. No, she told us that she had seen one of them guys again all dressed up and coming out of that big building they built where the mission stood. He was coming straight down the street toward her. Well, she marched right up to him and gave him a piece of her mind. She told him that now that she knew where he had been, she was going to go in there and tell everyone just what he had done to poor old Happy.

"The man recognized her right away. He told her that it was all a mistake. He asked her to not do anything until he could show her the proof that he had also been tricked. He asked her how to get in contact with her. Me and Goldie didn't like it, but the man told her that he was working to try to clear Happy's name.

"As it turns out, I got lucky. I ate some of Jack's chowder soup and got sick as a dog. Sammie told me that she would go with Goldie to make sure she was okay. Still, Sammie wasn't taking any chances. If everything was on the up and up, she would call Jack and tell him to give me the message. Jack has a private room in the back of his bar for...Aw, never mind. Anyways, I was using the room to stay in while I was so sick.

"They left and never came back. Ain't no one heard of 'em since. Jack told me that word was going around that I was a hot commodity and that I needed to make plans to find another place to stay. He wasn't sure how long I could stay there before word got out that I was there at his place.

"So I've been barhopping, but not the way I used to. I'm down to my last friend in the world, Mister Ingram. And I asked him to let me use the phone to call you in the hopes that you would come and let me confess my crime. When I leave here tonight, I don't have anywhere else to go." She broke down and started crying. "There isn't even a Gospel mission for me to go to anymore."

Alex's mind was in a daze. "Torie, is there anything else you can tell me? Who were these men? What were their names?"

But Torie was too far gone to be much help. Alex had the location of the building, and that was it.

Torie kept repeating over and over, "You and me, we're both just a couple of whores. Now we have to pay the devil for what we've done." Over and over she kept saying it until the words were seared in Alex's brain.

"Torie, is there anywhere I can take you? Do you want to go to the hospital? They can help you get sober."

"You and me, Mr. Ingram. Just whores, that's all we are. We sold our souls. We sold our souls to the devil for thirty pieces of silver."

Alex had to get out of there. Clearly, there was nothing he could do for Torie. He got up and left a large bill on the table, nodded at the bartender and then left.

Chapter 16

The next few days were actually worse. He did some research on the building Goldie had pinpointed and found two interesting names. Then he made some calls and did some more research on the company that had bought the property which had housed the Gospel mission. It was owned by a handful of shell companies, but Alex had learned how to maneuver through those until he found a corporation owned by a real person. When he read it, Alex immediately felt sick to his stomach. It was his old boss at the State Department.

Alex was determined to do something. But apparently his research and inquiries had not gone unnoticed. Two days later, he received an unmarked envelope in the office mail with his name on it. Alex opened it and found a single photo. When he turned it over and looked at it, he again became violently ill. It was Torie, or what used to be Torie.

He flung the photo down as if it were a hot iron, dropped to his knees and held the wastebasket under his chin for ten solid minutes. Thankfully, his blinds had been drawn in the office, otherwise someone would have called an ambulance thinking he was dying, and the photo would no doubt have been seen by someone else. Exhausted, he pushed the wastebasket and its stench away. His eyes were bleary from all the abdominal exertions, but he managed to spot the photo lying face up a few feet away. He forced his head to turn away as he crawled over to it and picked it up. He turned it face down and fumbled with the paper as he ripped it to shreds. He would never be able to remove that image from his mind.

"You and me, Mr. Ingram. We sold our souls, and now we have to pay the devil for what we've done." Torie's words haunted him.

A half hour later, he was still sitting in the floor trying to piece together what to do next when the phone rang. It was the receptionist for the paper. "There's a Torie holding on line three for you." Alex's blood ran cold. How? What? He managed to clear his throat enough to acknowledge that he had heard the message, then he pushed the button for line three.

"Alex Ingram, how may I help you?" he croaked.

"Mister Ingram. This is Torie." (It clearly was not.) "I'm calling to find out if I'm still a good friend of yours or not."

Alex understood the message. "No. I—I'm afraid I don't know anyone by that name."

"Aw, that's too bad." Alex's anger started to rise. The woman on the line was actually mocking Torie's accent. "I had a really hot tip for you."

"No, I'm not interested. Really, I must go."

"Okay, Mister Ingram. But if you ever want that hot tip, you just remember good ol' Torie." The line went dead, and so did any chance that Alex would ever write a story about how the Gospel mission was sold for thirty pieces of silver to an upper-level State Department employee because of a few cheap prostitutes.

Still, something changed that day. Just like Goldie, he couldn't get over what had happened to Happy. He knew that he would never expose his masters. He had reconciled himself to the truth that he was a prostitute. He looked back and realized all too clearly how he had been bought and paid for by shadowy government clandestine services and employees. All the stories had won him many accolades and not a few awards, but none of them were his own. He was merely a mouthpiece, a convenient vehicle for establishing someone else's talking points. But Happy was a real man who apparently had done a lot of good.

Chapter 17

Three years later, Alex's conscience overcame his fear enough that he actually started looking through public and private databases until he located one William Lewis, formerly of Philadelphia and lately of Shamokin, a small town northwest of Philadelphia with a population of less than a good-sized arena. Alex found an address for him as well as a phone number. He thought about many ways to approach the question of how to make contact but decided that he didn't want to get shot. He picked up the phone and dialed the number. Surprisingly, the phone was answered on the second ring by a woman on the upper end of middle age.

"Hello, this is the Lewis residence."

"Yes, uh, I'm trying to reach William Lewis, I mean Billy."

There was a pause and the voice changed to a more guarded tone. "And might I ask who is calling for him?"

"Uh, this is Alex Ingram, I'm with…"

"I know who you work for, MISTER Ingram." The tone was downright icy, and Alex was reminded of a handful of times when he had been called Mister Ingram in such a tone that had never been forgotten.

The voice continued, "If you want my advice, you will take one of your whole newspaper's Sunday editions and sh…" The voice broke off, and it sounded like there was a healthy argument going on while someone had placed a hand over the mouthpiece. After a lot of raised voices, the hand was lifted, and a male voice came on the line.

"This is Billy, Mister Ingram. What can I do for you?"

Alex couldn't believe his ears. He would not have been surprised to be cursed royally. What he did not expect was a voice filled with warmth. He was taken aback and couldn't find words.

"Mister Ingram, are you still there?" The voice seemed to turn away from the mouthpiece. "You done gone and scared him off, Sarah."

"No, I'm here. I'm still here, Mister Lewis. I just didn't expect, I mean, I really don't know what to say."

"Well, you can start by letting me know why you called. You obviously had to look to find me, but you found me. The question is, why were you looking?"

"Mister Lewis, some things can only be best said in person. Would it be possible for me to visit with you?"

Pause. "Sure, Mister Ingram. But I warn you that things might be a bit frosty depending on who answers the door. And call me Billy. This Mister Lewis doesn't suit me one bit."

"That's to be expected, Mist...I mean, Billy. I'd like to come up tomorrow if that's suitable for your schedule."

It was. The time was set, and Alex let the newsroom staff know that he would be out of the office. The next day found him knocking on a small but tidy wood frame house on a side street in the bustling metropolis of Shamokin. Billy himself answered and explained that Sarah had some shopping she felt needed to be done.

"To be honest, Sarah wasn't sure she could be in the same room with you and not resort to her carnal nature and become violent, so I encouraged her to step out for a bit."

Alex didn't get part of what Billy was saying, but he understood that it meant that he was less likely to be assaulted by an angry woman.

"I didn't realize that you were married, Billy. How long have you and Sarah been married?"

"Married? Sarah?" Billy slapped his knee and laughed out loud. "Sarah is my older sister, but she thinks she's my mama, God rest her soul. She's an old spinster, and I'm an old bachelor. I like to kid her that no one would have her or me but God Himself. Now come on in and have a seat here in the parlor." He ushered Alex into a quaint sitting room, which had obviously felt the touch of a woman's affection in its decor.

"Thank you for seeing me, Billy. I've never really been in a situation like this, and I'm not really good at making small talk."

Billy nodded his assent for Alex to continue.

"To put it bluntly, I was completely in the wrong in what I wrote about you. I thought I was doing the right thing at the time, but I came to realize a few years ago that what I had written was nothing more than a hit piece. I was deceived, but for my part I never did my part to dig deeper into the accusations which I wrote and caused to be published all over Philadelphia— and beyond."

Billy sat quietly. His eyes didn't stray from Alex's face.

"Billy, what I learned about you long after the fact is that you were never involved in any of the things I accused you of. In fact, everyone I've talked to who knew you personally has told me story after story of how you went out of

77

your way time after time to help the people who could never pay you back." Alex's voice broke. "Billy, I wanted to look you in the face and tell you I am so very sorry for what I did to you, your work among the poor and the hopeless in Philadelphia, your name..." He broke off and looked pleadingly at Billy.

Billy was silent for a time. Then he spoke in a quiet but firm voice. "And for my part, Mister Ingram, I forgive you."

They were three simple words, but Alex could not believe he had heard them. "Billy, I ruined your name. How could you just forgive me?"

"I beg to differ with you. Didn't you just tell me that there's a whole bunch of folk who remember me differently than you expected?"

Alex nodded.

"Maybe there were a bunch of folk who thought of me only what they wanted to. But the people who knew old Happy firsthand haven't much changed their opinion, have they now? And those who want to believe something different are going to believe what they choose."

Just like that, Billy was Happy again. And Alex realized that he had never stopped being Happy. He didn't really know how any man could undergo such a vicious and slanderous attack on his character and forgive the one who did it so readily. It was a miracle out of nowhere.

The day stretched longer than either man expected. Sarah eventually ran out of excuses to come to her own home. After an aloof greeting, Happy explained why Alex had come and shared the whole story. Alex apologized to Sarah directly for hurting her brother and for the pain he had caused her, too. That was enough to bring a tear to Sarah's eye, which she promptly wiped away as she hurried to make a "proper supper" for them all to enjoy.

Alex left with a lighter heart than he had had for many years. He also had a notebook full of details which he was already formulating into a story on the drive home. Over the next two days, he crafted what he believed was his best piece of work. Considering much of what he had published under his own name had been a regurgitation of someone else's story with his own bits added for flavor, it really was his best work in years.

When he submitted it to his editor for review, he was surprised to receive pushback.

"This is over and done with, Alex. It's kind of late to be issuing retractions, don't you think?"

"I don't think it's ever too late to print the truth, do you?"

"Let me run it up the flagpole and see if anyone salutes on it."

Alex waited for an additional three days. At the end of the third day, he was sitting in his office when the phone rang. "Torie on line five for you."

Alex paused and took a deep breath then pushed the button. "Torie, how can I help you?"

The woman's voice was hard-edged, and she was struggling to put an accent on it. "Mister Ingram. How is your health?"

"I'm well, thank you. How is yours?" If they were going to play this game, he would play along.

"I've been much better. I heard that you are digging around in a cemetery. You don't need any tips from Torie, do you?"

"No," Alex said firmly. "There is a man I hurt rather badly, and I want to set the record straight about him. It only seems fair so many years down the road."

"Mister Ingram, you of all people should know that life isn't fair. How many people get to enjoy your level of success? Have you thought about that?"

He had. Life had been more than easy for him most of his career. "This isn't about my career. It's about trying to remove a stain from a good man's name."

Laughter, more of a cackle, emitted from the phone in his ear. "Not a good idea, Mister Ingram. We don't want people asking questions about what happened to the Reverend. It might cause some problems."

"Listen, you have my word that this is not an investigative piece." The photo flashed back through his mind, and he involuntarily trembled. "My editor has already seen the story. It's about putting some shine back onto Happy's name. He deserves that."

"No, you listen, Mister Ingram," the voice grew stern. "Take it from old Torie. Some things are better left dead and buried." The connection broke. The call was over.

Alex hated bullies. He had run into his share of them growing up before puberty leveled the playing field with his own growth. The fact was undeniable that someone had leaked his story to a person connected to these phone calls. He picked up the phone and called his editor. "What's the word on the story?" he asked.

"The consensus is that we shouldn't run it."

Alex expected that. "Here's the deal," he said with as much conviction as he could muster, his body shaking with a combination of rage and dread. He had to say it before he changed his mind. "If you don't run that piece, I'm going to take out a full-page ad in three other papers and publish it myself. This is a chance for the paper to go on the record with my name. If you don't, you know how it will look. The paper will get a black eye because it was too afraid to print the truth by a senior journalist."

Alex had them boxed in, and he knew it.

There was a low growl on the other end and then, "I'll call you back."

Ten minutes later, Alex had his answer. The paper would run the story. It was going to be buried in the lifestyle section, but Alex would not accept any less than somewhere on the front page of the Sunday edition. He got his wish.

Chapter 18

That following weekend, the story ran. In it, Alex walked a fine line but was straightforward in his facts. Happy had been, he related, the victim of a smear campaign by someone who was opposed to his work and what he represented. He left out the details of Torie and her friends. He did not lead the reader to any speculation as to who had purchased the property later and how the transaction had been facilitated by the charges against Happy. But Happy was held up for the whole community to see and, this time, to admire as a man who had not lost his faith or his compassion for others.

His journey over the last eight years was chronicled. After a year of jail, bond and numerous public trial motions, he had left Philadelphia under a cloud when it was apparent that there would be no future for him to minister to those he felt called to serve. From there he had moved to Shamokin, where he found work as a volunteer counselor under the supervision of a lifelong friend who was willing to give him a chance. That had blossomed into work as a chaplain in the local jails and nearby prison. He had also managed to save the lives and quite possibly the souls of more than a few drug addicts the past seven years. Alex had managed to locate Goldie's younger sister, Lisa, who was holding a steady job and was happily married. She had never even felt a craving for drugs of any kind after her three-day stint in the hospital. Alex had concluded his article with her story and this quote:

> As I reflect on what I have learned about Reverend Lewis' life in the past seven years, a man who I wronged personally by not investigating further, but also a man who has not only forgiven me but has proven to be a friend equally to both journalist in an office and junkie in a gutter, I cannot help but imagine that in him I see a man on whose shoulder the hand of his Savior continues to rest in approval.

Again, news of Happy and the Gospel mission created quite the stir. For the poor and the down and out, it was like a breath of fresh air. Their hero had been exonerated after more than eight years. For the churches in the area, there was a mixture of some shame that they had been too quick to cast away one of their own so quickly as well as relief that a minister was receiving good press for a change. The story was hailed widely as what was right about Philadelphia and was depicted as the boldest story ever by a local journalist in a generation. Because of Alex's personal retraction and public apology, he and Happy both were invited to speak together before the top civic organizations and various Christian and interfaith gatherings. The current mayor, looking to never miss an opportunity, invited Happy to City Hall, where he issued a statement officially proclaiming that day to be "Reverend Billy 'Happy' Lewis Day" and gave him the key to the city.

It was a surreal time, and Happy took it all in stride. He was genuinely pleased to be able to breathe the air of the city he had served for most of his life without the stigma of the accusations hanging over him. When the whirlwind of appointments and speaking engagements were winding down, he asked Alex to go for a walk with him. As they strolled along the streets with Happy reminiscing about numerous encounters he remembered in his work among the hopeless in the various bars, dives and places of ill repute, Alex realized that they were headed toward the site of the old Gospel mission. He began to feel a bit uncomfortable, but he also understood why Happy would want to visit the place. The location held so many memories for him.

When they reached the address, Happy stood for a while just looking at the behemoth of a glass, concrete and steel structure which had erased the simple mission with its quirky combination of Gothic revival and Queen Anne architecture.

"Do you know who owns it currently?" Happy asked.

"Yes."

'What do they do in there now?"

Alex sighed. "They make money, a lot of it."

Happy kept looking at the building. Then, in public, he stretched both of his hands outward toward the building and began to speak in a fervent tone: "Lord Jesus, you know what this place used to be. You know what it is now. You see what they have done to your mission, how they have tried to derail your mission from happening in this city. I pray that you look down from on high and let them know that you still rule in the affairs of men. As I walked here, Lord, I saw people who are still hurting, people whose eyes are still empty of the hope that only you can bring. Turn this place into a house of hope and healing once again."

Alex was embarrassed both at the spectacle and the volume with which Happy had chosen to implore heaven. He looked around. Yes, people were staring. He had no doubt that half a dozen security cameras were capturing the whole thing. But when Happy finished his prayer, the strangest thing occurred. A bird flew out of nowhere and landed on the steel molding just above the engraved letters spelling out the name of the building. Alex was used to seeing pigeons, but there had been no birds around for the past fifteen minutes. Now here sat a lonesome bird. Alex looked more closely. It was a dove.

Happy noticed it, too. He smiled his big smile, looked up and said, "Thank you, Lord." Then he turned and said to Alex, "I'm ready to go back home now."

Chapter 19

The news cycle being what it is, it didn't take long for another story to capture the minds of the city. Happy had gone home to Shamokin, and Alex had sat around waiting for another story lead. He waited several days, but there were no leads. Days had turned to weeks. Weeks dragged into months. Months used their collective strength to flip the calendars over to years. Alex had been hung out to dry.

The most obvious proof was the immediate cessation of phone calls with solid intel on upcoming stories. Then, the invitations to travel the globe dried up along with dinner parties, both locally and in the DC area, where he had rubbed shoulders with the newsmakers, both public and private. One by one over a relatively short period of time, Alex was systematically blackballed from his former journalistic jet-setting lifestyle so suddenly that the isolation took a shock toll upon him.

While Happy had withstood one of the greatest tests to a man's character—the assassination of the character itself—Alex had no real moral compass to guide him. Instead, he found himself suddenly awash in a sea of self-loathing, fear, panic, depression and a litany of issues which would have made even the most seasoned psychiatrist earn his pay. He had known for years that he had been bought, not just by corporate America but by intelligence agencies and the pawns they controlled in the State Department. He had long ago realized that the State Department itself did not have all the resources to supply the depth of information on some of the stories he had received. But to face that fact now required him to look into the mirror in the mornings at the face of a man who had been just another mouthpiece for a deeper and darker organization that pulled the strings of a million puppets, it seemed. Torie's words haunted him the most when he tried to close his eyes at night: "You and me, we're just a couple of whores."

True, the fact that he had written the retraction on Happy and demanded that it be published counted for something, but it was only a temporary salve on a wound which stretched from one end of his soul to the other for the entire length of his career. When he tried to compare that one, honest good deed with the multitude of times that he had stifled the voice of conscience as he regurgitated the talking points year after year, it was as if he could see one side of Lady Justice's scales dropping under their combined weight. Alex despaired at the thought of how many years it would take him to even begin to balance the scales in his favor.

The fear set upon him when the gravity of his position began to be clearer. Sources were the lifeblood of any journalist, and he no longer had any. In the first few months, his editors had nudged him with questions about what he was working on and when they might expect an outline or rough draft. He had given vague answers at first to delay the inevitable, hoping that his transgression against his former masters would be forgiven. But the silence continued, and Alex realized that if a story were to be had, he would have to find one on his own. He did make several valiant efforts, but the truth, it seemed, was a hidden jewel. At the very least, it was in very short supply among those in the journalism industry.

After hitting dead end after dead end, true panic set in. It would come in waves. Sometimes they were predictable. At other times, the smallest thing would overwhelm him with another wave. It might be the buzzer in the office signifying the alert that final articles were due in fifteen minutes before the presses would begin to run. At other times, it would be a face on the television reminding him that he had traveled to Europe with that man or been invited to his home to hear the background for another story. Once, he had turned a corner and seen a poster for a reenactment of a political debate between a patriot and a Tory. In a flash, the conversation in the bar, the photo in the plain envelope and the phone calls from the fake Torie all came back at once. It was not until another pedestrian had repeated the phrase "Sir, are you all right?" several times that Alex realized he had been standing stock still for the better part of a half hour.

It was when Alex began to realize that there was no way out of his nightmare that depression overtook him. He found it difficult to get up in the morning early and go to work. Why bother? He started drinking regularly, something he had never done because of what he had heard over and over from his mother that it had done to his grandfather. But Alex began to find more comfort in the glass in his hand than he could find the will to work. At least it took the edge off the pain. It turned down the volume on Torie's voice. And, he began to tell himself, he deserved no better than to end up in the gutter outside the old Gospel mission. Perhaps that would in some way serve to atone for what he had done to destroy it.

Chapter 20

Five agonizing years later, it was this Alex Ingram who managed to shuffle to his desk, sit down in his chair and stare at the two monitors on his desk. He opened up his Internet browser and flicked through the latest stories of the day. To Alex, it was less about trying to catch up on the news as it was trying to guess what the real truth was. As he would scroll through the headlines of the major news organizations, he recognized name after name of the men and women whom he had seen at the summer conferences or who had attended them right along with him. He knew that they were like himself, shapers of the narrative rather than independent guardians of facts.

After ten minutes, he was tired of it again. He contemplated reaching for the bottle in his desk drawer, but the face of the man who had stared back at him in the mirror this morning was beginning to truly frighten him. Instead, he opened up his email program and began sorting through it in rote fashion.

At first, Alex didn't pay attention to the subject line. He got so much junk email that some days he would just drag it all to the trash bin in the email program. As his eyes rescanned the page, they focused on the subject line fully. It began with the words, "I thought you might be interested," which was the lead-in to every good Internet scam or porn site advertisement he had ever been unlucky enough to receive. That was why he had scrolled past it earlier. But the rest of the subject line read "in some background on the Flatley case." That at least got his attention enough to click on the email. He had never been offered male enhancement pills or a solar energy solution with the name of a real court case attached to it.

When he read the email, his heart jumped just a little. Could his exile be over? Was this a chance to get back into the good graces of his editors and, perhaps, his former masters?

His excitement was short-lived. The email didn't read like the talking points he had received for every other article. And there was no reason someone wouldn't just pick up the phone and call him. It wasn't like his number had changed in five years. Instead, the email read more like a series of bullet points combined with a list of questions. Still, Alex's journalistic instinct was stirred. He read the email through quickly and then slowly a second and third time.

First, he looked at who the email was from: "polkadotpanda." It was sent through one of the popular email servers which Alex had heard some of the younger reporters babble on about being secure and private. Whatever. He had never had time for subterfuge in his career when it was going strong. This panda bear, whoever he was, had some interesting thoughts he had shared. Alex looked at the bullet points:

1. The arresting officers involved in this case have been the same arresting officers on seven other drugs busts in the past year.

That wasn't news. That's what the narc squad was supposed to do.

2. In over half the cases, the offenders all received suspended or minimal sentences. In the other three cases, those arrested received full maximum sentence allowed by law, even the juveniles.

Again, this wasn't exactly earth-shaking. Who knew what deals were reached between the attorneys and the prosecutor, maybe in exchange for giving up information on someone higher up?

3. The judge in each of these cases was Judge Lewisburg, and the prosecutor was Aaron Mennheim, the DA.

That was starting to beat the odds. It was not uncommon for the same people to see each other in court on a regular basis, but all of these were pretty high-profile cases over the past two years.

4. The defendants who got off all are connected to narcotics operations in Southside. The defendants who received maximum sentences are all connected to narcotics operations in North Philly—but they were arrested in the Southside.

Alex was very interested now. Then he hit the list of questions at the bottom again:

1. How many cases have all of these people been involved in together in the past seven years since Mennheim was promoted to DA?

2. What are the connections between sentencing recommendations and actual sentences?

3. Is there a connection between sentences and criminal organizations?

4. Who is being protected and why?

The email ended simply with a request that Alex reply if he cared about the topic or was interested in pursuing it. "Fair enough," Alex thought. He hit the reply button, typed in the single word "Interesting" at the beginning of the subject line and hit the send button.

Then he sat and thought long and hard about what he had read. To pursue this story would require no small amount of research. He wasn't afraid of that. Even in his earlier days, he had done a fair share of legwork to round out the stories he was given. The question that was running through the circuits in his brain was frankly who it could possibly be who would be sending him a news tip. He hummed a tune and half sang, half whispered, "I set a course for winds of fortune…" and trailed off.

He picked up the phone and called the HR director. "Judy, do we still have interns in this office?" Judy was doubly shocked not only to hear Alex asking about interns but also to hear a crisp tone to his voice.

"Uh, yes, Alex. We have ten currently."

"How many can you spare for the next two weeks?"

"Let's see," Judy said as she looked at her master calendar. "I can give you three for all of that time and maybe a fourth one next week. He's finishing up a story with John."

"Send them up pronto," Alex said. He was about to hang up when he stopped and said, "And thanks, Judy."

Judy looked at the phone in her hand for five seconds before flicking the switch hook and calling down to the intern office. Within five minutes, three fresh-faced college students were gathered in Alex's office with an array of tablets and smartphones in hand. They weren't quite sure what to expect, since no one had worked with Alex their whole time at the paper, but they had all heard of his feats enough to be excited to work with him on any story he might have going.

"Okay, boys," Alex began. Then he glanced over and added, "…and lady. I don't know how familiar you are with the court databases we have available to us, but we're going to conduct a little exercise. I'll assign each of you a task, and I want your best effort. We'll have meetings here in my office once in the midmorning and twice after lunch to share what each of us has learned. Over here, we'll make a roadmap of our notes and the progress we make." He gestured to the whiteboard along one wall. Does anyone have any questions so far?

No one did. So Alex divided the workload of finding all the narcotics cases which Judge Lewisburg had heard during the past seven years, the narcotics cases that DA Mennheim had prosecuted in the same time period and finally, all the narcotics cases that any or all of three specific police officers and detectives had been involved in within the same time frame. "You have two hours before lunch, and I want to see some good, solid legwork by the time we meet back here at 1:00 p.m. Now get going."

After they left, Alex instinctively opened his drawer to pull out his own legal pad from his file folder and saw the bottle of amber staring up at him. His mouth watered. The craving for a drink was so strong. Alex flexed his fingers as they headed down toward the bottle. But then they stopped, almost as if they had a will of their own, or maybe muscle memory from years past was kicking in. In his head, he could hear Steve Walsh belting out the lyrics from *Carry On Wayward Son*. Which course would he set? Alex watched as his fingers reached in the file folder, pulled out the legal pad and slid the drawer closed on its rails. He smiled to himself as he began to sing right along with the lyrics.

Chapter 21

Western Italy

It was the last of the three warehouses which was causing Tina grief. Due to the aging electrical grid infrastructure, the power kept going out. This wouldn't be a cause for concern in most warehouse districts unless a company was dealing in frozen foods. But in her case, the loss of power in the middle of the operation of a laser-guided CNC machine, especially on a very delicate design, could wreak havoc and potentially ruin the whole thing.

Her operating budget was not unlimited, and the list of people she could trust was even more limited. Rather than delegate most of the operations, she had handled a myriad of details herself. Now she was speaking with a fifth company where she was finally able to order the largest diesel generator available which could handle the wattage requirements. Two 1,000-gallon tanks had already been located, ordered and were being shipped by freight trucks for delivery the next day. She did have a couple of other staff whose diverse backgrounds qualified them to handle the installation of everything once the pieces arrived at the warehouse. After getting a commitment to have the generator on site within forty-eight hours, Tina sat back in the secondhand office chair, pressed her face between her folded hands and closed her eyes.

After a few moments of sorting through her mental to-do list, she rubbed her face vigorously and opened her eyes again. The chic dress from her meeting in Rome had been replaced with jeans and a T-shirt. The auburn hair was pulled back and pinned in a quickly fixed bun. Efficiency mattered most now.

To make the most of her time, she opened her secure messaging app and again scrolled through the photos that Pietro had sent. He was nearing the halfway point. The man was a sculptor straight from myth. Not only was he gifted in his ability to see a piece, but his speed was unparalleled. Tina had spent time with him when they would talk about difficulties on their respective assignments. To pass the time while they were talking, Pietro would often pull out a hammer and chisel from his backpack along with a lump of stone and start tapping away at it. At times, his hands seemed to move as if he were a pianist who was so in tune with the instrument that his eyes seemed not to notice what the hands were doing.

Among all her colleagues, something had immediately clicked with him, and it seemed to work both ways. Pietro could be as tough as the rock he chiseled—she had seen it—but there was a side to him that was gentle. He was one of the rare people who, when he asked you how you were doing, looked at you in such a way that you knew he really wanted to know the truth. And, if he didn't think he was getting it, he would probe a bit more to find it.

She looked at the photos again and then saved them to an album. Then she opened the laptop on the desk beside her and synced the phone with it. It wouldn't hurt to practice with the equipment. After the photos were on the laptop, she opened up a 3-D modeling program and imported the photos. She arranged the photos in sequence so that they displayed the sculpture as if a person were walking around it in a circle and observing it in its entirety. Then she clicked through a series of menus to adjust the settings and answer questions about the nuances of combining the photos. Then she hit the final menu button, and the computer began the process of creating a 3-D composite of all the photos in a set of data which it would then be able to transfer to any of several types of machines for processing. It was really quite a clever setup, thought Tina. She had seen vendors around Europe selling custom 3-D busts or even miniature statuettes of the customer which were created by standard 3-D printers. But shop owners couldn't afford the type of equipment in the three warehouses. She wondered how many people were out there using the same type of setup to forge classical antique artwork.

A ding notified her that the program was done working. For her testing, she had reduced the scale to about half a meter in height. She walked over to the CNC and placed one of the small blocks of marble they had purchased for just this type of practice onto the center of the work area. Then she powered up the machine, donned a set of safety goggles and a respirator and began putting them on as she walked back to the computer. She looked at the profile summary of the job and then selected the CNC machine as the output device or "printer" for the job. After a slight delay, the CNC machine began to whir as the head was driven to its position. Tina wheeled the chair across the smooth concrete floor of the warehouse and sat down to watch the process. She glanced at her phone and made a mental note of the time for the purpose of seeing how long it would take to finish.

Tina was fascinated as she watched the marble chips and dust fly. The software was advanced enough to be able to cut off sections of marble from the outer edges rather than peeling away fractions of a centimeter at a time. As a result, chunks of marble were dropping off the edges at first before the software determined that it was time to switch to the more fine-tuned approach.

Just over two hours later, the machine beeped and began the process of retracting the head back into its locked position. Amidst the chunks and pieces of marble and the mound of dust stood a small statuette. Tina reached down and hefted the piece in her hands and turned it all around as she inspected it. She had reviewed the photos on her phone during the carving process, and what she held in her hands was a miniaturized version of what Pietro himself was carving. Since she had time, she went ahead and took the marble to a corner and adjusted the settings on a sand blaster which had been fitted to use a mix that included salt. Over the next half hour, she practiced different types of techniques Pietro had showed her. Slowly, the marble began to take on an aged and weatherworn appearance.

When she was finished, she reached inside a pail of dirt and clay mix and grabbed a handful. She rubbed the dirt over all of the surface area of the statue. It looked hideous. Then she placed it inside a small kiln and left it to bake at a low temperature for a few hours. In the interim, she continued working on a list of details which still had already been thought of but had yet to be implemented. One of the trucks arrived without a lift gate. Another truck at another warehouse had the lift gate but no winch and retractable boom. Down through the checklist she went, marking off items as they were finished and making notes besides the ones which yet required her attention.

By late afternoon, she removed the statue from the kiln with a pair of thick mittens. The kiln had done an amazing job to replicate the effect of centuries of dirt and grime being baked into a statue exposed to the weather. She could have waited for it to cool, but this was still a test run. She put a spray head on a water hose and began to remove the layer of baked on dirt with the pressurized stream. When it was completely washed and her clothes were thoroughly soaked with the constant spatter of dirty spray, she turned off the hose and looked at the piece again. It was amazing. She was no antiquities dealer, but what she saw looked similar to the pieces she had seen in museums all over Europe.

Tina closed up the warehouse for the night and headed back to her hotel. Room service after a hot bath sounded much better than a restaurant, especially the way she looked. The pace was about to pick up for all of them, and she knew she would need as much rest as she could when it did.

Chapter 22

Italy

For Pietro, he had established a rhythm early on to his work. This was desirable for several reasons. First, as an artist, the ability to find a groove was important. Second, he knew the general timetable which the Vatican had set for the project. Consistent work meant consistent visible progress. Third, there was his own schedule which involved Tina and the other warehouses. Fourth, there were the cameras to consider. He knew that they were watching him every time he entered the warehouse until he left. He had tested it easily enough. If he made a show of gesturing at the marble as if irate about something, within half an hour, someone would show up and ask how his progress was going. If he stood at the refrigerator and opened it and stared at it without pulling anything out, someone would drop by "just to check and see if he needed anything." And, finally, he needed his watchers to see him develop a pattern. If he worked sporadically, there would likely be more visits in person. But by showing up at 7 a.m. each morning, breaking for lunch from noon till 1 p.m. and then leaving sometime between 6 and 7 p.m., he was developing their rhythm as well as his own.

The city was big enough to have good public transportation, but not too big. Whenever he left the warehouse district, he altered his schedule enough that it was clear that Pietro liked some variety in his life. One evening, he might take a bus and head back toward the part of the city where he had leased a modest apartment. Before heading in for the night, he might grab a takeaway from a local shop. On another evening, he would exit the warehouse district and hail a cab. It would deposit him at a restaurant of one kind or another. Pietro made it to Dona's on more than one occasion. Still, some evenings he would simply leave the warehouse and walk for a long time. He had plenty to think about as it was.

The biggest thing his watchers noticed over the first few weeks was that Pietro had an appalling lack of social contacts. Being new to the area, that was to be expected at first. It wasn't that he was socially dysfunctional or unlikeable, but those who interacted with him noticed pretty quickly that he spoke and acted to some degree like a provincial, and even in a modern era, the farmhand was still seen as somewhat beneath the level of the town folk. Even the two or three ladies who tried to chat with him in the pubs he ate at found their conversations with him to be short-lived. Pietro did not seem to understand their interest in him, and this left them feeling alternately wounded in pride that they must somehow be lacking or disdainful that he was so simple to not be allured by their charms. Thus, Pietro answered questions, ordered food, bought the occasional small bag of groceries and visited parks, but he did not make many friends.

After three to four weeks, his watchers knew what to expect of him and had left off the surveillance after hours. By six weeks, they were hoping that someone else would draw the assignment to watch the cameras. And by eight weeks, things were fairly well set up for Pietro to rid himself of them entirely.

He began walking loops around the building, alternately crossing his arms and then massaging his temples as if lost in thought. He would mutter and turn to look at the statue. Then he would look away. On the third loop around the interior, he turned toward the air compressor and did a double take. He stopped in his tracks and stared straight at the camera. Then he walked toward it, tilting his head as if caught in curiosity. When he got closer, he reached out and touched it, jiggling the wires behind it. Then he covered his face and ran backwards, falling to the ground as he went. When he got to his feet, he pointed at the camera and began screaming at the top of his lungs. It would be twenty minutes before the nearest one of Giacobbe's men could make it to the warehouse, during which time Pietro never stopped yelling and gesticulating at the camera. Their sculptor was clearly upset.

Chapter 23

Philadelphia

It was a little after 1 a.m. on an early Saturday morning, and Margot was elated. Serious had been on an extended private messaging session with her. Their work was paying off. Over the course of several weeks of collaborative effort, they had been able to chart with an amazing level of predictability the sentences a criminal would get in one of several European courts based on the affiliation the criminal had with one of a handful of syndicates as well as the judges and prosecutors who were involved in the cases. This was damning evidence to a degree and pointed to some level of collusion which would be worth opening an investigation by an independent oversight body. But it was Margot herself who had risen to the challenge and suggested that they cross-reference names of anyone involved with the document dump known as the Panama Papers. This large treasure trove of over 11 million documents related to a shadowy bank in Panama uncovered the names of people involved in over 200,000 offshore organizations, many of which had been set up in order to launder money and hide it from governments around the globe.

One of the geeks in the group had created a script to take the names of all the people who were objects of their interest and search for them in the entire cache of documents from the Panama Papers dump. The names of nine judges, thirteen prosecutors and about the same number of defense attorneys were found. This information added to the case they were building by showing a definite intent on the part of these people to hide money, very likely ill-gotten gain.

In their chat session, Serious had commended Margot highly for her diligence in connecting the dots and her creativity in being willing to look at the big picture and think of other ways to find associated data and evidence. He told her that the leaders of the group believed that they had enough to move forward. They had identified a couple of investigators at Interpol and a handful of prosecutors scattered across the countries whom they believed were relatively clean or "at least as best as we can tell at this point." They would be releasing the information to each of them separately while informing each that the others were all going to be receiving copies.

When Margot asked what would happen if these people were dirty or had no desire to pursue the investigation of their peers or if they pursued the case but corrupt judges tried to derail them, Serious told her that each of the persons contacted was given an email address to respond to with a request to reply and to indicate whether or not action was going to be initiated and what the likely response would be. The recipients were also notified that if no action was taken, the data would be dumped to the public on a handful of sites which were known for being repositories of such data. Then, links to the data would be sent to a list of independent investigative journalists around the globe with an explanation as to the importance of the data. And the names of all the recipients would be included at that point so that their own inaction would become part of the public record.

S: So, if they are hesitant to act, they have a little more motivation to do so if for no reason but to save their own image or career. For some, they may pursue justice because they are on the right side. Others may do it to earn a promotion. Either way, if they act at all and the public sees corrupt justice systems exposed, we count that as a battle won in the greater war against evil. We try to give them adequate time to examine the information we send to them and present it to a judge and maybe even a grand jury to get the ball rolling before we make the information public. Sometimes we are asked to withhold the information from a public release because a prosecutor or investigator is really working on a sensitive issue. Where we can, we try to help in those situations.

M: Do you ever get asked to withhold the information because someone says they are pursuing a case but really aren't?

S: Yes. We always ask for proof of progress whenever someone asks us to delay a public release. If we don't get something to satisfy us that the information is really being used, we move ahead with the public release. And, of course, we have been threatened more times than I care to count at this point.

M: What kind of threats?

S: Death, usually. Occasionally we send the information to the wrong person, someone who may be involved. Sometimes we send the information in order to stir up the hornets' nest knowing that the public release is already set. A few people have gotten really creative in the way they describe what they would do to us if they found us. So far, we've played it by the book and been safe in how we've handled these projects.

Margot's spine tingled just a little when she read that. She was feeling high on emotion with the near completion of this group effort. She thought it might be a good time to be just a bit more personal with Serious. She wrote a message and added a hyperlink to a newspaper's website.

M: Check out this link. I'll wait for you to read it."

After a few minutes, a reply came back.

S: Hmm. This is very interesting. Seems like this reporter has taken the same approach to some of our own research.

Margot hesitated and then wrote back.

M: I may know someone who might have helped him.

Serious wrote back immediately.

S: You???

M: Yes. I wanted to do something that didn't involve a bunch of criminals overseas.

There was a pause before the reply came back.

S: Gandalf the White, please tell me that you do NOT live in Philadelphia or anywhere near there!!!

The triple exclamation points threw her for a loop. She was expecting a bit more affirmation than that. She had never told anyone online where she lived, but Serious asked a point-blank question and seemed concerned.

M: Well, I might live in the general area.

S: I don't think you realize what you've done.

M: What's the big deal???

She was beginning to feel defensive, and it was burning away the elation she had just been enjoying as if it were a hot sun on the morning mist.

M: I simply used the same tools you have been teaching me to use to try and make a difference in a place I care way more about than Romania or some European country.

S: Dear Gandalf the White, please do not take offense. I mean you no harm. But—there are people who do. As I told you at the beginning, this is not a game! There is a reason that we have worked on research projects which span the globe. The geographical distance is one of the boundaries we use to help to keep us safe. Working on corruption or illegal activities in our own backyard can cause us to become involved emotionally. That's when we can get careless.

M: I've been just as careful about this as any of my other research!

S: Have you? Is there anyone at all who knows what you are doing or knows of your interest in these issues?

Immediately Margot's mind flashed to a picture of Detective Carson sitting across from her in the coffee shop as she asked him her pointed questions about the drug bust in the paper. Her face grew hot. She sat frozen in front of her computer.

S: Well? Is there?

M: I don't know. Maybe. I haven't really told anyone what I'm doing, but I told you about the detective I met who was involved in one of the cases and how I asked him some rather detailed questions about it.

S: Such as…?

M: Such as what the recommendations were by the prosecutors in the cases where criminals got off scot-free.

She cringed as she typed it. How stupid could she have been? I mean, how many people would even think to ask a police detective a question like that?

There was no response from Serious. The more she thought about it, the more she worried. What had begun as a random encounter with a stranger now seemed like a gaping hole in a castle wall. With a flashing red sign saying, "Attack here!"

M: Serious, are you there???

S: Yes. I was looking through the other articles by this Alex Ingram. I wasn't sure if this was the only one or not.

M: No, this is the fourth article he's written on the topic.

S: So I see.

Margot's heart stopped beating as she read the rest of the reply.

S: Well, Gandalf the White, I think it's time we discussed your dead man's switch.

Chapter 24

For Alex, the buildup to the release of the first story had paralleled a reemergence from the overwhelming cloud which had consumed his life for the past five years. Hard work combined with a purpose was the closest thing to a deliverance from depression that he could have hoped for. He went to bed and slept and woke up refreshed and ready to work again.

His editors were delighted to see the old Alex emerge from the doorway to his career's tomb. Although he kept the major details until the very end, the outlines and drafts he gave to them elicited low whistles of approval. When the story was published, it was the equivalent of dropping a bomb in a field full of ripe dandelions.

Immediately, the judges and attorneys were put on the defensive. They had no idea it was coming. Their initial response was a cool downplaying of the story. There were, they assured the public via other traditional media, many factors which played into the decisions of crime and punishment, and one should not put too much weight on a story which was filled with circumstantial evidence and innuendos.

Alex expected no less. But he had learned a thing or two in the years of working for his masters. One of those tactics was appropriately named The Chinese Water Torture. Information would be released in small increments at regular intervals. With each release, the story was kept in the public eye, and the person being targeted was kept on the defensive. Plus, with the type of data he had been supplied by those masters, there was enough to drown most people. The cumulative effect of this method was to wear down the target and win a victory in the court of public opinion, if not in a court of law itself.

So Alex waited patiently as the sheer weight of his targets' reputations and influence in the Philadelphia area was brought to bear against him. Then he released the second article. In it, he had tied the criminal indictments of a particularly egregious offense that had resulted in the death of a minority shopkeeper and his wife to the pattern with Judge Lewisburg and DA Mennheim. The criminals had been released on a technicality. There had been a general uproar at the time, but when reviewed under the glaring light of a factual pattern of leniency, not just in general but on three of the criminals involved in that particular crime, the mood began to get very tense.

Murmurings of a two-tiered justice system began to be heard from minority community leaders.

The next skirmish was more personal. No fewer than two of the local television stations and two of the competing newspapers began to focus on Alex himself. "Who is the reporter bringing all these accusations against these established leaders in the community?" Alex found his name being smeared. He was an alcoholic, a has-been reporter who hadn't worked seriously in years. The idea was floated around by "anonymous sources" that Alex had never been responsible for his own career and may have indeed profited from an arrangement with ghostwriters. The viewers and readers were reminded that Alex had slandered and caused the ruination of another great community leader, the Reverend Billy "Happy" Lewis. Most of the media left out the fact that he had written the retraction story, but the ones that mentioned it only slanted it to point out that Alex had waited years before doing so. Here he was again, slandering respected leaders who had served their communities for years. Was he going to admit he had done it only for publicity at some point in the future? "I'm very concerned," the local congressman was quoted as saying, "that what is happening here is that we have someone who may be a little unstable, a person who has seen the end of his career and is grasping at anything he can in order to appear to be relevant."

Alex took it all in stride. Yes, it stung, but he at least recognized that his foes were circling the wagons because they realized they were under attack, not because they were on the offensive. They were using the classic echo chamber technique to amplify a set of common thoughts in order to shape the narrative. That meant he was getting somewhere.

At the height of the attacks against him, and when the fury seemed to be turning the public opinion against him, he released the third article. In this installment, Alex had been able to locate five current and former employees in the judicial system who were willing to go on the record to talk about discrepancies they had observed through the years between the cases prosecuted by Mennheim and tried before old Judge Lewisburg. It seems that more than one or two people had been troubled by what they had seen. Some of them kept notes, meticulous notes. One assistant had been privy to some of the private chamber discussions which had led to cases being decided away from the open courtroom. This person had a very fine memory of several of those cases.

People on the outside really began to take notice. This was less of a standard news cycle and more of a nail-biter tennis match. Each side would fire back a volley that was seemingly impossible to return only to find that the other side had managed to save the point by their own incredible backhand. But when the response to that article mostly involved a scattered attempt to discredit five individuals on a rush basis, Alex knew that he had them game, set and match.

Remembering what one of his masters had told him on the phone many years ago, "Take the kill shot," he released the fourth article before the other side could even begin to get organized. Alex had never even heard of The Panama Papers, but polkadotpanda introduced him to them and even provided links to the salient documents showing that Messieurs Lewisburg and Mennheim seemed to have formed an offshore corporation which had several million dollars' worth of transactions over the past several years. Coincidentally—or conspiratorially, Alex inferred—the dates of those transactions could be overlaid with precision within a month's time either way over the date of the judgments rendered in the major cases in question.

"Kill shot" was probably the best way to describe the impact this article had. Whole neighborhoods erupted in marches and demonstrations at City Hall. Traffic was shut down in the downtown area as mothers and ministers spoke into the mics of cheap PA systems and railed against the injustice which allowed those entrusted with administering justice to profit off the lives of those who had been exploited by the criminal element among them. In private backchannels, the governor threatened to send the National Guard if the mayor did not do something to restore order and find a solution. The mayor, ever the politician who would not let a good crisis go to waste, announced that he was demanding the resignation of those involved in such a heinous abuse of public trust and that he was calling for an independent outside investigation of the entire staff of the district attorney's office (whom he personally hated) and the local court system. The police, who were mentioned by name in the investigation, somehow escaped scrutiny. Part of this was that the attacks on Alex had weighed his reputation against those of the judge and DA. Part of it was the camaraderie among law enforcement, which keeps them from ratting on their own even when they're as guilty as sin. And part of it was the speed with which the chief of police announced that any officers involved would be removed from active duty "pending an investigation" by their internal affairs bureau.

Another factor that cut the whole drama short was the discovery of Judge Lewisburg's body hanging from the antique and very ornate light fixture in his chambers. A security guard coming through to open the building early that morning noticed an unusual shadow in the judge's etched-glass window in his office door. Knocking first, he received no answer. After using a master key to open the office, he took one look, reached for his phone and called the police station. The judge had left no suicide note, but his will had been meticulously placed on his desk alongside a list of signed checks made out to various local charities and synagogues. Judge Lewisburg, it seems, intended to enter eternity with the well wishes of as many people as possible.

All attention now focused on District Attorney Mennheim. For his part, Mennheim was terrified. He was a reasonably intelligent man and had lived a life filled with the benefits of ample financial pork despite eschewing the edible kind. Like many of the common criminals he put away, he simply never thought he would get caught. Scandal and prison represented an unknown quantity which he could not begin to fathom as representing his own future. He was desperate for a lifeline and was willing to talk, to make a deal of some kind, any kind, to avoid prison. He made this fact known to one too many confidants. In the attempt to escape one fate, he sealed another.

Before a special investigative counsel could be formally convened and organize a meeting with Mennheim for questioning, the Philly police were called to a park in the wee hours of the morning on a Saturday. A tramp had stumbled across a body. What started out as a routine call turned into about twenty police cars and ambulances all assembled to witness the cold body of one Aaron Mennheim. The ambulances were as useless as the police presence. He was quite dead, had been that way for at least two or three hours, according to the medical examiner, and would not be talking with anyone, at least in this life. Cause of death was officially determined as suicide by two shots behind the right ear with a small-caliber, pearl-inlay revolver.

Lest it be seen as cynical to compare the uselessness of the EMTs with the poor efforts of the police, it should be noted that while not dressing the part, Mennheim had lived the religious principles of an orthodox Jew and had never been known to walk more than a half-mile (the rough equivalent of a Sabbath Day's journey) from sundown Friday until sundown Saturday. The park in which his body was found, which was the closest secluded area anywhere near his home, was a good three miles' walk from his residence. Further, there was a general lack of curiosity as to how a person could manage to hold a revolver at close range and pull the trigger twice after the first one was already doing so much damage to the central nervous system's main processing unit. Not to be excluded for consideration was also the fact that Mennheim was a southpaw and had rarely even gestured in court with his right hand.

But there was the revolver lying near his body with his fingerprints on it. Some cases solve themselves. The overall result was a sacrificial delivery of the blood for which the baying mobs were lusting. Justice, it seemed, had been served on the two culprits by their own hands. The criminals, seeing their guilt had been exposed, had saved everyone a long and delayed process. It was a tidy solution, and the mayor let it be known to the police chief that the finding of suicide in both cases would be a welcome relief "so that the city can begin to heal."

The catalyst behind the investigation was once again hailed as a hero. Alex's editors actually ordered a cake with the words "Welcome Back" written in frosting and called the whole office together to celebrate their first glimpse of the old Alex in years. The four interns who had been involved in the research for the story received a small mention in the byline credits and considered themselves to have been the luckiest among their peers for the parts they played in unraveling the story.

For Alex, he felt newborn. He had resigned himself to his fate of watching his career die a slow and painful death. Now he was back in the game. Yet the deaths of Judge Lewisburg and DA Mennheim were unnerving to him because he knew that there was more to the story. A good reporter tells the story fully but never tells the full story. There are threads left hidden which can be picked up again in the future in order to develop new articles with their own subjects. This story had exposed the equivalent of a frayed Persian rug.

He had received additional tips from "polkadotpanda" tying the previously mentioned congressman, who had been so vocal in his attack of Alex, to both men via separate additional offshore trusts. That deserved a further look. Then there was the question of who was involved in the actual payments to the judge and the prosecutor for playing ball with them. Alex also had his own questions that he would have loved to have asked several of the police who had been involved in the investigations and arrests, but they weren't being helpful. The more he looked at what he had begun to uncover, the more it looked like a mass of interconnected webs. Alex had no doubt that back in the dark recesses of the hole lurked one or more very big, very powerful spiders.

Chapter 25

Layla, Saudi Arabia

The Datmari family was neither wealthy nor powerful. As noted with Hijan, most of its members were not particularly pious. In the context of a conservative Muslim culture, they could pray with the best. If they were freed from those cultural bonds, they could blend in. The one redeeming value which the whole clan had was a highly developed sense of family loyalty.

Thus it was, when Hijan's family received the sad news the following day of his unexpected death at sea due to, it seemed, a tragic accidental fall overboard caused by excessive inebriation, his family mourned loudly and longly for him. And when the period of mourning had passed and the tears were dried, his brother Hali called a family meeting that was attended by nearly everyone within two hops of Hijan's family ties. The general consensus among the group as they gathered for the meeting was that perhaps Hijan had come into some wealth which was going to be distributed to the group. Rumors swirled that he had saved his income over his many years at sea in an investment fund which had yielded significant returns.

Instead, when Hali quieted the crowd and read the contents of HIjan's email, they could not have been more stunned if he had just told them that Hijan had died a billionaire. Grief is an interesting emotion. It strongly craves the presence of the one who has been stolen. Death itself is an elusive foe which humans are taught to respect and even fear from an early age. But when grief is presented with a tangible representative of the great Robber, it can metamorphose into the hottest of rage within a split second. There is no doubt that, were Captain Andar present or even anywhere near the attendees of the family meeting, his life would have been over before he could have mounted a protest.

Hali let the emotions play out as person after person expressed their violent desires. He had, after all, had time during the whole mourning period to begin to process the news which they were just now receiving. His cousin, Bandar, who had also received a copy of the email, now joined him at the front of the room. "Brothers and sisters, we are family. We are Datmari. When someone strikes one of us, we all feel the blow. When someone kills one of us, we all die a little. We know that we must act to avenge our brother. Our only question is how we should respond."

For the next two hours, the group sat as member after member proposed one idea after another. Hailed as interesting but quickly dismissed as impractical were plans to storm the container ship disguised as pirates, the idea of commandeering a coast guard cutter and boarding the ship under cover of law, and the suggestion that Captain Andar be invited to visit their city in order to officiate at Hijan's official funeral service. As the group began to get their collective bearings, the ideas began to be more practical, if not particularly gruesome in some of their implementations. Hali and Bandar mainly served as guides to the discussion.

Eventually, the conversation turned toward an examination of pertinent facts. The ship had left China and was headed to a destination. Along the way, it would be in motion and difficult to board. It had to stop eventually. The shipping containers which so concerned Hijan weren't going anywhere by themselves. Their best solutions lay in the intersection of the ship with a port. Captain Andar himself would be present, along with the containers. Perhaps the owners themselves would be located, or at least their representatives.

The leaders among them decided that those who were relatively good with technology would begin to work in earnest. Some would locate the ship, track it and find out its destination. Others would begin looking for employment opportunities at the destination port. Some would put the word out among the community at large to see if anyone had relatives in that location who could be relied upon for housing, local contacts or logistical support. Since they had no idea of the current timetable for the movements of the *Ahil*, it was made clear that time was of the essence.

And so it was that, as Captain Andar charted his course from the southern edge of China to the Adriatic and the northeastern edge of Italy, others were charting right along with him. He would reach the Suez Canal in about a week and a half. From there, it was a left across to Italy and then a straight shot up the eastern seaboard. When Captain Andar made his routine checks on the special containers, other people were scouring the Internet for any type(s) of blueprints for his type of ship, and still others were beginning to explore the underbelly of the Internet for clues as to what Captain Andar might have picked up in China which was so valuable to him that he would kill someone to protect its secret. When Captain Andar lay down at night for his rest, at least a dozen people were staring at computer screens or writing messages to contacts working on support and logistics. And when Captain Andar let his mind wander to how he would use the money he was going to make, there was always someone thinking about how to make his death as long and painful as possible. Somewhere in the near future, two worlds would collide because of a man's ability to be bought.

Chapter 26

A honeypot sounds like an innocent prop in a children's storybook about bears. In modern terms, a honeypot is usually a computer that is attached to the public Internet with minimal protection. It may be loaded with programs and website software which are out of date enough to be current but vulnerable. The data on it may be fake or genuine, but if the latter, it is benign enough that no real loss would be caused by its seizure. In short, it is an invitation to hackers and investigators to come through any door or window they can. Meanwhile, in the background, the server is running software which is analyzing and logging all the attacks and successful intrusions. It may also be connected to a special type of network device which analyzes the traffic before it even reaches the server itself.

Honeypots have a variety of purposes. Researchers use them to determine what types of software vulnerabilities are being used the most. Security vendors use them to try and make their firewall and network protection products better. Hackers even use them to try and learn from their peers anonymously. People with something to hide may use them as an outer perimeter tripwire. In the latter case, a tripwire honeypot is a cheap way to find out when someone is interested in someone or something the owner would prefer to remain secret.

To the one doing the searching, it's not easy to determine if the server on the other end is legit or a honeypot. It requires a gut instinct or administrator-level access to be able to make those types of determinations. When Margot began her research on the local issues related to Judge Lewisburg and the District Attorney Mennheim, it led her to Congressman Fitzpatrick. In the Panama Papers, she had seen his name in two separate offshore trusts individually with each of the other two men. But the connection between them was unclear. This led her to dig deeper, and her digging led her to a site which purported to have information about the congressman's rapid wealth increase. (After all, if a person serves in Congress for ten years at an annual salary of $174,000, even if he saved it all, his net worth on that salary would be $1.74 million. For a congressman to have a net worth of over $30 million with no previous significant business holdings and only a public servant's salary should raise some red flags.)

Alas, Margot's searches on that site's database and the clicks she made throughout the pages were all set to ring the doorbell at the haunted mansion. Her Internet addresses were duly recorded, and given that they were all from the Tor network, the person assigned to monitor that particular honeypot decided to wait. When she forwarded some of the links to Alex, he clicked on the links from his work computer. The newspaper's Internet addresses were statically assigned and always remained the same. This address was easily traced back to the paper. At this point, the monitor began to send some messages up the chain.

And so it was that other calls were made up and down the line. Two days later, the newspaper publisher informed the IT manager that the parent conglomerate was sending in an outside auditing firm named GroupBeat to do a routine risk assessment. The IT manager was, like many geeks, a bit peeved at having his fiefdom invaded but acquiesced to the leadership while maintaining a wary eye at the intruders. They poked and prodded on the network, ran tests, checked for patches, scanned for vulnerabilities, and asked to spot-check individual machines. One of those was Alex's workstation, during which the auditor, himself a former spook with one of the alphabet agencies, installed a couple of programs in the background. One of them was a keylogger which would record in the background everything Alex typed on his keyboard. The other was a small service which would only wake up at 3 a.m. and call home to a server hosted in Romania. It would upload the contents of the keylogger file, and it would remain running for five minutes, effectively holding open the back door to Alex's computer so that an operator could connect to it and issue commands.

From that point on, all of the research that Alex did on his computer was uploaded once per day and was reviewed thoroughly by one or two of the former spooks who worked for GroupBeat. They had been on the right side of the law enough to know what to look for on both sides. When they saw items of interest related to the congressman, they passed it up the chain to the client. From there, it was determined that Alex was not the completely dependent dullard he had been chalked up to be. The reporter was pulling from a wide array of experience and was beginning to ask questions about investment portfolios and foundations and fundraisers with foreign nationals and other matters of debauched interest.

There was a debate of sorts as to the best way to handle old Alex. His demise in the midst of such a stellar investigation could be problematic. True, his computer could be wiped remotely during the daily open window, but he had interns working with him. What did they know? How much of the investigative reporting was being written with good old-fashioned paper and pen? And who was feeding Alex tips? The polkadotpanda email address had shown up in the midst of the keylogging. Currently nothing was known about who was behind that account, but GroupBeat's leadership was "reaching out" to contacts they still had at the NSA, FBI and other agencies to try to gather what data they could. They were also reviewing their list of assets to see if they had anyone in a tech administration position at the email provider whom they could activate for a request on any details regarding that account.

This was going to take time. The problem was the congressman. He was useful but unstable. If he began to feel the heat, he might determine that it was in his best interests to make a deal to save himself. If Alex could be convinced to back off, it would solve all the problems. The person behind polkadotpanda apparently had no significant voice or he/she would have been publishing the information under some other format.

The call came to Alex on a Monday morning. He felt rested from a good weekend. He had actually stayed away from the office and had enjoyed a couple of days on the town. When he picked up the phone, a man's gravelly voice greeted him. "Alex, this is Bart from back in your days at State. How you been doing?"

Alex was stunned. He hadn't heard that voice in well over five years. In fact, that voice stretched back even farther. It was one of the early voices from the phone calls which helped to make his career. But Alex remembered a promise he had made to himself, and he pressed a button on his desk phone's keypad. The phone system's recording function was now activated.

"Bart Nicholson? Is that you?" He wanted to establish a name along with the voice.

"One and the same. It's been a while."

"Sure has. How can I help you, Bart?"

"I've been hearing good things about you, Alex. Seems like you lost your way for a little while, but you've come roaring back. Just like the old days."

Subtle. But clear.

"Yeah, things just seemed to dry up for me for a long time." Alex could play the game, too.

"About that," said Bart. "I'm wondering if you are interested in maybe getting together sometime real soon. There's some big news coming up that I wanted to share. I couldn't think of anyone I'd rather see get the story than you."

"I bet," Alex thought but didn't say aloud. Instead, he said, "Thanks, Bart. But I'm in the middle of a story I've been working on. I think it has a chance to be as big as anything I've worked on." It was a bit of a push on his part, but he wanted to see what he had stirred up.

"Sure, Alex. I've been reading your articles. Good stuff. But you could dig and dig and end up at a dead end. I'm offering you something major—

108

global, even. I can't think of anything more important than news related to the future health of our nation."

There it was. "Dead end." "Future." "Health." Somebody didn't like where he was digging.

"Well, Bart. I don't know. I sure am interested in big news. You know me. How long do I have before you pass it on to someone else?" Alex was stalling for time.

"This can't hold for more than two days. How about I call you back then?"

"Sounds fair," said Alex. "I'll think about it." He paused and then added, "Thank you, Bart."

"Sure thing, Alex. I'll call you in a couple of days. I'd love to have you back on the team."

The receiver went dead. Alex couldn't remember if he was supposed to press any other buttons. He didn't think so. He looked around his office. He wasn't the most technically challenged person, but he knew that he was out of his element. Something didn't feel right, and he was going to go with his gut.

Without doing anything else, he walked out of his office down a couple of flights of stairs and down the hall to a door marked "Information Systems." He knocked, heard a reply and stuck his head in. "I think I've got a problem." Alex said and closed the door behind him.

Chapter 27

Italy

There was a knock on the door to the warehouse. When no one answered within a minute, Giacobbe's man inserted the key and unlocked it and let himself in. Pietro was still yelling and pointing at the cameras (he apparently had found two of them). At first, Pietro did not want to acknowledge him, but after shouting himself, the man was able to get Pietro's attention and saw Pietro's eyes focus on him.

"I was coming by to check on you and couldn't get anyone to answer the door," he said innocently. "What is the matter? What is wrong?"

Pietro looked at him as if he had never seen him before. It was a wild-eyed sort of stare, and it unnerved the man sufficiently. He glanced at Pietro's strong arms subconsciously and felt even more ill at ease.

"I cannot work here," Pietro shouted. "I am being spied on!"

"What are you talking about?" the man asked.

Pietro stalked toward the compressor and then pointed at the two cameras. "These cameras! These spy cameras! I cannot work with someone spying on me!"

The man tried to reason with him, but Pietro was not listening. So he excused himself, placed a call and waited for someone higher up than him to come and try to take charge of the situation. Within half an hour, Giacobbe's car pulled up to the warehouse door. His man reaffirmed what was happening. Giacobbe opened the door and walked in. He tried to affect a fatherly or brotherly smile as he approached Pietro, who was now sitting in his chair and rocking back and forth with his arms wrapped around himself.

"Pietro, it's Signor Manco. My employee tells me that you are upset over the security cameras here in the warehouse. Is that true?"

He waited for two minutes and then repeated himself. Eventually, Pietro seemed to find his way out of the haze long enough to turn and look at Giacobbe with a questioning gaze. "Signor Manco. Why are you here?"

For the third time, Giacobbe repeated his question.

Pietro tilted his head as if hearing him for the first time. Then he turned

110

away and said, "Yes. That is it. I am being spied on! I cannot work here while I am being spied on!"

Giacobbe tried to ease the tension. He laughed a little. "Pietro, no one is spying on you. Those are security cameras which have been here for years. You shouldn't let a little thing like that bother you."

Pietro's head turned toward Giacobbe. He stared at him with that wild-eyed expression, his eyes searching Giacobbe's face. Then, rushing to the base of the sculpture, he picked up a piece of marble the size of a thimble. Holding it between his fingers, he strode back to Giacobbe and said, "Signor Manco, do you see this piece of marble?"

"Yes, Pietro, I do."

"To you it is but nothing, a scrap of stone. But to me it is the greatest of obstacles. As long as it remains in place, the sculpture can never become what it is meant to be!" Pacing back and forth, he continued, "One by one I find the obstacles which are shielding the true beauty and remove them. What you have done with these cameras, this spying, is to shroud the whole piece in my mind. I cannot see any longer what is inside of the stone because of them!" He threw the piece down in anger and then burst into sobs. "I'm sorry! You must forgive me. I want to do nothing more than to complete this piece on time for His Holiness, but my mind is dark." He continued sobbing.

Giacobbe was faced with a decision. In truth, none of his men who were monitoring the cameras had ever reported anything other than what was supposed to be happening. Pietro worked. He occasionally sat and stared at the marble. He would make coffee or drink juice and eat an occasional snack. His phone, they were certain, remained on one of the side tables. He appeared to only use it to look up images of classical sculptures or to read about classical music composers based on the WIFI traffic they had been monitoring.

Moving toward Pietro, Giacobbe placed his hand on his heaving shoulder and spoke in a gentle voice. "Pietro, this warehouse has been in use for many years by one of my companies. The crime in this area, well, it does happen. We only wanted to be certain of the safety of your work. You have my word that the cameras themselves are only monitored after you leave in the evenings." Pietro's sobbing continued.

"However, I understand that this upsets you greatly. In order to avoid causing you any grievance, I will have them removed immediately. Your peace of mind is of the utmost importance to me, and had I known that this would be a problem, I would have removed them before you began your work."

Pietro spoke through his lessened sobbing, "Thank you, Signor Manco.

Thank you. I shall try my best to refocus. It may take some time. I hope you understand."

"I do, Pietro. I do. But we mustn't forget our schedule." Giacobbe pulled his phone from his pocket and made a quick call. "One of my men will be here shortly to take care of this problem."

"Thank you, Signor. I must leave for now. I cannot stay here until they are gone."

"Of course, I understand."

Pietro turned and walked slowly to the door. He looked back once, a sad expression on his face, and then he exited the warehouse.

Giacobbe waited until one of his hired geeks came to remove the cameras. "Do you want to simply hide them better or maybe use a smaller camera?" the man asked.

"No," Giacobbe responded. "I can't chance him stumbling over another camera. That could ruin the whole project. He knows what he is doing, and we can't afford to endanger his work. We'll have to do more frequent checks in person, but I'll work that out with Pietro in a day or two."

While his man worked on removing the cameras, Giacobbe strolled over to the sculpture in progress. It was shaping up very nicely. He could make out the rudimentary form of a person. The head was beginning to take shape. What appeared to be one arm was stretching out from the body upward and toward the front. The bottom of the marble beneath the figure was shaping up to be a square block. He stooped to pick up one of the many fragments which littered the area and looked at it. Pietro said these fragments were an impediment that had to be removed in order to uncover the true sculpture beneath them. Well, maybe Pietro could serve to remove the impediments preventing the flow of large sums of money to the Vatican, his organization and everyone involved along the way.

His man called his name. The cameras were gone. He tossed the piece back into the pile. They were close, and who knew what opportunities lay beyond?

Chapter 28

Philadelphia

Margot was being much more careful now than she had been before. Frankly, her chat with Serious had scared the wits out of her. Serious explained some of the practical dangers to which she had exposed herself by working and researching on corruption local to her own place of residence.

S: Nations work together and share data, but given the scale of global traffic, especially with the use of multiple layers of protection, it makes it much harder for Country A to detect an actual user in Country F, especially if the traffic is routed through and bounced around Countries B, C, D and E. But when you begin looking at things locally, it gets tougher. Yes, you are still trying to use tools to cover your tracks. But your ISP is your first point of entry to the Internet. And if that ISP is in bed with one of many government agencies, or if someone from those agencies is checking traffic, they can determine that out of 1,000 users, only two or three are making their first connection to a VPN server somewhere. Don't you think that those users will get more attention than the rest? After that, it's a matter of whether or not they have the capability of tracking threads of traffic out of the VPN server—or whether they have someone on the inside.

That shocked Margot.

M: What do you mean?

S: Gandalf the White, for a wizard you are naïve. Do you think everyone working at a tech company swears an oath of loyalty to consumer privacy? Or do you think that they can't be bought? Or blackmailed? These people are very powerful and very rich. And how do you know the VPN server you use isn't a front for the CIA or any number of other government agencies, US or foreign? It's an open secret that the Chinese government owns a large proportion of the VPN companies.

113

Margot felt sick. She thought she was being safe, and a bit clever.

Another message from Serious appeared.

S: You're probably thinking that you're doing what I and others recommended. In reality, security online is an illusion which is measured in various shades, but mostly it is still an illusion. Those of us who have been doing this for a long time use many of the same tools in different combinations. But we also realize that if we make the wrong people or government angry, we can be located.

M: Then how do you deal with that pressure, knowing that your life may be in danger?

S: I'm no longer afraid to die. I know I'm going to die someday anyway. I'd rather die for something worth living for than pretend to live a life consumed by emptiness.

It sounded poetic in a way, the kind of quote that would be in a movie or a book. It didn't help. Margot was terrified.

M: So, what is the dead man's switch you mentioned?

S: All of us who have been doing this type of research have one or more of them. A dead man's switch is an action which is taken or a secret or set of secrets which are revealed if a person dies suddenly or under mysterious circumstances. It involves entrusting your secrets with one or more persons who would be willing to carry out your requests in the event that you disappear or die. Some people give one person an encrypted file and give the decryption key to another. They may not know each other. The first person is instructed to send the file by email or post it publicly. Then the second person is responsible to decrypt the data and disseminate it. Other people may use a thumb drive or another type of media and give it to a relative or friend or even a lawyer. What matters is that you put the deepest and darkest of secrets you are working on in your dead man's switch. If you are ever uncovered or kidnapped, the fact that you have this in an unknown place can buy you time or possibly save your life. Having more than one copy is also a good idea.

They chatted a while longer with Margot asking some technical questions and Serious answering and offering some words of comfort along the way. After their communication was over, Margot sat and thought long and hard about her life. She really didn't have anyone that she knew well enough to turn over her life's work to them. Her parents had divorced when she was in college. While she supposed she loved her parents to some degree, they had always lived in their own worlds with Margot being a bit of an afterthought. When they divorced, they seemed to travel deeper into orbits that were further away from Margot's interests. They didn't call her. She didn't call them.

Because of the way she had been raised, Margot found it difficult to make friends. Some people, when they are emotionally starved, tend to latch onto anyone who will give them the time of day. Others retreat into their shell a bit deeper. For some, they live in a detached state where they crave human contact but just do not know how to find it. For people like Margot, the experience makes them stronger, and they find an inner strength which allows them not only to function but also to thrive without close relationships—at least most of the time.

Still, when it came time to count the people whom she could turn to with a life-or-death emergency, she was having difficulty counting from zero to one. Margot began to feel depressed. She started to go down the mental path of asking what she had done with her life in the way of relationships, but halfway down the path, she realized that it was a dead end. Even though she was depressed, she was also feeling a deeper-abiding sense of fear which was goading her into action. She dismissed the depression and began to ask herself practical questions as to what she could do to find people she could trust with her dead man's switch whenever she had completed it.

After much thought, she decided on one of her coworkers named Cassandra Beeler. They weren't particularly close, but Cassandra somehow seemed different than the rest of the staff. She seemed a bit more serious about life in general, and she had even offered to help Margot when she was overloaded with work. It wasn't much to go on, but it was the best she had.

That was one. She thought of the apartment manager but figured that he would be one of the first persons to actually pass along anything she gave him to someone claiming to be in authority or law enforcement. Well, it was time to think outside the box. She started mentally tracing her steps to work and around her neighborhood. One building kept coming to mind. She could see the image in her head but had never paid much attention to it. She thought it was home to some kind of community outreach program. Tomorrow she would leave a little early and check it out in more detail.

Her mind wandered around the city some more until she remembered the coffee shop where she had met Detective Carson. She had avoided it for some time. Was she afraid of him for a reason? She didn't have any facts to go on. If he were clean, he would be a possible second person to entrust with her dead man's switch. She would have to ponder that one a bit more. In the meantime, she made three copies of all her research, past and current, and put them onto thumb drives. After that was finished, Margot looked at the clock. It was 2 a.m. She sighed. The nights seemed to get shorter.

Chapter 29

When Margot asked to speak with Cassandra at lunch, she wasn't really sure how to begin the conversation. It did not turn out to be an issue. Cassandra begin talking first. She talked about work, the local news and touched on how her brother was faring in his ROTC program in high school.

"He wants to be an air force pilot, but I keep telling him to remember what pilots use for birth control."

Margot looked puzzled. "What do they use?"

Cassandra stared at her with a deadpan expression. "Their personality."

There was a pause, and then Margot burst into laughter. "Oh, girl, you got me with that one." She relaxed inside. Perhaps talking to Cassandra would be easier than she thought.

They chatted a bit more after that until the waitress brought their food. Then Cassandra asked, "What did you want to talk about, Margot?"

Margot took a deep breath and sighed.

"That bad, huh?" asked Cassandra. She seemed genuinely interested.

Margot said, "I don't know how to really begin, so I'll just blurt it out and then try to explain things in a little more detail. What I need is someone who can keep something safe for me in case I..." she trailed off. Maybe this wasn't going to be so easy after all. She took another deep breath and looked Cassandra in the face. "In case I die or disappear unexpectedly."

Cassandra's eyes studied Margot's face, her expression impassive. "Okay. Margot, do you mind telling me what you've gotten yourself into?"

Margot hesitated. She was about to cross a threshold. She hardly knew Cassandra. But something inside her was yearning for a deeper connection with another human. Could she trust Cassandra? At this point, that was something she did not know. But would she trust Cassandra? That was the question which she faced. Cassandra was still looking at her, patiently awaiting her reply. Well, at least she wasn't looking at her phone every five seconds like most of the rest of her coworkers when they were on break. If she had people skills, maybe that meant she cared about people.

"I'm a bit of a loner." She waited for a wisecrack, but none came. "Almost a year ago, I got interested in some topics I found online. The more I read, the more I realized that there is a lot of corruption going on, not just here but all

117

over the place. I wanted to do something about it, so I teamed up with some other people to coordinate our efforts. It's been really rewarding because we've made some impact with what we've done. But somewhere along the way, I decided to start looking at what was happening right here. You know, clean up in my own backyard.

"Part of my research led me to discover that certain prominent people were engaged in some pretty bad things."

Cassandra interrupted her. "Do you think you could be a bit more vague?"

Margot looked at Cassandra. There was a hint of a smile on her lips.

"I mean, if you're going to tell me this much, you might as well share some of the juicy details."

"Do you remember the story that came out not long ago about Judge Lewisburg?"

Cassandra nodded.

"That was one of the things I researched and found."

"But I thought that story came out because of that reporter at the Daily."

"I, uh, I shared the research with him and asked him if he would be interested in covering it."

Cassandra squinted one eye and looked at Margot with her head tilted. "Are you telling me that he got that story only because you dug it up?"

"Yes. I know it sounds crazy, but that's what I've been doing for months. I don't go anywhere and do anything because I..." Margot paused. "I don't really have any friends other than my online friends."

"Say for a minute that I believe you; what do you want from me?"

"Well, to be frank, one of the people I research with yanked my chain the other night and helped me to realize how much danger I could be in if my identity were exposed." She stopped and looked imploringly at Cassandra. "The people involved in these types of corruption are powerful. Very powerful. And rich. They don't think anything of removing threats to their enterprises. My friend told me about a type of safeguard. They call it a dead man's switch. If anything happens to that person, information gets released publicly so that whoever was responsible ends up paying for it in the end."

"And you want me to guard whatever it is you have?"

"Yes."

Cassandra was quiet as she chewed slowly on a bite of food, a pensive look on her face. Finally, she said, "Well, I guess I don't have any choice but to say yes."

"What do you mean?"

"This weekend at church, my pastor was preaching on the story of the Good American."

Margot looked confused. "I don't know much about the Bible, but I didn't think America is even mentioned."

"You're right," Cassandra said. "He was taking the story of the good Samaritan and putting it into modern terms. Just like in that story, there were plenty of people who saw a need and could have done something to help, but they made excuses and did nothing. Finally, a Samaritan helped a stranger, a Jew who probably looked down on him, when no one else would care. He challenged us to not be busy Americans but to stop and help others in need. Anyway, this morning before I left for work, I prayed and asked God to show me who I could be a good American to today. I guess you're it."

Margot didn't know what to make of that, but Cassandra was saying yes to her request. "Thank you. That's great." She reached into her purse and pulled out a small thumb drive. She laid it on the table between them. "If I do die suddenly or am in an accident, really if I die of anything other than old age, you can look at this. There's a file named 'Instructions.' It has a list of details on what to do with the information contained on the drive, various people to contact and their email addresses and such."

"Do you not want me to read it otherwise?"

Margot thought about it. "I'm not telling you you can't. If I'm giving it to you, I have to trust you that you're not going to post it somewhere with my name on it. But I have to warn you that what is on there could make you very depressed, and some of what these people do is so evil that it could make you throw up everything you just ate."

Cassandra's eyes widened. "Are you being serious?"

"Dead serious." Margot thought about what she had just said. "But I hope it doesn't come to that."

Cassandra picked up the thumb drive and eyed it cautiously. She put it in her pocket and looked across the table at Margot. "Me too."

Chapter 30

Philadelphia

Glenn Dalton was, like many IT gurus, quirky and tended toward overprotection with his kingdom of servers and network devices. When GroupBeat sent their high-dollar consultants to "audit" his network, he was peeved, if not downright suspicious. But he also knew his place. IT people are seldom called upon for their real opinion and are generally expected to implement the latest technology that the upper echelon heard about at a conference, even if it is junk.

But out of curiosity, he did a brief bit of research on GroupBeat. What he found left him perplexed. It was a nebulous company with murky connections. True, the website was brilliantly done, but other than being loaded with buzzwords and photos of the senior management, there was no real way to find out just what GroupBeat did from their site. A little more online searching turned up the fact that GroupBeat had some Defense Department contracts. That was also confusing. The newspaper was respected and did have a national readership, but it wasn't like they housed the Crown Jewels. Still, it wasn't entirely unheard of for a large IT company to have staff involved in smaller gigs to fill in the cracks or to learn the ropes. The only other information he could find was that they seemed to have a heavy presence in Romania for reasons unknown to him.

So Glenn did what any self-respecting geek would do. He tightened the settings on his firewalls, ran network-level and workstation-level scans on the machines and kept a weather eye on his logs. Most firewalls are designed to allow traffic from the inside out but keep the bad guys on the outside from getting in. But that does not mean both sets of traffic cannot be logged and analyzed.

Still, it was a couple of weeks later on a Monday morning, coincidentally the same Monday morning Alex received his phone call, when he found it. While reviewing the firewall logs, he stumbled across a strange blip of traffic at 3 a.m. to an Internet address which, when he looked it up, was assigned to a network provider in Romania. That was enough to pique his curiosity. When he looked at the corresponding address that was sending the traffic, he discovered it was Alex's workstation. IT workers know who the problem children are on any network, and Alex was not that guy. He wasn't continually loading the latest emoticon packs or clicking on strange links promising him a fortune in diamonds if he helped a certain heir bypass his country's repressive regime. No, Alex used his computer for work and nothing else, strange as it might sound.

While he was mulling this over, he heard a knock on his door. After inviting the person in, he was surprised to see Alex at his door. Alex said, "I think I've got a problem." Then he shut the door and sat down in the chair across from Glenn's desk.

"You've been hacked," said Glenn matter-of-factly.

Alex stiffened. "How do you know this?"

"Let's take a walk," said Glenn. "And leave your phone here," he added, taking his own phone out of his pocket and placing it on the desk.

Alex complied, and the two of them walked down the hallway and took the elevator to the basement where the boiler was located. Other than being a bit dank, the basement provided a constant hum of noise which rarely ever abated. Alex looked around with curiosity etched on his face. He hadn't been to the basement since his original building tour as a new employee.

"Alex, I have reason to believe that your computer is sending out information at a set time every day—3 a.m. to be exact."

"What does that mean?"

"It means your computer, like ET, is calling home. I've looked up the address, and it's somewhere in Romania. I've been looking at the logs for the past hour, and it's been happening every night at the same time ever since..." he trailed off.

"Since when?"

"Since GroupBeat came through and did their 'risk assessment' of our network. They asked to spot-check some individual machines. Yours was one of them. I can't prove it right now, but I suspect they installed something on your machine at that time which is probably gathering all of your data and sending it out to another computer over the Internet."

Alex swore under his breath. "Are you sure?"

"I won't know for certain until I do a more thorough analysis of your machine, but I scanned everything multiple times after they left. Nothing showed up as far as malware or viruses. Whoever is behind this is using some high-level tools. And that's just it: this GroupBeat company has DoD connections and contracts."

Alex swore again. "That means they've got almost everything I've been working on." He rubbed his temples. "What can we do to fix this?"

"First of all, it would be helpful to know who we're really dealing with on this," said Glenn. "What are you working on which would have caused someone to go to all this trouble?"

"A few pieces, actually," said Alex. "Any one of them would be enough to make some powerful people mad. But I've got an idea as to which story is probably the most important one."

Glenn thought for a minute. "There are really only a couple of options. I can maybe find what they installed and remove it. But that would alert whoever is behind this that we know what they are doing. The other way is to pretend that you don't know what's happening and feed them misinformation. It's been happening forever in military planning."

Alex pursed his lips. "Let's go with that. But how can I keep working on my stories without them knowing it?"

"That's pretty easy. I've got a few laptops that are clean. We'll get your work from the daily backups. They won't even know we've done it, since everyone's computer gets backed up. None of the laptops were touched by those guys. Do you have another email address you can use other than your work email? They probably have access to that by now and are watching it."

"Yeah. I've got a couple of other addresses I use from time to time."

"Tell you what, why don't you create another new one, just in case?"

"I can do that." Alex went quiet for a bit. "Glenn?"

"Yeah."

"Thanks for your help with this. I'm in over my head with all this technical stuff."

"No problem, Alex. Those jerks should have stayed away from my network."

Two days later, Alex was sitting at his desk. He started humming the old Andy Williams tune: *Charade*. Then he picked up his desk phone and dialed a number. He pressed the record button on the phone. A voice answered on the other end.

"Bart? Hey, it's Alex. I'm in. What's the story?"

And so it was that Alex began down the path of his newly chosen double life. During office hours, part of the time he would be in his office, dutifully typing away at a story chosen for him by his previous overlords. He added his own thoughts to the main points sent to him. He made calls and interviewed key people. He typed what he knew would be acceptable. Then he would read through his work email making sure to delete without reading anything which came from polkadotpanda. He had written to the person from his new address and had explained in brief his suspicion of that address being monitored. The person was supposed to keep sending emails to his work address asking repeatedly why he was not responding any longer. He knew that at 3 a.m., someone would be reviewing everything he did that day on the machine.

Sometime around 10 or 11 in the morning, he would leave his cell phone in his office and make his way down to the furnace room. Off in a corner beyond the boiler and behind some dilapidated print equipment sat a small intern's desk equipped with a desk lamp and a laptop. Glenn had installed a wireless repeater which was piggybacking on the open network of the coffee shop nearby. For all practical purposes, the laptop didn't exist on the paper's network.

There, Alex would sit for hours and labor over a web of details involving the power brokers in Washington and dozens of other cities around the globe. No interns. No research department to help him look up the details. Other than his communications with polkadotpanda over his new email address, he was reduced to being his own gumshoe. It was hard work, and it would take him longer, but Alex was satisfied.

At the end of the day, Alex would save his work only onto a thumb drive, not the laptop itself. Then he would back up his work onto a different thumb drive. One he kept with himself. The other he would place back in the recesses of one of the old, unused printing presses. Anyone reaching back into that area would find the slightly crusty corpse of a rat which had long since breathed its last. Glenn was the only other person privy to its location. Returning to his office, Alex would check his phone messages, retrieve his cell and head home for the evening. It was a dangerous game he was playing, and Alex wondered how long he could keep the façade going.

Chapter 31

Italy

Pietro walked up the long alleyway to the warehouse. The journey from his apartment gave him time to think through a myriad of problems and logistics as well as make certain that he was not being tailed. He knew that a shop near the corner on the way out of the warehouse district was loyal to Giacobbe and no doubt reported his comings and goings. Two to three times per week within an hour of leaving, someone would visit the warehouse and inspect his work. Once per week, Giacobbe himself would show up, sometimes with Father Donati, and check the progress.

Pietro did not mind the after-hours intrusions into his workspace. He could observe them even if they could not do the same with him. The warehouse was clean. Of that, he was certain. He had double checked and scanned it to verify there were no more cameras or even any microphones. When he was working, he now had complete solitude. After the flare-up over the hidden cameras, Giacobbe had agreed to send a man over two times per week at a prearranged time in order to check the stock of snacks and beverages. Pietro kept the door locked, and even though the man no doubt had a key or access to one, he always knocked and waited for Pietro to open up the door to let him enter.

As he approached the door and entered the warehouse, his mind wandered back many months ago to when they had been in the planning stages. He and Tina had spent countless hours going over every contingency they could think of. It all depended on timing at the end. They both knew that the Vatican leadership had been bleeding cash at an alarming rate. Through a combination of intel and recommendations made to Vatican leadership by third parties, the idea of faking treasures of antiquities in order to sell them to gullible bidders was accepted as something worth looking into.

Many people would be happy to just shake loose a few bad apples in church leadership and be content with that. Pietro knew there was more, much more. So did Tina. No, in order for this operation to be successful in their eyes, it had to snag a whole netful of the largest fish plus snag some tentacles of the hidden creatures who lurked in the shadows.

While their team itself was small, their funding was large. The Internet economy had created billionaires and multimillionaires out of the unlikeliest of people. As a result, there were a decent number of people in the world who were both very rich and very concerned about the future of the world and the level of corruption in the established structures of power. Then, there were the hidden gems who served in all levels of government, banking and religion. They had names and faces and histories, but they were largely ignored by their employers. They shouldn't have been. The most secure facilities in the world have to be cleaned by janitorial staff who have the literal keys to the kingdom. Trash bins are filled with secrets. Computer passwords still get taped under the bottoms of keyboards. Executives talk loosely in the backs of limousines or at their desks while the invisible perform their functionary roles.

In 2006, Julian Assange had tapped into those people when he established Wikileaks. In 2010, James O'Keefe had established Project Veritas with a focus on hidden cameras capturing executives, political organizations and media leaders speaking their private thoughts and secret sins. Others had branched into researching publicly available records in order to connect the strands of relationships among organizations, foundations, charities and other entities which were used to launder money in quantities that would make the Mafia blush.

Overall, the effect was that people worldwide were waking up to the fact that their leadership in pretty much all countries were corrupt, self-serving puppets who obeyed a handful of globalists whose desire was to enslave the whole earth to their whims. Further, people were beginning to realize that they were not alone in this understanding. Nor were they powerless. The lowliest could accuse royalty of sexual assault and be heard. Such things were unthinkable in past generations.

As these invisible men and women observed and discovered the depths of wickedness to which their entertainers, leaders and corporate moguls were beholden, they copied documents, shot photos, took videos, made notes and began the process of exposing the darkness. Like rats or roaches, the effect was powerful. Some people sued those who exposed them. Some committed suicide, unable to live with the fact that the public knew of their abuse of children or their unfettered pilfering of public funds. Some resigned in disgrace. Some fled, never to be heard from again. Some died of natural causes, if multiple bullets to the back of the head could be termed natural. With all of the successes, there were still plenty more rats and roaches. And somewhere back of all of them, there were the kings and queens of darkness who remained hidden. Like Moriarty, they sat at the centers of their webs and pulled strings at all levels of society.

Pietro looked at the statue before him. It was a silent piece of stone that was slowly taking shape. It had a story to tell, a story which would serve as an oracle speaking against modern-day evil.

He picked up his hammer and one of the fine detail chisels and began to work on the legs. With steady work, he would be done within a week, two at the most. After the legs were completed, all that remained was the inscription on the base. Then, it was time to deliver the finished goods to his patrons.

One week later, Pietro stood in front of the statue. He had asked Giacobbe's man to pass along the request that he not be disturbed and that no one come to review the statue until he was finished. He stated that since he was so near completion, he needed complete mental concentration and also wanted to make the best of impressions only after he was satisfied that the statue was ready for inspection.

Giacobbe had complied with his request. Pietro's camera had picked up no visitors of any kind. He had also installed a couple of other tools for maintaining privacy, but neither had picked up any intrusions. This had given him ample time to record in minute detail the dimensions of the statue as well as take a detailed series of photographs with a digital SLR until every centimeter had been thoroughly documented. When this was completed, he encrypted the whole bundle of information, uploaded it to a server and sent a note to Tina that it was ready. Now he had little to do except clean up and pretend to be busy while she began the process of creating the clones.

Chapter 32

Western Italy

Tina was at the third warehouse. She had visited the other two earlier in the day to check on the progress. All was going according to plan. It was a good thing they had done several dry runs, as they had exposed some programming flaws which had to be overcome. Other than that, she and the rest of the crew stayed busy with water hoses and air compressors keeping the work pieces free of debris. The laser cutting edge would recognize debris and cut through it again, but they had calculated that adding the human janitorial element would save time in the long run. So they slept in shifts and kept the marble chunks as clean as possible. Tina had also mandated that they keep filling up trash bins with the scraps which would be carted to the dumpsters and emptied on a routine basis. She wanted each site to be completely clean and devoid of any trace of their presence or the actual work that had taken place.

The CNC machine was programmed to take off user-defined manageable chunks of material so that very large pieces of debris did not drop down below onto the floor or even the sculpture itself. Once the rough outline was formed, the machine began the fine-tuning of the object. This created much more dust, and smaller chips of marble accumulated with it around the base to form a volcanic rim from which the statue itself seemed to be erupting. At this point, the crew had to continually wear respirators in order to breathe safely. They also began using industrial vacuum hoses to clean up the waste.

After four days, all three of the statues were in the rough completion state. All they lacked were the final detailing, their unique inscriptions on each base, and the sanding, polishing and aging. Tina had stayed in contact with Pietro via email to keep him abreast of the progress.

At this point, Tina set the "fudge factor" for each of the statues. By assigning a unique number to each statue, the final details would vary enough that the statues would not be exactly the same. Certain lines, contours and textures on the surface would be slightly different but obvious to a trained eye. This was necessary to avoid arousing suspicion that the statues were created by a machine.

Tina looked up at the one she was working on currently. It was amazing to watch the grooves appear in the hair, to see the detail around the eyelids and the ears take shape. Once the statue itself was completed, she would enter in the text for each base.

It was time for her shift to end. Her colleague was waking up from his nap in the far corner away from most of the dust. After giving him an update on what was needed, Tina retired to the corner, where she lay down on her cot.

She closed her eyes and tried to force her mind to relax and rest. Instead, the smiling face of her younger sister Davina intruded on her thoughts. It was the same every night. Her sister had been laughing and having such fun at the playground. She was on the swing set, her favorite part of the park. Tina had been watching her as she swung higher and higher, wearing that bright yellow jacket she adored so much. Davina would turn her face to Tina and make goofy faces and then laugh. It was just the kind of thing an eight-year-old enjoyed.

Tina had gone to the contraption with the ladder on top that was parallel to the ground. She relished the challenge of being able to hold on to the bars and swing herself two rungs at a time until she reached the other side. She had just completed her fifth circuit when she happened to glance over at the swings. Davina wasn't there. Still hanging onto the bars, her eyes quickly scanned the rest of the park. No yellow jacket. No Davina.

Tina hung onto the bars a few seconds longer while her mind processed what was happening. Then, in the distance, she saw a flash of yellow. She opened her grip and dropped to the ground. She could feel the gravel crunch under her feet, which were moving as soon as they hit. Running as fast as she could through the park, out the entrance and down the tree-lined avenue, she could see a man dressed in black opening a car door and ushering Davina inside. Tina yelled her name as loudly as she could, frantic. The man turned and looked at her. They locked eyes. Even at a young age, Tina was struck by how cold and hard his eyes were. Without a word, he slammed the car door and hastened around the car and into the driver's seat.

Tina was running with all her energy, all her effort focused on reaching the car door where Davina was. The engine turned over and sputtered. Again, the driver switched the ignition off and on. The engine sputtered again and caught. Exhaust blew out of the pipe in a blue cloud. Tina lunged for the door handle and began to open the door. There on the seat lay her sister. Her eyes were glassy as she stared off into space. Tina looked up at the man as he turned to take stock of the situation. Tina saw those eyes drilling into her, and she saw his clerical collar. None of it made sense. As she hesitated, the man gunned the motor and slipped the clutch. The door jerked from her hand, its momentum causing it to slam into the fender of a car parked in the next space. The tinkle of glass from the taillight of the other vehicle, the thump of the door hitting, and the screeching of metal as the door was dragged along the whole side of the other car were sounds she never forgot. In that moment, a young girl raised by a pious family screamed with all that was within her, "God, please help my sister!" The car left Tina in a cloud of blue exhaust, some dust and a short lifetime of memories.

The police response was swift. Tina provided all the details they needed to begin their search. The car was located. Davina was not. The police identified the owner of the car, a priest in a nearby parish. Tina was asked to pick out the driver in a lineup. Standing behind the one-way mirror, she shuddered and gripped the hand of her father as she picked out the man whom she had seen abduct Davina. There was no doubt in her mind it was the same man.

Everything was clear-cut. But suddenly it wasn't. After the police formally interviewed the priest in question, Tina's family was informed that she must be mistaken. She doubled down on her assertions. The police were equally firm, to the point of being belligerent. Tina had picked the wrong person, they told her parents. Tina did not realize the underlying truth of the words which the detectives spoke. Power had met impotence, and power had won again.

Davina never came home. Tina's world was flung into a tailspin. Why didn't her parents demand justice? She knew the man was guilty. Why did know one believe her? What if she had not been on the bars and had stayed with Davina?

One day, she lashed out at her father with a barrage of questions and accusations. Her father was a particularly devout man. Instead of responding in anger to her or being overbearing, he got down on both knees and pulled her into his arms. "My dear," he said softly as he stroked her back with his strong hand, "the Bible tells us about these situations. It says sometimes the laws are not enforced, justice is the loser, and that wicked people win over the righteous."

He put his hands on her and held her at arm's length. Tina's chin trembled, and she looked down at the floor. "Look at me, child," her father said. Tina looked up at him. Tears were brimming in his eyes. "Your mother and I love you and your sister more than life itself. If there were anything we could do to bring her back, we would do it in a heartbeat. Do you believe that?" Tina nodded. He continued, "But sometimes very wicked people have so much power and influence that they can get whatever they want. We live in a time and place where that is true. We are the powerless, the weak, those who cannot get justice even though our hearts cry for it. It is a burden that no man should ever have to bear." He looked at her, and the tears flowed freely now from his eyes. "Much less a tender child like you."

They both wept for a long time in each other's arms. Tina understood the best a child could that no one who could do anything cared enough to make a difference. It was her brutal introduction to the dark world of corruption in high places. In that time of her life, she determined that no matter what else happened, her future would be devoted to fighting that corruption with everything she had to give.

She had studied everything she could get her hands on concerning law, criminal justice and investigative work. As her skills grew, she turned her attention to the organization which had not only enabled a child predator to operate but had actively protected him. Through her research, she found that the priest was deeply connected to one of the more powerful orders within the church hierarchy. She was disgusted to learn that after a run of almost ten years in the nearby parish, he actually had been promoted and moved to another city. From that point on, he had disappeared. On instinct, Tina had looked up the missing persons reports in the city where he moved along with the surrounding towns and villages. Like clockwork, the number of missing children had an uptick of almost one per month on average after he relocated. Tina was sick to her stomach. But there was still nothing she could do about it.

Her life choices led her to go through police academy training, where she rapidly made detective. Then she had moved to an international crime-fighting task force within Interpol. There, she had begun to blossom as someone who had the ability to pick up multiple seemingly disparate threads and find the connections between them. Because of the breadth and depth of their investigations, their team size was kept small, and the number of people in leadership who knew of their work and particular missions could be counted on one hand. Even Interpol, it seemed, did not discount the danger of corruption's long reach among its rank and file or even the leadership.

Tina sighed and brought her mind back to the present. Every night it seemed to be the same. Davina had lived with her more intimately since her disappearance than she would have had she never been taken. Mercifully, sleep finally found her in the late hours of the night. She drifted off to the sounds of marble chips dropping to the floor. In her dreamy state, they formed a pathway down a long avenue. At the end, she could see the back of a little girl in a yellow coat.

Her teammates took her phone and muffled it with a blanket so that she would not be disturbed. They covered her next shift when it came. Each of them knew that she did not rest easily and were happy to oblige her when she did.

Chapter 33

Shamokin, Pennsylvania

Reverend Happy awoke again while it was dark. He did not have to look at the clock, but he did anyway. It was 3:33 a.m. The same as the past two nights. The dream was just as vivid as it had been the other two times. Or maybe it was a vision. Did dreams have color, or was it just visions? He was too tired to care, but he was wide awake, nonetheless.

"Okay, Lord. You don't have to keep on thrashing this old mule. I reckon I know what I'm supposed to do now." He had dressed, prayed a while and was making a pot of coffee when Sarah came into the room. She looked just as prim after getting out of bed as she did when she went to do her shopping.

"And just what are you doing up so early?" she demanded.

"Just having a little talk with Father," Happy replied.

"Hmm," she snorted. "What are you talking about that has got you out of bed three nights straight?"

She didn't miss much. "I've had a dream about Mister Ingram three nights in a row. Same dream. I think the Lord is wanting me to give him a warning, maybe check in on him."

"You don't owe that man a thing," Sarah replied tartly.

"Not a thing except the continual debt to love one another," Happy replied just as quickly.

She hated it when he answered her with the Bible. She couldn't argue with him then. "What do you plan on doing?"

"I'm headed down to catch the bus and go see him," Happy said matter-of-factly. "I should have done it the first day. But I guess I'm getting slow or senile for the Lord to have to speak to me three times about something."

Sarah bit her tongue. There was a time when she would have chided him over every little thing, but the truth was, time had mellowed her with age, and the chip she had held on her shoulder over injustice toward her family, and especially her brother, had gotten too heavy for her to carry. She had come through her own time of grief and anger and finally had chosen to relinquish her right to judge other people to the one true Judge. She admired her younger brother for his gentle spirit and his willingness to seek the path of peace, even if it cost him personally.

Happy was watching her face. "You not going to try and talk me out of it?"

"No," she said. "But I will pray for you."

Happy smiled at her. He knew she loved him. He had watched the transition she had undergone the past few years with patience. In her own way, his big sister had grown up.

A few hours, a long ride and a lot of asphalt later, Happy found himself seated in a waiting room at the newspaper's offices. After a short wait, the receptionist called his name and instructed him which floor to get off the elevator at and how to find Alex's office. While he was riding the short journey up the elevator, Happy sighed and said, "Well, Lord. Here goes. I hope Mister Ingram is willing to listen to me. Either way, find me as your willing servant."

Mister Ingram, it turned out, was delighted to see Happy. He gave him a hearty handshake and pointed to a leather sofa in one corner of the office. "Let's sit here. It's way more comfortable than the chairs."

After they were seated, Alex looked at Happy and said, "Happy, I'm glad to see you. What brings you to Philadelphia? I wouldn't think you come here every day."

"Well, Mister Ingram, to be frank, you're the reason I'm here."

Alex looked puzzled. "Please, call me Alex. But I don't understand. I don't remember asking you to come."

"No. But you're the reason I'm here."

"Perhaps it would be better if you explained..." Alex said.

"The past three nights, I've had a dream, the same dream every night. The dream is about you, Alex. After waking up this morning at precisely the same time, I realized the Lord was trying to tell me something. I had to come and talk to you in person and give you a warning."

Alex's brow furrowed. "A warning? About what?"

"Well, I'm not exactly sure about what. I was hoping I could tell you the dream and it would make sense to you." He paused and looked at the bewildered expression on Alex's face. "That's how these things work sometimes."

Alex shrugged. "Okay, Happy. Go ahead."

Happy settled back in the sofa and looked at Alex. "I warn you. Some of this is going to sound strange. But just let me tell it until I'm done."

Alex nodded.

Happy settled into the sofa, shifted his eyes up toward the ceiling as if remembering and said, "In my dream, I saw a great big old chasm, looked something like pictures I've seen of the Grand Canyon. I've never gotten to go there. In the distance, I could see what looked like a wire of some kind stretched out over this chasm. As I got closer, I could see the figure of a man walking along that wire. The closer I got, I could see more details. First of all, I saw the man's face. It was you, Alex. You were way out in the middle of this wire over the chasm. In your right hand, you had a laptop computer. This may sound weird, but It had a coffee cup attached to it with some kind of computer wire."

When he said that, Alex's face tightened. "Go on."

"Well, in your left hand, you had a bottle. It was...well, it was a liquor bottle, Jack Daniel's whiskey. I could see the label. You was also holding two pills with that hand, kind of clutched between your fingers and the bottle. I didn't see any details about those, just that there were two of them.

"You were kind of hunched over walking on this wire, and on your back, there were two newspapers. One of them was just as shiny as glass. It was pretty, at least as pretty as a newspaper can be. But it was small, about the size of a little town's weekly edition. That other one was the biggest newspaper I ever seen in my life. It was bigger than you, but it was ugly. It was dirty, filthy like it had been drug through a sewer, and I don't know if you're supposed to be able to smell things in dreams, but it stunk to high heaven.

"Anyways, you was carrying both of these on your back. As I watched you, you were struggling to keep your balance. Every step was a burden to you. But you kept putting one foot in front of the other."

Happy paused again. Alex looked at him. He half expected him to smile and say it was all a joke, but he had never seen anyone look as serious as the old minister was at that point. Happy looked him straight in the eyes.

"Then in my dream, I looked down and saw what was beneath you." His voice grew quiet. "It was the fires of hell. I've never really seen hell, but I've read about it plenty, and I knew right then that if you were to fall, it would be the end for you."

Alex swallowed hard. "What happened next, Happy? Tell me."

Happy continued, "I looked behind you and saw the shape of a man coming after you on that wire. I didn't see a face, nothing I could recognize, but I know it was a man. The only thing I saw was his hand. He had a ring with the number thirty-three on it. Does that mean something to you?"

Alex stiffened. "Yes, yes it does."

"That man was agile, and he was coming for you. I just knew that he didn't

133

have your best interests at heart. He was coming faster than you were able to walk. Just about when he got to you, I heard a voice say, 'Tell Alex where his help comes from.'"

Alex said, "Who was speaking? Was it the man you saw?"

Happy shot him a glance. "No sir. That one's easy. Your help comes from the Lord, the Maker of heaven and earth."

There was an uneasy silence between them. Finally, Alex asked, "How do you know it was God?"

"Because the Bible says, 'Whoever calls on the name of the Lord will be saved.'"

Alex sat quietly for another few minutes. Happy seemed to be in the zone. He had a peaceful expression on his face, still tinged with a bit of concern.

The more Alex thought over the dream, the deeper was his sense of foreboding. Either Happy was lock, stock and barrel involved with the people he was investigating, or there was an unexplained accuracy to a random dream he had had—for three nights in a row. Nobody but Glenn knew about the laptop he was using rather than the PC over at his desk. And a coffee cup attached by "a computer wire of some kind?" That was unreal. Then there was the man with the ring. The stress of living his double life had begun to take its toll on him. He was drinking again—not as much, but more than he was comfortable with. The pills with no name, the two newspapers. The symbolism was way too accurate. Although he did not like the direction that path took him, he had to acknowledge the fact that it was at least a possibility that God was real. The question was, why did a God up there care about Alex Ingram?

As if reading his thoughts, Happy spoke up and said, "You're probably wondering, 'Why me?'"

Alex nodded.

"Alex, it took a lot of nerve to do what you did when you retracted your story and printed the truth about me. Many a man wouldn't have done that. Maybe God saw something in you that showed you were on the right path, headed in the right direction. And maybe He knew that you needed a nudge to get you over the edge of the finish line."

"I hope I'm not dying yet, Happy."

"I don't mean the finish line of eternity. I mean the finish line where you finish trying to do everything on your own and ask God for His help, where you finish living life Alex's way and give living God's way a try. Now, I know you're thinking that here comes Happy trying to convert me to religion. Ain't nothing further from my mind. But if I could do anything for you, it would be to introduce you to my best Friend, the One who has always stuck with me through thick and thin."

Alex looked at Happy's face. There was no wild-eyed religious fervor. He had learned long ago to read quite a bit about people from their dress, mannerisms and their faces. Most of the people he dealt with, you could never trust their words. What struck him the most was the calmness in Happy's demeanor. Happy was simple. Not in the way one would describe someone who was mentally challenged: he was simple in a beautiful way. It was as if the man was who he really was and who he really was supposed to be all out there in the open. Something in Alex really wanted what Happy possessed.

His office phone rang. The noise jarred Alex, though Happy seemed to never even flinch. Alex said, "Excuse me just a minute." He stood and walked to his desk and picked up the phone. "Alex Ingram." It was one of the interns telling him that she had some background material ready for him to review for one of the stories from his handlers. "Okay. I'll call you when I'm ready for you to bring it in."

Alex hung up the phone, sat down again and looked back at Happy. He had not moved. Nothing had changed. He was still in his zone, as if he were suspended between heaven and earth with a foot in both places. Alex could walk in or walk on. He chose to walk on.

"Happy," he started, "I can't tell you what it means to me for you to make the trip to come down and tell me your dream. It's a lot to process. Everything you said was spot on. I'm not sure that I'm ready to make any big decisions just yet." There was a bit of a business edge in his voice.

Happy studied his face for a few moments. "Alex, it's like I said. I'm not trying to convert you to a religion. Any choice you make has got to be your own. But before I go, do you mind if I say a word of prayer for you?"

"No. Go right ahead."

"Let's join hands," Happy said, reaching out for Alex's hands.

Alex wasn't married, and he wasn't a particularly touchy person, so the sheer fact of letting a grown man hold his hand seemed awkward. But he pushed his arms forward from his knees and let Happy grip his hands in his. The ease with which he gripped Alex made it obvious that he had done this plenty of times before.

Alex waited for Happy to bow his head, but instead, he tilted his face up and turned his eyes upward. He began, "Father God." Strangely enough, Alex's fingertips began to tingle. That was weird. "You gave me this dream

135

to share with Alex, and I've done it. He's heard everything You told me to tell him. I know that You have been mighty good to just show him what he needed to know, but I'm asking you to be extra merciful to Alex. I'm asking you right now, in his hearing, that you confirm this dream to him three times over the next three days, just like you did with me. Let him know how serious his predicament is, not just in this life but also in the one to come. I'm asking this in the mighty and precious Name of your Son, Jesus Christ."

When Happy said those words, Alex felt the tingle run through his whole body. It lasted for just a few seconds while Happy held his hands in silence. Happy looked up at him and said, "I'll be leaving now." He let go of Alex's hands, and the tingle left. Alex didn't know why, but he suddenly felt a wave of sadness.

As Happy left the office and walked down the hallway toward the elevator, Alex thought long and hard about what had just happened. Happy had said three times in three days. Well, he would wait and see.

Chapter 34

The first confirmation to Happy's dream came later in the afternoon. Alex had been down in the basement working on his private research on the laptop when the WIFI dropped suddenly. His eyes went down to the corner of the screen where the network indicator was. The WIFI indicator showed it was in "searching" mode. Right next to the icon was the clock. It was 3:33 p.m. A laptop with a coffee cup connected to it by some kind of computer wire. The number 33. And 3:33 p.m. Not a.m., but still the same time Happy had his dream.

It was enough to set Alex on edge, but the reporter in him was curious as to what, if anything, would happen next. It was the next day when things took a more sinister turn. Alex had just arrived around 7 a.m. to find the office abuzz. People were running around with the kind of energy that only accompanies a big story. "What's going on?" Alex asked one of the other reporters as he was bustling past.

"You haven't heard about Representative Fitzpatrick?"

Alex did a double take. "No. What happened?"

"He was found dead. Apparently, a murder-suicide between him and some high-class madam in DC. Lady went ballistic on him for some reason. Stabbed him thirty-three times. Then she did herself in with the same knife."

Alex went cold. That number was not random. It was a warning to anyone involved with the congressman: "Shut up, or you're next." He had no doubt that the lady involved was murdered. The police would investigate, find nothing and move on. The poor congressman would be eulogized, buried, and his sins, which were many and profound, would be buried right along with him. At least they would unless Alex pressed forward with his story.

The following day, after a rather fitful night's sleep in which he could not seem to find rest no matter how many pills he took, Alex left late for the office. He was in no mood for a third confirmation to Happy's dream at this point. But somehow, he knew it would be coming. He decided to throw a monkey wrench in the works and change his plans for the whole day. Instead of going to work, he would roam around the city, maybe visit a park or a museum, enjoy the fresh, exhaust-filled air of the downtown. This all seemed to be centered on the office, so he would avoid going there at all costs. He looked at his phone and saw three missed calls. They could wait.

His wanderings eventually took him past Independence Hall where he observed a tour group. He paused to listen for a bit, intending to move on. The guide was apparently answering a question. "Yes, it's true that there was a strong Masonic influence among many of the founders of our country. The land on which Independence Hall was built was owned by William Allen, the Grand Master of Pennsylvania. The cornerstone was laid by old Ben Franklin himself, who was Grand Master of the local lodge. And, interestingly enough, legend says that the Liberty Bell cracked when it was tolling to mark the passing of Supreme Court Chief Justice John Marshall, the Past Grand Master of Virginia."

"Maybe that happened to show that true liberty is completely incompatible with secret societies," said a tall, distinguished-looking man in the rear of the group.

"Maybe so," said the tour guide. "Who knows? Over here, we have..." his voice trailed as he turned away and the group moved on.

That gave Alex pause. He watched the group move on and then turned himself to walk on. It was then that his cell phone buzzed in his pocket. He looked at the number. It was one of the editors at the paper. He pushed the answer button.

"Alex here. What's up?"

"Two days in a row we get bombshells, only this time, it's too close to home."

"What are you talking about?"

"Glenn Dalton, our IT guy. He just got arrested here at the paper for hacking and for possession of illegal pornography."

Alex froze. "What did you say?"

"You heard me the first time. Bunch of guys in suits came pouring in and swarmed his office. They spent time with Dixon and the assistant publisher explaining things. Funny thing is, they asked specifically if you were available for questioning. Do you know anything about all of this?"

Alex's mind raced. Why would someone arrest Glenn? Even more, why were they asking for him?

"Alex, you there?"

"Yeah, uh. Wow! This just catches me by surprise. I know Glenn is our IT guy. He's helped me out on a few occasions with questions about computer problems. I'm not sure why anyone would want to talk to me about Glenn though. Did they give any indication what they want?"

"No. Apparently, the guy who spoke with Dixon had a list of credentials a mile long. Said they had been watching Glenn for a long time. Hey, you going to be back in the office today?"

"I wasn't planning on it. I was taking a day off. I haven't done that in a long time. Does Dixon need me?"

"I don't think so. The guys already left with Glenn. I'm sure if they want to talk with you, they know where to find you."

That last statement left a chill on Alex. He managed a half-hearted laugh. "Yeah, I'm sure they do. Well, I'll see you tomorrow then, I guess."

"Okay, Alex. I figured you'd want a heads up. Bye."

Alex put the phone back in his pocket and turned and looked back toward the Liberty Bell. Imperfect though it was, it seemed to stand for something. Three confirmations in three days. Wasn't that what Happy had asked his God for? Alex scanned the sidewalk behind him. He half expected to see someone sneaking after him. No, Happy had said the man on the high wire was just about to get him in the dream.

Alex put both hands in his pockets and walked slowly along the sidewalk. He knew in the back of his mind that if someone from the government wanted to pick him up, they were probably already tracking his phone. He thought his best move was to go back to the paper after hours and see if anything had been disturbed. The main staff would be leaving in another thirty minutes or so. It would take him longer than that to walk the distance.

On the way back, he thought of a dozen different courses of action, but none of them seemed to be worth pursuing. He went in one of the back doors of the building. He thought of going to his office, but really, he wanted to find out if anyone had disturbed his workspace in the basement—or discovered it at all. Rather than take the freight elevator, he opted for the stairs, reasoning that they would be quieter.

As he made his way down the stairs, his insides grew tense. Something seemed just a bit off. Questions kept running through his head. Was Glenn really involved in hacking, or was it a setup? Why had the law enforcement people, whoever they were, asked for him?

When he made it down the final few steps, he paused at the doorway and listened. Regardless of fire codes, the basement door was always left propped open. Now it was shut. Alex turned the handle softly and slowly and then pulled the door open. The hinges creaked in protest. A door left alone for decades does not like to have its habits changed any more than people do.

Alex peered into the cavernous basement, but nothing seemed out of sorts. He could prolong the inevitable, but Alex knew that he had to find out if the laptop had been discovered and, especially, if the thumb drive was undisturbed. He walked down the rows of files and abandoned equipment until he came to the section where he had been working. When he turned the corner, his stomach clenched. Seated at the desk where he had been working was a man. At the sound of Alex's approach, he turned and looked up. Alex froze. The man had a thick head of red hair parted down the middle.

"Good evening. Alex Ingram, I presume?" said the man as he offered his hand.

Alex reached out and shook the man's hand. "Yes, I'm Ingram. And you are...?"

"FBI. Special Agent Mulvancey. I was wondering if you were going to show up today or not."

All of Alex's alarm bells were going off inside. First of all, why was this man waiting in the basement if he didn't know if Alex was coming? Was he planning to spend the night? Second, why was he alone? Didn't these guys work in pairs? Third, why was the laptop missing?

The man continued, "So what brings you down to the basement after hours, Mister Ingram?"

"I was..." Alex paused mid-sentence. He realized he didn't have an alibi or excuse of any kind. Then his mind slipped into business gear. "Hey, what is this? An interrogation? What are you doing here, for that matter?"

The man smirked at him. "I'm here because your IT manager decided to pull a few stunts with your company's computers. We caught him hacking into some systems and downloading some pretty objectionable material. Because of that, our orders were to do a complete sweep of the premises to see if there are any other machines which may be part of the crime scene."

"Glenn Dalton, a hacker? I don't believe it."

"You don't have to believe it. His computer was filled with images and videos of some pretty whacked out stuff. He'll probably be going away for a long, long time."

"I still don't believe it. But what does any of that have to do with me?"

"We're not sure. Maybe nothing. But before we took him into custody, Mister Dalton had made three phone calls to you this morning. We're wondering what could be so important that he tried to reach you that many times in a row. Do you know?" He drilled Alex with a classic FBI stare, waiting for him to respond.

Alex stared back. "Yes. As a matter of fact, I do."

"Do you want to share that information with me now, or do I need to get a warrant?"

Alex did not like this man. He was brash, rude and pushy. No wonder Goldie had referred to him as "Mr. Creep."

"It's really none of your business, or the FBI's for that matter. But if it would help get you out of my hair sooner, I'll tell you."

The man grunted. "Sure. Go ahead."

He kept staring at Alex, but Alex had worked around law enforcement his whole career.

"Glenn was working with me to get me a laptop I could use to work on here or away from the office. He was probably calling me to let me know that it was ready."

"Three times?"

"How should I know? Maybe he had some questions about what I needed."

Mulvancey glared at Alex. "We found a laptop here. Would that be your laptop?"

"Probably. Where is it?"

"We took it for analysis, purely a precaution, you understand. It wasn't attached to the network and didn't have any clear connection to any employee. When we opened it up, your name was on the login screen."

"Then that's my laptop."

Mulvancey looked around. "Why here? Why in the basement, Mister Ingram? Seems like a pretty out-of-the-way place to put a laptop. Don't you hotshot reporters have your own offices and workstations?"

"Sure, we do. But I wanted to have the ability to go somewhere quiet. It gets noisy up in the offices sometimes, and I find it hard to concentrate for long times compared to when I was younger. Glenn suggested the basement. He brought me down here and showed me this area. He said he'd leave the laptop for me whenever it was ready."

Mulvancey glared hard at Alex again. "Well, I guess we'll see what the lab says after they have a look at the laptop."

Alex shook his head. "You Fed types are all the same, aren't you? I haven't done anything wrong, and here you are trying to tie me into this thing somehow. I still don't believe Glenn is guilty of whatever you say is going on, but even if he is, you've got nothing on me because I'm not part of it." He looked around and then said, "Well, if the laptop isn't here, then I don't need to stay any longer. Unless you have a warrant, that is."

Mulvancey got up from the chair. He was a bit taller than the average person, and it was obvious that he had grown accustomed to using his height

141

as an intimidation factor throughout his career. He started to intrude on Alex's personal space, but Alex simply turned and began to walk away.

"Mister Ingram," Mulvancey said to him. "I seem to recall your name being involved with a story some years back." Alex stopped but didn't turn around. "I've written lots of stories. If you read the newspaper, you will have seen my name dozens of times."

"This story was something about a do-gooder organization in the bad part of town. Seems like some women accused the preacher of doing some pretty bad things. Didn't you write that story?"

"I did," Alex replied. "But it was all a lie. I later wrote a retraction."

"Did you now? I just remember the main story. Whatever happened to the women who accused the preacher? I don't seem to recall hearing about them any more after that story."

There it was. The threat. The undercurrent of danger. It took all of Alex's willpower and nerve that he could muster to not turn around and charge the man in a blind rage. Assaulting a federal law enforcement officer was probably still a crime even if he were a stone-cold killer. Instead, Alex forced himself to draw a breath and relax. He could hear Mulvancey walking toward him.

"I never met them again after it was all over. Maybe they moved away. For all I know, they could be dead."

Mulvancey walked past him. As he headed back toward the basement doorway, he said, "Hmm. Yeah, I guess you're right. Well, Mister Ingram, you have a good rest of the evening. If we find anything amiss on that laptop, you'll be hearing from us."

"In that case, I won't be hearing from you again," said Alex.

"I hope so, Mister Ingram. For your sake, I really do hope so." Mulvancey walked out the door, and Alex could hear his footfalls on the steps.

Chapter 35

Alex waited a full minute, collecting his thoughts, and then walked up one level and found an in-house phone. He dialed the front security desk and asked if Mulvancey had actually left the building. When he received confirmation, he walked back down to the basement. Before he left the building, he had to find out if his hiding place was still secure.

When he entered the basement, he walked the entire length looking for anyone else. Not seeing anyone, he walked down the aisle to the abandoned printing press and reached his hand back into the recesses of the darkness. His heart skipped a beat. The dead rat was gone or moved. He stuck his arm in further and began to pat around the entire area. Again, his heart skipped when his hand touched an envelope. Slowly, Alex extricated the envelope. It was smudged with dirt and ink but looked brand new. It bore the paper's logo in the return address corner. There was no name on the front. It was sealed. It felt like there was a thumb drive or something like it inside.

Before opening the envelope, Alex stuck his arm back in the press further and felt around. He felt the carcass of the rat. Just beyond it, he found his thumb drive. Whoever had put the envelope back there had probably been in a bit of a hurry and was not worried about decorum. It had to be Glenn. If it were anyone else, they would have taken the thumb drive.

Alex was relieved and stressed at the same time. His hiding place had not been located. But where was Glenn? Who really had him in custody? What would he tell? Alex envisioned Glenn hanging up by leather straps while being beaten by thugs in military uniforms. He shook his head and blinked his eyes. Watching movies never helped during times like this.

He needed to find out what Glenn had left for him, but he couldn't use his office computer to check the contents of the thumb drive. And Glenn wasn't around to help him. He also became conscious of the fact that he was still in the basement. If someone walked in on him, it wouldn't look good. Alex put his extra thumb drive back in the hiding place. It hadn't been found yet, and he really didn't need to carry two copies with him.

All the way up the stairs, the load Alex was carrying seemed to weigh on him heavier with each step. Nobody at the paper knew what he was really researching. If they knew, some of them would run away instead of wanting to help. The bigger names were, for the most part, just as bought as he had been most of his career. He couldn't go to the police. From what he had seen, it was a gamble to find the right person who would take the information and not use it against him. He didn't even have a wife to yell at him and tell him he was foolish to be putting their lives in danger for all of this. And he was in danger. He sensed that now more than ever.

If he had had any doubts left after listening to Happy recount his dream, they were gone now. "They" were closing in on him. How did Happy put it? "I just knew that he didn't have your best interests at heart." That was an understatement. Torie's face flashed in his mind. He couldn't put the memories of the photo of her out of his mind permanently. No amount of booze or pills had ever helped. These people were sick.

Then he thought of the laptop itself. What would they find? He had never saved a document to the hard drive. Glenn had drilled him on the importance of keeping the laptop "clean," as he had put it. But what else was there? He had used the privacy mode for all his web browser research. How good were these people? If it really was the government, what tools did they have available? Could they pull up private browsing history somehow? Would there be any traces of what he had written in the word processor?

By the time he got back to his office, he was a wreck emotionally. He sat down on the sofa he had sat on just three days ago and thought back over what had happened since. Pretty much his entire life had been turned upside down. Some people would have a strong fight or flight impulse. Alex just felt an overwhelming sense of hopelessness. How could he fight shadowy figures who were part of an organization which included so many powerful people in banking, law enforcement, and the government? For all he knew, the organization was the government.

He needed help, and he didn't know where to turn to find it. Well, that wasn't completely true, he thought. He looked across the sofa to where Happy had sat. He could hear Happy's voice. "Your help comes from the Lord, the Maker of heaven and earth." Was it really true? Was there a God up there somewhere who really existed? Then his mind raced back to where he was three days ago. He knew he had a choice to make, and he could walk in or walk on.

Alex didn't know much about this, and he couldn't bring himself to turn his face up to the ceiling like Happy did. Almost like a whipped puppy, with his head lowered and his eyes looking up, he spoke aloud, "God, I don't really know if you are there. Happy says you are. He says that you want to help me." His voice faltered. "I need help."

With those words, a pressure that had been building inside of him for years erupted. One man, alone in his world, sat on a sofa in an office of power and began to sob. Once the tears flowed freely, waves of grief pounded him. His life and the breadth of his career paraded in front of the review stand of his conscience, and he hated what he saw. He saw himself hobnobbing with the rich and powerful. He saw himself as a young reporter eagerly lapping up the instructions of his handlers as they guided him on how to craft his stories from their talking points. He saw himself sitting at bars asking for another drink, and he remembered the emptiness which ached inside of him. On and on the images marched. And then he saw himself seated at a table with Torie Spalding. Torie's makeup was in shambles, and her speech was slurred as she said, "You and me, Mr. Ingram. Just whores, that's all we are. We sold our souls. We sold our souls to the devil for 30 pieces of silver."

There comes a time in each man's life when he has to face a reckoning. Alex had run from his years ago. Now he had nowhere left to run. "God," he said. He was barely able to form the word because of the convulsing of his body. "I don't deserve your help. I'm so sorry. I'm sorry for everything."

Tears and mucus had merged to turn his face into a disgusting mess, but the spirit inside of him had never looked more beautiful. In that moment, something happened. His tears still flowed, but he felt as if he were back in his mother's arms and she was consoling him as he cried over a broken toy. Could God really fix a broken heart or a broken life?

Outside, the world passed on. Money changed hands. Drivers sped down the highways to their next destination. Surely, somewhere, the rich were oppressing the poor and justice was being denied to the powerless. But time had stopped for Alex Ingram. He knew that he had stepped into the place where Happy lived. He didn't want to leave it. He felt sorrow, but he also felt comfort. He knew that his life was in mortal danger, but he felt safe. The reporter part of his mind tried to analyze everything, but a deeper part of him he had never really explored seemed to be putting a finger to its lips and shushing him to be quiet and experience this on a different level. There it was. It was peace. He had a sense of peace that he simply could not logically explain.

He sat there: for how long, he did not know. When he finally looked up at the clock on his wall, it was approaching midnight. Nothing else in his life had changed. He still had a tightrope to walk. He had a story to research. He surely had someone who was coming after him. Glenn was still locked up somewhere. What was his next move supposed to be?

"Go see Happy."

Those three words dropped into his mind: not audible, but unmistakable. Alex looked around his office and got up from the sofa. He retrieved a pen and paper from a desk drawer and wrote a note to the pool secretary explaining that he had urgent personal business to attend to and would be away for a few days. He left the note on her desk and then stopped by the men's room to clean up. On the way out of the building, as he passed by the security guard's station, the guard looked up and saw him leaving. "You have a good night, Mister Ingram."

Alex stopped and looked at the guard. "Oh, I will," he said. And he knew that he would.

Chapter 36

Indian Ocean

Captain Andar had just finished inspecting the special cargo. He knew that it was valuable, but he did not really know why. While he was tempted to take some of it for himself, he weighed the consequences in his mind and decided that if he delivered it all intact, he might be given a chance to make future deliveries and earn even more money. Still, he was tempted. But the people who shipped such cargo were not the kind of people he wanted to cross.

Returning to the bridge, he gave the crew foreman the okay that it was permitted to resume duties in the cargo hold. He always cleared the hold for the captain whenever he needed to inspect the cargo. Captain Andar knew that there were questions among the crew, but he also knew that after Hijan's untimely disappearance, no one else was likely to intrude into matters which did not concern them.

As he took over the wheel, he thought of the payoff. If he were able to make just a few more of these runs, he could retire with a nice nest egg. He even mused about the idea of investing the money into some property where he could have a nice garden and enjoy a view of the sea.

While his mind wandered over the money he had not yet been paid, Hali Datmari was counting out a stack of bills to a man who worked in the water authority over the Suez Canal. After much debate, it was decided that working within the Muslim community in a Muslim country would defer some of the risks. The contact they had was on the Port Said side, but he himself had other contacts who worked at Port Suez. It would be dicey to make everything work, but it was their best shot at getting justice for Hijan.

For a substantial sum, they were being provided uniforms of the police force, temporary "jobs" as security staff and access to the *Ahil* during the journey through the canal and before it reached the open waters of the Mediterranean. Other contacts of their relations were providing them with room and board and the loan of vehicles. The less they had to hire through official channels, the less they could be traced. Still, the four men who were going to be part of the police boat crew knew that there was a chance that it would be a suicide mission of sorts, suicide including the potential for being stuck in an Egyptian prison for the rest of their lives.

Hali had, of course, volunteered to lead the mission. The four men had each traveled to Suez, where they had reunited and begun a crash course in their new roles. Receiving regular updates via their relatives back home, they knew now that the *Ahil* was less than three days away. After discussion with their contact, it had been agreed that they would trust him to bribe the right person at the water authority to make sure that their boat was able to intercept the *Ahil* before it began its journey up the canal. They would board the ship under cover of a standard, routine inspection or some such ruse and then proceed from there. As he squinted against the harsh sunlight reflecting on the water, Hali wondered if their mission would be successful. They would know soon enough.

Chapter 37

Philadelphia

Margot was at a crossroads. After the surprising and untimely death of Congressman Fitzpatrick, she had paused her investigation. After all, what was the point? He could no longer be arrested or questioned. He no doubt was a link in a bigger chain, but how big of a link was he? His suicide sounded like death by a thousand cuts.

She had emailed the reporter at the paper several more times through his new email account. He had thanked her for the information she had provided him and indicated that his own research was going well. Then he had gone silent for several days.

Serious was involved in another round of research that did not particularly interest her. While he was still available to chat, there was not much to chat about. Maybe it was time to dig deeper locally. After all, she at least had an idea of some of the names and locations rather than having to start from scratch all over again.

She stared at her screen, which was currently at an empty Tor browser page, and thought back to the deaths of Mennheim and Lewisburg. The police had never really been questioned or put under scrutiny. She knew that the trail of corruption had to be deeper than just at the judicial level. So Margot decided that for her part, rooting out corruption on the other side of the thin blue line would be the best way to help her community.

Her first efforts were to research all the names of the officers who had been involved in the cases with Judge Lewisburg and DA Mennheim. She found a total of twelve officers who had been involved regularly in the arrests associated with the drug cases. Out of those, two were in the homicide division, five were in narcotics, and the other five were a mix of detectives and patrol officers. Notably, none of them had been charged with any type of crime related to the investigation. The internal affairs bureau apparently liked to keep a tight lid on their dirty laundry.

Margot decided to do more research on the officers themselves. As she perused their social media pages using a fake account she had created for that purpose, Margot was amazed once again how much personal data people post online willingly. While she was scrolling through one of the officer's pages, she saw a post which read, "Home team 2 kikes 0." It was an offensive slur, and she was surprised that it was still online. She looked at the date of the post and compared it to the growing list of facts and details in her spreadsheet. Her pulse quickened when she realized that it was posted the day after DA Mennheim's "suicide."

She quickly scrolled through the rest of the posts but turned up nothing until she got near the very end. It was a group photo. Several men, some of them in uniform, were brandishing weapons. As Margot examined the photo, she saw something that tugged at her mind. Sticking out of the waistband of one of the men was a small pistol of some kind. She could just make out what looked like the chamber of a revolver. The handle was pearl inlay with a unique design etched into it. She searched through all of her notes but still found nothing. Her mind kept nagging her that something about that was important. After another thirty minutes of searching online, she found the details of DA Mennheim's death and saw where he had committed suicide using a .22 revolver with a pearl inlay handle. Maybe it was a coincidence. Maybe not. The design on the handle looked to be custom, and that would at least be a good indicator as to a match.

To get more background on the photo, Margot tried to identify the people in the photograph. It took switching back and forth on social media accounts, but she was able to match six of the seven men with names of the officers who had been involved with arrests in the cases which were part of the Lewisburg/ Mennheim scandal. The seventh man was a wiry looking man with pointed features. He reminded Margot of a cartoonized sewer rat. The look on his face was a mixture of sly, devious, and cruel with a hint of congenital suspicion. More than anything, Margot saw a strong look of pride in his features, almost as if he were daring anyone to tangle with him. Even though he was not quite as big as the rest of the men, he was in the center of the photo with his arms draped up and over the shoulders of two of the beefiest guys. The caption someone had put to the photo read, "Band of brothers. Together again."

That added new information. All seven of these men had been in the military, presumably together. As she began scouring through social media pages again, Margot found references on two of their pages to Afghanistan. She also found another photo of one of the police officers in military desert battle dress uniform with the rat-faced man. The caption said, "Me and Little Poppy after a successful raid on the enemy compound." Little Poppy. The nickname raised some questions in her mind. Was he little because of his size or because there was a Big Poppy or Daddy Poppy somewhere? Was the poppy a reference to the plants used in the production of heroin which made up so much of Afghanistan's export? Why have a nickname that referenced a drug plant?

Intrigued, Margot focused on trying to find out more about who the rat-faced man was. After three more hours, she hit pay dirt. Using a reverse image search, she found another copy of the image posted to a military news site. The caption to the photo said, "Sergeant Earl Scoggins and men beat AQ against insurmountable odds in the nick of time." The story gave the rest of the details. The seven men in the photo had been involved in a brutal firefight with Al Qaeda around the border area of Pakistan during a nighttime patrol. The Al Qaeda fighters had almost thirty men against the smaller force. Neither side seemed to gain an advantage, but the US forces knew that they were near enough to the border that the enemy would be reinforced soon.

Using a combination of intense gunfire and the occasional grenade to distract the enemy, Sergeant Scoggins had left the rest of the men while there was still some cover of darkness. Alone, he had gone downhill for almost half a mile, skirted the enemy positions, and then climbed up the side of the mountain. There, using only his standard issue rifle and secure local radio communications, he coordinated with the team to unleash a burst of fire each time he was ready to shoot. He had managed to snipe twelve of the Al Qaeda members before they realized what was happening. That was because eleven of the twelve were headshots. The twelfth man managed to cry out loud and long enough that his compatriots realized they were under attack. About half of the remaining fighters had charged toward Sergeant Scoggins' position, but his teammates provided cover from behind. All eight were mowed down from both directions.

The remaining AQ fighters decided to live to fight another day and fled in two small groups of approximately four each. Unfortunately for them, the US troops had anticipated this and had already split into two groups of three and were waiting behind clusters of boulders when each group came within distance. After the brief skirmish which followed, they regrouped with Sergeant Scoggins and did a basic but hurried assessment of the dead. Hearing motors in the distance, they departed the area to a higher and more secure location where they watched as a convoy of six Toyota pickups loaded with .50 caliber guns and supporting AQ fighters reached the area. All the men agreed that if Sergeant Scoggins had not taken decisive action when he did, none of them would be alive. For his efforts, Sergeant Scoggins was awarded a medal and had his exploits recorded in the paper Margot was reading.

"Earl Scoggins," Margot murmured to herself aloud. "So that's your name. I wonder if you are mixed up with what's going on here in Philly."

Because she was off work the next day, Margot decided to make a fresh pot of coffee and pursue things further. She was young. Sleep would come when she was exhausted.

The problem she encountered was that Sergeant Scoggins was a bit of a ghost. He had no social media accounts. Undaunted, she went back to the other six men's accounts and began to follow their own links and look deeper at the companies and people they followed. Four of the accounts had links to articles about Briarwood Properties, LLC. One was a short story in a local newspaper which noted that Briarwood had purchased the property formerly owned by Gospel to All People, popularly known as the old Gospel Mission.

Margot looked up the articles of incorporation for Briarwood Holdings, LLC. It was owned by another corporation, Trantwa Holdings. Like Alex, she followed the trail until she came to a real name. Although it did not mean as much to her personally, she was at least able to write down the details and note that the person had an extensive career with the US State Department.

Little else was said publicly about Briarwood Properties, LLC, or the parent corporation. It was not clear what the company actually did. Surely people worked at the location. But what went on inside?

Margot put that on hold and decided to drop back to the rest of the police force members who were part of the same military unit as Sergeant Scoggins. The one who had the pearl-inlay revolver in his waistband. He was in the narcotics squad and, as such, was not subject to the same haircut requirements as regular officers. On his social media page, he looked like he would fit in with most any street gang or band of hoodlums.

He obviously made arrests. That much was clear from the court cases and his records. But as she had shared with Alex earlier, some of them were given harsh sentences, and some of them were let off easily.

She was beginning to lose sight of the forest because of the trees. Margot closed her eyes and asked herself, "What is the connection here? What would Serious tell me to do?"

She began to look over the arrest records and the court documents. As she reread the details, it was if someone twisted a lens and brought it into focus. All of the persons arrested and given harsh sentences were dealing in heroin and other drugs. The defendants who got light sentences may have been dealing in meth or cocaine, but heroin was never mentioned. Were they not dealing in those drugs at all, or was there heroin involved but not mentioned? Why were heroin dealers targeted so heavily?

She thought back to her research in Europe. Serious had told her to "think turf wars" back then. If these police officers were targeting heroin dealers, were they protecting other dealers? She mused over the details she had uncovered in the past several hours. "Little Poppy" had to mean something. It wasn't a nickname a guy would usually want to have ascribed to himself. The coincidence of that nickname and formerly being a sergeant stationed in

Afghanistan seemed significant.

Margot looked over at the heavy curtains in her bedroom. She could see sunlight blazing around the edges. She had stayed up all night again and still had a long way to go.

Chapter 38

Italy

Father Donati was in a very happy mood. He hummed a tune to himself as he smoothed his hair and checked his appearance in the mirror. In just a few minutes, Giacobbe would be dropping by to pick him up to go to the warehouse for the unveiling of Pietro's statue.

The whole happenstance had been not just luck but also, one might venture to say, an act of Providence. Pietro's appearance on the scene had come at exactly the right time. Everything he had done up to this point continued to exceed both his and Giacobbe's expectations. Most importantly, the few images they were able to send before Pietro had requested absolute privacy met with the wholehearted approval of the Holy See.

Along with himself and Giacobbe, there were going to be two representatives of the Vatican present. Pietro had been informed of this, and he had been offered and had accepted a suit of clothes provided by none other than Signor Giovanni for the occasion. If all went as planned, then the statue would be shipped privately to the Vatican, where it would be "found" and then privately auctioned to the highest bidder. Based on the preliminary photos they had sent, the rumor had already been placed in the art collectors' world that the Vatican may have discovered a new piece which was a unique marble sculpture, one they would be willing to part with for a princely sum. Several Arab sheikhs were expressing an interest, as were a few of the Asian mega-millionaires.

Father Donati walked down the stairs of his apartment and sat down in his parlor. He checked his text messages. There was one from a parishioner wanting to discuss his performing a wedding for a family member. Another was from a person whose father was requesting last rites as soon as possible. Still another was a text from one of his classmates who had advanced in leadership in their order. He had chosen to move to the USA for a unique assignment. He was sending an update on the progress of his work.

His thoughts were interrupted by a knock at the door. Father Donati glanced out the window through the thin curtains and caught sight of Giacobbe's auto. Opening the door, he greeted Giacobbe and followed him to the vehicle. It was obvious there were no other occupants, since he had driven a convertible.

"Will our guests meet us at the warehouse?" Father Donati asked.

"Yes. I've sent a driver for them. I didn't think they would enjoy the rush of air as much as yourself."

"Probably not. It might lift their miters right off their heads," Father Donati said.

Giacobbe laughed at the thought. "This is the day, Prete. From what my contacts are telling me, the interest in the rumor of a new and exquisite piece is already above 200 million euros."

"Have you given thought as to what you will do with Pietro after this project?" asked Father Donati.

"Our share of this will be enough to pay him the rest of his life. If he wants to continue doing private commissions on sculptures, he can make as many as his heart desires."

Father Donati was pleased to hear that. He knew that some people who had been involved in projects with Giacobbe and his organization ended up at the bottom of the sea or a mine shaft. While he had no personal connection with Pietro, the man possessed such skill that he would hate for it to be cut short without a chance to blossom further. In a way, he felt a bit of priestly responsibility for him, since he had discovered the man and his gifts.

A short time later, they were at the warehouse. The other car was already there, idling in the sunshine with its air conditioner running. Father Donati exited first and greeted the two men as they exited. Pietro had agreed to noon as the time for the unveiling, and it was just a few minutes shy of that time. Giacobbe knocked on the warehouse door and waited until the locks clicked on the other side. Pietro opened the door and greeted Giacobbe and Father Donati with a smile.

"Thank you so much for coming. I am looking forward to showing you the finished product. As an artist, this is one of my biggest joys: to see the look on the faces of those who see my work for the very first time."

"And I cannot express our excitement to see what you have created," said Giacobbe.

"Nor can I," said Father Donati. "These two gentlemen are Father Axelrod and Father Sopelli. They represent your true client this morning."

"It is a great honor that you are here," said Pietro. "I can only hope that you are pleased with my work."

"If you are only half as good as Father Donati here claims, then I am sure we will be impressed," said Father Sopelli with a chuckle. He was a rotund man with florid cheeks. He looked toward the center of the room, where the sculpture stood shrouded in lightweight gray cloth. Everything had been cleaned to perfection. Lights on stands were arranged around the sculpture at different heights and angles. "What can you tell us about your work before we get to see it?"

Pietro smiled and said, "Thank you for asking. Most people want only to see and then ask questions. The sculpture I have worked on is one that has been in my mind since I was a child. I've never had the opportunity to work on material large enough and for long enough to allow me to bring it to reality." He paused and looked off into the distance. "It almost feels as if this image has haunted me for many years."

There was silence for a few moments. Then Pietro returned to the present. "What you will see is a representation of the greatness of the mysteries of our faith. I think of it as the rebuke of satan by the glory of God. It is, I believe, my greatest work."

With that said, Pietro walked over to the sculpture, reached up to the front of the cloth and pulled it down with a flick of his wrist while he himself stepped back out of the lights. Like water, the cloth flowed down the front of the statue until it was left in a nondescript puddle at the base. Pietro watched the four men as they stood gazing at the sculpture.

Father Sopelli gasped audibly. Father Donati's face split into a broad grin. Father Axelrod's face remained impassive for several seconds and then his head nodded several times, and he smiled. Giacobbe brought steepled fingers up to his mouth and then said, "Most impressive!"

There before them was the figure of a man clothed in a long tunic and standing upright. The right arm was bent at the elbow above the waist and was extended slightly about half an arm's length from the body. The fingers of the right hand were curved in a natural repose with the index finger raised as if making a point. The left arm was bent and tucked in at the waist with the forearm and hand clutching a tablet. The face was the most striking feature. It was a mixture of nobility and grace, mixed with a certain sternness and fire. The features were altogether devoid of carnal anger or base emotion. Rather, the countenance evoked a sense of purity of heart which was about to unleash wrath.

Each of the men sensed something of its message, and had they known what it truly represented, they would have fled from the building at that instant. But men of the world are ensnared by their own passions. To the four men viewing the sculpture for the first time, it represented the possibility of wealth and power, not the loss of it.

At over two meters tall, the figure itself was a bit larger than life and was standing on a square base about a meter high. On the base was written in letters about fifteen centimeters in height the single word "MYSTERIUM." There was ample space below that word, but the rest of the base was blank.

Ever the simple sculptor, Pietro quietly watched the faces of the men as they relished the exquisite detail. After the initial assessment, they walked around the statue slowly and began to notice the texture in the clothing, the folds of cloth along the arms, the nails on fingers and toes, and the finer lines within the hair and beard. They gestured and talked among themselves as they made their first tour around the piece.

The figure itself was well structured but did not appear overly muscular. The strength was more so that which comes from authority. The way the figure held the tablet was indicative of the source of that authority. As one approached the statue, there was a faint lettering on the tablet that looked like a written language but which none of them recognized. Instead of standing in repose as if in military rest, the figure had the right foot extended as if advancing toward the observer. With the lights trained on the statue from different angles, it had the appearance of a speaker alone on a stage.

"Mysterium," said Father Sopelli aloud as if musing. "Pietro, why did you choose the word you did for the base?"

Pietro stared at Father Sopelli for several seconds, his eyes focusing both on the priest as well as beyond him as if lost in thought. Then he answered very quietly, "Because that's how I remember it in my mind."

"Remember it? You sound as if you've seen this statue before," Father Donati said jokingly.

Pietro's face grew ashen as he slowly turned to Father Donati. "I...I have," he said, blinking his eyes. He began to breathe rapidly.

"Pietro, are you feeling all right?" asked Father Donati with a look of concern on his face.

Pietro appeared to have lost all sense of his surroundings. He did not respond to Father Donati. Instead, he walked to the statue and stood in front of it just a couple of meters away, his eyes searching it as if seeing it for the first time. "It's not right," he said. "It's not right."

He knelt down and ran his hands along the base. "There's something missing. I can't remember what it said. I can't remember."

Then he got back up and backed away rapidly. He brought his hands up toward his face and looked at them as if they had been burned by touching the base. His fingers opened and closed. He began to breathe so rapidly that he was almost to the point of dry heaving.

The four men were staring at him wondering what was happening. This was no ordinary burst of emotion. Something deeper was at play, and they could only watch as it happened before their eyes.

Then Pietro looked slowly back up to the statue. His eyes traced the figure until they stopped on the extended right arm. "It wasn't there. No. It was never intact."

Before anyone could say or do anything, Pietro raced to his worktable and picked up a large mallet. He strode back to the statue with panic on his face and shouted, "It was broken! The arm was broken!" With one fluid motion, his arm swung from overhead from his side and smashed into the forearm near the elbow. With a mighty crack, the hammer met the marble, and the marble lost the battle. It fell to the floor with a resounding, solid thud which echoed in the cavernous warehouse.

All four men had begun to rush forward to try and stop what they realized was going to be a destructive blow, but it was too late. Consequently, they were surrounding Pietro when he had finished his swing. His fingers slowly loosened their grip on the hammer and dropped it to the floor. With a look of sheer horror on his face, Pietro said in a low but sorrowful voice, "I remember." He looked off into the distance. "Momma. Daddy," he said. Then he crumpled to the floor.

Chapter 39

The response by the emergency services had been swift and efficient. Pietro, the emergency technician had said, had been in and out of a delirious state during the ambulance ride to the hospital. Although he was not violent, he was strong, and his ravings threatened to imbalance the vehicle. The medics were forced to administer a mild sedative.

After a description to one of the doctors of the happenings, the assessment was made that Pietro was likely experiencing a form of shock or PTSD from a relapsed memory. Just what that memory was would have to wait until he regained consciousness. For now, he needed rest and an IV to keep him hydrated.

Unfortunately for Giacobbe and the trio of priests, when he did regain consciousness, he did not seem to recognize anyone. He stared off into space and repeatedly said, "Father Darien, I remember. Father Darien, I remember."

While there was a calloused discussion about cutting their losses and taking the statue and moving on, Father Sopelli was of the opinion that Pietro's comments seemed to indicate that he had actually seen a similar statue somewhere in his past. Based on the brief background sketch Father Donati could provide, it seemed more prudent to pursue the recovery of what memory Pietro had in order to determine if such a statue really existed. Father Donati was given the charge of contacting Father Darien to ask him to come with haste to visit his former ward in order to provide consolation and to minister to his needs. Within twenty-four hours, he was by Pietro's side. He asked to be alone with Pietro in order to ensure a bound of privacy which Pietro would perhaps need in revealing the root cause of his sufferings.

So it came to be that three days after Pietro's sudden spell at the warehouse, Father Donati and Father Darien were having coffee in the afternoon in the hospital cafeteria to discuss what had been discovered.

"It's really quite a remarkable tale," said Father Darien. "I made copious notes because I felt it would be important in his recovery to be able to check the details in order to see if any news of the fate of his parents could actually be determined."

"And he says that his parents were archaeologists?" asked Father Donati.

"Of a sort. You have to remember that he was very young at the time, maybe four years old, maybe five. Whatever they were, they were on the trail of a significant discovery. He does not remember the actual details of how his parents learned about the statues, but they talked about it constantly and at great length. He does recall that there was only one reference they could find about them in all of their research. His parents said that it would be the most earth-shaking discovery for an entire generation."

Father Donati interrupted him. "Did you say statues?"

"Yes. As Pietro recalls, his parents' research showed that there was a total of three statues. They were crafted almost identically. They were reputed to have been commissioned by Constantine, although that is debatable ultimately based on their age and style. The rumor surrounding them was that they contained information which would lead to the utter ruin of some people and, the phrase he remembers was, 'the endless wealth and freedom' of other people."

Father Donati sat in silence. This explained much about Pietro and the sculpture to which he had given birth. Still, there were many more questions to be answered if they were to be able to maximize this opportunity for the Vatican. The thought passed through his mind as to whether or not Giacobbe needed to be included in this information. But the man had too many contacts which would prove to be invaluable along with a history of knowing how to operate in the darker areas of the world. Yet he needed to be cautious in his line of questioning. He opted for the human angle first.

"And Pietro's parents. What of them?"

"As you can imagine, such a find would doubtless have enemies among those who would be ruined. Pietro recalls bits and pieces of worried conversations between his parents. They certainly received threats against their lives. He doesn't remember all of the details, but they were chased a couple of times. He remembers the automobile rides quite clearly.

"Eventually, his parents felt that they had thrown their pursuers off the track. They were able to locate one of the statues. Pietro said it was in a most ingenious hiding place. It had survived for over a thousand years without detection. This is the statue he actually saw. Sometime during its history, its arm had been broken. He saw the arm lying with the statue while his parents were busy recording the details about it. They left the statue where it was and were preparing to locate the other two, which they felt would be simpler now that they had found the first one, when disaster found them.

"They never kept their notes with them on their person for fear of the details being discovered by someone else whether by accident or intention. They had returned to their hotel when someone began breaking down the door. Pietro's father was blockading the door while his mother rushed Pietro out of bed. He was a bit groggy, but he still remembers the look of panic in her face. She ripped the bedsheets off the two beds and tied them together quickly. She was attempting to create a means for them to climb to safety from their room, however high it was. The last thing Pietro remembers of his father was two men clad entirely in black breaking down the door and beginning to overpower him. They had weapons. His mother grabbed Pietro, told him to hold onto her neck and began climbing down the bedsheets. One of the men came to the window and was attempting to pull the sheets back up to capture her. Either she let go or lost her grip. They fell, with her shielding her son. He survived, miraculously. In this state of shock, he ran until he could run no longer. Eventually, he was discovered by a person who called the local council services who brought him to our orphanage."

"So do you believe that his parents were operating that close to your area?"

"Not necessarily. The council is some distance away, but one of the members had reason to know about our orphanage and suggested us. For our part, we were told that he was a young orphan who had apparently suffered severe emotional trauma, of what nature they could not say. His parents were never found, by the way. I intend to do a bit of checking to see if there were any reports of violence in the hotels in that area around that general time frame, but I would not be surprised if it had been covered up. You know how things go unsolved in our country with the long reach of the criminal element."

Father Donati nodded. "It's a shame, to be so young and have that level of violence to affect him." He paused and then asked, "Does he remember anything else about the statues? Surely if those could be found it could possibly lead to the identity of his parents' killers."

"I'm not sure. He had finished talking about the details I had shared when he seemed to relapse a bit. The nurse suggested that he be given time to rest more. I want to help him as much as I can, but I do have some pressing matters to attend to. Perhaps you can accompany me on my next visit and see if he remembers you or any other details from the present. If so, then it is possible that you could continue the counseling that he will need in the coming days."

Father Donati was pleased at that suggestion and had to conceal his glee. "If I can be of assistance to this young man after such an incident, I would be happy to help."

Father Darien nodded. "Thank you. Let's plan to meet at six this evening. Pietro should be awake by then."

When they met together later that day, Pietro was subdued but alert.

When he saw Father Donati accompanying Father Darien, he put his head down and said, "Father Donati, I must say how sorry I am for destroying the piece that I was working on for your friends."

"There, there, my son," said Father Donati. "Father Darien here has explained everything in its entirety. You have nothing for which to apologize. I'm glad to see that you are awake and healthy, although I am sure that you have a road ahead of you which will be difficult at times to navigate."

"And that's why I asked Father Donati to accompany me here this evening, Pietro," said Father Darien. "There are some pressing matters I must attend to back at the orphanage. Since Father Donati has been so helpful to look after you in this parish, I had every confidence that I could ask him to step in and be the ears which will listen to you and the heart which will be open to your pain during the coming days and weeks."

Pietro looked back and forth between the two men slowly. When his eyes finally rested on Father Donati, he lowered his eyes. Father Donati read the expression well and spoke up. "Pietro, I can assure you that not a single person is angry with you or holds you responsible for what happened earlier this week." He paused. Pietro's eyes were still cast downward. "Pietro, do you still believe in absolution?"

Slowly Pietro nodded.

"Do you have anything you would like to confess?"

"I acted rashly. I had no right to break the statue. I...I should not have let my emotions overwhelm me to that point." Pietro ran out of words.

"Then my dear child, please listen when I say that you are absolved of your sin, if call it a sin you must," said Father Donati. His seminary training had kicked back in without hesitation. Inwardly, he felt pleased that he could still perform the functions in which he was trained.

Pietro raised his eyes and looked at Father Donati. "Thank you, Father," he said.

"You are most welcome."

Father Darien interjected, "Well, now that that is settled, I believe I will take my leave. I've a ways to travel before getting back. Pietro, I will inquire after your well-being with Father Donati. If you need me for anything else, please do not hesitate to send for me."

"I will, Father. And thank you for coming," said Pietro.

After goodbyes were completed, Father Donati said, "Pietro, I want you to know that I will be willing to help you in any way in the search for your parents."

"My parents are dead," Pietro responded.

"How can you be sure? Father Darien said…"

"Father Darien wasn't there. I was. I saw their weapons. I have no proof that my father is dead, but I do not doubt it. My mother…" He paused and then finished, "I know they are dead."

Father Donati let him have some time to reflect and then asked, "If you are sure of that, then how best can I help you? What would you like me to do?"

Pietro looked straight at Father Donati and said the one thing that he was hoping to hear. "The people who murdered my parents will only be brought to justice if the original sculptures are discovered and unveiled. More than anything, I would like to see that done."

Again, Father Donati had to suppress his delight. He managed to convey what he thought was a somber expression and tone. "If that is what would bring healing to you, my son, then I will pursue every means to that end."

"I feel that I cannot ask you to endanger your life. The people behind this must be very powerful and wealthy."

"Nonsense. Is not the church also powerful?"

"God's church has the full authority of heaven," said Pietro.

"Exactly! I'm sure I speak for all of us who were part of this project you were working on when I say that you will have everything you need to see this through. Do you have any idea on where to begin?"

"Yes, I do, Father. One of the gifts I have possessed my entire life is to remember things perfectly, at least with certain things. One of those is sculptures, as you know. But it also includes sketches, drawings and maps. My parents did not openly discuss many of the details of the locations of the statues, but twice I saw them as they were studying the map. Really, it was more like a sketch. But it was accurate enough to help them locate the first statue."

"Do you remember any of the details of that map?"

Pietro looked at the priest quizzically. "I remember all of it. I also remember where they hid some of their notes." Father Donati raised an eyebrow. "Their notes?"

"Yes. They had a system they used which proved to be effective at hiding their research in the event that one of them was caught or captured. It was safe, virtually foolproof and was available in most places they ever worked."

"Where was that?"

"The local library. I believe that there is a good chance that I could locate the notes, if they had not removed them, if I were to go to the library in the city where we were."

The priest sat silent in thought for a few moments. He knew that Giacobbe would want to be involved in the matter, but he also felt that he should give Pietro the space he needed to work through the trauma which he had suffered in the past few days. He felt it best that he let Pietro decide.

"Pietro, for us to undertake this course, it may be necessary to include the men who commissioned you to work on the sculpture. After all, they have more resources at their disposal in the way of transportation, help—and money, of course."

Pietro thought for a moment and then said, "I would not mind if Giacobbe himself were part of our search. I do not know the other men as well as you do. Still, if you believe they must be part of our search, I would welcome any help they can offer."

"I will let Giacobbe know. He is a man of some resources. I believe the others will be content to let us help you. As soon as you are well and able to leave…"

"I am ready now," Pietro interrupted. "I am a grown man able to look out for myself. What happened was…a shock. But now that I remember, there is nothing I can do which will change the past. I can only hope to alter the future."

"Then I will call Giacobbe while you ring for the nurse," said Father Donati. "He can come pick us up within the hour, I'm sure."

Pietro nodded as he reached for the buzzer. As he called the nurse station, his mind lingered on the fact that with the press of a button he was setting into motion the final parts of a plan which had been in the making for a long, long time.

Chapter 40

Almost five years earlier, Pietro, whose real name was Nicola De Lisio, had been contacted by the section head of Interpol. He had been approached by an anonymous source inside the Vatican who had information he wished to share. This person was in a high enough position, or a position with enough clearance, to be able to access financial, written and electronic records for much of the Vatican. The information was related to crimes against children, sexual exploitation, money laundering, bribery, extortion, coverups—in short, a litany of sins for which the whole of the Roman clergy would be kept very busy for months or years sitting and listening should confession ever be made.

This person had been forthright in his approach and candid in his motives. He and all of his siblings had been abused by a series of priests as children and teenagers. For reasons known only to himself, he had chosen the priesthood as his profession. Once within its ranks, he had witnessed acts he would only initially describe as "unspeakable." Over the course of decades, his soul had struggled with the contradiction of the public persona of his peers and leaders versus the corruption he saw on a daily basis.

Finally, "something happened" which flipped the switch. He would no longer be complicit. He realized that simply speaking out would result not only in ostracism but in the loss of his life. Of that he had no doubt. "They kill without compunction those who oppose their plans," he had written. Instead, he believed that using his position and access in order to obtain evidence would be the best use of his life and the only reasonable way he could begin to offer penance for remaining silent.

Rather than do a document dump to some place such as Wikileaks or to a journalist, he wanted assurance that the crimes he was documenting would be prosecuted and those responsible would be brought to justice. That is why he contacted the section chief at Interpol. He had done his research, and to the best of his knowledge, that part of Interpol and the chief himself could be trusted.

His faith and research were not unfounded. Although every organization has its bad actors, and infiltration is sometimes more powerful than invasion, Stanley Worthington was an upright man who took his commitment to law enforcement with a wholehearted measure of devotion. He had responded to the initial inquiry, had followed up with every precaution to protect the identity and life of the person and had eventually been rewarded with a face-to-face meeting in Vienna. At that meeting, he was given a thumb drive with a trove of documents. Stanley also provided him with a list of telephone numbers and generic email addresses and several file upload server addresses where more data could be shared in the future with as little risk as possible.

Their contact was a very methodical and organized person. The data was organized into folders according to classification of crimes. Within each folder, such as "Sexual Exploitation," were individual folders for clergy and leaders. The names in the subfolders were numerous and included high-level officials up to and including various popes.

It was at this point, in the early stages of the investigation, that Stanley had contacted Nicola and asked him to head up the task force which would be charged with cataloging, investigating and building cases against those named in the documents. Nicola had invited Tina to join the task force as its second member, and together, they had chosen a few others whom they knew they could trust implicitly. Together, they had read, studied, scrutinized and followed up on the information provided for over a year. It was in the middle of the second year of the investigation that they began to realize not only the enormity of the task which lay before them but also the seemingly insurmountable task of seeing justice done using traditional law enforcement methods. As Tina had so accurately put it, "The corruption is so deep, so endemic, that finding a single prosecutor, judge or a jury which would pass sentence on each of the many people involved would be next to impossible."

At that point, they began to think outside their standard operating procedures. "What if," Nicola had mused, "we not only continue to pursue the legal cases, but we also place the evidence in the highest court in the world?"

"The Hague?" Tina asked.

"No," Nicola said. "The court of public opinion."

The group was uncertain of the idea at first, but the more they brainstormed, the better it sounded. There were quite a number of independent journalists and news organizations who would be willing to pursue the stories in detail once the data was made available. If the whole world, or at least a sizable percentage, were made aware of what they knew, then the guilty would be tried and sentenced in ways that the judicial system could never affect. Plus, they ran a much greater chance of seeing traditional justice served if the matter were so public, so widely known that those involved in the prosecution of crime would be afraid not to handle the matters properly.

After the decision was agreed upon, the plan began to take shape. Stanley had agreed to it only after a consultation with their contact. If a man was risking his life to bring about justice, Stanley reasoned, he should have some say in what that justice would look like. The contact actually applauded the decision by the group because he understood full well the power and reach of his own organization. If anything were to change long term, it would have to come about by a grassroots cry if not an outright rebellion by the rank-and-file clergy and a majority of those considered to be laity.

Over the next two years, the groundwork was laid to make use of the Vatican's desire to make substantial money off the books. Through Stanley's contact, they both learned of and nurtured the desire to sell forged artwork and sculptures which would appear to be historic or undiscovered pieces. With Nicola's natural gifting at sculpting, his role in the drama was preordained. Their search for an honest, clean priest led them to Father Darien, who, in the hopes of seeing real change and cleansing in the higher ranks, agreed to cooperate and provide the appropriate backstory for "Pietro" when called upon.

The documents had included a rather interesting section on the Don's network and how it was tied into numerous relationships within the Vatican's network. The team assigned another trusted group to work with them by focusing their attention on the Don's network. This led them to the discovery of Giacobbe Manco's importance in the organization's art dealings along with evidence on other, more debauched facets of the Don's businesses. Tina herself had served in a couple of important roles for that group as they began their probing and surveillance of some of the key players.

After five long and challenging years, their plan was finally coming to fruition.

Chapter 41

Shamokin, Pennsylvania

"I don't care what your feelings are; the truth is, you have to learn to listen, really listen, to what God is saying to you."

Happy paused as he was weeding outside his home and wiped the sweat off his brow with the back of his weathered hand. Sarah had made it clear that the two men could talk just as easily to one another outside "doing something useful" as they could inside over coffee.

Alex exhaled a sigh as he kept tugging at weeds, or what he hoped were weeds. The truth was, he had never done much manual labor. He found it... diverting. He wondered what other simple pleasures he had missed out on over the years while he was hobnobbing with politicians and business leaders.

"But I don't know how to listen. I don't know what I'm supposed to hear. I don't even know if God wants to speak with me," he said. He sighed again.

Happy looked at him with his head cocked sideways. "Didn't your Daddy and your Mama ever talk to you when you was a boy?"

"Of course they did."

"What did they talk about?"

"Mostly about being successful, making good grades, staying out of trouble."

"But they did talk to you, didn't they?"

"Sure. But what does that have to do with this?"

"Everything! Too many people who believe in a God think He sort of wound up the universe like a clock and just let it run. That ain't what the Bible tells us about Him at all. He's been intimately involved with His creation ever since the beginning when He made it.

"He made man in His image, Alex, and anything that is so special to us we don't just leave it alone to fend for itself. When you had that experience in your office, you were born into God's family just like you were part of your Daddy and Mama's family—even more so because this one is eternal. And just like our parents want the best for us, God does, too. That's why He speaks to us. He wants to guide our lives if we'll only listen."

Alex sighed again. There seemed to be so much about life that he didn't know. After that night in his office, it seemed like he had stepped into a new world. But, like any new experience, some of it was challenging and even unsettling at times.

"How do I know when God is trying to speak to me, Happy? You seem like you have this down pat."

"Why did you call me and ask to come here?"

Alex didn't even have to think about that one. "Because you were on my mind as soon as I finished crying."

"Were there any words? Or did you see my face? How exactly did you know you needed to call me?"

That required a little more thought. "Well, I saw your face in my mind. And I felt, no, I heard just three words in my mind: 'Go see Happy.' It felt right. I somehow just knew that it was what I needed to do."

"So inside of you, you had a sense of peace and a sense of rightness about doing that, is that correct?"

"Yeah. I'd say that sums it up."

"Then I'd say that you understand more than you allow about what it means to hear God speaking to you. God don't always show up in a big thundercloud with angels blowing trumpets. Most of the time it's what the prophet Elijah described as a 'still, small voice.' It may be an impression, a few words in our mind, but as God's children, we know that it's the right voice."

"But how does that help me in my day-to-day decisions?"

"It's the same. For instance, what would you say your biggest decision facing you is right now?"

"Whether or not to pursue this story I've been working on."

"Now, I want you right now to ask God to give you that same sense of peace and rightness about this decision." Happy looked at Alex, waiting for him to respond.

"You mean right now?"

Happy nodded. "You can ask Him in your mind, but I would encourage you to speak it out of your mouth. Sometimes, we take things more seriously if we speak them out where we can hear them ourselves."

Alex was about to bow his head, but he remembered what Happy had been telling him the past few days. Lifting his eyes up to heaven, he said aloud, "God, I want to do the right thing about this story. It's a dangerous path, and I could get into a lot of trouble if I do. But maybe it will help someone else if

169

I expose what I know. Please show me what to do." Then he added what he had heard Happy say so many times the past few days, "In the mighty name of your Son, Jesus."

He looked at Happy. Happy was still looking at him, waiting.

"Well?" said Happy.

Alex was about to say, "I still don't know what to do," but he stopped before opening his mouth. He did know what to do. "Happy, I just saw a picture of myself with a powerful searchlight shining it on a nest of snakes. While I was shining the light, other people saw them and came to help destroy them."

Happy smiled. "That sounds like what the Apostle Paul wrote about in his letter to the Ephesian believers. Over in chapter five, he said that we are not supposed to be participators in what he called the fruitless works of darkness. Instead, he said we are to expose them. Then he said that everything exposed by the light is perfectly clear."

Alex nodded. "It makes sense. I have an opportunity that most people will never have. I have the platform to draw the attention of sometimes millions of people depending on the story's coverage and whether it is picked up in syndication. God didn't tell me what would happen if I do. But I know that it's the right thing no matter what happens."

Happy looked intently at Alex. "I think it's time I gave you the letter."

"What letter?" asked Alex.

"Just follow me," Happy said as he carried the weeds to the trash can and dumped them.

Without another word, he walked inside. He washed his hands in the kitchen. Alex followed him to the living room where Happy motioned for him to take a seat while Happy went to his room. A few minutes later he returned with an envelope and handed it to Alex. Alex saw that it was addressed to Happy, but it was in Happy's handwriting. The postmark was from several years earlier. It was sealed.

"Open it," said Happy.

Alex took his keys from his pocket and slit the edge of the envelope. He withdrew a single sheet of paper folded into thirds. There was no writing on the backside. He unfolded it and looked at the salutation. His face and hands began to tingle as he read:

Alex Ingram,

I'm writing this letter to you without knowing whether or not I will ever be able to give it to you in person. When you wrote the story about me and the mission, I confess that it was one of the hardest times in my life. I used to have such a terrible temper when I was a young man before I met the Lord, and it was real hard not to let it come back again.

In the middle of all of it, I believe the Lord spoke to me and asked me this question: "Would you be willing to endure this cross if you knew it would result in Alex's salvation?" When He asked me that, I knew what my answer had to be. He did the same for me, and I had to be willing to do the same for you.

The other thing God spoke to me was that you are a man who will fight deadly serpents. I don't know what that means, but I sincerely pray that it comes true. I also pray that God delivers you from the real serpent. If and when this letter makes its way to you, I hope you find some comfort in these words.

Happy Lewis

Alex's eyes left the page and looked at Happy questioningly. He looked back at the letter. "Happy, you mean to tell me that years ago..." He broke off. He didn't know whether to cry or laugh. His emotions were running in all different directions. He sat stunned.

"Alex, you've been a marked man. What I mean is that God has had His eye on you for a while. Maybe this letter was to make sure you never doubt that or question it."

"Yeah," said Alex. "I get it. Thank you, Happy. I would love to stay with you longer and keep learning from you. You are an incredible man. But I know what I'm supposed to do, and delaying it any longer now would be wrong on my part."

"You're welcome, Alex. Any time."

The next hour was spent with Alex packing and bidding his farewell to Sarah. He gave Happy a burner cell phone "just in case I need to contact you privately."

Happy accepted it reluctantly. "Alex, if you're so concerned about secrecy and your safety, don't forget prayer. God knows how to ring my number if you need help without anyone else knowing."

Alex let Happy accompany him to the bus stop. To be truthful, he enjoyed his companionship. Given the paucity of sincere relationships in his life, the fact that this man was willing to spend time with him really meant something. After he had purchased his ticket with cash, Alex felt a pang pass through him. He had a wave of emotion come to him much like the first day he went to school. He turned to Happy and said, "Happy, I guess it's goodbye. I...I don't know if I'll ever see you again."

Happy smiled his same comforting smile. "Alex, for believers like you and me, there's never truly a goodbye. There's only 'see you later.'"

Alex thought about what he said and relaxed. With those words ringing in his ears, he boarded the bus that would take him back to his destiny.

Chapter 42

Gulf of Suez

Captain Andar watched the patrol craft approach. On board would be the pilot who would take the ship through the Suez Canal. And then, once through, it was a short journey to his final destination. He was almost there. His mind began to relax and thumb through the money which would soon be his.

When the small boat came near the ladder, Captain Andar sent out his first mate to welcome the pilot aboard. However, when he returned, he was accompanied by five men instead of just one. Four of them were dressed in the uniform of the canal security force with the notable addition of balaclavas covering most of their faces. Momentarily startled, his first thoughts leaped to the shipping container, but he quickly recovered and said, "Gentlemen, what seems to be the problem?"

"There's no problem, Captain," said the pilot. "There has been some violence by extremists, and we have received a credible threat against convoys over the next two days. Because of that, each ship in the convoy will receive a small detachment of security to ensure the safety of the ship's crew and cargo as they pass through the canal."

"I've heard nothing of this," said Captain Andar.

"Precisely," said one of the men in uniform from behind his mask. "Otherwise every terrorist would also know our plans. This is a joint operation with the government security forces who will monitor the situation and keep the canal security teams apprised of any trouble. We are here as a last resort."

Captain Andar started to worry in the back of his mind. If there were any trouble, it could lead to a thorough examination of his ship and its cargo. That was the last thing he needed. But if he played things right, with luck there would be no trouble and the guards would actually serve as protection for his special cargo.

"Thank you," he said. "What do you require from me and my crew in order to do your jobs? Do you need food? A cabin?"

"We require nothing along those lines, Captain. All of the crew are to remain below decks in their quarters or on their stations. No one is to be allowed above deck. I and my men will patrol the deck mostly, use the facilities as needed and generally stay out of sight and out of your way. We are not advertising our presence. If trouble comes our way, we want the element of surprise."

"Very good. I believe I shall retire to my quarters for the journey through the canal."

"That will not be possible, Captain," said the man. "Because of the potential for a threat to appear unexpectedly, we are requiring each captain to remain on the bridge in the event orders need to be given. You will, of course, have opportunity to sit and rest on the bridge. I'm sorry for the inconvenience."

Captain Andar bristled at this, but he was determined to make it through whatever was required to reach his final port. "As you wish. Shall we proceed?" he said to the pilot, motioning to the controls.

"After you give the appropriate orders for your crew," said the man.

Once that was completed, the pilot nodded and moved to the navigation seat while the four men silently departed. If Captain Andar had been paying closer attention, he would have noticed that at all times, one of the men was in visual contact with the bridge to ascertain that Captain Andar stayed where he was supposed to. They were all wearing earpieces and radios—that was no cause for alarm in and of itself. The other three used the cover of darkness to begin making their way to the hold. Two went in advance while one lingered and brought up the rear to ensure that none of the crew were following them. They weren't. Captain Andar had been sufficiently surprised that he had been unable to notify the first mate to be on the lookout for anything amiss. The crew had made the Suez run many times and knew that it would be a slow and boring journey in which they would change shifts once. Those lucky enough to be off duty were sleeping, and the skeleton night crew were on station at their jobs.

Thus, the two forward scouts reached the hold with no opposition. The *Ahil* was in position to be second in the convoy which was just forming. The engines were beginning the task of moving the freighter along at a slow pace, their massive power sending a steady throbbing along the hull. Once in the hold, they crept quietly along the outer walls looking for two containers sitting off by themselves. At the opposite end, they found what they were seeking. But unlike Hijan, his brother Hali was a bit more cautious. Before approaching the containers, he took time to scan the area around them. There, nestled among the beams of the hold, were a series of motion sensors directed toward the containers. He looked further but saw no cameras. Quietly, he discussed the problem with his cousin Jandir. Since they were in the hold, they had lost direct radio communications with Chinar up on the deck. Instead, he radioed

Katib, their rear guard, and asked him to move back up their path until he could reach Chinar. He was to verify that Captain Andar stayed on the bridge. If Katib's position allowed him to radio down into the hold, he was to maintain that central position. If not, he was to ensure that Captain Andar did not leave. If Chinar reported otherwise, Katib was to move downward into the hold until he could warn Hali and Jandir.

When that was settled, the two crept along, backs pressed against the wall, until they could see the wiring for the motion sensors. Fortunately, the sensors were a basic kind which had no battery backup and did not generate an alarm if they lost power. Jandir pointed to the power cords as they snaked down the rear of one of the structural beams. From there, they were plugged into a simple surge-protected power strip. Hali smiled as he pressed the off switch on the strip. The motion sensors were dead in the water.

After another check of the perimeter for sensors or cameras, the two men approached the containers. The doors to the containers were locked tightly with stout padlocks. They had expected as much. Like Hijan had done, they climbed to the top of one of the containers and proceeded along the top of the box. Hali did a whispered check on the radio. Katib answered and did a relay check with Chinar. Captain Andar was still on the bridge with the pilot.

Hali looked at the hatch and found the release mechanism for the hatch cover. They had discussed many possibilities as a family as to what was in the mysterious shipping containers. Everything from nuclear weapons to guns to jewels had been raised as a possibility. Hali was nervous as he loosened the seal and raised the lid.

The same dim light Hijan had seen greeted him. Cautious now, Hali lowered his head until he could peer fully into the container. Although not a particularly devout Muslim, Hali swore multiple oaths when his eyes took in the sight. There below him were young Asian girls cramped together clothed only in shorts and t-shirts. The oldest of them appeared to be just twelve or thirteen. Each had an ankle cuff affixed by a chain to the floor of the container. Hali craned his neck further. In one end of the container there appeared to be a large chemical toilet and a shelving unit with rations of food and water. Also at that end was a cot with a young lady who was unchained and fast asleep. The girls were lying on thin blankets. Hali did a quick count. There were at least eighty girls in this container.

Removing his head from the opening, he put his finger to his lips as a warning and motioned to Jandir to look inside. Jandir's reaction was much the same as Hali's. Neither of them had been expecting to see what was actually before them. Although not all of the girls were asleep, none of them seemed to notice or care about the hatch being opened. Hali pondered that and then realized that their stares were blank and glassy. He guessed that they were sedated enough to keep them under control and very likely also to keep them quiet.

All the way up to this moment, Hali's plan had been simple: get on board, discover what was in the containers, confront Captain Andar, and kill him to avenge Hijan's blood. Now, the discovery of a living cargo, enslaved and literally in chains, altered everything. Well, at least, it altered some of the plan.

Before closing the cargo hatch, Hali pulled out his phone and snapped a bundle of photos. Then he recorded a video for about twenty seconds. Putting the phone back, he quietly closed the hatch. Ten minutes later, they had confirmed the same situation with the other shipping container. Hali then shot photos of the containers themselves. After doing a quick comm check with Katib, he informed him that they were headed back on deck. Almost an hour had passed, and the cover of night was quickly slipping away. Hali sent Jandir to the entrance of the hold while he restored power to the motion sensors.

As they made their way up the stairs from the hold, Hali thought of his own two young daughters and how he would feel if they were stolen from him. A switch flipped in his being. In his mind, every one of those girls in the container were his daughters, taken from a loving home with parents who wanted to see them grow up, get married and bear their grandchildren. Captain Andar must pay a very dear price, but there were other people involved. That made the decision on how to proceed much more complicated. He needed to think, and he needed to do it quickly.

Chapter 43

Philadelphia

There comes a point in the life of a digital soldier where reality gets fuzzy, or rather, it merges with the digital. Margot had spent so much time online doing research that the world and life she had encountered there had taken over much of her waking moments. Because of her natural inclination toward introversion, this accelerated until she was having difficulty connecting with the fellow human beings she encountered during the workweek.

What she had found in her research was enough links to give a proper DA or some investigative agency the groundwork they needed to roll up what Margot figured had to be a significant drug import and distribution network in Philadelphia. That also meant it was supplying all of the other major cities. The problem was that Margot did not know whom to trust because she had not spent any time developing relationships in the real world.

In the digital world, people were a set of data represented by transactions of various kinds. Emails, shipping manifests, flight numbers, online profiles—all of these could be assessed and evaluated. People seemed way more predictable online than they did in the real world.

On this particular day, a Tuesday, she had clocked in at work, begun her morning tasks of checking the orders which needed to be processed and had begun setting up the prescription tickets. Shortly, there would be a rush, if you could call it that, of septuagenarians and a few octogenarians smiling and thanking her as they picked up the pharmaceutical equivalent of prunes and salts. Margot couldn't help but smile as she imagined some of her customers sitting around and talking about their latest colonic happenings.

Just after she had finished that chore, the general phone began to ring. Since the other employees were occupied, Margot picked it up and answered.

"Draper Pharmacy, how may I help you?"

"Yes, my name is Detective Deshawn Carson with Philadelphia PD. I'm calling to verify if you have an Elaine Norwood on staff there. Would you be able to help me?"

Margot's blood ran cold. She heard herself suck in her breath and hoped that she had not done it loudly enough to be heard.

"Hold one moment please while I let you speak with the manager."

She touched the hold button and placed the receiver down on the work counter. Her mind was racing. When she looked up, the room was beginning to spin and tilt. She couldn't pass out here, not now.

Why was Detective Carson calling to ask about Elaine Norwood? What was going on? He had to be investigating something in order to track that name she had given. Worse yet, she had the horrid luck to have answered the phone. Did he recognize her voice?

The phone beeped twice at her. He had been on hold for 30 seconds.

Margot dialed the pharmacy manager's extension and explained that someone was calling to verify employment. Although not regular, such calls were routine enough. And they usually didn't involve the police. Elaine had been offered a full-time position elsewhere a couple of weeks previously out of state. Maybe that would keep things obscured.

She went back to the work counter and placed the phone handset back in the base.

"Excuse me?" The voice was frail and accented.

Margot turned and saw a diminutive Asian lady standing at the counter. She looked almost like a child but with silver hair neatly coiffed high on her head. Her head and shoulders reached above the service counter, but not much else was showing. The appearance startled Margot, but she quickly recovered.

"How may I help you today?" she asked the lady as she approached the counter.

"I'm here to pick up a prescription. The name is Li. L-I. Mrs. Grace Li."

"Just one moment." Margot went to the baskets, which were arranged alphabetically, and looked through them until she found the right one. She picked out the bag and returned to the counter.

"Here it is." She placed the bag on the surface and started to turn to the register. "Is there anything else I can help you with today?"

"No. But I can help you if you like."

Margot turned her eyes back to the woman's face. The woman's eyes were dark and inscrutable, but there was a power in them which seemed to be burning into her own. Quickly, Margot glanced down. She wasn't sure what she had seen, but it scared her.

"I'm not sure I understand."

"You are troubled. You are carrying a heavy burden. I can help you. I want to help you."

Margot's eyes were drawn back to the woman's face. The same steely gaze met her. It wasn't harsh, but it was still more powerful than Margot was able to endure. She glanced downward. The woman had on a printed T-shirt. Margot could read the words "Jesus the way to Heaven."

"I...I'm not sure what you are talking about."

In return, the woman just continued to drill into her with her eyes. Margot felt more vulnerable than if she were living out one of her recurring nightmares of being at a party in only her underwear.

"I need to help the other customers."

The woman looked slowly to her right and then to her left. The store was empty. That rarely happened.

"Please, I have to go back to work now." Margot realized that she was actually pleading to be released from those eyes.

The woman paused and then nodded almost imperceptibly as if listening to an order from someone. She reached into a vintage purse and pulled out a calling card. She offered it to Margot.

"Do not lose this. You will need it."

"Thank you. I'll keep it safe."

Margot rang up the sale. Mrs. Li paid cash, thanked her and then turned and walked out of the store. Margot half expected her to turn around and offer some parting words, but she left as quietly as she had come.

"That was strange." The voice came from behind her. It was the manager. Margot thought she had witnessed the encounter with Mrs. Li, but she had just walked up. "I've had plenty of people call for employment verification, but I've never had anyone ask me to describe the employee."

Margot felt as if something wrapped itself around her lungs. "What do you mean?"

"That detective with the police department. I told him that we had an Elaine Norwood who worked here but that she had left for a new job a couple of weeks ago. Instead of hanging up or asking me where she had moved, he asked me to describe Elaine."

"What did you tell him?"

"I said she was about five and a half feet tall, long red hair and green eyes."

Margot's chest grew tighter. "What did he say to that?"

"He said, 'That's what I thought,' and thanked me and hung up. It was really weird. I wonder if Elaine is in trouble."

Margot didn't hear the rest of the comments. She could only think of Mrs. Li. Something about that woman was more real than what she had experienced anywhere else. She seemed otherworldly. To top it all off, she had offered Margot help, and foolishly, Margot had refused it.

Chapter 44

Italy

The armored limousine-style SUV was navigating the busy streets of the town until it came to the central business district. Giacobbe was seated in the rear with Father Donati and Pietro. In the front were the driver and extra bodyguard as they headed to one of the smaller towns Pietro believed was the location they were seeking. Pietro was describing a clock tower that he vividly remembered from his childhood. They had checked out two possible locations that turned out to be duds. This one was not their last option, but it was their best one after a bit more searching on the Internet. Pietro's memory came in snatches here and there. They were fortunate that he had recalled as much as he had. Giacobbe ordered the driver to pull to the shoulder and halt as the clock tower came into view.

"Well?" he asked. "Is this the one?"

Pietro craned his neck and then opened his door and stepped out. The other two men got out and joined him. He stood staring for several moments and then looked at Giacobbe.

"Yes. I'm sure of it."

Both men sighed in relief.

"Where to now?" asked Father Donati.

"The library. There are only a few places they would have left their notes."

They got back into the vehicle, and Giacobbe instructed the driver to proceed to the library. Once there, the driver stayed with the vehicle while the bodyguard accompanied them into the library. Pietro asked the librarian where the historical archives were which contained the early church fathers. After receiving a perfunctory answer, the group headed upstairs into a corner room with glass walls. This was the research area where rare volumes were stored.

His parents, Pietro explained, knew that every town and city had a library, no matter how small. Most of them would have at least one set of ancient texts. While he was talking, he was looking through the shelves. He found the section devoted to the early church fathers and continued scanning until he reached up and pulled out a volume.

"Here we go. This is the volume that contains Tertullian's works. He was one of the authors my parents loved to pick because they had found that he was one of the least-referenced early church fathers. Because of that, they could leave notes amongst his works with little fear of detection."

He looked at the table of contents and then began thumbing through the tightly packed pages until he came to the chapter heading titled "On Idolatry." The significance of the selection of that particular treatise by Tertullian was apparently lost on the rest of the small group. Still, Pietro could enjoy the private humor. He turned the page as he continued talking, "Chapter four: Idols not to be made, much less worshipped. And here it is."

The other men crowded around to see a small brown envelope barely taped to the page. Because of its complete lack of exposure to light and air over the past decades, it still looked as crisp as the white pages which surrounded it. Pietro carefully lifted the envelope away and then opened it carefully. It was not sealed but simply had the leaf tucked into the body. From it, he withdrew a single sheet of paper, unfolded it and placed it on the table beside them. Sitting on a chair, he motioned for the others to do the same. The bodyguard remained standing near the entrance to the room.

Pietro looked at the paper and mumbled to himself quietly as he worked through the notes written in pencil on the page.

"What does it say?" asked Father Donati after a few minutes.

"It says that after locating each of the statues, they hid them again until they could safely remove and reveal them to the art world."

"Does it say where?" asked Giacobbe.

"Actually, it does. It's in a shorthand or code that my father and mother used to use. It's pretty simple." Here, Pietro turned the page on the table and allowed the other two men to look at where he was pointing. "As you can see, they removed the vowels. The first set of letters is usually a city or region. This one is 'Frm,' which is likely Formia. The next part can also be part of the place indicator. This is 'PNDMA,' which would be…"

"Parco Naturale dei Monti Aurunci," said Giacobbe.

"Yes," said Pietro. "So this location is near Formia in the park. After that, they would write more and more details. From the looks of it, there is a certain section in the park. My parents were trying to hide the statues, and so they used the tools that were available to them to hide the statues as best as they could. I remember they had an old truck with a frame and winch, which was strong enough to lift and lower a statue. They didn't want to leave them in their original locations in the event that their enemies discovered them and destroyed them. By relocating them, they felt that they were buying time. If they are still there, their work will not have been in vain."

"What are the other locations?" asked Father Donati.

Pietro looked at the paper intently for a bit more and then answered. "This one has a single letter 'p,' but it is lowercase. The initials after it are NPALM."

A bit of thinking and searching on phones gave National Park of Abruzzo, Lazio and Molise as the general area and Opi as the closest town. The last was determined to be San Gregorio Matese and the Parco Regionale del Matese.

The rest of the details were in cardinal directions, distances measured either in meters or kilometers, and reference points. It was not the most difficult of codes, but one would have to have found the notes first and then cared enough to try and decipher it. Giacobbe wondered how many other libraries contained similar notes from Pietro's parents or if these were the only ones, since they had perished after leaving the notes here.

Pietro folded the note paper and placed it inside his voluminous pockets and then returned the volume to the shelf. Given the lateness of the day, Giacobbe made the decision to travel to Formia and find a hotel for the night. Once this was accomplished, the group settled in. In their trailing thoughts before sleep found them, they each envisioned the vastly different types of spoils which awaited them.

Chapter 45

Pennsylvania

Glenn Dalton was proving to be difficult to deal with. In fact, he was a downright nuisance. Rather than being a moderately educated IT flunky, he was actually brilliant. Why he settled for a career working at the newspaper when he could have been making many times the salary as a security consultant was a mystery.

For starters, he wasn't intimidated by the "men with badges" routine. Innocence has a way of emboldening the common man, and Glenn knew that he was innocent of the lurid charges the FBI agents had drummed up against him. They were charging him not only with possession of but also distribution of child pornography. Glenn had never been bent or twisted in that way and would have quickly reported any of the users on his network had he ever encountered it.

Next was the man's prescient actions he had taken to protect not only his own network but also his own self. As part of a normal backup strategy, he made volume snapshots of the hard drives of his own workstation and servers along with the rest of the newspaper staff's machines. Because these types of backups are done at the disk's block level instead of the file level, they record everything on a hard disk. These snapshots were stored in an offsite location which was known only to him. Of course, this was good practice in the event of fire, flood or storm. It was also a genius move in the event that someone were to be framed by the FBI.

When the corrupt agents raided the paper's offices and apprehended Glenn, they simply picked up all the machines in his office (there were three of them) and presumed that they could load whatever incriminating evidence they wanted onto the hard drives. This they did, of course, at their leisure, while Glenn sat in a cell awaiting a bail hearing.

After charges had been filed, a lawyer had been contacted and the whole ruination of Glenn's life had been set in motion, the lead FBI investigator came to talk to Glenn. He assured him that even though the case against Glenn was looking pretty bad, he believed that they could get the charges dismissed or a sentence reduced if he was willing to help them. It was Alex, he said, that they were really after. They were sure that he had been involved in some shady dealings, and they wanted to know everything that Glenn knew about what Alex had been up to.

That sealed it for Glenn. He didn't understand the level to which this corruption rose, but he knew that things were stinking on a big level. There was no way he was going to be coerced into framing someone else while he himself was being framed. Though Glenn considered most lawyers to be shysters who were mostly part of the problem, he had made the acquaintance of a couple of attorneys through the years who seemed to be regular guys who just happened to practice law. He had randomly picked one of them and was not disappointed by the interactions they had had so far.

Glenn had kept abreast of the General Flynn case enough to know that while the government was legally obligated to produce all exculpatory evidence to the defendant or his lawyers, they routinely did not do so. In fact, as the Flynn case so clearly manifested, the FBI could and would manufacture incriminating evidence, hide the things which would help a defendant and lie outright to cover up their own illegal actions. Because of this, Glenn was working with the lawyer to establish a baseline not only of his innocence but also of the government's illegal conduct. If they wanted a fight, he would give it, even if he went down swinging.

For the handful of corrupt agents who were tied into the organization which was particularly worried about Alex's investigation, the response was not what they expected. What they anticipated was that they would come in hard and heavy, frighten Glenn and get him to spill the beans on everything he knew about Alex. They figured he was the likely person to be helping Alex, who was not known to be particularly computer savvy. It wasn't the first time evidence had been planted on a target computer, and who was to say whether it had been there an hour, a day or a year?

When he didn't break or even budge, they figured giving him some time in the jail system would soften him up a bit. Subsequent conversations with him by one or the other agent did not prove to be fruitful. After almost three weeks, their higher-ups were beginning to ask pointed questions. When Glenn's lawyer demanded that a copy of the evidence along with the chain of custody on all hard disks be handed over to him for review coupled with a detailed log of how their investigation of the hard disks was conducted, things got downright worrisome.

While evidence could be tainted given the right opportunity or circumstances, there were procedures in place. The fact that the computers had sat in one of the agent's office getting files copied to the hard disks for a twenty-four-hour period before they had been checked into the system would not fly well. But the software they used to plant the child pornography was efficient enough, and it would not only ensure that the files had older date and timestamps, it would also plant various cookies and traces of Internet activity around the system folders for standard web browsers.

Alas, Glenn was the consummate privacy-oriented geek. He loathed Google's products in general, and he distrusted Microsoft almost equally. His own choice for web browsing extended even beyond Firefox and Opera to little-known browsers such as Brave and very often the Tor browser. The fact that the FBI agent seeded the folders for Google Chrome and Microsoft Edge and Explorer browsers on his PCs was more damning to their case than it was helpful. Once Glenn examined the evidence in the company of his lawyer, he realized what was happening and also could share the details of what would serve as multiple avenues of his defense.

Whether it was divine providence or a geek's paranoia, Glenn realized that he was potentially in danger. In the company of his lawyer, he requested that all bed clothing be removed from his cell. Anything which could be twisted, tied, or fashioned into a good old-fashioned noose for suiciding oneself was removed by one of the jail custodians. With one of the jailers present, Glenn had his lawyer record a video of himself clearly stating what he had done, why he had done it and declaring that he was not suicidal, was not depressed and was confident that he would be found innocent of all charges against him.

When this news made its way up the chain to the FBI agents who were involved with the case, there was a general sense of panic. This was not how things were supposed to be trending. They had just had a meeting a day or two previously where the idea was floated that the suspect could commit suicide due to the overwhelming feeling of guilt. This would present an easy tie-off of one Glenn Dalton as a loose end. With this new development, they were looking at a discovery phase which could prove to be troublesome for their careers, if not their own lives. Their masters did not brook failure easily.

Thus, it was decided that with the help of a friendly judge, Mr. Dalton could be granted a speedy bail hearing, a ridiculously low bond amount, and then once free of prison bars, he could be dealt with in one of any number of ways. Muggings happened all the time in Philly. Break-ins occurred routinely. Both of those sometimes proved to be fatal if the victim struggled. Even food poisoning could be fatal. Something could be done. Something would have to be done with Glenn Dalton.

A little over three weeks to the day from when he was arrested, Glenn Dalton found himself leaving a courtroom in the company of his lawyer and not a jailer. For some reason, he kept feeling the urge to look back over his shoulder. It was a feeling he just couldn't shake.

Chapter 46

Suez Canal

The sun was growing lower in the west as the *Ahil* neared the end of its journey through the canal. Another hour and the journey would be completed. Captain Andar's time on the bridge had been largely uneventful. The pilot had engaged in small talk occasionally. The security troops would occasionally step in to check on things before leaving to patrol the decks. Captain Andar had caught glimpses of them only rarely. They appeared to have found places to tuck away out of view. That was better than advertising their presence, he supposed.

Just then, the door opened, and the leader of the security team stepped through.

"Captain, may I speak with you privately?"

The pilot looked over at the man and then at Captain Andar. "Go ahead," he said. "I'll let you know if I need anything on the bridge."

Captain Andar got up from his chair and followed the man out of the bridge and then down a flight of stairs onto the upper deck.

"What seems to be the problem?" he asked.

"Are you aware of any crew members who may have extremist views or ties to extremist groups?"

"None. What's going on?"

"One of my men was doing a routine search of the rear cargo hold and found a suitcase which he thinks may contain an explosive device."

Captain Andar began to grow uneasy. While his first thought should have been the safety of his crew, his mind instead raced to the thought of losing the €200,000. "Where is this suitcase?"

"It's down in the rear hold near the engine room."

"Let me get the first mate."

"No!" said the man firmly. "Until we can determine more about what is in the suitcase, no one else can be involved to prevent the possibility of alerting whoever is responsible."

"But I insist. My first mate has been with me for over ten years. I would trust him with my life."

"And I do not trust him with mine. My responsibility is to ensure the safety of this ship in the convoy. If this ship is sabotaged and sunk near the entrance, apart from the potential loss of life, it would disrupt traffic for days or weeks. I assure you that if we need to speak with the first mate, he will be next on the list."

It made sense in a practical way. With an hour to go, if anything were going to happen, it would be soon. They passed another of the security team on the way down who commented that everything was still secure. As he followed the security man down across the decks and down the various flights of stairs, Captain Andar began to mentally sort through crew members to see if he could think of anyone who might be the culprit. He was still focused on those thoughts when they entered the rear cargo hold. The throb of the engines was noticeably louder.

As they turned a corner, the security team leader moved to the side so that Captain Andar could see. There before him was a standard storage trunk which could have been used by the galley crew or even the maintenance crew. The fact that it was on the boat was not unusual. Its location in this rear cargo hold was strange. The other two security team members were flanking the trunk where they had obviously been waiting for Captain Andar and their leader to return.

As the captain turned to ask the leader a question, he was startled to see that the man had pulled a cell phone from his pocket and was pointing it toward him as if he were filming.

"What is the meaning of all this?" said Captain Andar.

"Have a seat on the trunk, Captain, and I will explain it to you very carefully."

Captain Andar noticed that the other two men had shifted the angle of their rifles from a resting position. He also noticed that the rifles were fitted with suppressors. He walked over to the trunk and sat down facing the leader. The other two men covered him from an angle on each side.

"Now," said the leader as he pulled a long blade from a sheath inside his clothing. "I am going to ask you a series of questions. If you hesitate or refuse to answer, I can assure you that it will be very unpleasant for you. Do I make myself clear?"

Captain Andar nodded.

"Good." He moved closer to Captain Andar and held the camera lens just an arm's length away from his face. "You will speak loudly and clearly. Let's begin by having you state your full name and your current profession."

Captain Andar glanced to each side at the men who stood silently. He licked his lips and swallowed hard. "My name is Josef Andar. I am captain of the *Ahil*, a cargo ship which mainly traffics between the Orient and Europe." Since there was no response, he continued. "I have been in command of this ship for the past fifteen years."

There was a nod. "What was your last port of departure and your current destination?"

"My last port was Qinzhou in the Quangxi province of China. It's on the Gulf of Tonkin. We are headed to Chioggia in the northeast of Italy."

Another nod. "Tell us what your cargo is."

"We have several shipping containers filled with electronics and appliances. Some of the containers contain clothing. There are a few which contain food."

Silence. No nod. The hand with the knife shifted so that the blade was pointed toward Captain Andar.

"State very clearly what your 'special' cargo is."

Captain Andar's heart began to race. Could they really know? He decided to try and bluff his way through. "We also carry a shipping container which is refrigerated. It has been used to carry a bottle of Lay You for auction, but other than traditional brands, we don't have any special alcohol on this voyage."

In the dim light, Captain Andar saw the man lash out and the knife blade flash as it raced toward his abdomen. He gasped. It stopped just short with the tip near the buttons of his shirt.

"State what special cargo you are carrying in the two shipping containers in the forward hold."

An involuntary shiver ran through his body. These men knew. He didn't know how they knew, but they knew. He glanced around this section of the hold again, but there was no one to be seen other than the three security men. The low throbbing of the engines would serve to muffle out any shouts for help.

He swallowed again and began speaking in a plaintive voice. "At the last minute in Qinzhou, we took on two fifty-three-foot shipping containers. They contain..." His voice faltered as he began to really think about what he had been facilitating.

"Go on."

"Children. They each contain eighty girls along with their guardian."

"Describe the children."

"The girls are Uighurs. The Chinese government has no use for them

189

because they are Muslim, you see. Most of them have been kept inside camps within China. Rather than exterminate them, their leaders have chosen to sell some of them. At least that is what I was told."

Hali's blood began to boil at hearing this. He had heard a little about these fellow Muslims and the plight they faced within Communist China. With this one statement, Captain Andar had sealed his fate.

"How much are you being paid to carry the girls?"

"I was offered €200,000 for this job."

"How many times have you done this?"

"This was my first time. I swear to that. I was hoping to save some money for my retirement. Now I wish I had never agreed to do so."

Captain Andar was beginning to sweat profusely. Part of it was the heat in the hold. Part was from the steely glint he saw in the man's eyes as he questioned him. He had heard of the notoriety of Egyptian prisons, and he had no desire to discover the truth of the tales.

"Who offered you the money? Give me names and details."

"It was a man I used to work with at another shipping company. He goes by the name Franky. I don't know for certain, but I think his last name is Francone. He showed up at the ship in Qinzhou right after we arrived and said he had a proposition for me. I listened to him. He said that his boss wanted to test a new way of moving the girls and that I would be paid €40,000 in cash if I agreed and the balance once the girls were delivered."

"Who is your contact once you reach port?"

"He gave me the name Pagano and said that he would arrive with the customs inspectors. He apparently was to ensure that the cargo was not searched or hindered. After the ship has cleared all the customs and begun unloading, I would be told where and how to unload the containers."

"Who else is involved with you on the ship?"

"No one."

"What about your first mate? Surely he knows something."

"As I said, he has been with me for many years. If he suspects anything, he has not voiced it. He has minded his own business and stayed out of mine."

Hali thought about all he had just been told. There was little more to be learned from this man. Here before him was the epitome of unbridled greed. That Captain Andar thought so little of Hijan's life to kill him over this secret was clear. If he was willing to sell the souls of one hundred and sixty young girls into who knew what kind of slavery, Hijan would only have been a minor inconvenience to him. He switched off the camera on his phone and made sure that the video had recorded properly. Then he pocketed it and squatted down in front of Captain Andar. Slowly and carefully he removed his balaclava, revealing his facial features.

"Captain, I want you to look at me very, very closely and tell me if you recognize me."

Captain Andar looked confused at first. How would he know this man who had only appeared on his ship less than twenty-four hours prior? Hali watched as his eyes roved over his face searching his features. Then he watched as recognition appeared in his eyes. Then fear. Then terror.

"You're...It can't be. I..."

"You're right Captain. I cannot be Hijan Datmari because you killed him. You killed him because he found out what you were doing, and you did not want anyone else to know."

Captain Andar's eyes were a mixture of horror and perplexity.

"How do you know this? You cannot possibly know this."

"My name is Hali Datmari. Hijan was my younger brother."

At this declaration, Captain Andar exploded from his sitting position and attempted to grab the knife from Hali's hand. Hali struck the captain across the face with his fist, knocking him backwards. The other two men joined in with their rifle butts and heavy boots and quickly subdued the captain. After securing his legs and arms with zip ties, Hali asked him, "Where is the €40,000 you were paid for my brother's blood?"

"It is in the safe in my quarters."

"Where is the key?"

"It is in my wallet inside my jacket."

After searching and retrieving the key, Hali held it in front of him.

"Captain, Hijan left behind a family who love him very much. I am taking the money to help to pay for the care of our parents. Hijan was very loyal to them and would want to know that they are cared for."

Captain Andar only stared.

"What are you going to do with me?" he asked. "Are you going to turn me over to the police?"

"And risk your posting bail and possibly fleeing? No. Our family has been planning to avenge Hijan since we learned of his death. He sent me an email telling me of his suspicions about you just before you killed him." He motioned to the trunk. "This is going to be your new home. You may think of it as your retirement home."

Captain Andar struggled to no avail as the other two men picked him up and placed him in the trunk. After a short but somewhat laborious trip to the nearest deck, the trunk was unceremoniously dropped over the side, where it disappeared from view for a few seconds before bobbing back up. Then it slowly began to sink as the wake of the big ship pushed Captain Andar away from what had been his temporary slice of life on earth and into his new reality of eternity.

Chapter 47

Philadelphia

It has been said that "a man without ethics is a wild beast loosed upon the world." Earl Scoggins was close to fulfilling that quote. To be sure, Earl had some ethics. He believed in loyalty, at least loyalty as he defined it. If he had one redeeming trait, that would surely have been it. But loyalty, like emotions and even love, can be misguided in its devotion to that which is in itself evil.

Currently, his loyalty was first to himself and then to the men who paid his very comfortable salary. In return, he made sure that their operations went as smoothly as possible. In practical terms, that meant overseeing the flow of heroin from his contacts in Afghanistan all along the way until they reached Philadelphia, where the shipments were catalogued, cut, assorted to top distributors and occasionally delivered to high-profile figures who couldn't be seen associating with the riffraff dealers. He was also involved in maintaining order, which occasionally meant cracking a head or two, sometimes worse.

He had directed the hit on District Attorney Mennheim in order to tie up the loose ends. Indeed, he and one of the dirty cops in the photo Margot had seen had paid a personal visit to Mennheim in the wee hours of the morning. After not finding any firearms at his home, they had used the cop's .22 pistol because it was not registered to anyone they knew.

Life was not as active as Earl liked it, but his bosses threw him the occasional bone because they knew he relished the hunt. When he checked his email for the day, he perked up. After some digging and footwork, one of their contacts in the police department had managed to locate one of the people who had been poking around for information online. It was a female—not that much of a challenge, Earl supposed—but they were giving him latitude as to how he handled the job. They wanted to extract as much information as possible from her in order to find out who her contacts were and just what she knew and what she had been doing with the information she had. After that was accomplished, he could use his creativity on the hit. The email included a couple of photos taken with a telephoto lens along with the addresses of her workplace and her apartment.

A second email amended the first by stating that it had to occur at the target's apartment this coming Friday. The contact had shadowed the target enough to establish a pattern. She always went home straight after work and did her research on the computer into the late hours of the night, sometimes staying up all night. She had little in the way of friends or contacts outside work. Plus, she had no security alarms at her apartment.

Earl grinned his little weasel grin and laughed to himself. It might be easy, but he was going to make sure it was fun. He was already imagining the ways he would get her to talk.

Chapter 48

Margot had been feeling unsettled all day long. Something just didn't feel right. After her encounter with Mrs. Grace Li, she had felt more aware—of what, she did not know. It was if a veil had been partially removed from her eyes. She couldn't see anything clearly, but she knew the veil was there, had been there and was still blocking her vision. It was frustrating.

Normally, she would be looking forward to getting off work in a few minutes and spending the entire weekend doing her research. Pretty much the whole day, she had been cloaked with dread. So when Cassandra asked her to have supper with her at one of the nearby restaurants, Margot actually felt a sense of relief and heard herself saying, "I'd really like that."

After work, they went to the restaurant, a local shop that was famous for its chili and hotdogs, and ordered their food. They sat in one of the booths and sampled the chips and dip entree. In the cacophony of background music and patrons laughing and talking boisterously, Margot would normally be able to let the day slough off of her, but the undercurrent of tension was still there.

"Margot, is everything okay?" Cassandra asked her. Cassandra was staring at Margot's hands.

Margot looked down. She was holding a chip with dip on it. The dip had been spilled on the table because her hand was shaking. She wasn't even sure how long she had been holding the chip.

"Margot?"

Margot looked up from her hands into Cassandra's eyes. They were filled with concern.

"I'm sorry. I've felt really weird all day long."

"Are you sick?"

"No, not that kind of feeling. I've felt like something bad is going to happen. I don't know why. It's just a feeling I haven't been able to shake. It's...I don't know how to handle it, Cassandra!" She looked away as tears started to rim the edges of her eyes.

Cassandra put her chip down and laid her hand on top of Margot's hand. Slowly, she guided her hand to the plate, where Margot let the chip drop from her grasp. It was so simple a gesture, but it was a gesture of friendship nonetheless.

"Margot, can I say a prayer for you?"

Margot nodded. At this point, she would have accepted a lucky rabbit's foot, henna tattoos or a funny hat, anything to help with this feeling.

Cassandra closed her eyes and said, "Father God, please help my friend Margot. I don't know what she is feeling, but you do. If she is truly in danger, help her to know that. Please protect her. Please protect her from all harm. I ask you to do this to show her your goodness, in Jesus' mighty Name. Amen."

There it was again. In her mind's eye, the veil shifted. Margot knew in her gut that she was in danger. She didn't know how or where or when. But the feeling of dread had crystallized from something vague to a clear sense. At the same time, the dread itself had left her. In its place was a somber feeling, a sober feeling. Weird. Did prayers really work? Something had happened. She described her feelings to Cassandra, who nodded as if she understood.

"I believe that God heard my prayer. He is able to protect you, Margot. You need to know that."

Margot shrugged. "I don't know what I believe. I know I feel better than I did five minutes ago."

Cassandra smiled at her. "Then let's eat." She looked up as the waiter arrived with their order.

After a satisfying meal, Cassandra offered Margot a spot on her couch if she wanted to spend the night at her place. Margot declined.

"I've got some leads I need to follow up on and hopefully finish part of my research." As she said it, the dull ache grew stronger. Should she retract that and take Cassandra up on her offer? No. She was a big girl. She couldn't live running from shadows no matter how she felt.

Cassandra stared at her. "Suit yourself. If you change your mind, call me. On second thought, I'll call you around 9 p.m. If you don't answer, I'm going to call the police."

"No. Don't do that!" Margot saw Cassandra's startled expression. "It's just that what I've found in my research proves that quite a few of the police are involved in all of this."

"All of what?"

"I'd rather not say right now. It's on the thumb drive I gave you, at least some of it. I've found so much more since I gave you that to keep."

Cassandra eyed her carefully. "Sometimes you worry me, Margot. Well, I'm still calling at nine, and if you don't want me to call the police, I'll have to figure out something else."

"It's like I told you in the beginning. The best thing you can do is to follow the instructions on that thumb drive."

Cassandra sighed. "You're being impossible, you know. But I'll do whatever I can to help you. I hope you believe that."

"I do."

After paying their bill, Cassandra walked with Margot to the bus stop. They chatted until the metro bus pulled up, disgorging a crowd of youth ready to hit the weekend night life scene. Margot stepped up into the side door and grabbed a strap as she turned around. She waved at Cassandra as the bus lurched forward. Cassandra watched the bus drive away until it turned at the corner of the block.

"God, watch over her. Please." she said.

Margot walked to the door of her apartment. She was about to put her key into the lock when the ache inside surged. She hesitated. Part of her wanted to run screaming from the apartment and find a safe place to hide. She rolled her shoulders and unconsciously jutted out her chin. She was not going to let her feelings run away with her.

Sliding the key into the lock, she twisted the deadbolt and then unlocked the handle next. Most of the time, she kept her blinds and curtains drawn just for privacy. Because of that, she always left a small night light on in the hallway to her bedroom. It didn't illuminate much, but it served as a reference point when it was dark.

She stepped in and turned to shut and lock the door behind her. As she turned around, she realized something wasn't right. Furniture had been moved. She couldn't tell what, but she knew something was out of place. Her adrenaline started to pump as her hand reached for the light switch.

Just then, a hand grabbed her wrist. She started to jerk away, but the hand folded her arm down to her waist and jerked her backwards into a person while the other hand capped her mouth and nose tightly. A voice in her ear hissed, "Don't make a sound if you value your life!"

A tremor surged through her body. She knew that voice. She had heard it before. Once at a coffee bar and then again on the telephone at the pharmacy.

Chapter 49

Margot was trembling from shock. Since Serious had enlightened her to the dangers of her chosen occupation, she had known viscerally that it could be dangerous. Yet she never really believed it would happen to her.

Instinctively she started to struggle and kick, but the hand around her waist pulled her tighter while the hand on her face mashed her nose and mouth almost to the point of pain.

"I said be quiet!"

Her mind raced wildly, and then it stopped as if time stood still. In a split second, three things went through her mind. First, she saw a picture of herself talking to Mrs. Grace Li and heard her say, "I can help you. I want to help you." Then she saw herself at the table with Cassandra and heard her praying, "Please protect her from all harm." Then, she read the words on a computer screen where Serious had just typed, "Pray."

Margot was past rational debate on the topic of the existence of a deity, beneficent or benign. Whimpering underneath the hand muffling her words, she simply said, "God, help me."

Some people claim to hear audible voices from angels or God. The next words Margot heard were again whispered in her ear. "I'm here to protect you."

"That was an unexpected answer to prayer," she thought. But her body relaxed just ever so slightly, and she quit struggling.

"I want you to face the door while I turn on the light. Then I need you to not turn around while I explain what's happened. Then, when you're ready, you can turn around. You promise me you're not going to scream or try anything stupid?"

Margot nodded.

The hand relaxed off her waist and steadied her on her feet. The hand on her mouth and nose slid down and away and felt for the light switch. The soft glow of lamps came on, but the lighting seemed different somehow. As the hand was removed from the switch and retreated past her, out of the corner of her eye Margot saw bloodstains on the coffee-colored skin.

"In case you haven't already recognized my voice, I'm Detective Carson.

We met at the coffee bar some time back."

"Yes. I know."

"Good. And you are Margot Jackson, sometimes also known as Miss Elaine Norwood." There was a hint of a smile in the tone. "I'm not completely sure why you lied about your name to me, but I have my guesses. Tonight confirmed a lot of those theories for me."

Margot remained silent.

"There's no sugarcoating it, Miss Jackson. A man came to your apartment to kill you. Based on what I've seen, I'm going to guess that he had much more intended for you than just a simple murder. I would also imagine that he has been here since early afternoon, if not right after you left this morning. He had plenty of time to prepare for what he planned to do."

Margot's breathing began to quicken.

"Without telling you everything, I knew that your life was in danger today. I didn't know who was going to be here, so I came prepared. I'm glad I did."

He paused for a moment. Margot thought she heard a stifled grunt. Then he continued.

"If you don't want to see anything, you can walk right back out the door. But I think you need to see what you have gotten yourself involved with. I do have to warn you that it's kind of messy. What do you want to do?"

In reply, Margot slowly turned around. Detective Carson stepped to one side to allow her full view. She gasped in spite of herself. The furniture had been knocked aside. Two of the three lamps were on the floor. One end table had been completely crushed with all of the legs splayed out. Oddly enough, when she saw it, Margot thought that she should have bought better-quality, solid wooden furniture. A couple of pictures along one wall were missing. One was on the floor face down; the other was peeking out from the edge of the sofa, which was itself several feet out of place.

"I'm sorry about your apartment. Couldn't be helped."

As she scanned the living room, her eyes rested on a pair of black boots sticking out of the end of the hallway leading to her bedroom and bathroom. Instinctively, she began to walk toward them. As she got closer, she saw the form of a small man dressed all in black from neck to toe. He even had on tight-fitting black surgical-style gloves.

The carpet around him was not the pristine white it had been that morning. It was a dark red all around his torso, which was slightly propped up against the wall. The head drooped on the chest. Behind him, there was a smear mark on the cream-colored drywall that followed the body downward.

Margot followed the trail with her eyes up to where it began next to a neat hole in the wall.

Her lips began to tingle, then her cheeks. She realized what was happening and took a couple of deep breaths and shook her head. She couldn't pass out. She wouldn't pass out.

She got down on her knees, being careful to avoid the blood, and leaned down and looked into the man's face. The lifeless eyes were locked in an odd mixture of rage and shock. The face was set with a look of defiance. It was as if the man's brain had refused to accept death even as it took him.

"I don't have an ID on who this man is. But I hope to find out soon enough."

"Don't bother looking," said Margot, not looking away from the face. "His name is Earl Scoggins. He was in the military in Afghanistan. His friends called him 'Little Poppy.'"

"How do you know…" Detective Carson started to ask. Then he stopped mid-sentence. "Never mind. You've done your research, I see. I've heard his nickname a few times but had never laid eyes on him until tonight. He's a bit of a mystery figure who works for some pretty powerful people."

"Who are involved in bringing heroin and other drugs into the US using Philadelphia as their base of operations."

Margot said it matter-of-factly. Again, Detective Carson was surprised.

"How did you…?" Margot pointed to the corpse as her voice trailed off. She turned to look up at Detective Carson.

"I picked the lock, just like he did, no doubt. Then I knocked on the door really loud and said 'Housekeeping!' and waited a couple of seconds and opened the door. Then I flicked on the light and walked into the room like I was delivering something. Then I walked back to the door, turned off the light and closed and locked the door from the inside. Anybody listening could hear that deadbolt slide back into place.

"After that, I crept over behind that chair and just waited and listened and watched the best I could. After about ten minutes, I heard the sound of his boots on the carpet as he started coming down the hallway to check things out.

"I had my taser out and ready. When he got into the living room, I fired the taser and hit him directly. He stiffened and grunted, but he didn't go down. That's only the second guy in my entire career that a taser didn't seem to phase one bit. The other one was high on meth at the time. This guy was just plain tough. That's when things got ugly.

"He had pulled the barbs out of his body and threw them to the side. He rushed me and we both fell down on the floor. It was hard to see with it being dark, but I could tell he knew his stuff. He was reaching for something, which I figured out pretty quickly was a knife. I grabbed his arm and did my best to keep it away from my vitals, but he got me a good swipe on my arm while we were struggling."

Margot looked at his left arm and realized it had been bleeding from a nasty gash.

"Oh, let me get you something for that. That has to hurt!"

"Yeah, it does. But it'll have to wait. I got most of the bleeding stopped before you came. There's more you need to see, and then we have to figure out how to deal with this."

Detective Carson offered her a hand and helped her to her feet. He stepped over the body and walked the few feet to the bedroom door. He stepped to the side and let Margot enter. What she saw only made her feel sicker in her stomach.

A chair had been placed in the middle of the room. Beside it, there were several short lengths of rope and belts. On the bed itself was a leather tool pouch filled with all sorts of weird-looking tools. They looked like the types of things she had seen when visiting the dentist or what she had seen in an ER on the occasional hospital drama she happened to watch. The pouch had been unfolded and several tools already set out as if in preparation for surgery.

"What was he going to do to me?" Margot asked in a quiet voice.

"What do you think he was going to do? He planned to strap you to that chair and find out everything you know about what this group is doing. And then he was going to kill you."

The tingling started flooding her cheeks and lips again. Margot thought about sitting on the nearest rest, but there was no way she was going to sit in that chair at the moment or the bed with those torture tools. She turned and steadied herself along the wall—the clean one without the blood smear. By the time she reached the body and started to step over it, her head was swimming. Detective Carson put an arm around her and lifted her up just as she was starting to aim for the carpet.

"Easy there. You don't need to plant your pretty face on any of the furniture."

Margot said nothing as he guided her to one of the chairs that had not been turned over. He eased her into it and said, "I'm going to get you something to drink. What do you have that you want?"

"Water," she managed to say woodenly.

Her mind vaguely processed the sight of him moving into the kitchen and the sounds of cupboards being opened and closed and then the tap being turned on. When he returned, he had a glass of water in one hand and a sopping wet dish towel in the other.

"Here. Put this on your face and the back of your neck. It'll help with the effects of the shock you're experiencing."

Margot didn't respond immediately. Detective Carson looked at her and then quickly dropped to a knee and began dabbing her face with the towel.

"Miss Jackson, listen to me. You've got to snap out of it. I know it's a lot to process, but I need you here fully awake. Miss Jackson! Come on. Snap out of it!"

After a minute or two of having her face and neck bathed in icy cold water, Margot's eyes pulled back from deep space and centered on Detective Carson's face.

"These people...they're evil," she said.

Detective Carson looked at her intently. "Yes. Yes, they are. But tonight, there's one less evil man, and you lived to tell the tale."

Margot looked back at him. Her eyes began to fill up with tears.

"Thank you for saving my life. I can't imagine what would have happened if you hadn't come."

Detective Carson knew what was coming and braced himself for it. Margot burst into tears and threw herself against him, her body heaving with sobs. He had seen it plenty of times. Those who survive great peril and endure horrific mental stress eventually have to find a way to vent their pressure valve. He put one hand on her back and just held her as she heaved and sobbed and blubbered. One thing he did wish was that she would stop squeezing his hurt arm, but overall, he would pick this outcome any day over many of the other ones he had witnessed throughout his career. And sometimes the hugs came from the down and out who didn't bathe frequently. Margot had the scent of lilac.

As he held Margot, his eyes gazed around the apartment. It was a wreck. His mind had been processing options for being able to cover up or clean up both the apartment as well as his presence there. Too much was at stake.

The sobs were subsiding. He looked down at Margot's dark hair and thought about what an exceptional young woman she was. He wondered if she would have to die in order to clean up the loose ends. He sincerely hoped not.

Chapter 50

Cassandra put down her cell phone. She had dialed Margot's number five times. There was no answer. She had texted her asking her to call. There was no response.

She had been ready to dial the police several times, but she remembered Margot's plea. And what if the person who responded to the call were dirty? Would she not be putting her own life in danger? She had more questions than answers.

She went to her desk and pulled out the thumb drive Margot had given her. It wasn't the original one, as Margot had given her an updated copy just a couple of weeks prior. Margot had told her to look for the document labeled "Instructions" and to read it thoroughly first before doing anything in case she ever had to use the thumb drive. In it was a list of step-by-step instructions for setting up a VPN account and at least two different secure email boxes the same way she had. Margot stressed in the instructions that only after doing this was she to proceed.

When those precautions had been taken, Cassandra noted that there were two email addresses she was supposed to contact. Unbeknownst to Cassandra, these were Alex Ingram and the anonymous user Serious. Margot had laid out a template detailing what to say and had given links to several different online storage services where she maintained current copies of her research. Cassandra was not to send the same link to both parties. That would protect them a bit more, she had written.

With a heavy heart, Cassandra copied and pasted the text into the email:

Hey.

If you are receiving this email, it's because I have gone missing and a friend has been asked to activate this dead man's switch. You know me online as one of several aliases including polkadotpanda or Gandalf the White. In real life, I'm Margot Jackson in Philadelphia currently residing at this address:

(Here, she inserted Margot's home address.)

Attached is a relatively recent photo of me.

You may not be able to help me or find me, but hopefully you can honor me by continuing or publishing the research I have done on one of the biggest drug traffickers in this part of the US. While my computer may or may not be seized or compromised, you can find the latest copy of my research at:

(Here Cassandra inserted one of the URLs Margot had listed).

To verify the authenticity of this email, I have left my friend a copy of our private tripcode.

(Here Cassandra pasted the unique encrypted hash for each of the two recipients.)

If this is a false alarm or if I am simply in hiding, you will hear from me again sometime in the future. If not, I want you to know that I gave this my all.

Here is a private email address of another trusted source:

(Here, each of the recipients was given the private email address of the other).

It's up to you to communicate, but one of you is a journalist who can help spread the word. The other is a researcher like myself but way better.

After hitting send on each of the two emails, Cassandra reviewed the rest of Margot's instructions. She was not to initiate a missing person's report for at least three days. There was a chance that she was simply hiding out somewhere. If she were dead, it wouldn't help her anyway, and if she were alive, it might cause problems and get the wrong people looking for her. If she did not turn up after one week, Cassandra was to contact her two parents at the telephone numbers listed.

Cassandra was free to download her research from one of the other URLs not sent to her contacts. She could read anything Margot had written with the understanding that she would probably find it very upsetting and potentially dangerous. Margot had suggested that after sending the emails she simply dispose of the thumb drive and thus have no way of being forced to give the information to anyone else. She closed the document by writing, "Thank you for agreeing to do this. I've never had a friend like you, and I wish I had spent more time getting to know people like you throughout my life. You'll never know how much your caring attitude has helped me."

She had done what Margot asked, and she had refrained from calling the police. But nothing would stop her from dropping to her knees and beginning to ask God to somehow help her friend. He could do the impossible.

Chapter 51

Unknown Location

The user known as Serious was reading generic new posts in one of the message boards when an email notification dinged. Serious cautiously eyed the sender address. It wasn't from anyone Serious recognized. But it was the subject line that demanded attention. It read simply, "Dead Man's Switch Activated."

Clicking on the email, Serious read it, heart growing heavy with each sentence. After scrolling down to the attached photo, Serious smiled in spite of the soberness of the moment. Serious spent the next four hours downloading and then reading through the main highlights of Margot's research. She had outdone herself. Still, there were numerous avenues that could use more digging. Serious composed an email to a trusted list of anonymous warriors and explained both the situation and the challenge. Unless Serious was mistaken, there would be fifty to a hundred people poring over the documents and adding to the research within the next twelve hours, all in a brand-new private message board Serious created just for that purpose.

Chapter 52

Philadelphia

In the end, Detective Carson left it up to Margot whether she would live or die. He described some of the ramifications of going into a witness protection program and what it meant. Her death could be faked, and her life as Margot Jackson would end. But she would have to leave Philadelphia and the state completely. He had his own feelings on the matter, but he knew that a choice of this nature had to be made with full disclosure.

Either way, he made it clear that for the present, Margot would have to leave her apartment. First, it was now a crime scene, and second, the people who had sent Earl Scoggins knew where she lived. It was doubtless that they would try again in spite of his failure. He told her to start packing whatever she considered to be essentials while she thought about it.

Margot listened and thought intently about what he had described as the two paths in front of her as she packed up toiletries and personal items. She looked through her closet and dresser and picked out some of her most practical clothing to take with her. Her eye landed on Mrs. Li's calling card. She put it in her pocket.

She looked around the apartment one more time as she prepared to leave. Her two tote bags were stuffed. Her laptop was small and was in a separate bag slung over her shoulder. It had been a little over an hour since she had entered the apartment. She had heard Cassandra's phone call, but Detective Carson had advised her not to answer the call. Margot knew what that would trigger, but it could not be helped.

"I don't want to go into witness protection," she said. "I can't live the rest of my life not being...me."

Detective Carson looked at her for a few moments. "I understand. Some people find that option as a relief. If you change your mind in the future, you can revisit the idea."

Margot nodded. "Sure. I don't think I ever would, though." She looked at the body in the hallway. "What about him? What happens next? If you call it in, his buddies on the police force will know what's going on."

"I've thought of a way to handle it. You met me on the street outside.

You recognized me from a chance meeting at a coffee bar and told me that you had a funny feeling and asked me to check out your apartment. When I entered the apartment, this man attacked me. We struggled. He pulled a knife. I shot him. As an officer of the law, I'm entitled to carry and use this weapon against anyone threatening me or anyone else with deadly force."

"Won't they bring me in for questioning?"

"Eventually. I'll tell my superiors that you were traumatized and needed to get away from the scene. When they want to speak with you, I'll let you know. You can come in with a lawyer and hopefully some kind of protection. Just working this crime scene will take a while, and when they start to pull details on who this guy is, I'm sure it will rattle a few cages."

Margot sighed. The adrenaline rush was over, and the crash was starting to kick in. She was suddenly very tired.

Detective Carson phoned a friend who he said would take Margot wherever she wanted to go. The man showed up just a few minutes later. As Detective Carson escorted her to the parking area, he asked that they remain in contact by email, or she could call him whenever she was ready. With that, he told her he had work to begin.

After Margot left, he went to the body and searched the clothing until he found a smartphone. He held it up to the dead man's face and unlocked it. He mentally made a note that if possible, it was a good thing not to shoot an attacker in the face or head for this very reason. Once inside the phone, he turned off all the security and facial recognition features so that it would remain unlocked. Then he pocketed the phone, pulled out his own and called in his report asking for the homicide unit and a medic for himself.

As Margot departed the apartment, she had to shake off the feeling that she was in a dark tunnel. Her mind was slowing down, but she still had a sense of security protocols which she felt needed to be followed. After they had traveled a couple of miles, she asked the driver to let her out. He was concerned to do so, but Margot insisted. Once free of him, Margot hailed a cab. She paid cash for it to take her a couple of miles in another direction. While she was in the cab, she used a secure browser on her phone to look up Mrs. Li's address. She cross-referenced that with the bus routes. When that was completed, she powered off her phone.

She asked the cab to let her out near a bus stop. She paid cash and rode on three different buses until reaching Mrs. Li's neighborhood. It was a quaint but well-to-do area. She walked down the street checking the numbers on the gates or the houses until she arrived at the address. The house was well lit both inside and out. She opened the small gate and walked up the path to the porch. Plants and ornamental bushes dotted the small yard. She climbed the steps, took a deep breath and then pushed the doorbell. She could hear a classical tune playing in the background from inside the house.

After about twenty seconds, she heard a deadbolt retract and a handle turn. The door opened wide. Mrs. Li stood before her, framed against the bright light spilling from inside. It reminded Margot of the type of iconic scene which would end a movie or be found in a painting.

She looked down at the petite woman and said, "Mrs. Li? I'm Margot, from the pharmacy. You gave me your card. I need your help."

Her face an inscrutable mask, the dark eyes boring into Margot's own, Mrs. Li stepped to the side, motioned an invitation with her arm and said, "Come in, child. I've been expecting you."

Chapter 53

Alex got his email Saturday morning, having gone to bed early Friday night. After he read through it, his first step was to call his contacts at the morgues and see if there were any unidentified females or any bearing the last name Jackson. That proved fruitless, which was neither a bad sign nor a good sign yet. Then he called up his buddy at the paper who worked the police report beat and asked him to keep an ear open for any female homicide victims or missing person reports for any females last-named Jackson.

Then he opened one of his burner laptops he had picked up after the FBI visit and connected to the Internet using one of his burner phones. Like Serious, he spent time looking through the document summaries and delving into the occasional set of details. As he realized the amount of work Margot had done, his mind could hear Brody saying, "You're going to need a bigger boat."

He tried to think of anyone outside the paper whom he could ask to share the load, but the names which came to mind were all compromised in his opinion. He could ask for more interns, but that would draw attention. He was still trying to fly under the radar.

Margot had offered a contact she trusted. He knew that if he ever referred someone to Happy, that he could be trusted implicitly. Out of options, he wrote an email to an unknown person which said:

> If you get this message, you have probably also already received an email regarding our mutual friend's dead man's switch.
>
> Full disclosure: my name is Alex Ingram, and I'm the journalist our friend mentioned. Because of unique challenges, I don't really have anyone I can ask locally to help me with this load of materials. Some of them I have already been exploring in conjunction with our friend, and it looks like some of them we both were exploring without the other's knowledge.
>
> At this point in my life, I know that I have to pursue this as far as I can even though it may cost me my life. Previously in my career, I would have run from this level of conflict. You can save yourself time reading through all my articles checking on my background by

looking at my hit piece on the Old Gospel Mission and then my later retraction. I made some people very angry with that and went through a dark time. Now things have changed in my life. I've realized that whatever else I do with the rest of my career, this is my calling. I want to expose corruption and bring down the house of cards these dirty people live in.

I think that I can get much of this material published, but I have to have impeccable research on every detail that goes into print. Working alone, it would take me months if not years to make this happen. If you are willing to help and can help, I would really like to speak by phone. I've played this cloak and dagger game for months now and have learned a little bit about it, but I can get a lot more done a lot quicker if I could just speak to you. I would need help on the "how" part of the equation.

Alex reread the message and then sent it. He sat for a few moments, pondering what to do next. An overwhelming urge to pray came over him, so he closed his eyes, leaned back in his chair and did just that.

Chapter 54

The person known as Serious was just beginning the day. This included checking email. Serious smiled after reading the request for help. Yes, they could add a bit of research and documentation to Alex's stories.

The person composed a reply to Alex that included a link to and instructions for downloading Signal, a secure messaging app. After doing that, Alex was to call the number included with the email. This would ring Serious directly so they could talk over a secure, encrypted connection.

After doing that, Serious did some digging on Alex, read the articles he had mentioned and made a decision that Alex was someone who could be trusted, at least to a reasonable degree.

Within the hour, the app rang, and the two began talking. Serious opted not to give a name or location. Alex was used to dealing with anonymous sources and didn't really mind. When he realized that Serious represented dozens of anonymous researchers, he felt like cheering. When he heard that Serious had already gotten posts to the new message board he had created for Margot's research, he did cheer.

The two of them spent three hours talking. Part of the time, they were looking at the research Margot had done. Part of the time, Alex discussed his own research. Then they agreed on a basic plan of attack on which items were the most important to get into print first.

Alex was mentally gauging the possibility of having something ready for the editors in two weeks. When he asked Serious if that was a realistic possibility, Serious replied that knowing who was helping on the project, it would more likely be 24-48 hours. Alex was stupefied. He was used to flogging interns and getting results in weeks and occasionally days depending on their personal interest in a story, but two days or less?

Serious suggested that he begin writing the story and make notes for items which he felt needed more documentation. He could send Serious an email or call on the app, and Serious would manage the anonymous diggers on the message board. He also offered to give Alex a login to the site so that he could post directly, but Alex declined for the moment, stating that it might prove to be too overwhelming.

The conversation ended with the two discussing the search for Margot. Alex shared what his sources on the ground had been telling him, which was no news. Serious inquired about Alex's thoughts about the area in general as a local. Alex replied that the neighborhood where Margot lived was not the best, but it wasn't in the hood either. Margot had shared about her job, so the choice of her apartment was close enough to be convenient but far enough away to generally require public transportation of some kind.

Serious stated that some of the diggers would start looking into anything they could find on the area. Alex was encouraged to keep asking for information locally without unnecessarily arousing suspicion. Then the two finished the conversation with a promise to speak again Sunday around noon Alex's time.

After they finished their conversation, Serious sent an email to a couple of people who had been fruitful in the past. They were particularly good at finding unsecured doorbell cameras and accessing poorly secured municipal surveillance systems or even business security cameras. Serious supplied the address for Margot's apartment and asked for everything they could find in the past 24 hours and then additional footage as they saw fit. Including the one photo Margot had shared, Serious mentioned that this one was personal and involved someone who particularly deserved help if at all possible. There was also a mention of a bounty in cryptocurrency if they could expedite it and get satisfactory results.

Late that night after hours of research, Serious' inbox notification alerted to a response. One of the persons had had a very successful hunt. He had sent a link to a file sharing account with a load of images to download. Two of the parking lot cameras in Margot's collection of buildings were using default authentication passwords. With a little more work, the person had gotten into the stored footage. They were each set on five-second increments, but they were not synchronized. Thus, a person moving in frame in one camera might be slightly further down a sidewalk in the other camera.

While there were several people coming and going over the course of the day and evening, Margot arrived at 8:35 p.m. There was more coming and going over the next hour and a half as the sky grew darker. Then Margot reemerged from the building with a couple of travel bags in each hand and another bag over her shoulder. A black man holding his left arm was with her part of the way. She approached a man who had just pulled into the parking lot a couple of minutes earlier who was standing by his vehicle as if waiting for someone. Then the next photos showed her getting into the car and the car leaving. She appeared to be going of her own free will, so that was good. She had two bags with her. She was leaving her apartment in haste. What had happened inside?

Serious kept scrolling through the images. There it was. Fifteen minutes after Margot left, a bevy of official vehicles converged on the premises. There were three squad cars, what appeared to be two unmarked vehicles and an ambulance. The black man holding his left arm met them on the sidewalk. He was not in uniform, but Serious had a hunch that he possessed a badge by the way he carried himself.

Several people headed into one of the units. The injured man began to be looked after by the two emergency services workers while a man from one of the unmarked vehicles appeared to be talking to him. Eventually the two men on the sidewalk headed into the apartment building. Serious kept scrolling through images until getting to the ones where a van pulled up and unloaded a gurney. Given that it had no emergency lights, Serious guessed it to be a medical examiner. This hunch proved correct when later images showed the gurney being wheeled out with a form on it draped entirely in a sheet.

Serious sat and reflected on the images. Margot was alive, and Serious offered a sincere prayer of gratitude for that. Someone with at least a semi-official status had been involved in her departure and perhaps even her protection. Someone was dead, again possibly related to Margot and the man in the images. This marked a severe turn in the level of seriousness to the research she had been conducting. Margot would no doubt reach out in her own time. For now, the best option they had was to produce solid components for a story which Alex would be in charge of putting before an editor to have published. These people needed to be brought down.

Chapter 55

Gladwyne, Greater Philadelphia

Fury. Pure, unbridled fury is what John de la Rouche was feeling. He epitomized the image of the cultured aristocrat, quintessentially in control of everything around him. Now he could not even stop his own hands from shaking. Even his left cheek muscle was twitching involuntarily. He looked down with wrath at the newspaper in his hands and flung it violently across the room. It was a display of emotion that he had not shown in over fifty years.

Who was Alex Ingram to think that he could betray those who had brought him to prominence? Who was this media company to think they could publish such a story about him? He had worked out at the gym that morning, had a hearty breakfast, showered, dressed and was preparing to head to the office when he had picked up the morning edition. The headline had blared at him "TRANTWA HOLDINGS PROBED" and had immediately arrested his attention. The byline had Alex Ingram's name. That was quite concerning. There was a photo of the office building sitting where the Old Gospel Mission house had been. The story explored some of the financial details of Trantwa Holdings based on the Panama Papers.

There was documentation linking the group to a OneDel Freight, a freight company with routes from Europe. Alex had provided enough links to clearly imply that OneDel was simply a front for Trantwa Holdings. But the story went further and alleged that the cargo carried by the freight company actually originated in Afghanistan. Inferences were made that the cargo might have actually originated in the local poppy fields of that country. Had Mister de la Rouche known that Glenn Dalton's thumb drive had provided a couple of key links in this chain of connections, it would have pushed him over the edge.

With each paragraph, the story dug deeper into the activities and influence of Trantwa. A breakout feature on another page listed "the players" for readers to become acquainted with. His photo was there, along with a note that he had retired from an extensive career at the State Department. The names and photos of everyone on the board of directors was printed along with a brief background as to who they were and what positions they had held—most of them in the federal government. A single line at the top of that section had encouraged the readers to "Pay attention to each of these names so you will remember them as more information is revealed in future stories."

The level of research was immaculate. He could not find anything in what he had read which could be immediately refuted or countered. He had no idea who all was helping Alex, but this was something that had been going on for a long time. His FBI man had assured him that nothing on Alex's office computer or laptop indicated that he was writing anything other than what he was being fed, and as a result, Alex had moved to the edges of their radar as they focused more on the girl who had been probing them on the Internet. Yet there was no way that this article had been written off the cuff.

The promise of "future stories" echoed in his mind, but it was the photo on another part of the page that had caused him to snap. There, staring at him defiantly, was the photo of Earl Scoggins. "Ex-Military Member Killed in Alleged Murder Plot" blared the headline. The byline was also Alex Ingram. John read through the article. In it, Alex gave the briefest of details. Scoggins had served with distinction in Afghanistan and had since moved back to the US, where he resided in the Philadelphia area. He had no known job, but banking records (where did they get those, John wondered) obtained by this reporter showed that Scoggins had received regular payments from OneDel Freight, which established a possible link between him and Trantwa Holdings.

Scoggins had been killed in a fight with a local police officer who had been asked to accompany a female Philly resident to her apartment to investigate a noise she heard before entering it. Upon entering the apartment quietly, the officer had surprised Scoggins, who had attacked him with a tactical knife. The officer had managed to pull his service weapon and neutralize Scoggins. Further investigation of the apartment showed that he had apparently planned to detain, torture and presumably murder the female resident. Police were attempting to determine a motive for the crime.

John's vision tinted with red as the capillaries in his eyes throbbed with blood. He was vaguely aware of the pages of the newspaper scattered in front of him like random leaves across a path on a fall day. In the distance, a bell was tolling ominously. As his mind began to refocus, he realized that his desk phone was ringing. He walked slowly toward the phone and placed the receiver to his ear.

"John de la Rouche speaking."

"Hello, John. This is Martin." It was his lawyer.

"Good morning, Martin."

"Have you read the paper this morning?"

"I just saw it."

"John, this is a bad bit of press for the company. I'm prepared to file a libel

215

lawsuit in your behalf. I believe we can get out in front of this and quash this in a court today or tomorrow at the latest if we act quickly. Would you like me to proceed?"

His cell phone buzzed in his coat pocket. "Just a moment, Martin," he said as he pulled out the cell phone and tapped on the text messages. There was one new message from a weird number. He tapped on it with his thumb and almost dropped the phone. He swore under his breath multiple times as he stared at the single photo. There he was, unmistakably him, on one of his visits to the castle in Europe. He remembered it all too well. The other people in the photo and the age of the people along with what he had in his hand would get him the electric chair—if he were so lucky. Below the photo was a brief line of text:

`"We have it all."`

His mind raced. Who were they? He knew who was there at the party. They were mostly the same people who were at all the other parties. They were all bonded together. No one would betray their oaths for certainty as to what would happen if they did. Yet that photo was undeniable proof that someone had leaked or been compromised somehow.

"John? John? Are you there? John? Is everything all right?" Martin's voice was straining through the speaker of the landline's handset.

Slowly, John brought the receiver back to his ear. "Martin, something's come up. Don't do anything till you hear from me."

"John, what's going on? We need to move quickly on this to get—"

John placed the handset back in the cradle carefully, deliberately. He was being overcome with a feeling of fear and helplessness. It reminded him of being in the headmaster's office at boarding school or the handful of times his father was home and had dressed him down with a tongue-lashing. He had sworn that he would never allow himself to be put in that position again by anyone. To this point, he had kept that promise through ruthless dealings and his political and business acumen.

He looked again at the cell phone in his other hand. Who were they? What did they want? They couldn't be the police. He would have already known it. Too many tripwires were out there for a man of John de la Rouche's stature to not know when someone came digging. That's how they had found the girl. Maybe that was it. Maybe it was her or people associated with her. It had taken a considerable amount of time and resources just to locate her. And now they were perhaps faced with another person, or five, or fifty?

John knew what would happen if that photograph or any others like it were made public. And if they had his photograph, did they have pictures of any of the other guests on these trips? Their numbers included heads of state, businessmen and women at the highest levels of global commerce, military leaders, entertainment industry leaders and iconic media personalities. Heads would roll, literally, if the public were made aware of their unique ways of entertaining themselves.

He contemplated suicide for about ten seconds. It was an easy way out. Leave others to deal with the repercussions of their choices. Then he remembered one of his last initiation rites. In a dimly lit room, he had been cloaked and hooded but had been allowed to stare down and straight ahead of his feet. He had to walk over a full-sized cross with the body of a man lying upon it. He knew what it represented. He was trampling underfoot the cross of Jesus the Christ. At the time, he had thought it the foolish antics of a bunch of post-fraternity men. When he had finished walking on the cross and the man upon it, he had come to another man standing in a crimson robe edged with black. The man had held out to John one of the oldest and boniest hands he had ever seen. He never saw the face. His instructions were not to look up unless told to do so by the man behind the trampled cross. He knelt in front of the cadaverous hand and grasped it with both of his.

"Having trampled upon the body and cross of the Son of God, what say ye?" inquired an elderly and equally frail voice.

"My lot has been cast, and I have chosen my portion," John had responded as he had been instructed.

"Is it final?"

"Aye."

"And with whom are ye bound for eternity?" The voice sounded hollow.

"With him who conquered the Son of God by death."

At that point, the gnarled hand had squeezed both of his until pain shot through his arms. The voice changed to a guttural tone, a cross between a growl and a deep bass mixed with about a thousand years of tobacco habit. "Then from hence ye are mine!"

A surge had gone through John's body. In private one-on-one conversations with other members, he had learned that not a few of them had lost consciousness at that point. John did not. But he knew something had happened. He had never believed in the supernatural before. Yet after that rite, he felt himself to be "more." He counted it as a net gain and had never looked back throughout his career.

Here in his own home, he knew that the voice he had heard was awaiting him at death, and he had no particular desire to hasten that meeting. Suicide was not an option. Fight or flight? He had to decide soon.

Chapter 56

Formia, Italy

Formia is a small coastal city of just under 40,000 inhabitants which is situated about halfway between Rome and Naples. Man-made stone barriers protect a row of inlets at the sea and provide a safe haven for those who enjoy the water. The town itself is a mixture of old and new architecture interwoven with modern streets and classic narrow alleyways.

Pietro and his acquaintances enjoyed a clean room and a hearty breakfast at a hotel located on a promenade that overlooked the harbor. Father Donati found Pietro on the patio staring out at the morning's activity, a cup of coffee in one hand, while the other held the notes they had found the previous day.

"Good morning, my son," Father Donati greeted him. "How are you feeling this morning?"

Pietro turned his head at the sound and smiled his simple smile at the priest.

"I am feeling rested, thank you."

"How are you holding up amidst the memories?" Father Donati asked. Though he was not particularly concerned with Pietro's feelings, he took very seriously the practice of his priestly training. He had been drilled on the fact that the people cared a great deal that a priest fulfills the proper functions of his office, and thus he took pride in his ability to discharge his duties regularly.

Pietro weighed the question as he took a sip of his coffee. He looked at the priest with genuine sadness in his eyes, not from the loss of his fictitious parents but from the deficiency of compassion which he had continually observed in the man before him. It was because of men like the priest that men like Pietro had to exist. This brought a deep sigh from inside him. The priest took this as a sign that he had reached Pietro on a spiritual level and was pleased.

"The memories are what they are—just memories. I will never have my parents with me again. I am sure of it. There has always been something at the back of my mind weighing upon me. Perhaps our search will be rewarded, and I can finally put my parents to rest."

Father Donati had no response to that but instead ordered a cup of coffee himself and sat with Pietro quietly, observing the fishermen below preparing their boats for their day's work. They were joined shortly by Giacobbe, his bodyguard and his driver. Giacobbe ordered breakfast for everyone, which they ate while planning the course of action for the day.

While smartphones are useful, there is nothing like a real map that can be spread out on a table. Pietro had picked one up in a shop the previous evening before it closed. He now unfolded it and pointed at a location in the park outside the city.

"This is roughly where we need to go. There is a road that will take us close, and then we will need to hike or take bicycles with us. Bicycles would be quicker." He looked at Father Donati. "It would probably be about an hour by bicycle or perhaps three by foot."

Father Donati understood. "I am not as fit as I once was, so perhaps I will stay with the automobile."

Giacobbe gave the driver instructions to rent bikes and purchase water and some prepackaged food for the trip. After everything was ready, the four of them set out on the road leading into the park.

The Aurunci Mountains Park is a beautiful place. It is filled with mountains, some of which are covered with dense forests and some with a seemingly unending procession of rocks, the variety of which are just as capable of breaking an axle as they are an ankle. It is the kind of scenic location where you would be just as likely to see a swarm of honeybees as you would a field of vivid red flowers. On the right mornings, if you ascend to one of the peaks, you can look out over a sea of fog as it blankets the valleys and towns below and see the other mountaintops proudly holding their heads above the layer of white.

This day, the sky was bright blue with a hint of cirrus clouds high in the atmosphere. After the driver stopped the car at a pullout beside a meadow, Pietro unloaded the bicycles and got them ready to go up the trail.

Giacobbe motioned to the valley below. "At least you'll have a scenic view, Prete."

Father Donati grunted. He did not want to be left out of the loop, but he also knew his limitations. If he tried to hike or cycle to where they were going, he would likely be coming back down on a stretcher.

"I'll spend the time in meditation," he said. He leaned back against the plush seat and closed his eyes. With the windows down and a slight breeze, he would soon be asleep.

The other four men did not waste any time starting up the trail. It was actually a service road and was a relatively gentle slope, but it was uphill, nonetheless. Still, each of them walked enough weekly or daily to be in good shape. They traveled thirty minutes before stopping for a break. After two hours total, they were near the target area. Pietro pulled out his phone and looked at a GPS app. He started cycling across a flat, rocky section. The others followed him.

Eventually he stopped and pulled out his notes. After consulting them, he looked around, pointing first one direction and then another and then another.

"The notes say that when that peak over there is at 268 degrees on a compass, we have to find the spot that that peak over there intersects at 210 degrees. And that third peak in the distance should be in a line on the same spot at 100 degrees."

Pietro did not wait for a response. He started walking until he was in line with the first peak on the appropriate reference angle. Then he looked up at the other peaks and then began walking slightly downhill to the west. The other two men followed him on foot.

The hillside split into an incline on their right while still being a broad expanse for them to walk downward. Pietro kept looking up and then checking the compass app on his phone. After another minute of walking, he stopped.

"I wondered why none of the reference points were to the north. With the hillside blocking the view, the only thing my father could see would be these peaks to the south. This is it."

Giacobbe looked around. "I don't see anything," he said.

"What do you see?" asked Pietro.

"Rocks. Plenty of them," said the driver.

"Look closer, especially at the hillside," said Pietro.

Where they were standing, there was what appeared to be a natural cleft in the hill. Over the course of time, it appeared that water had eroded rocks which had tumbled down into a jumbled mess. The hill itself was about ten meters high. The rocks themselves were in a pile about half that. The other two men looked. Giacobbe spoke first.

"These rocks have been placed here. It's made to look like a small slide area, but the hillside is actually intact. There is no sign that these rocks have broken off and fallen into this area."

He looked at Pietro who smiled and said, "Now we get to move stones." Looking at the driver, he added, "Plenty of them."

After an hour of removing stones from the heap, the men were ready for a break. Pietro had volunteered to go back to the bicycles and retrieve the knapsacks, which contained their water and snacks. After a respite, Pietro stood and stretched.

Giacobbe motioned to the pile and said, "How much more, do you think?"

Pietro appraised the pile carefully before responding. "It could be flat rather than standing up."

Giacobbe looked very sourly at the pile. "In that case, we will need more help."

"Why don't we work for another hour or two? We will still have time to get back down the mountain before the sun sets."

"Okay. We can't leave our priest alone for too long. He might succumb to boredom," Giacobbe said.

The four began working with renewed energy knowing that they had a fixed time limit. Pietro had a goal since he had a general idea how things were laid out based on his conversation with Tina. After about forty-five minutes, the driver said, "I've found something."

Pietro, Giacobbe and the bodyguard shifted to where he was working. In the place where he had just removed a stone was a smooth marble surface. After pulling away another dozen stones, the hole was enlarged enough that they could see an edge where two surfaces met. Pietro stepped back and looked at the pile.

"It has to be on its side. There's not enough room for the statue to be standing up."

"That settles it," said Giacobbe. "Let's cover up the hole. We'll have to bring men and equipment." He looked around. "The path is wide enough for a truck here. We just have to make sure we can make it all the way up the service road."

"I'm sure that we can," said the driver. "There are big rocks occasionally, but they would have built it to accommodate army trucks back in the war most likely."

"Okay then," said Giacobbe. "We're going to have to have a big truck to remove it—and plenty of men to move those rocks."

The three spent another thirty minutes covering up the hole and adding in enough extra so that anyone mildly curious would be unlikely to stumble upon the statue. Going down the mountain across the rocky slopes was only slightly easier than riding up, due to the need to keep their speed under control while avoiding any particularly large boulders jutting from the ground. They reached the meadow just as the sun was beginning to dip below the horizon.

They found Father Donati perched on the rear of the car, sipping from a flask of coffee and looking out over the valley below.

"I was about to send out a rescue party to look for you," he said with a smile. He looked at the expressions on the men's faces. "It was a successful trip, no?"

"It was," said Giacobbe. "We can talk about it in the car and over dinner. I'm famished. Let's head back to the hotel."

Chapter 57

The next twenty-four hours were a flurry of activity elsewhere, but for Pietro it was mostly a time of waiting and watching. He had studied Giacobbe from a distance, but now he was able to do so closely. He was included in a few of the discussions, but it was obvious from the way Giacobbe took charge, gave orders and delegated lists of supplies to various people over the phone that this was not the first piece of antiquity that he had handled or relocated. As an artist himself, Pietro had an interest in seeing the flow of the illicit trade in stolen art to diminish. But that was secondary to the goals they were pursuing. Nevertheless, if all went well, at least one of the major pipelines for stolen art would be cut off.

By the next evening, Giacobbe had assembled two different teams of men. One group of four men had brought a four-wheel-drive truck with a flat bed. Attached to the frame was a squat but very stout-looking boom. The second team of four were in a much heavier truck. It also had a flat bed with numerous piles of equipment lashed down along with some large rugged totes. There were also two recreational four-wheelers in the middle of the bed.

All of the men looked physically fit and hard. Pietro guessed that not a few of them were ex-military. They worked with precision as they checked and double-checked their equipment using lists on clipboards. Pietro was impressed by how quickly they operated while not exhibiting a sense of urgency. They were practiced, that was for certain.

At their meeting that evening, Giacobbe laid out the plan.

"As soon as it gets dark, we head out. The lead four-wheeler will scout the road ahead and make sure there are no surprises. Then the two trucks will follow. Another four-wheeler will bring up the rear." He looked at one of the men and asked, "Have you checked all the comms gear?"

"Double-checked and working."

"Good. You can see that clouds have been moving in all day. The weather forecast shows cloudy with a light rain forecast for the night. That means we should have less of a chance of being discovered or interrupted."

"Will Pietro and I be going?" asked Father Donati.

"Your presence is not required, but you are welcome to ride on the backs of the four-wheelers if you would like."

"I should like to be there and see it when it is uncovered for the first time in decades," said Father Donati. "Pietro?"

"Yes," said Pietro, nodding. "It would be good to see it. Who knows? There may be some other clue there as to who was after my parents."

"Then it's settled. I suggest everyone tries to rest for the next couple of hours."

Three hours later, the trucks were in position as the four-wheelers were unloaded. Pietro watched as two of the men unlatched one of the totes and began handing out night vision goggles and communications headsets to the members of the party. He noticed that the two leaders of the teams each had a pistol in a belt holster. Pietro pitied anyone who happened to cross their path tonight, although he doubted it would happen.

"Prete, you will ride with me up front," Giacobbe said. "Pietro, you will ride on the rear four-wheeler. Let's go."

With that, the vehicles started through the meadow and up the service road. It was easier than riding the bicycles, but it was not much quicker due to having to navigate around rocks in the dark using only night vision equipment. After about forty-five minutes, they arrived at the location around half past ten.

Immediately, the teams began to work in three groups of two all around the edges of the pile. The man closest would lift a stone and then pass it to the man next to him, who would heave it as far away as he could. It was loud, but this was a fairly secluded spot of the park. Every twenty minutes, one team would take a break while the reserve team took over. Thus, the removal process continued hour by hour with the statue's shape slowly becoming visible.

Shortly after midnight, one of the men grunted something inaudibly over the radio.

"What is it?" asked Giacobbe.

"Look at this," came the response.

The others came closer to the pile. A hand was reaching upward through the debris with one finger pointed to the sky. A thrill of excitement passed through Giacobbe and Father Donati.

"Continue, but be extremely careful," he said to the group.

They stood around for several more minutes and watched as the hand extended into a forearm, then a complete arm and then the beginning of a torso. The whole effect in the greenish glow of the limited light of the night vision equipment was as if an alien creature or a ghostly shadow were emerging slowly from a grave.

The teams continued until shortly past three in the morning, when the entire object was free of debris. Giacobbe ordered a break for everyone while he, Father Donati and Pietro approached the statue. The base was facing outward with the figure pointing inward and slightly uphill. Even in the limited light, the figure was remarkably similar to what Pietro had carved.

The three stood in silence for a couple of minutes. Then Giacobbe said, "Pietro, I don't know which is most remarkable: this statue or the fact that you were able to carve another one from memory."

"I would say this one is," said Pietro quietly.

"Well, now that we have uncovered it, it is time to move it. We can examine it in more detail later."

He gave the order, and the crews began the next phase. Totes were opened, and heavy straps were placed underneath the statue every few centimeters. These were interconnected with other cross straps so that it resulted in a web of support. The truck with the boom was backed as closely as possible to the statue. The boom was raised and extended above the object. A girder was attached to the boom, and the straps were connected to the girder after the slack was removed. Then the hydraulics engaged, and the lifting process began. Slowly, the straps began to flex and become taut. A couple of adjustments were made to ensure the weight was being distributed evenly. Then the whole piece lifted off the ground.

Once it was free, the boom went higher until the statue was clear of the surrounding piles of rocks. The truck eased away from the area a few meters until it was away from the hillside completely. At that point, the second truck was backed into position, and the process was reversed. The statue was lowered until it was near the truck bed, the truck position was adjusted, large pieces of rubber and foam were positioned beneath the statue, and then the statue was placed onto the bed and its supports.

When it was finally in place, the teams swarmed the truck and covered the statue with heavy blankets and then tarpaulins. Loading straps secured it to the deck. Then, from the front of the bed, they pulled out metal poles and began attaching them together. Pietro watched with interest as they formed the frame of a canopy over the bed, which was then covered with yet another tarp. To a passer-by, it would be just another delivery truck driving down the highway. The removal and loading had taken less than an hour. Pietro made numerous mental notes and determined that he would have to tell Tina how they could improve their planning should they ever have to do something like this again.

"Right," said Giacobbe. "Two of you will drive this truck down to the road with the priest and myself while my driver and Pietro lead the way on one of the four-wheelers. The rest of you will put the rocks back into a pile as close to what it was as possible. When you are done, the second four-wheeler will lead the way out for your truck. Park the four-wheeler in the meadow where you see the first one. They will be picked up later."

And so it was that, within a day, the first statue was delivered without incident to the warehouse where Pietro's sculpture still stood with its broken arm. Pietro was not invited to be a part of that delivery. Giacobbe and Father Donati wanted a chance to compare the two side by side. They were extremely similar, but because of the algorithm which Tina used to introduce the fudge factor, there were clear differences and subtle changes. It was apparent that they were looking at different statues and not an exact replica.

"It's truly remarkable," said Father Donati as they were ending their comparison. "That so young a child could be that impressed with an image such that it stayed latent in his memory all these years."

"And to be able to reproduce it from that memory is an even greater gift," said Giacobbe. "But this is not the statue he saw."

"How do you know that?"

Giacobbe pointed to the intact arm. "There's your proof. The statue he saw was apparently missing that arm or he saw the broken piece. And the base. The inscription is different. That means there is at least one more statue still out there. Maybe two if his parents' notes are accurate."

"Then it is imperative for us to find them," said Father Donati.

226

Chapter 58

One week later, the two men were standing in the same location surveying four statues in a row. Pietro's was still in its original spot. To the left, the three other statues were aligned next to each other. All were spaced about six feet apart.

Finding them had not been that great of a problem, given the accuracy of Pietro's parents' notes. The chance of someone finding them without the notes would have been slim to none, depending mainly on providence or luck. The recovery of the other two had been a bit more challenging due to their locations.

They had one scare when a pensioner whose passion was night photography was spotted coming down a trail. There were a few tense moments as the decision was being made as to how to handle the old lady. Pietro saw the muscles tense in the teams' leaders. Quickly, he volunteered to walk toward her and take care of the situation.

"After all," he explained, "I don't think she will be afraid of me."

Giacobbe assented, and Pietro hurriedly met her before she was too close to the area where they were working. Pietro engaged her in conversation, said he had been out walking and had accidentally run across a wild boar. He had managed to elude it, but he was concerned for her safety. (He really was.) Could he escort her back down the way she had come? She profusely thanked him for his concern and allowed him to walk with her some ways back to where another path would take her into a safer part of the park. Pietro did not doubt that he had saved her life, and he was happy to prevent innocent blood from being shed.

Other than that, the operations had gone smoothly overall in spite of the locations. Now Giacobbe and Father Donati were standing in the warehouse looking at the three newly arrived statues side by side. A broken arm lay in front of the base of one of them. This was their first opportunity to really observe them undisturbed and at leisure.

The statue on the right with the broken arm was closest to Pietro's for comparison. On the base was the single word MYSTERIUM in large letters. The statue in the middle was the one they had recovered first. On its base were the words BABYLON MAGNA. The third statue on the left had the words MATER FORNICATIONUM.

"It's a reference to the Book of the Apocalypse," Father Donati was explaining to Giacobbe. "The original Latin from the Vulgate was 'et in fronte eius nomen scriptum mysterium Babylon magna mater fornicationum et abominationum terrae' or 'And upon her forehead was a name written, Mystery, Babylon The Great, The Mother Of Harlots And Abominations Of The Earth.' The sculptor chose to leave out most of it for brevity knowing that the reference would be unmistakable with even just two of the statues."

"So you're saying that they should be read from right to left?"

"Or the statues could be repositioned left to right. Either way, the phrasing shows the correct order for the statues."

"What about the rest of the Latin script?" asked Giacobbe pointing to the words in smaller letters.

Below the word MYSTERIUM was written "FINEM MYSTERIUM." On the second statue on the second row of script were the words "VAE VAE VAE." The third statue had the inscription "INITIA SUNT DOLORUM" on the second row.

"The first reads roughly 'the end of mysteries' or 'mysteries end,' something like that. The second one simply says, 'woe, woe, woe.' The third is also a reference from Scripture, perhaps. It says, 'beginning of sorrows.'"

"Hmm. Quite a collection of phrases, don't you think?"

"It does seem to indicate that these are no ordinary statues created simply for artistic enjoyment," said Father Donati.

"The final question remains about the rest of this...gibberish. I don't know Latin half as well as you, but even I can tell it doesn't appear to be words as much as random numbers and letters."

"Yes. I can't say that I understand its purpose any more than you at the moment."

The men stood silently and stared at the bottom of each statue's base. In a smaller size of letters were three sets each of numbers and letters. On the right statue were these:

```
N E III VI N II D N
II II I V N IV V F
V I A D N VI A VIII
```

The middle statue had this set:

```
I IX N N N III VII C
I I III VI N II D V
V VIII B III N VI F III
```

The statue on the left had these lines:

```
III  V  IX  IV  N  V  VII  VIII
III  V  VI  E  N  V  VI  B
III  F  VI  I  N  V  F  VII
```

"It's obviously some kind of cipher or code. It's going to take someone with experience in riddles or ancient ciphers to help us," said Giacobbe. "Is there anyone at the Vatican who can help with this?"

"I'll ask. It does make me wonder about the rest of Pietro's story."

"What is that?"

"The part about a mysterious group of people who were chasing after his parents and who would stop at nothing to destroy the statues and the secrets they contained."

"Who do you think it could be?"

"It's hard to say. There are all sorts of shadowy figures and groups throughout Europe. Even our own Orders within the church have their share of dark secrets." Father Donati grew silent. "We could be opening a can of worms by revealing these statues."

"More like a can of money, don't you think?"

"There are some things more important than money."

"Prete, really, you surprise me," said Giacobbe as he turned to look at Father Donati. "Here we are with an unfathomable amount of wealth in front of us, and you are having second guesses? If one forged statue could have been worth nine figures, how much will three genuine matched statues bring? Half a billion? More?"

The thought of the money intruded upon Father Donati's subconscious musings. Something was stirring in the depths of his mind, but, as he concluded, even Holy Scripture says, "money is the answer for everything." Surely with enough money, they could find a solution to both the riddles and whatever threat they represented.

They both snapped photos of the base of each statue. Father Donati sent discreet inquiries through Father Axelrod and Father Sopelli. Giacobbe sent a copy to the best computer guy in their organization.

"Do you think Pietro would be able to help us?" asked Giacobbe.

"It's worth a try. The statues are valuable as they are, but if they point to something dark and secret, I'm sure that someone would pay perhaps even more to bury that information. Or we could use it to our own advantage. If someone were hunting them as recently as the seventies, no doubt such an organization still exists."

An hour later, Pietro stood beside the men looking at the statues. He was awed, but for different reasons. Tina had done a magnificent job on her end. He could see slight nuances which were caused by the fudge factor in the CNC machine's programming. Her team had aged the surfaces well. They looked old.

"I don't remember much about this part of the statues," he was saying to the other two men. Pointing to the one with the broken arm he continued, "Now that I have seen this one, I remember that there was more writing on the base, but it did not stand out as much as the one word."

"Do you think your parents would have left any more notes about the significance of the code?" asked Giacobbe.

"Perhaps. I will have to review the notes in more detail. I don't recall ever seeing anything or hearing them talk about such things." Pietro paused as he knelt and looked closely at the bases. "Have you thought about a contest?"

"A contest? A contest for what?" asked Father Donati.

"Maybe someone can figure out what they mean. If you had a contest and advertised it, maybe people would see it as a competition to try and discover the meaning." Pietro shrugged. "A lot of smart people out there."

Father Donati turned behind Pietro's back and looked at Giacobbe. He tilted his head. "That's not a bad idea. We could do a big press release about finding the statues and then make a big press conference where we invite all the world media. We could offer a bounty, a sizable one, to ensure that we get the best minds working on it."

"We could offer to pay in Bitcoin or any form of payment the winner chooses in order to allow the hacker community to participate," said Giacobbe.

Their conversation and brainstorming continued as Pietro examined the bases, seemingly oblivious to the touch he had made on the lead domino in a long progression. A smile worked its way to the edges of his mouth. They had bitten. The hook was set. Now they would swim the direction they thought they had chosen to go.

Chapter 59

Port Said, Egypt

The *Ahil* passed through the upper end of the Suez Canal and began making headway through the waters of the Mediterranean. The first mate had been told by the pilot that Captain Andar had to be evacuated from the ship due to a sudden onset of what appeared to be kidney stones. Since he had been in his quarters, the first mate had no reason to doubt the veracity of the tale. He simply took over the duties and began to calculate in his head the overtime pay he would rack up. One engine had started to overheat as they exited the Canal, so he had ordered it shut down. The rest of the trip would be slow, but they would arrive nonetheless.

Night had already fallen in Port Said. Hali felt a sudden pang of sadness at the thought of his brother. He realized that because of his anger, he had never been able to fully grieve his loss. He thought of the young girls in the shipping containers. Surely their parents were grieving for them. Someone was missing them. He wondered if he had done the right thing by allowing the ship to continue without raising the alarm. But stopping the ship in Egypt would have raised too many questions about their presence on the *Ahil* and just how they came to be there. No, it had to be this way. Besides, this way the people on the other end of the line could possibly be caught.

Hali located a public phone and made a call to Interpol and asked for someone who could help with a tip in Italy. After being passed around, he was connected to an investigator who had jurisdiction over Western Europe. Hali told the man that he wanted to pass along a tip on human trafficking taking place at the present time but wished to remain anonymous. Several thousand kilometers away, the officer assured him that this was perfectly acceptable and casually pulled a pad of paper in front of him to begin taking notes.

Hali stressed that the information had to be acted upon immediately and that it involved the safety of 160 Chinese Uighur girls. When he said those last two words, the officer gave him his undivided attention. Over the next few minutes, Hali gave a brief but detailed report on what they had seen on the *Ahil*. He described in detail the location and description of the shipping containers themselves. Even though the call was being recorded, the investigator took notes furiously and asked a few questions for clarification.

When he asked if the captain of the ship was aware that the nature of his cargo was known, Hali snorted.

"Yes. But he will no longer be a problem for you—or anyone else."

"What do you mean? Is the captain on board the ship?"

"I'm afraid not."

"Has he escaped?"

"Escaped? Not likely. He has already faced justice for his crimes."

"Did you kill him?"

"You are recording this call, yes?"

"Yes."

"Then I have nothing more to say about the captain."

The officer was unsure how to proceed. He wasn't sure if he was hearing a confession of another crime or if someone was staging a hoax, but Hali answered his dilemma by asking for an email address in order to send a video recording of the captain's full confession. He assured the officer that it would guarantee the legitimacy of the tip.

After the call, Hali uploaded the video to a file sharing site using a newly created account and sent a link to the officer's email. Then he took the cell phone, a burner, and removed the SIM card. He tossed the card down into the gutter and dropped the phone into a waste bin.

All that remained for him to do was close out accounts with their contact in the Canal Authority. That man would pay the pilot for his silence and return the uniforms which had been taken from one of the depots. Then each of the men in the party would board different flights over the next three days to return home. Hali's parents would benefit from the money he had taken from Captain Andar's safe, but mostly they would rejoice in the news that their son's blood had been avenged on his killer.

Chapter 60

Philadelphia

For fourteen days straight, the stories steadily had kept coming. Alex had never been more euphoric. The real journalist in him was living his dream. He was writing stories that mattered. Although it would have bruised his journalistic training decades earlier, he had been meeting with Detective Deshawn Carson of the police department. They were comparing notes, mostly from Alex's side, but the detective occasionally made a comment or pointed Alex in the right direction based on what he knew.

Apparently Detective Carson had been working undercover on special assignment by the US Marshals against his own police department for some time and had built a sizable trove of evidence, which he was using to methodically build numerous cases to prosecute the corruption he had observed. The person known as Serious had located him the weekend of Margot's disappearance and had recommended that Alex contact him immediately. Now he was sharing stories two to three days prior to publication so that Detective Carson could prioritize warrants for arrest and mitigate flight risks.

One set of articles detailed the flow of heroin and other strong narcotics into the Philly area. Another revisited some of the convenient suicides by judges and prosecutors and other persons who had been associated with the crime scene in one way or the other. That led to a set of articles detailing "side-by-sides" in which convictions and sentencing were compared between offenders. Alex had a good way of relating technical information, which was usually thought boring to the average reader, such that they understood it. It was clear to those reading the news in Philadelphia and beyond that there was a two-tiered justice system in place. If you were part of the big club, you could get away with literal murder. If you were not, then simple possession would send you up the river.

The pearl-inlay revolver used in Mennheim's "suicide" was even tied to one of the policemen on the force. The design was determined to be custom. The gunsmith who created the handle acknowledged that he had done a whole set of commission pieces for a group of military members returning from Afghanistan. They wanted something to remember an event that had shaped their lives. Only one of the pieces was pearl inlay, and he had never repeated the design for anyone else.

With murder and narcotics charges flying, the best part of Alex's day was reading the roundup from the bookings and arrests. These were people who had been on the public payroll for most of their lives. Now their crimes were being laid bare. Some editors opined that actual punishment would likely be slim due to corruption in the judicial system, but several shots had been fired across the bow there, too. No fewer than five judges in the city had already been arrested. Seven more had resigned suddenly.

The stories had been picked up by the various wire services. They were being published nationwide and as far away as London and Hong Kong. Interview requests came from all over. The paper had to transfer two dedicated secretaries to handle the incoming flow of calls and letters. At the insistence of his publisher and because it would help the paper, which had always stood by him, Alex gave as many interviews as he could, but he limited them to one hour per day, and they were generally no more than five minutes each in length.

While he was being touted as the current generation's Woodward or Bernstein, Alex remained noncommittal. All he would say consistently is, "I had help which I cannot, of course, divulge." The anonymous people who had contributed to the research felt the nod and knew their own part had been acknowledged.

After two weeks, several things happened to bring about a natural break. The first was the overall shock value of the news which had been unleashed. The public had been engrossed in the mass corruption which infested their community. The nation had paused to look at it as well and had wondered how much it was mirrored across the country in their own cities. But having observed the evil, most people were not conditioned to be able to keep handling the truth in such large doses. Even a loving mother has no real desire to clean up the kind of diaper that comes up out of the top and bottom of an infant's clothes. There seemed to be no end to this mess.

Second was the fact that there was a backlog of arrests and indictments which was beginning to crowd the system. Detective Carson assured Alex that there was more evidence that he was privy to which could not be published for fear of jeopardizing some higher-profile cases. He gave Alex his word that as long as he was able, he would keep following the leads which Alex had supplied in addition to his own investigative work. Based on what he had already seen, Alex believed him.

Third, there was a bit of foreign news that had gradually attracted the attention of the world. It seems that a set of ancient statues had been suddenly discovered in Italy. The Vatican was offering a huge reward for anyone who could help to decipher the meaning of their inscriptions. While most people saw their chances as remote as that of winning the lottery, the mystery served as a welcome relief to read about.

Thus, with mutual consensus, Alex's publisher and editors agreed that it was time to let this story cycle play out with younger writers having a chance to follow up on the remaining trails of the story. It would give them exposure and a chance to add to their own bylines. Alex would have time to rest, do more interviews or follow up new stories as he saw fit. In years gone by, Alex would have bristled at the thought. Now, with his different perspective on life, he both saw the wisdom of it and looked forward to getting more than four hours of sleep per day.

As he was explaining this to Serious, Alex was surprised to hear that Serious was ready to turn attentions to the statues.

"I believe that there is more to them than meets the eye. I am not yet sure of their significance. Nor am I certain that we can decipher the inscriptions, but I believe that we are to at least focus on them for now."

Alex wished Serious good success on this new venture and expressed an interest in staying in touch on a routine, if not regular, basis. Serious responded by stating that if they did have good success, Alex would have a first scoop on any story that came out of it. And with that, they parted digital company.

Chapter 61

Cyberspace

The announcement and subsequent unveiling of the statues a few days prior had taken the art world by storm. Officially, the statues had been found in one of the catacombs underneath Vatican City, which helped to establish their ownership. The narrative was that they had been sealed behind a wall and that a routine maintenance had discovered a major crack which required a repair. When the workers began the removal of the debris, they had discovered a cavity that had been covered up for who knew how long. Inside this were three statues of currently unknown age and origin. Rather than simply move them to a private room in a museum somewhere, the Vatican had decided to share them with the world. Oh, and by the way, there was a mysterious component to the statues that would be revealed at the worldwide unveiling.

Everyone loves a mystery, especially one with ancient origins. When the Vatican announced a ten million-euro bounty to anyone who could successfully crack the secret code, one the best cryptographers the Vatican could hire were unable to decipher, it took less than a New York minute for the word to spread globally.

In less than twelve hours, the website which had been set up to serve as a clearinghouse for the public to report their attempts and successes had completely crashed. Two of the major software companies offered to host a collaboration site, mainly to tout their abilities. The Vatican agreed to allow the transition of the site as long as they would play nicely together. For once, they agreed and even allowed anyone to connect into the sites through an open API. The comments came fast and furious, but the new platforms weathered the storm. There were numerous message boards which were created where people discussed everything from biblical prophecy to the treasure of Caligula to theories involving aliens and shapeshifters. Everyone from the nerds to the New Agers claimed to have insight into the meaning of the statues.

Still, no one could come up with an answer to the mysterious numbers and letters on the statues. The amount of computing power spent trying to run decryption schemes during the next few days is still unknown, but the participation graphs on all major cryptocurrency exchanges dropped significantly. Why mine Bitcoin when you could potentially hit the jackpot quicker and easier? But the jackpot was hiding deeper than a simple decryption algorithm could uncover.

Yet, instead of discouraging people, the public awareness increased. The whole thing took on the life of the search for Mr. Wonka's fabled golden tickets. The eyes of the world, grown weary from the continued political news and routine global upheavals, needed a distraction that would give them something to cheer for. Even the major news networks worldwide devoted time to update their audiences on the progress and recent theories related to the statues.

Thus it was that the eyes of the world were fixed firmly on three pieces of marble when a cluster of anonymous Internet researchers began to look at the statues together, partly out of the sheer challenge of breaking the code and partly out of a curiosity as to whether or not these statues would tie into any of the other research they had done on the Roman system. With less than ten total, the bounty, if they won it, would go a long way toward paying off debts, buying an epic gaming system or helping their charity of choice.

They decided to meet in a gaming voice and chat server channel they had created years ago. It was hosted by one of their members, and they each had enough trusted level access to be confident that the machine was as secure as they could reasonably make it. By talking through their initial questions and assessments, they hoped to get a leg up on the competition. What follows is a rough transcript of the salient parts of their discussion.

17-Tips: What do we know about the hard details on the statues?

CADDurt: The Vatican anticipated that people would have detailed questions, so they've provided high res pix of each of the statues from every conceivable angle. They used 3D mapping technology, so we can rotate, tilt and zoom to see any detail we want. They also have exact dimensions of the main measurements and points of references in case that matters.

Burfer: Does the type of marble give us any reference on the age? How do we know these things are legit?

17-Tips: We don't. That's why we're looking at everything from the ground up. The Vatican from all appearances thinks they are legit, but they could be lying through their teeth.

Hubbl3: Why? What would be their end game in doing so?

17-Tips: No idea. But we can't rule it out as a

possibility. I think everyone else has started from the ground level of their being authentic.

Burfer: I'll start looking into the marble itself then, colors, finish, aging.

TechFrog: Make sure you look at the bottom of the base, too.

Burfer: Hadn't thought of that. Why?

TechFrog: Just a hunch. How many people would forget to do that?

Burfer: Probably most of them.

TechFrog: If we're starting from ground level, that's the part that sits on the ground.

17-Tips: What's everyone else working on?

CADDurt: I'm looking at everything I can related to the Latin that we can read. If there's a pattern or clue in the actual wording, I hope to find it.

Burfer: Don't forget to look at the Gematria. There might be something there.

CADDurt: Hmm. I doubt it. I mean we're talking about potentially thousand-year-old statues, right? But I'll run it through some calculators and see.

17-Tips: Serious, you've been awfully quiet. You're the one who wanted to have this meeting and see if we could break this. What are you thinking?

There was a significant pause, but all the other participants waited. They had learned that Serious did not rush into things, nor was Serious likely to speak quickly or frivolously.

Serious: In my mind, I keep seeing these statues lined up as the lead domino, each at the head of a long line of dominoes. Once their secret is revealed, it will bring about a predictable but unstoppable sequence of events. I also have a sense that one of us may have to go public with our findings in order to achieve maximum impact.

TechFrog: Are you being serious?

It sounded ridiculous as soon as it was spoken, but the other participants were each thinking of the ramifications of losing anonymity.

Serious: We'll cross that bridge when we come to it.

238

In the meantime, let's get started with our respective areas of research. I suggest we meet at noon and midnight GMT. That seems to work with the different time zones we are in.

Burfer: What are you going to be looking at, Serious?

Serious: I plan to focus my attention on the actual coded portion.

TechFrog: Do you need any help with that?

Serious: I will. I would welcome your help.

Hubbl3: What do you want me to work on?

Serious: Why don't you and Gandalf the White work on trying to verify the story about the finding of the statues.

Hubbl3: That's going to be a challenge. If it's not true, the Vatican is one of the world's best at keeping secrets. I'll get started on it.

17-Tips: If the story is false, someone somewhere has to have seen something. People talk because generally people can't keep secrets. Social media, local newspapers, police reports, anomalies of any kind.

Hubbl3: On it. Serious, how is Gandalf the White? Still safe?

Serious: Yes.

Hubbl3: How will I contact her?

Serious: She has a new email address. I'll send it to you. You can work with her directly. If there is nothing else, let's begin.

Chapter 62

Margot woke up with an inexplicable craving for hash. While the dish takes on diverse forms around the world, at its core is a mixture of usually common ingredients which typically comprise the leftovers of the working class. In the United States, those ingredients are commonly meat, potatoes and onions. The ingredients are cut up into pieces and fried together. Margot's grandmother used to add in a mixture of extra spices that earned her the culinary respect of her generation's community and Margot's lifelong memories. It had been years since she had tasted something that good.

Maybe it was being with Mrs. Li and her mostly vegetarian diet. Maybe it was the sense of displacement she was feeling. For whatever reason, her mouth actually began watering as she thought about it. She had not left the premises and had no intention to do so yet. That fact alone intensified the craving.

All that morning as she sat in front of her computer working on her research with Hubbl3, her stomach growled. For breakfast, Mrs. Li had cooked eggplant with fresh tomatoes and basil. It was quite tasty. But it wasn't hash.

They had run into some interesting information. The tunnels and catacombs had been used during the world wars, and several maps documented their existence. The Vatican had not pinpointed the location of the discovery of the statues, but they had given enough statements that the location had to be within a certain section of the city. Unfortunately, that section was mapped and riddled with enough tunnels that it seemed improbable if not impossible that there would actually be a room or cavity large enough to hold the statues while still remaining a hidden secret for such a long time.

That was the problem with a lie. Somewhere, there lay facts which would destroy fiction if a person sought for them long enough. Margot and Hubbl3 had just finished their conclusions when it was time for the midday conference call with the rest of the team.

After hearing from most of the rest of the group, Hubbl3 shared the current status of their research on the authenticity of the story of their discovery. Hubbl3 stated to the group that he rated the probability of the story being a lie at around ninety percent.

Serious spoke and asked, "Gandalf the White, what do you think?"

Margot had been half in and out of the conversation and answered abruptly, "All I can think about is my grandmother's hash."

There was a moment of silence and then laughter ensued, along with interjections and comments by the others.

"I'm serious," protested Margot. "Ever since I woke up, all I can think about is hash, hash, hash."

"What did you just say?" asked Serious.

"I said all I can think about is my grandmother's hash."

"No. Repeat what you just said after that."

Margot looked sideways at her laptop. "You mean ever since this morning, all I can think about is hash, hash, hash?"

"Yes!" said Serious with excitement. "Three plates of hash. Three sets of hashes. Three hash codes!"

TechFrog spoke up. "That doesn't fit. How can an ancient statue have hash codes? They weren't practical before the age of computing."

Burfer said, "Yes, but if what Hubbl3 says is accurate, they may not be that old."

CADDurt interjected, "When I looked at the Latin phrases, I went ahead and did my best to transcribe the coded portions. I wasn't sure sometimes if a 'V' represented a letter or a number or if an 'N' was a letter or number. But I can tell that if the statues are old at all, they can't be older than the eighth century."

"Why is that?" asked 17-Tips.

"Because Latin did not have a zero as a placeholder. The first person to use it widely was the Venerable Bede. He used the letter N for the word 'nulla' alongside the traditional Roman numerals. In fact, as late as 1259, Italy had passed a law stating that bankers were forbidden to use the newfangled Arabic zero in their bookkeeping."

"So what did you come up with?" asked TechFrog.

"Each statue has three lines with what could be eight letters and numbers if I am transcribing it correctly. Let me post them in the chat window." A few seconds went by, and then the following appeared.

N E III VI N II D N = N E 3 6 N 2 D N

0e3602d0

II II I V N IV V F = 2 2 1 V N 4 V F

2215045f

```
V I A D N VI A VIII = V 1 A D N 6 A 8
51ad06a8
```

"Here's the first statue's coded inscription," he said. "Again, I wasn't sure whether to transcribe 'V' as the number five or as the letter."

"Let's go with the numbers," said Serious. The following rapidly appeared in the chat window:

```
N E III VI N II D N = 0e3602d0
II II I V N IV V F = 2215045f
V I A D N VI A VIII = 51ad06a8
```

"Can you post the rest?"

"Sure," said CADDurt. "Let me clean them up first to match this theory." After another minute, the chat window displayed the other two coded inscriptions.

```
I IX N N N III VII C = 1900038c
I I III VI N II D V = 113602d5
V VIII B III N VI F III = 58b306f3


III V IX IV N V VII VIII = 35940578
III V VI E N V VI B = 356e056b
III F VI I N V F VII = 3f6105f7
```

"Well, I've got to admit they sure do look like hashes. But decrypting a hash isn't going to be any easier than any other cipher."

"Give me a minute or two," said Serious. "I want to check something."

"It's still pretty far out to think that this is real," added Hubbl3. "I mean, the chance excavation story was starting to look pretty suspicious, but this is even crazier."

After that, they waited in silence for a few minutes. After an interlude, they could hear Serious' voice on the microphone mumbling a "Yes!" quietly. Everyone began craning to listen. They heard, "Yes, another one. Let's try the second set. Yes, again. And the fourth line. Now the third set." There was a long pause and then, "Impressive!"

"You going to enlighten us or just keep us in suspense?" asked 17-Tips.

"Sorry," said Serious. "You may not believe this, but it checks out. I took each of the hashes and began asking how they relate to the statues as a whole. On each of the statues, there are two distinct Latin phrases on separate lines. All three of them are this way. Burfer, what would you do if you wanted to send a message and make sure the person on the other end received exactly what you sent?"

There was a pause, and then Burfer responded, "No, you're kidding me. You're not saying that these hashes correspond to the readable text, are you?"

"I am," answered Serious. "I took the word MYSTERIUM and tried it in lowercase at first, but that didn't work. But if you take it in all caps as it is written and run it using the Adler32, you get 0e3602d0 exactly!"

"No way!" said CADDurt. "That's impossible!"

"Try it yourself," said Serious. "I'll wait."

There was a pause as several sets of hands opened browser tabs or terminal windows and began pecking away at the keyboards. The collective exclamations over the group audio were proof enough that Serious' theory was correct.

Margot had been following with interest but was still completely in the dark. "Would someone please explain what is going on—in layman's terms?"

Serious responded. "It's pretty ingenious, really. Whenever a developer creates new software, or when a person wishes to send a compressed file, they need a way to allow persons to verify that the contents of the file or the software have not been tampered with. After the file is completed, the developer will run a cryptographic hash against the file to produce a checksum."

"Great!" interrupted Margot. "Layman's terms, please."

"What that means is that each file has its own unique digital fingerprint, just like you have a unique physical fingerprint. If I want to verify your identity, I look at the archived set of your fingerprints and then check your fingerprints when you show up at the door to a bank vault. If they match, you are who you say you are. With computer files, if you run the file through one of the many algorithms out there, the results will be completely unique to that file."

"Okay," said Margot. "I've seen people include a checksum file in some of the research I've done, but I never knew how they got them or their importance. But all of those are really long. I thought all of the encryption stuff produced results that were just as long."

"That's the beauty of the Adler algorithm," said Burfer. "It only produces eight-character results. Very lightweight. It has its disadvantages, of course, but rather than writing something out which is thirty-two characters like MD5 hashes, eight is a distinct mark in its favor.

"Every one of them check out," said TechFrog. "I've tried all six of the Latin phrases, and they all match the six of the nine numbers we have."

"What does it mean?" asked Margot.

"It means that the Vatican got played," said Burfer.

"We don't know that for certain yet," said 17-Tips. "They could still have a plan or long-term play going on here."

"No, I think he's right," said Serious. "Not just because of the evidence we've found so far on our own. But I still see these statues in my mind at the head of different lines of dominoes. I don't think the Vatican knows what they have. It's the last line on each statue which holds the key."

"But how are we going to find out what that is?" asked TechFrog. "Even knowing that it's an Adler32 hash, the last line could be anything. You know that. We could spend years trying to run Latin phrases through the hash generator to try to find it."

"How do you know it's Latin?" asked CADDurt. "It could be any language."

"Good point," said TechFrog. "At which point our dictionary of words and phrases just got exponentially bigger and nigh to impossible to decrypt."

"I don't think we have to find the answer at all," said Serious quietly. "I think the answer will find us."

"That's rather cryptic," said Burfer. "What do you mean by that?"

"If we are correct in our assumptions that the statues are not truly from antiquity, then someone went to a whole lot of trouble to play this out. We don't truly know how or where the statues were acquired by the Vatican, but they are going to a whole lot of trouble and expense to promote them. If the Vatican believes they are legit, then whoever designed them thinks the coded portions are very important. Put yourself in their position. If you created a checksum with a cryptographic hash, then you know that the chances of someone cracking the hash in reverse is going to be nearly impossible. What would you do if you want to get the message out?"

"I see where you're going with this," said Hubbl3. "You wait until someone figures out the first part, and then you communicate with them and tell them what the hidden part is."

"Exactly," said Serious. "If someone has done the heavy lifting, they establish their validity. With all the attention focused on these statues, whoever is behind this is guaranteed maximum reach with their message. I believe that all we have to do is announce that we have solved the first part of the puzzle, and then we need to provide a way for the party on the other end to contact us."

"How about Alex Ingram?" asked Margot. "He has the ability to make this international headlines with his position at the paper."

"I think it's the logical choice," said Serious. "Mr. Ingram has proven that he is willing to go the distance on very important stories. Are we all in agreement?"

The group voiced their consent. Serious offered to write up the analysis into a cohesive and factual format. After further reflection, the group decided that throwing out a teaser of a future public statement would make for greater fanfare rather than simply sending the details for Alex to publish.

As the meeting was ready to conclude, Hubbl3 spoke up. "Well, Gandalf the White, when this is all over, I want to offer to use part of my share of the reward money to treat you to your choice of hash from any restaurant in the world."

They all laughed, including Margot, until Burfer concluded the meeting by stating quietly, "If this plays out like we think it will, I think the Vatican would prefer to reward us quite differently."

Chapter 63

Italy

A day after the meeting at the warehouse, Pietro had asked Father Donati if he could be given a relatively small block of marble to keep busy with while events with the statues played out. While he had faith in the abilities of the people who were working hard to decipher the statues' code, his group had agreed on an outlier of four weeks at most before moving the story along through their own efforts. In the meantime, he had another piece to work on for his own personal reasons.

Father Donati spoke with Giacobbe, who immediately dispatched one of his associates to pick up whatever Pietro requested. A piece of white marble approximately one-half meter wide and deep by about two-thirds of a meter long was delivered two days after their last meeting at the warehouse. The statues were already gone. Father Donati was busy working with the various representatives of the Holy See. Giacobbe had stayed involved long enough to ensure that the major media organizations had picked up and were propagating the story, and then he turned his attention to more pressing business matters. No one cared to check on the sculptor at the warehouse, nor did Pietro expect their gaze to return upon him any time in the immediate future.

He had seen the photo one time, but Pietro had a remarkable memory. He touched the play button on the radio. Then he took up a large chisel and began to take off the outer edges of the marble block.

Chapter 64

Chioggia, Italy

Giacobbe was juggling multiple priorities. Currently, he was in his armored SUV with a driver and bodyguard as they headed to Chioggia in the northeast corner of Italy. Since the abrupt removal of Aldo Serafini from the organization, the Don had elected to spread out the doll business to aspiring men such as himself in order to see who was best suited for the job. This was a test of each man's organization, his contacts and network of other criminal entity leaders. Giacobbe's turn had arrived, and he had worked through an old friend who had contacts among several less-than-savory sea captains. One had agreed to ferry the cargo for a reasonable sum.

Now the shipment would be arriving within the next twenty-four hours. While all of the arrangements had been made and the onshore crew downline from him knew what to do, he was torn between staying away for safety and being on hand to verify the handoff of the goods to the client. In the end, the opportunity to become the man in charge of the doll business outweighed the risk. There could be no fouling up this one chance only to see the business pass to one of his peers. It was widely understood that whoever controlled the doll business would be the most likely candidate to replace the Don whenever the time came.

His phone rang. It was Father Donati telling him that a group had come forward to announce that they had cracked part of the code and would be giving a press conference the next day. Giacobbe pressed for details. Father Donati related that an American newspaper in Philadelphia had just released a story across the wires timed to coincide with the printing of their morning edition. He would send him the link, although there were no real details to speak of. The one thing that gave the story credibility was the name of the reporter himself. Alex Ingram had broken many news stories through the years, was a respected journalist and had been contacted by the group as an intermediary. The journalist was only authorized to say that he had seen a fraction of the evidence and was convinced that the group was genuine. The purpose of the story's release was to allow ample time for international news organizations to either send their own reporters or work with local stations and media outlets to serve as their representatives for the press conference, which would be held in the newspaper's spacious main conference room.

Interested parties were advised to begin making arrangements. Each major news outlet would be afforded one seat in order to provide maximum coverage of the event.

Giacobbe thanked him and then returned his thoughts to the present. The freighter was due to arrive at 6 a.m. the following morning. He would observe the unloading of their two containers at a distance. Emil Pagano would be on board to make sure that the customs end of things was handled and that no one would hinder the offloading with obtrusive questions. If there were no issues with the offloading, Giacobbe would accompany the semis to the warehouse where they would conduct an inspection of the goods. If all was satisfactory, then and only then would the contacts for the customers be notified to come pick up their percentage of the merchandise.

He looked at the details on his phone. The Castle would be taking the lion's share: eighty of the girls would go to the Count at his spacious estate. Another twenty-five percent would be taken by a laboratory network. The balance of them were allocated to a less-than-savory group which he had once heard Aldo refer to as "the breeders."

He knew that two of the other men in the Don's organization had handled things a bit differently, but Giacobbe had chosen to have all three of the organizations present at the warehouse at the same time. For one, he wanted the second and third in line to see the quality of the merchandise the Castle got to choose from. His point was to have them understand that if they increased their price per unit to a larger amount, they could move to the head of the line and get first pick on the next shipment. In this way, he intended to spark a bit of a bidding war, which would increase profits and give the Don yet another reason to consider him as the permanent owner of that business. Additionally, the quicker they moved all of the girls out of the warehouse, the less exposure he would have.

Giacobbe had made it clear that, just like the narcotics they supplied, no one was to sample the merchandise. "Nobody in the organization gets hooked," was a mantra every member was made to understand. Still, he was a bit excited to see what the shipment looked like. The driver spoke up then. They had arrived at their hotel in Chioggia.

Chapter 65

Italy

The next day in a hotel located in the business district, Pietro placed his bag on the floor and the sculpture on the table. He wiped his brow more from habit than from sweat and looked at the finished piece. Artists pour a bit of their soul into every work they create. For Pietro, he would contend that his spirit had bled into this one.

He wasn't sure it would survive more than a minute or two after its unveiling. Nevertheless, it had to be created. In a moment like this, art was obedient worship more than an expression of creativity.

Father Donati had texted him the previous day that a group in America was making an announcement this afternoon. Perhaps this was the day he could learn more about the statues. Would Pietro want to join him at the parish manor for the broadcast? Pietro had declined, saying that he did not want to get his hopes up and would wait to see whether or not the news was real.

He looked at the time. The broadcast would begin in five minutes. Much depended on what was revealed. He sighed deeply, sat down in an upholstered chair and turned it so that he was facing the sculpture. As he focused on it, his eyes began to moisten with tears. It was almost too much to bear.

Chapter 66

Tina was, however, watching the broadcast. It was part of her responsibility to keep an eye on all things related to the decoding of the statues' message. The hardest part was selecting a channel. Every major media corporation was covering the press conference. It was being livestreamed on numerous social media sites.

The conference began promptly at 9 a.m. Philadelphia time. It was opened by the publisher of the paper, who welcomed everyone and thanked them for coming. He recognized several of the big names on hand for the occasion. It was obvious he was not used to doing this type of thing. Then he began his introduction of Alex Ingram, who had been on their staff for almost two decades. During that time, he had been the lead on more headlines and blockbuster stories than anyone could remember. At that point, one of the television journalists actually coughed loudly. The hint was taken, and the publisher quickly concluded his remarks and yielded the floor to the reporter everyone had assembled to hear.

Alex thanked everyone for coming and then got down to business. Tina liked what she saw. It was hard to tell much about a person from a bio photo on a company website, but the man in front of the cameras was energetic and well-spoken. He stated that he had been contacted by a group of Internet researchers who had been working nonstop to decipher the code. While he understood that many individuals or groups worldwide had been making similar claims, he believed that this group had actually done so based on a portion of the information they shared with him. This group was largely anonymous even to one another, but one of their members had elected to come forward publicly in order to share the information and to answer questions in person. With that said, he picked up a remote and clicked a button. Two large screens which had previously been displaying a stationary image of the statues with the chryon "Riddle Solved" flipped over to a video conferencing app. On the screen was an empty chair in front of a plain white background.

"The video and audio of this session are being recorded and will be made available via a web download after the press conference has concluded," said Alex as he placed a small earpiece and microphone over his right ear. "Are you there?" he asked into the mic. "Can you hear me okay?"

"I'm here, and I can hear you fine," answered a female voice as a figure moved into the frame. Tina watched with much of the world as a young African American lady sat down in the chair and looked directly into the camera. Tina was struck by her strong cheekbones and the broad smile she flashed as she greeted the participants.

"My name is Margot. I work online with a group who call ourselves 1329 Collective. We love to do research and solve puzzles. When the Vatican offered this latest challenge, our group was interested on several levels. The first was purely from the standpoint of the challenge itself. Who doesn't like a good riddle? The second was from what we originally perceived was a historical perspective."

The word "originally" made Tina's ears perk up.

"If these statues were able to offer an insight into another era, we wanted to be able to share their message. The third reason for our interest is that several of our members have worked on puzzles related to the Vatican in the past."

Tina stroked her chin softly. Was this a subtle hint? She and Pietro along with the rest of the team knew the chances were that anyone had the potential to uncover the mystery. Could it be that these people were interested in more than the money and fame? Did they share a common goal? She listened closely as Margot continued speaking.

"What we have uncovered has led us to the conclusion that the statues, while excellent pieces of art in and of themselves, have been created in the past twenty-five years."

There was a buzz of voices in the conference room that could be heard over Alex's mic. His voice could be heard next saying to someone, "If you leave now, you'll regret it. Have a seat and listen to her. She knows what she's talking about. Pardon the interruption, Margot. Your statement caught everyone off guard here."

"That quite all right, Alex. I'm going to display several things on the screen and talk about what each of them mean. The presentation should only take about fifteen to twenty minutes, and then I will take a limited number of questions."

Her image disappeared and a map appeared on the screen. As Margot spoke, she used the app's tools to point to and highlight portions of it. "This area here is the general area where the statues were said to have been discovered. The Vatican was intentionally short on giving an exact location. Some attribute that to basic security measures on their part. We are confident that it is because the statues could not have been there to begin with."

The image changed to a close-up view of the same area.

"As you can see, this area is where the train station is located. This particular section of the Vatican was bombed on November 5, 1943. While no one was injured, there were damages to the tunnel infrastructure. That, coupled with the bombing of July 19 earlier in the year, had left any tunnels or catacombs with brick or block walls severely damaged. If you look at this next image, it is a map of the known utility tunnels at the time of World War II. This next image is a drawing of the maze of catacombs running under this section of the city. This third image is an overlay of the two. Based on all the public data, and I realize that the Vatican may not have released everything about what they have going on underground, the footprint required by these three statues is not readily available. As you can see, the distances between catacombs, train paths and various other tunnels makes for a tight space in this particular area. During the bombing, entire walls collapsed and had to be repaired. The Vatican's statement was that the statues had been found sealed behind plaster and were positioned as if they were on display. Assuming for a moment that each statue had a spacing of two feet between the next, this would have to be at least sixteen feet or even as much as thirty feet if they were spaced proportionally to their height.

"Further, there is the question of how the Vatican could have raised the statues to the ground without excavation, none of which has been reported in the past few years on the grounds. The weight of each statue is around ten thousand pounds, or roughly forty-five hundred kilograms. If they had been located in one of the tunnels connected to the train or utilities, we could envision a forklift being able to handle such an operation. However, the Vatican was specific that they were located in a catacomb. None of the catacombs in this section of the city have the necessary access to allow anything of their weight or magnitude to be navigated to the surface."

Margot switched the screen several times and added commentary.

"These images show the access locations for the catacombs. As you can see clearly, each of them is accessed only by flights of stairs which have no doubt been repaired over the years. Regardless of their strength, they could never sustain the weight of a single statue. We also questioned whether the shafts leading into the earth for each stairwell were capable of having a statue raised by a cable and strong winch. This also is impossible. The stairs in this image make their way down the outer rim of the shaft. As they make the turn at each corner and continue to descend, the distance between the steps and guardrails is three feet, or about a meter."

Alex looked around the room. People were sitting stoically, with several taking notes. Margot had not yet won over her audience, but she was beginning to command their attention.

"We began to ask why the Vatican would not be forthcoming about the location of the discovery of the statues. One simple theory is that they were discovered elsewhere. While this is ultimately a matter of discussion for the Vatican and the Italian Carabinieri, we felt it was worthwhile to explore all theories. In doing so, we requested the help of likeminded researchers within Italy. We received one tip which sounded anecdotal in nature. A retired lady who loves night photography was in the Parco Regionale del Matese when she happened upon a rather strange sight. Late at night, she observed a group of men with a truck that had a winch with what sounds like a boom from her description. She watched them for about fifteen minutes as they were removing a large statue from that area of the park. Curious as to what it may have been, she was going to approach the men and ask them questions and offer to document their work. One of the men instead came to meet her and guided her back up the path with instructions to come back another night. She told a few people in her community about the experience. After the unveiling of the statues by the Vatican, she swears that what she saw that night from a distance looked to be the same type of statue. Her story made it into the local paper where it had been read by the researcher who sent us the tip.

"I realize that such a story would be dismissed as rather shaky evidence in a court of law. We asked the researcher to locate the lady if possible and to determine the exact location of the occurrence. Her memory is stellar, and she was able to lead our colleague directly to the spot. He took several photos and GPS coordinates which he relayed to us.

"When we looked at the current satellite images of the area, we could tell that the rocks in that spot had been repositioned recently. Using the tools available, it does appear that something of substantial mass has been removed from that place. You can see the location both before and after in these side-by-side images."

Tina was intrigued as she sat in her hotel room, eyes transfixed on the television. These people were good. She had no idea who they were, but she wished they were part of the team.

In the parish manor, Father Donati began to feel uncomfortable. He knew that men more powerful than he would be scrambling to formulate their own press release to counteract what the young lady was saying. It was what she said next that made him feel weak in the stomach.

"One point of interest we are not yet able to explain," Margot continued. "When we were reviewing the archival satellite photos, we discovered that the site appears to have changed even prior to this date. These side-by-side images show the site three months ago. As you can see, the stones appear to

253

be a jumbled mass three months ago. Sometime in the past two months, the stones were placed in a more orderly manner. If the images are correct and not out of order, it could be that a statue, if our night photographer is correct, was placed there and then later removed."

At that point, one of the press pool tried to interrupt for a question, but Alex motioned with his hand and said, "Just a moment, Margot." To the reporter, he said, "Let her finish. She hasn't gotten to the really good part yet. Sorry, Margot. Go ahead."

"No problem. I realize that this is intriguing. The real question that you are probably wondering and what the Vatican has offered a reward for is to find out what the encoded portions of the inscriptions mean. What I have shared is a foundation for you to be able to appreciate what I'm going to tell you about them. They were absolutely written by someone within the past twenty-five years."

Margot then took the time to show photos of each inscription and describe the process of converting them to an eight-character string. She then displayed on the screen the finished results of what each statue's complete inscription would look like. After that, she walked through a thorough but easy-to-understand description of what a hash code or a checksum looks like and why it even matters.

"We are convinced that these sets of digits are themselves the result of a modern-day hash code algorithm. Whoever created these statues left the simplest yet irrefutable evidence of this theory: each of the two Latin words or phrases matches the first two encoded lines when they are passed through the Adler32 algorithm."

Here she opened up a browser window to a free online site for creating hash codes and entered in the word MYSTERIUM in all caps, selected the Adler32 algorithm from a dropdown list and hit the Process button. The resulting code "0e3602d0" was displayed on the screen.

"As you can see, this matches the first line of Latin code on this statue. Now, I understand that there may be some skepticism on the part of those listening and watching, but I can assure you that every single line checks out exactly the same."

Here she took the phrases and entered in the other five one at a time and compared the results with the corresponding lines.

"To the Vatican, I would like to announce that we have solved two-thirds of the encoded messages beyond question. We are asking for two-thirds of the bounty to be paid by Bitcoin to the following address before we go public with any other information about the third lines."

A long string of letters and numbers was displayed on the screen.

"Alex?"

Before Alex took the floor, he looked around the room; half of the media were on their phones calling or texting their companies. The other half were leaning forward.

"Thank you, Margot. As promised, she will now take questions for a few minutes before we conclude this conference."

Hands shot up and voices rang out. Alex picked out someone near the front, a woman from one of the local Fox affiliates.

"Just to be clear, are you saying that all of this has been one elaborate hoax?" she asked.

"I'm not saying that at all. Someone put a lot of time, money and effort to create the statues. The fact that they went to all this trouble indicates that whoever did it is very serious about having their message heard by the world."

Alex pointed to a man in a Harris Tweed coat midway back.

"Margot, John O'Donald with the BBC. A question and then a follow-up if I may. If what you are suggesting is indeed true, do you have any idea who is behind the statues?"

"Our group has a theory, but we do not plan to release that until the Vatican has shown good faith by paying out a portion of the bounty."

"Fair enough," he said. "You've given us an impressive amount of research which I'm certain will be reviewed thoroughly by people more qualified than myself. That being said, I'm sure among the people watching there are some who will be asking if this is all the evidence you have. Someone will no doubt find a reason to dispute what you have said. Do you have any further evidence that the statues are indeed contemporary other than this hash or algorithm you spoke about?"

"That's a great question. To recap, we have reasonable evidence that the statues could not have been discovered in the place the Vatican indicated. Second, we have an eyewitness who saw a group of men removing what she was certain looked to be the same statue as one of those presented publicly. Third, we have satellite imaging which documents the absence, presence and then removal of something in the same location. Fourth, we have a six-for-six perfect match on the hash codes themselves. For those lines to be created any time prior to the mid 1990s and somehow match an as-yet-to-be created mathematical algorithm using a machine known as a computer which also had not yet been invented matches the probability that you and I will both take our tea on Jupiter this evening."

The group roared with laughter at that, including John himself.

"But I can see where that might not convince some people. For the pure skeptics who believe in infinitesimal probabilities actually occurring, we have other items which lend proof to the fact that these statues are a contemporary creation. I will share one of those with you. When we examined the photographs of the underside of the statues, we found that two of the sculptures have indicia of modern marble cutting tools. Specifically, on two of the bases, there are markings that correlate to the type of toothed saw blades which are used in many quarry operations. We were not going to share this unless necessary, as we saw it as a possible fraud detection tool for antiquities experts. These two photos show a distinctive line which, when magnified as much as we could do with the photos provided by the Vatican, match the markings left by marble cutting bandsaw blades. Two explanations for this is that either the creators of the statues did not think they would be noticed, or they left the markings there as a proof to be discovered. Our group leans toward the latter."

The room had gotten quiet again. In her hotel room, Tina realized that this girl and her friends were scary good.

Someone from CNN asked, "Do you think the Vatican will take you up on your demand for payment of two-thirds of the bounty?"

"We believe the Vatican has no choice but to do so. The whole world is watching, and the Vatican still would like to know what the message of the statues is, which someone spent all this effort to make known. That it is of vital importance to the Catholic Church is evident by the fact that they were given carte blanche access to the statues. Someone must care very much about the Catholic Church. I have no doubt that as we speak, there are plenty of people who are running programs to try and decode the last line of text on each statue. I'm just as certain that the chances of guessing the message of the last three lines is more remote than tea on Jupiter, at least during our lifetime with our existing computer capabilities."

They followed up by asking, "Is this simply about the money for you and your group?"

"No, it isn't. But the Vatican made a promise, and our group believes that people should be held accountable. That's a good thing, right?"

Tina noted the laughing tone in the young lady's voice, but the eyes remained steady and serious. There was more to who this group was, even if she could not know what all they had done. It was at that point that she made the decision to work with these people for the next stage of the operation.

Alex looked at his watch and said, "I believe we have time for a couple more questions. Cathy with Global News, let's take yours first and then Chandra with United American News."

"Thank you. Margot, I am having a hard time overcoming the facts you have presented. You make a very good case. In a court of law, however, a good lawyer would attempt to discredit your star witness with regards to seeing a statue late at night. Maybe her eyesight is not so good, or maybe she confused a work crew removing a fallen tree in the dark. I'm playing devil's advocate here, but you understand what I'm saying."

"I do," said Margot. "I can see where a reasonable person might question the memory, vision or cognitive abilities of a retiree." It was spoken with a bit of dry humor. "Really, if you want far-fetched, try running the gematria on those Latin phrases. But, in all fairness to your question, a reasonable person might have the same doubts of most any person given the circumstances and the claims. I might do the same—if I had not seen her photos."

At that statement, a fair number of people across Italy gasped right along with the reporter. There were photos? More than a few high-ranking priests would be confessing to each other later in the day the sin of swearing after hearing that.

"You remember that the reason she was in the park at all was because of her interest in night photography. Whereas we are used to standard daytime or flash photography, night photography relies only on the available light after sundown. She was gracious enough to share some of her work, and her skill is well above a novice. She had a small lightweight tripod, which she carries with her on these excursions. She was able to shoot several good-quality photos in which a truck with a boom can be seen lifting what is unmistakably a statue from ground level up to about a forty-five-degree angle. In one of the photos, there are markings on the base which a bit of image enhancement software reveals to be similar in structure to the writing on the Vatican's statues. It was after shooting the photos that she thought of offering to document the work closer up."

"Follow-up, if I may," Cathy said. "Are there any people who are recognizable in the photos?"

"Not to us. These are long exposures, so the movement of some of the people blurs their image beyond recognition. There are a few men—they appear to all be men—who are standing pretty still the entire time. We imagine that they would be the people in charge. Perhaps someone will be able to recognize them, but we do not plan to release the photos until we hear more from the Vatican on the bounty. Today we are prepared to share a tightly cropped image showing just the statue in one of the photos."

Here she switched to an image. For those unfamiliar with night photography, the image seemed grainy. The photographers watching were quite impressed with how much detail the pensioner had managed to capture just with the ambient light from the truck and the illumination of a handful of flashlights being played across the work area. The angle of the statue showed the base with writing just visible. On the far side of the statue one could see an arm pointing out into the night sky. The resemblance was too close to dismiss out of hand.

"Whatever you make of it, it certainly was not a fallen tree," said Margot.

"Last question, Chandra," said Alex. "I know you'll make it a good one."

"Thank you, Alex," said Chandra. "Margot, you indicated that decoding the remaining lines of text would not be easily done. Are you currently in possession of the words or phrases which make up the mysterious last three coded messages?"

"No," said Margot matter-of-factly. "But based on what we have learned so far, we hope to be very, very soon. Alex?"

"That's all we have, folks. Thank you for coming. Hopefully you have your stories. If not, you can read about it in the evening edition. We hope to have a few extras in there for you."

The room began to clear quickly. In the bustle of bodies, Cathy approached Alex and stood patiently in front of him as he shut down the laptop and began to pack it into a bag. He looked up and half-squinted at her.

"What?" he asked.

"You've been on a tear lately. First the Trantwa Holdings articles and now this. Do you ever sleep?"

"I can sleep when I'm dead," Alex said with a smile.

Cathy reached out and touched his arm. "Don't say that," she said, suddenly becoming serious.

Alex stopped smiling and looked at her.

"What's the matter?" he asked.

"I've heard a few rumors here and there that you've made some pretty powerful people mad. Alex, if what I'm hearing is true, they really do want you dead."

Alex studied her carefully. He did not tell her that in the past week, a car had almost successfully run him over as he walked to lunch. Someone had shouted a warning, allowing him to dive to the side in time. He thought he had caught just a glimpse of red hair as the driver roared off in the distance.

Instead, he said, "I know. A prophet told me the same thing some time ago."

She pulled her hand off his arm. "Don't make fun of me, Alex!"

"I'm not. He really told me. He had a dream: well, several actually. It scared me. But it also got me on the right track so that now, at least, I'm not afraid to die whenever it does happen." He looked at her again and said, "I also know that I'm doing what I have to do, what I was made to do, exposing this corruption."

Cathy looked up at him with her vibrant dark eyes. "Alex, I never told you this, but I want to say it now. You're the reason I'm doing what I'm doing. We had to read newspapers back in prep school for our world events class. You had just started your career here at the paper. Your writing inspired me to look beyond my local community. It made me want to help other people to learn more the way you did. Throughout my journalism degree, I kept reading your stories. You've...changed—in a good way, I mean. What was it, Alex?"

Alex felt her hand on his arm again.

"I got tired of having my soul rot from the inside out being a mouthpiece for someone else's words. Oh, and I don't like being bullied." He sighed. "There's more to it than that. It's a long story. If you would like, I'll tell it to you over coffee or a meal sometime."

She squeezed his arm gently and let go. "I'd like that," she said. "Soon."

Chapter 67

A continent away, Tina shut off the TV with the remote. She repeated to herself what she had heard the young woman say: "We don't have the last lines, but we hope to very, very soon—based on our research." She bit her lip. The young lady had posted three different email addresses, probably new ones created just for this project, that people could use to reach them. She also had included a public encryption key in order to allow communications to them to be encrypted.

Pietro and the rest of the team had ceded the decision-making on this to her based on her judgment from the field of those who found the secret to the coding, in case there were multiple individuals or groups. She opened up her computer and logged into one of her own email accounts. After typing in one of the addresses, she began to write.

To the 1329 Collective:

Congratulations. We are impressed. Your speed of discovery is above par. The press conference was handled with excellence.

We would like to make some suggestions which we hope you will see the wisdom in following to the letter or with minimal changes.

Wait three days from today and then announce a press conference to be held three days later.

Note that this is to coincide with the birthday of the Pope the next day and that the announcement is being made to honor and celebrate his legacy.

Announce that at this press conference, you will make public the complete, decoded message from each statue.

Emphasize that the answer to the riddles will bring peace and healing to many people around the world.

After you have done these things and the press conference is made public, you will receive more information from us.

To show that we are acting in good faith, have a look

at the satellite photos over the past few weeks and months at these locations:

(Here Tina inserted the GPS coordinates for the hiding places of the other two statues).

Tina used the public encryption key Margot had shared to encrypt the email. It was as secure as she could make it. Then she sent the message.

Chapter 68

Chioggia, Italy

The *Ahil* was sitting high in the water. Her many cargo containers had been unloaded with precision, albeit not with the speed or care which Hijan would have managed. The first mate acting in place of the captain had called ahead and requested a temporary stevedore with the necessary skills to take over the job. The customs inspectors had busied themselves with the paperwork and then left with the exception of the one named Pagano who asked for a cursory examination of the cargo holds. Now he stood on the deck near the forward hold as the last of the containers was being removed.

When the crane operator had cleared the hold with the exception of the final two, which were set apart from the rest, Pagano called up to him to pick them up slowly and to be extremely careful with them. The crane operator acknowledged and set about attaching to the first container. When it was in his grasp, he put the winch in a lower gear and gradually eased the container up from the floor of the hold. Two flatbed semis had been moved into place alongside the ship. He swung the container out and over the edge of the ship and rotated the container until it was lined up with the trailer. After lowering it onto the trailer, he watched as that semi immediately moved forward and allowed the second to shift into its place. The second container was offloaded similarly.

He looked down at the customs inspector, who gave him a wave and then made for the gangplank. He watched as the inspector made his way to one of the trucks and spoke to one of the drivers. Then the inspector got into a car and led the trucks away. The crane operator shook his head in disgust as he retracted the boom and began the shutdown procedure. No doubt someone was going to have to endure an annoying inspection by the port authority.

The stevedore would have been surprised to see the customs inspector lead the trucks through a maze of other vehicles coming and going. With his official car in the lead and an occasional wave or nod to the staff in the inspection facilities or gatehouses, Pagano guided the semis out of the port without any interference. His job was simple, and it paid handsomely considering the short amount of time involved in handling the safe movement of various cargo containers. He never asked what was in the containers. He did not care to know. It was better that way and probably safer.

When they reached the destination, he honked twice and waved his hand out the window. The lead semi answered with a flash of headlights. Then Pagano drove around the corner to head back to the docks. At €5,000 per container which he shielded from prying eyes, he had just made another €10,000.

The lead semi-trailer slowly swung into the recesses of the open warehouse bay. After adjusting from the bright morning sun to the gloom of the warehouse, the driver saw one of the onshore crew directing him forward to the opposite end where an exit door was shut. The second semi pulled into the warehouse and was parked near the rear of the first. A passenger vehicle pulled into the warehouse and drove off to the side. Then the bay door was shut.

A passenger from the front of the SUV got out and opened the rear door. Giacobbe stepped out and strode across the warehouse floor. The leather soles on his shoes barely made a noise as he approached the six warehouse crew and the two truck drivers with his bodyguard and driver.

"Is everything ready?"

The foreman nodded. He pointed to several large cattle troughs filled with water along with tables stacked with towels and an assortment of inexpensive hospital gowns.

"All right then. Let's get to work." Giacobbe motioned to the containers. "Bring the stairs and open them up."

Two men each rolled portable stairway platforms the width of the containers and set them in place at the doorways. The foreman and Giacobbe mounted the stairs. The foreman pulled out an envelope from his pocket and extracted a key, which he inserted into the padlock. After removing the lock, he retracted the bars holding the doors shut and slowly opened up the container. He coughed and stood back for Giacobbe to have a better look.

Giacobbe wrinkled his nose and then covered it with a perfumed handkerchief from his blazer pocket. His eyes looked over the faces and bodies of the young girls as he assessed the overall welfare of his cargo. They stunk and would have to be cleaned up, but there was no stench of death or decay. That was good. No one paid for a dead one except him. The Don had made clear that since the choice of transport was up to Giacobbe, all the risk and loss were his to bear.

He turned and looked down at one of the men. "Get started with this lot." Then to the foreman he said, "Let's inspect the next container."

While they made their way to the second container, four of the men moved into the first. The female guardian for that container barked a few syllables in a Chinese dialect. The girls, some of whom were sleeping, sat up and placed their backs to the wall of the container. She then began unlocking the chains which bound them and instructed them to stand and face the doors once they were able.

The men motioned them to follow them down the stairs and across the short distance to the cattle troughs.

"Tell them to strip and bathe," one of them said to the guardian. She gave the order in Chinese. Several of the girls looked down in shame, but the guardian simply walked to the front of the line and began undressing herself. She then got into one of the troughs and began washing with the soap and rag which was on the table next to it. After that, it was not a problem other than keeping the girls from overcrowding the makeshift tubs. A community bath was not, after all, uncommon for them.

The men handed out soap and rags as necessary. They also distributed towels to those who were finished. Then they did their best to match sizes for the simple cloth gowns with each of the girls.

At the other end of the warehouse, the same scene was being repeated. Giacobbe walked through the group, pausing occasionally to check a face or back for bruising or any other visible ailment.

"How do you keep them calm throughout the voyage?" he asked one of the guardians.

"I sing to them and tell them stories. And I remind them that they are being given a great opportunity in a new country. They are going to be mothers and wives and be given good jobs. If they are lucky, their families will be able to join them in the future." She looked at Giacobbe with her dark eyes and added, "They believe me. After a few days they stop crying."

"Stone cold," thought Giacobbe to himself. He admired the quality in a man but found it distasteful in a woman. Still, he had to appreciate her position. From what he had learned, the families of these guardians lived or died depending upon their success on each voyage. The ones who failed were made to watch as their family members paid for their mistakes. She was doing what she thought was best for those she loved, and who could stand up to the mighty system of the Chinese Communist Party?

Within an hour, all of the girls had been bathed and clothed. They were given water and a light snack, which kept them busy. The foreman had pointed out the toilets in the corner to the guardians. As would be expected, a steady stream of traffic continued to and from them.

Giacobbe pulled his phone from his pocket. He had it set to silent while they had been busy. As he prepared to call the buyers and have them come to inspect and pick up their consignments, he noticed a text message from Father Donati. He had half forgotten about the press conference. Perhaps it was news from him. He pressed the button to read the text. A frown came across his face and his brow furrowed the more he read. A group had claimed to decipher part of the encoded text. This proved, according to them, that the statues were forgeries or recently created works of art. The Vatican was reviewing all of the evidence they had presented. There was much confusion currently, but the general mood in Rome had turned from elation to caution with panic peering around the corner.

Giacobbe swore. How could this be? It did not make any sense. He looked up and saw again the two groups of girls. He had work to finish. He would find out more later. Before he made the calls to the representatives of the buyers, he sent one quick text message to Father Donati. It read simply, "Find Pietro. Will talk soon." It was the last time they would communicate.

Within the next hour, a caravan of semi-trailers and limousines entered the confines of the warehouse. Giacobbe greeted each of the representatives with an offer of coffee or wine. It was a beautiful day outside, and everyone seemed to be in a cheerful mood. There was one woman leading one group and two men each leading the other two groups along with their assorted drivers and helpers.

"As you can see, your shipment has arrived safely and in very good condition," said Giacobbe gesturing with his hand to the girls. "They have been bathed and are ready for your selection." Nodding to the woman he added, "The highest bidder does, of course, have the right to first choice. I invited you gentlemen here early so that you can see the quality of the product should you desire to up your price for future shipments."

"One question, if I may," said the man from the laboratory network.

Giacobbe nodded.

"Have they all been tested for disease? In our last shipment, we had several units which were riddle with STDs and some deficiencies in the blood quality."

"All of them have been tested prior to shipment here, but in the future, if you wish to make top bid, you would be welcome to run a quick test on each unit you choose. Now, if we may continue..." Giacobbe motioned with his arm for the group to approach the girls.

The buyers began to move toward the girls and were ready to commence business when the lights in the warehouse suddenly went out. There was a general commotion as the Chinese girls uttered exclamations. Giacobbe shouted to the foreman to find out what was going on.

"Everyone remain calm," he said loudly. "It may be a breaker. We'll have it checked out shortly."

Lights began to shine in the darkness as Giacobbe's workers and the buyers turned on their cell phone flashlights. After checking, the foreman reported that the electrical panel was all in order. "It may be that a transformer has gone down in this part of the city. It happens from time to time."

"I cannot wait, Mr. Manco," said the woman with a firm tone. She represented the Castle. "I need to make my selections as soon as possible to stay on the timetable at the border crossings."

Giacobbe looked at the foreman, who simply shrugged. They had not planned on a power outage and did not have an available standby generator.

"Open the two bay doors again," said Giacobbe. "We'll use the natural light. It should be sufficient for your purposes, yes?" he looked at the woman.

"Quite so," she answered.

The foreman motioned to three of the other workers. They followed him to the bay doors with their phones illuminating the way. Chains rattled and clacked as the doors were slowly hoisted. The sudden brightness of the outside caused those inside to squint as they instinctively turned toward the light.

There was a sudden shout and then the loud crack of a gunshot. Before anyone could react, men dressed in body armor and carrying assault rifles raced through the opening. Giacobbe was stunned as he took in the sight. His foreman lay still on the floor, a pistol by his body.

"Everybody on the ground now!" shouted a burly policeman. "Now! On the ground! Do as I say! Anyone attempting to flee or resist will be shot! Place your cell phones on the ground away from your body and do not reach for them again."

Giacobbe looked around frantically. The buyers were doing the same. But uniformed figures kept streaming through the door. There looked to be about thirty in total. Fighting them would be suicide. Escaping would be impossible. Still, one of the bodyguards for the laboratory's buyer attempted to pull out his weapon. He was cut down before he could even bring it level. These were not the local police, and they meant business.

Slowly and carefully, Giacobbe raised his hands and dropped to his knees. Police ran past him into the depths of the warehouse, clearing it and taking up positions. He leaned forward and hesitated. The warehouse floor was dirty.

A boot placed squarely on his buttocks shoved him down and forced him to ruin his favorite jacket. He carefully placed his cell phone on the ground and pushed it aside as he lowered his face to the bare concrete. It stank of diesel.

His eyes focused on the face of the lady from the Castle who lay on the floor near him. Her expression was a mask of scorn and fury. "You're dead, Manco. Do you hear me?"

"No talking!" shouted one of the officers as he gave the lady a firm kick.

Giacobbe turned his face away from her to the other side and closed his eyes. Boots echoed across the floor amidst the confused voices of the young girls. Then strong hands were lifting him from the concrete and jerking his arms behind him. While his hands were being tightly cuffed, he vaguely noticed that the officer in front of him was telling him that he was under arrest for human trafficking. As he was marched out of the warehouse, he glanced back one last time. One of the little girls was sitting on the floor with her arms wrapped around her knees, rocking back and forth. She was thousands of kilometers from home, alone and very likely missing her family, but she was free. Now Giacobbe and the rest of his party would get to experience the chains.

Chapter 69

Father Donati was worried. Giacobbe had told him that he had business up in the north of the country which was urgent and that he would not be back for a few days. But he knew the importance of this project. It was not like him to not respond to repeated text messages or voicemail.

"Find Pietro," he had instructed. But Pietro was nowhere to be found. The warehouse was locked and, upon inspection, empty. The area where Pietro normally worked was clean. On the table was a handwritten note which read, "To Father Donati. After hearing the news, I am confused. These people claim that the statues are new. But my parents were searching for them for many years before I was born. I am going to look for some answers. Pietro."

A visit to Pietro's apartment had turned up nothing. The landlord acquiesced to Father Donati's request to be let in under the assurance that he was checking in on one of his flock who had been depressed. One look around at the spartan surroundings quickly answered the question that Pietro was not there. There was food in the refrigerator but no dirty dishes. Everything was in order. But given that Pietro did not seem to own many possessions, he was not surprised to find the apartment so bare.

In the midst of his search for Pietro, Father Axelrod had called demanding answers. People higher up were pressing him. Father Donati had given a complete recounting of everything. Nothing made sense. The leadership was trying to determine whether or not the statues were genuine antiques at all. Maybe they were, but perhaps someone had gained access to them in the past and had added the encoded portions. That seemed to be the most logical answer. It was the way the Vatican was going to initially respond in a tersely worded release.

There was a growing unease in Father Donati's mind. He was a man of action and planning combined, but he felt himself being drawn inexorably into deeper waters. There was no little irony in the fact that he sought no aid from a Higher Power. Instead, as he returned to the parish manor, he told himself that the best course of action was to continue his daily routine and wait to hear from Giacobbe and to keep trying to reach Pietro by phone.

Chapter 70

Unknown Location

Serious read the email from the anonymous sender. It had taken a bit to find it. The inbox of each of the three email accounts was chock full of an array of messages. Some offered congratulations. Others expressed jealousy or outright hostility, calling the group a bunch of liars. A small set of messages had invisible tracking images embedded in them. These were designed to provide as much of the location of the person reading them as could be determined. Serious was using an email client with full text mode and noted their existence but did not worry about them.

Eventually, the letter from Tina was opened. Serious read it with interest. It seemed that they were on the right track. If someone were truly playing the Vatican, they could be using anyone else in the process. There was only one way to tell and that was to move forward. There was no realistic chance of decoding the Adler32 hash codes without knowing what the original words or phrases were. Much prayer and research through many years had led to this point.

The GPS coordinates did indeed prove to be interesting. Each location bore the same evidence of recent excavation of sorts. One could tell that something had been removed. Backing up just a few more weeks or months, it was also apparent that something had been placed in each spot.

The group would meet in a couple of hours. Serious had no doubt that they would all be in agreement to proceed as requested. That left some time to pray and seek for wisdom and direction.

Chapter 71

For the next seventy-two hours, the news cycle was dominated by the announcement from the press conference. The allegation that the Vatican was involved in the removal of antiquities outside of Rome or Vatican City was a source of irritation to the leadership. There were multiple requests for interviews. Then there was the whole disputation on whether the statues were, in fact, old enough to be antique, much less something which would fall under the definition of classical antiquities. Newspapers and magazines all over the world printed extra copies to meet the demand. Talking heads on television moderated civil debates or, at times, outright verbal altercations between experts with strong opinions on both sides. The media conglomerates did not really care what the truth about the statues was because the controversy itself was generating an immense amount of revenue from the interest.

The group known as the 1329 Collective suddenly appeared on every form of social media available—in multiple forms. They quickly gained rapturous followings until Alex was asked to post a statement that they were, in fact, not on social media in any form. Still, there were hangers on who were convinced that they were receiving hourly messages and posts from the greatest hackers on the planet.

Partly due to the fact that the Vatican had no legitimate answer for how the decoding of the six lines of letters and numbers matched what had been announced and in no small part due to the continued questioning by the press if they had followed through with Margot's request, the Vatican bank released payment of €6,666,666,66 to the Bitcoin address Margot had provided. If anyone at the bank saw any humor in sending a sum equivalent to an unholy trinity of the beast's mark in Revelation, they did not choose to make it public.

The arrival of the money changed the dynamic for the 1329 Collective. Serious waited to see if anyone else would make recommendations first and was not disappointed. Burfer suggested a media buy in major markets. If everyone agreed, it would cost probably close to $100,000 US, but the impact would be greater. The group agreed, and three of them set about making inquiries and seeking commitments from the advertising agencies which controlled the properties they were seeking.

After three days, Alex's paper printed a story with his byline which stated that 1329 Collective had broken the code for the remaining three lines. With the birthday of His Holiness approaching so closely, they were deferring an announcement until the day before in order to honor his office and the legacy of the Catholic Church. They had assured Alex in the strongest of terms that the final lines contained a message that would bring hope and healing to people all over the world.

This generated another round of media coverage, the kind where the experts gave their opinions at length on something about which they had no factual knowledge. It did not matter. People were eager for any scrap of information, any clue. Even the Vatican was in a holding pattern. They had about thirty different press releases prepared based on every conceivable angle their public relations department could imagine.

When Serious checked the email accounts after the story ran, there was a second encrypted message from the anonymous sender. It was long and detailed. There were photos. There was a brief backstory. Then there were three individual lines of text. Serious read them and began to weep uncontrollably.

Chapter 72

The day before the Pope's birthday is always a busy time. Pilgrims come from all around the world to celebrate. Hotels are filled to capacity. The tourism, dining and hospitality businesses all rejoice with heartfelt gratitude.

The crowds were abuzz because of the forthcoming announcement about the great statues. The mystery was going to be revealed. Every television was tuned to a news channel when 6 p.m. approached.

The American newspaper had printed a notice the day before that in lieu of a live press event, 1329 Collective would be releasing a video. In the digital age, it made just as much sense. The Internet had in many ways leveled the playing field and decimated the ability of media conglomerates to tightly control the narrative in the same way they had done prior to its global availability. The video would be livestreamed simultaneously on about seven different social media platforms. In deference to the mainstream media, the group had created twenty different virtual servers around the globe running streaming software. Media companies were contacted and invited to connect to these private servers to receive a high-quality feed, which they could broadcast if they chose. The article also noted that the video would be streamed live in Times Square, London, Paris, Tokyo, Hong Kong, Mexico City and a host of other large and medium-sized cities. After seeing the content of the message, the group had opted to increase their ad buy. It was, after all, only fitting that the Vatican's money should be used to publish the message as far and as wide as possible.

Seven people had labored over the content and format of the video. A couple of them were quite skilled at editing software. In the end, it was a group effort that was sprinkled with the excellence and eclectic touches of each of the members.

At precisely noon United States Eastern Standard Time, six p.m. local time in Italy, a global decibel meter would have recorded a drop in the noise levels around the world. Traffic came to a halt around the large electronic billboards. Office workers looking over their shoulders for their bosses realized that they were in their offices with their own doors closed. Bookies bit their nails waiting to see if the odds they had given on possible outcomes were going to make or lose them money. In his private apartment, the Pope sat in a plush chair facing a large screen. The poorest families in the slums of Central and

South America gathered around cell phones.

The presentation began with a video of the Pope smiling and greeting crowds. The music of "Happy Birthday" faded in. The sound of children's voices swelled. Various angles and levels of zooming in on the face of the Pope flashed on the screen.

A male voice with a South African-tinged accent began to speak.

"Two thousand years ago, the most consequential man to ever live walked upon this Earth. What started with a small handful of devoted followers who were persecuted, sometimes to the point of death, has grown into a worldwide movement."

Accompanied by videos of large crowds of churches, Billy Graham crusades, pilgrims in Saint Peter's Square and other such footage, the voice continued.

"Only someone with divine insight could have foreseen such incredible growth. The followers of Jesus Christ have brought comfort and hope through their consistent commitment to the truth that all people are created in the image of God, male or female, brown, black, white, yellow, old, young, born or unborn. They have continued to suffer untold persecution at the hands of political regimes that do not acknowledge the existence of God or the right to worship freely as each person chooses."

The screen displayed footage of hospitals, leper colonies, the Red-Light District and other images as the narrator kept speaking.

"The man named Jesus Christ was a healer, a man who showed compassion on multitudes. He healed lepers. He allowed prostitutes to touch Him with fearful and tear-stained hands. He held children and blessed them. He made time for everyone. He showed no favoritism. He who made all people equal treated them that way.

"This leader of love had His life ended by a system of religion that was opposed to His message and was jealous of His power. If we can be certain of one thing, He did not live and die so that people would create another system of power which would lead to oppression or injustice."

The screen changed to display the statues from numerous angles: close up on their features, far away and zoomed in on the inscriptions.

"The statues unveiled have a clear message and a hidden one. The first line of each statue is a direct quote from the Bible in the Book of Revelation chapter seventeen. In it, an angel appeared to the Apostle John and declared that he would show John the punishment that was coming upon the great whore. This prostitute was dressed in scarlet and had a name written on her forehead which is represented on these statues: MYSTERY, BABYLON THE GREAT, THE MOTHER OF FORNICATIONS. This woman is a city that rules over the kings of the earth. All the world and kings of the earth have freely enjoyed her vile sins.

"The statues then tell us that instead of keeping things a mystery, they bring an end to the mysteries. To Babylon which has been so great, there is a pronouncement of 'Woe! Woe! Woe!' Because it is pronounced three times, one for each member of the Holy Trinity, the matter has been settled by Father, Son and Holy Spirit and is unchangeable. The final statue that memorialized the Mother of Adulteries promises that she will experience the beginning of birth pains and deep sorrow."

The screen began to display headlines of scandal and fraud, video clips of various defrocked and disgraced leaders.

"The Man who forgave His enemies while hanging upon a cross could be very stern. In one instance, he actually took up a whip and drove out moneychangers from the temple and those who bought and sold animals. As He overturned their tables, He said that God's house was to be called a house of prayer for all nations, but the leaders had instead turned it into a den of thieves."

The headlines continued to change across the screen. They included the reports and statistics of human trafficking and sexual exploitation of children.

"He also gave one of the sternest warnings when He said that if anyone, and He gave no exceptions to this based on status of wealth, religion or popularity, if anyone were to offend a child or cause them to stumble, it would be better for that man if he had a millstone hung around his neck and that he be cast into the deepest part of the sea."

"Thieves, adulterers, predators and murderers have established themselves in positions of power throughout history under the guise of piety and religion, not just in Christian churches. It's the result of corrupt human nature. Because of this, the weak and the powerless cry and groan under their oppression. They see the injustice but can do nothing against religious systems which control the very fabric of their society and extend into every facet of power; the police, judges, lawmakers, kings and queens and even local church leaders all pay homage to the system that feeds them."

"Today, thanks to the message of these statues, we offer a message of healing to you who have been abused, robbed, molested, trafficked and exploited under the guise and cover of a cross which stands in direct opposition to how you have been treated. The background and provenance of the statues will be proven later. We have released that to the reporter Alex Ingram to disseminate. For now, we give you the final three messages hidden in the statues."

The screen flickered with digital effects. The first code appeared in large letters. It transformed from the Roman numerals and letters into regular digits and letters. Then it spun and twisted, the letters dropping in like the reels on the payline of a large slot machine. When it was finished, the text displayed was:

THESINSOFTHEVATICAN.COM

That slowly moved to the top of the screen as the second inscription began its transformation process. In the middle of the screen appeared this text:

THEMONEYOFTHEVATICAN.COM

Before it had moved to its location under the first line, the third cipher was already in motion. When it was finished, the screen displayed this:

THEGUILTYPRIESTS.COM

The narrator's voice began again. "Some will question how this can be a promised message of hope and healing. Each of these sites is filled with information which, if pursued, will lead to the exposure of wickedness, injustice, exploitation, murder, fraud, theft and a host of other lawless acts, all done under the cover of religion. For those who believe in justice, the only way to gain peace is to punish the guilty. For those who have been victimized, the path to healing begins when the guilty are punished. Each of these websites is hosted on multiple servers to prevent their being removed by those in power who are guilty. The material on them is extensive, detailed and, in most cases, very easy to understand. The verification for the data comes from the records of the Vatican itself. While the originals may be destroyed in the coming hours, days or weeks, rest assured: they are stored digitally in safekeeping all over the globe."

The screen changed to a picture of a millstone.

"To those who are guilty, you already know who you are. If you choose to forego the legal process and save the taxpayers in your respective countries the burden of trials and attempt to escape the justice of men, make your peace with Almighty God, for you will certainly face His justice."

The screen changed again to a photo of all three statues standing on display side by side. In the background, the strains of Happy Birthday could be heard playing faintly with the accompanying voices of children. The voice of the narrator came one last time and spoke as the image slowly morphed to a cross against a field of black, which gradually changed to bright white.

"We wish a happy birthday to every victim of the religious system which has destroyed your lives. May this day be the beginning of hope, peace and healing to you, a true rebirth. May this icon and image come to truly represent the deliverance and freedom it was intended to from the beginning."

Fifteen minutes from start to finish. Fifteen minutes to conclude years of investigative work. Fifteen minutes to shine the spotlight on deep corruption. Fifteen minutes to derail the political aspirations of power-hungry men. Fifteen minutes to rip apart the prison gates.

The world was collectively stunned. In a house in the Midwest, a housewife slumped to the floor beside her sofa and began weeping. A former altar boy turned grown businessman clenched his fists until his knuckles turned white. Sighs, groans, weeping, venting of anger, they all swirled into the atmosphere of eternity and added to the weight of the woes which had been pronounced upon those who had worn the cloth of the shepherd while feasting upon the flock like a pack of wolves.

The next thing that happened was that a few million people logged into the websites and began to explore what was displayed for all to see. The first site was a detailed list of corrupt practices going back at least fifty years. There were names of persons involved, dates, photos, quotes and all sorts of imaginable evidence which had been catalogued methodically.

The second site detailed the expenditures which the Vatican bank had made over the past two hundred years. A cursory examination of those books was enough to convince the reader that this was not going to be a list of purchases of communion cups and robes. Lavish hotels, private jets, entertainment purchases of every sort, the most expensive of foods, and other unnecessary items were detailed. Then there were the lists of payoffs to victims of assault and abuse. There were lists of fraud, waste and embezzlement. Billions and billions of dollars were meticulously documented. The optics of asking for donations in the light of all of this was going to be extremely difficult.

The final site had the names of tens of thousands of priests along with the allegations the Vatican had received against each of them. There were scanned pages of handwritten notes by leaders at all levels in which their personal recommendations were noted. The reality of how much all levels of leadership knew about the abuse and sexual exploitation of every age group of both male and female members was staggering. There was also a complete archive of photographs of groups of priests, presumably at private parties, engaged in all sorts of behavior and in all manner of dress.

Each site was professionally designed so that a person visiting could explore easily. Social media buttons were available to share any content with dozens, hundreds or potentially millions of a person's followers. Prominent on each site was a "Download all content for archive" link. Within the first hour, there were over a million downloads, not a few which came from the IP address space reserved for the Vatican.

Although the leadership desperately attempted to get the sites shut down immediately, there were too many servers spread across multiple countries. The domains themselves were vulnerable to seizure by a friendly superpower, theoretically, but the damage was done. The technical advisors shook their heads and told the leadership that there was no way to put the genie back into the bottle on this one.

It was going to be a very long night for many people and a long road ahead for victims, lawyers and investigators.

Chapter 73

Italy

Father Donati turned off the television and sat in silence. He still had heard nothing from Giacobbe. He wondered if he had somehow gotten wind of what was going down and had managed to save his own hide by fleeing the country. He had no way of knowing that at that very moment, one Giacobbe Manco was dressed in prison garb and was housed eight to a cell in an overcrowded jail as he awaited trial, or that he was doing his best to remain tight-lipped about the charges against him in order to avoid the fate which has met many child abusers or human traffickers in the prison population.

He did not really expect a call from Father Axelrod or Father Sopelli. They had their own problems to worry about. This was out of his hands; it was out of all of their hands. He could not remember a time in history that the church had faced such a momentous hurdle. Maybe it was a wall, or maybe it was really a dead end.

There was a knock at the door of the parish. More out of habit than any real interest, he rose to answer it. In front of him stood Pietro, carrying a box in his arms. It made sense, he supposed.

"Come in, Pietro," he said. "Or is that really your name at all?"

"You may call me Pietro," he answered.

He showed him into the sitting room and motioned to a chair. Pietro sat with the box on his lap. It appeared to be heavy.

"Congratulations! You fooled me. You fooled us all. I'm not sure what you hope to accomplish with this, but I have to admire your level of play-acting."

Pietro sat quietly. He was almost the same as before, but somehow, he no longer looked like a peasant. The eyes were much more intense.

"You came here for a reason. You have something to say, no doubt. Say it."

Pietro opened the lid of the box and tilted it forward. He pulled out a heavy piece of marble covered with a cloth and place it on the table separating them. Without a word, he pinched the cloth at the top and carefully withdrew it, revealing the figure underneath.

Father Donati looked at it. In spite of the circumstances, he still found

278

himself almost breathless at the artistic quality. The piece was standing vertically and depicted a man half in and half out of water. This figure was about half the height of the total piece. There was a chain around the man's neck leading to a millstone, which he was trying to pull out of the water. The hands and muscles were straining. There was a look of terror on the man's face, a face Father Donati recognized. It was his own.

Immediately behind the figure of the man was the face of a young child, a girl. She looked innocent except for her tears, which were flowing down her face and filling the turbulent sea. Other than her tears, her face was tranquil. It took a couple of minutes. A flicker passed through Father Donati's eyes.

"You do recognize her, then," said Pietro.

"The little girl with the yellow coat," said Father Donati. A cloud passed over his face.

Pietro sat silently.

"So that's what this is about? This is all about one child? You would destroy an entire organization over one man's sins?"

Pietro said, "Her name was Davina Colletti."

"Yes, Davina. I remember her well."

"Give me one reason at all why I should not make you atone for her right now," said Pietro quietly. There was something in his voice which made it clear that it was not a threat.

So Father Donati answered him. He gave him the only reason that Pietro would have accepted. As Pietro rose and turned to go, pointing to the statue, he said, "I made this for you. Perhaps you will find it to be an altar of stone."

He left Father Donati sitting in his chair staring at the statuette. As he made his way along the streets, he called Tina.

"Tina, it's Nicola. Can I meet you at your hotel?"

She agreed. When he arrived a little later, she greeted him with excitement about how the operation had gone and the news reports she was already beginning to receive about its impact. Pietro did not reciprocate. Tina looked at him and asked, "What's the matter, Nicola? You look as if you've seen a ghost."

"I have," he said. "Tina, sit down."

She looked at him strangely and tilted her head at him as she took a seat.

Nicola knelt down before her and took her hand gently. Looking into her eyes, he said, "Tina, I have news I'm not sure you are ready to hear. Your sister is alive."

Chapter 74

Six weeks later
Philadelphia

The doorbell rang. Margot heard Mrs. Li say, "I will answer it." She could not hear her footsteps but knew that she had made it to the front door when she heard the locks click open.

It had been a strange ride. Mrs. Li was what she would have described a few months ago as "way out there," but getting to know her had helped Margot to see just how solid of a woman she really was. At the outset, she had provided food and shelter for a young lady who had just been traumatized. She had listened to Margot as she opened up about her experience and then, over time, her life. When Margot ran out of words, Mrs. Li sat with her in silence. When Margot burst into tears, she placed a tissue in her hand. She served Margot in dozens of ways both small and large.

As Margot began to research again, she gave her space and time. When she appeared on television at the press conference, she smiled at her and told her that she was proud of her for her accomplishments. Margot began to realize that this was what a mother was supposed to be like, and she responded in kind as she shared more and more of her life journey. Mother, mentor, friend, Mrs. Li was all of those. Margot felt like a potted flower which had just been transplanted into a garden with plenty of room to grow.

"Margot, there is someone here to see you." It was Mrs. Li's voice from the front of the house.

Who could that be? She had communicated with Cassandra and let her know that she was alive, but she was still technically in hiding. The number of people who knew where she was living could be counted on less than one hand. Curious, she walked out of the den where she had been working on her laptop and entered the formal sitting room. There sat Detective Carson. He rose as she entered the room.

"Detective Carson!" She was a bit taken aback. "It's good to see you."

"It's good to see you, too, Margot."

"What brings you here? Am I needed for a court appearance already?"

He looked uncomfortable. Margot wondered what was wrong.

"I, uh, well." He glanced at Mrs. Li. She looked him up and down and said, "I believe I will go make some coffee," and left the room.

What was going on?

"Detective Carson, is something wrong?"

"Deshawn, please." His voice softened. "I, uh, wanted to check in on you and see how you were doing."

"I'm fine?" Margot said drawing out the words into a bit of a question. Something clicked. Margot started laughing. She put her hand over her mouth.

"Deshawn Carson, did you come here to call on me?"

He looked at her sheepishly and grinned. "Well, um, yes I did."

She looked at him and smiled broadly. "I'm glad you did. Now, let's have a proper seat, and you can tell me everything that's on your heart."

Chapter 75

When Happy answered the phone a few days prior, he heard Alex's excited voice on the other end.

"Happy, you've gotta come to Philly. I've got a surprise for you."

Regardless of prodding and guessing, Alex would give him no clues what this was about. Sarah was invited to come, too. After tying up some loose ends, at Alex's direction, they each packed a few changes of clothing and headed to the big city. Happy found himself waiting in the reception area again and thought about the big changes that had taken place since he had last sat here. Alex was his brother in the faith now. He was working with a purpose, and he had been instrumental in shining the light on more than one mess of snakes.

Instead of calling them up to his office, Alex came down to the reception area and greeted both of them warmly. "I've got a taxi waiting outside. Come on with me."

"Alex, you haven't even given me the tiniest clue why we're even here."

Alex grinned at him. "You'll find out," was all that he said.

He made small talk with Sarah and Happy for a few minutes. "Stop here," he told the driver. "We'll walk the rest of the way."

When they got out, Alex started walking down the street. Happy did not have to be told where he was. They were in the old part of town where the mission used to be. Emotions ran through him in waves as they turned the corner and he saw the behemoth of a building where the old church facility once stood.

"Well?" said Alex pointing to it and smiling. "Do you like it?"

"Mister Ingram," Sarah said with a bit of ice in her tone. "I'm not sure why you've brought us here. You know this place brings my brother nothing but pain now," she said, gesturing with her hand.

Happy looked puzzled himself. "Sarah, let's not jump to conclusions. I'm sure Alex has his reasons."

Alex looked at Sarah and said, "Really? Well that's just too bad. I was really hoping that he would like his new Gospel Mission facility. Or didn't you see the name on the building yet?" he asked in a teasing tone.

Sarah opened her mouth, but no words came out. There on the building were no longer the words Trantwa Holdings. Instead, in gleaming gold letters were those other two words, Gospel Mission.

Happy just started laughing. He laughed and laughed and laughed until tears were running down his cheeks. Alex looked at Sarah. She had tears running down her cheeks, too, and her lips were quivering.

"Brother Alex, I'm sure as a reporter, you have a story to tell me about this," Happy said finally.

"I do, Happy. But why don't we step out of the weather and get inside so I can show you what's in the building."

Alex pulled a set of keys from his pocket and unlocked the front door. Flipping on the lights, he ushered the other two in. Walking from room to room, he unfolded the story. The leader of a group of people who had helped him on a recent story was apparently a praying person. In the midst of doing an exposé on Trantwa Holdings, this person had felt a strong urging to do more research on the site of the building Trantwa had built. In the course of digging, the person had uncovered a news article from well over a hundred years ago. In it, the announcement was made about the opening of a Gospel mission facility for the down and out. It was hoped that the site would be of some use in the encouragement of those who had fallen upon hard times. What had caught the eye of the person was one statement at the end. As a matter of journalistic record keeping, the author of the article had noted that the land had been given "in perpetuity" for this purpose.

Quite a bit of time was spent coaxing and begging city employees to ransack old boxes of deeds until the original deed to the property was located. In it, the grantor had given the property over for the express and sole purpose of serving as a Christian Gospel mission. The strictest of terms had been laid upon the deed. It could never be sold or bought for any other purpose. After having the city attorney review it, along with another independent legal firm, a motion was entered into the court to vacate the previous deed by Trantwa Holdings. There was no one to dispute it, as John de la Rouche had not been seen in weeks. He appeared to have fled the country. If he ever did appear, Alex told them, he would have more warrants for his arrest than any man would ever wish to face. The judge nullified the deed, which meant the ownership passed back to the previous owner.

The city was in a quandary as to how to proceed. Alex reminded them that the previous director of the mission had been given the key to the city and was therefore in good standing as the likely candidate to pick up where he had left off so many years ago.

"That is, of course, if you are willing," said Alex as he held Happy's gaze.

They had just finished the tour of the main floor and were standing in a massive conference room that could easily serve as a worship room. Happy looked back at Alex.

"Do you remember that prayer I prayed the last time I was here?" he asked.

"How could I forget, Happy? You embarrassed the daylights out of me praying out loud in public like that with your hands raised and your voice on full volume."

Happy chuckled. "Well, it seems that God has answered that prayer. He showed that He still rules in the affairs of men, and He has made a way for this to be a place of hope and healing. How could I say no?"

"Mmm-hmmm," Sarah said, shaking her head at him. "You just gonna up and leave me like that?"

"Oh, no," said Alex. "I haven't showed you your apartment upstairs yet, Sarah."

"My what?" she said.

"Your apartment. The people who built this place had living quarters on the top floor." He lowered his voice conspiratorially and leaned toward her. "Might I add that they used only the best in everything they built up there."

"You expect me to leave my petunias and rose bushes for an apartment in the city where there ain't no green stuff around?"

"Oh," said Alex, "Did I forget to mention that on the roof of this building is a fully equipped greenhouse? It seems that the previous owners felt the same way you do about plants."

Happy reached out with his finger and poked Sarah on the forearm. "The Lord's given you manna, and without you even having to ask for it, he's provided you quail. You gonna argue some more or are you gonna recognize when the cloud is ready to move to a new location?"

Sarah pursed her lips and straightened herself. "Well, I could give it a try."

"Let's go see the rest of the building," Alex said. "After that, we'll run by the city attorney's office. There are some legal documents to sign for you to take possession. Then, if nobody has any objections, I'd like to interview the new owner and his assistant. I have a story to write before this afternoon's deadline."

Chapter 76

Tropea, Italy

Nicola sat on the warm, pristine sand of a beach in Tropea. The bright sun shone on the clear turquoise water of the sea. The gentle lapping of the waves was punctuated by the occasional cry of a gull. Beside him, stretched out on a beach towel with bits of sand clinging to her auburn hair, lay Tina soaking up the rays. It was the first real break they had been able to take in several years. Nicola had suggested they go to a quiet place where they could relax and process things together.

The last few weeks had been more intense than the even the weeks prior to the unveiling of the statues. The whole team had assembled together for a debriefing with Stanley Worthington. Their after-action reports had to be written and submitted for record-keeping purposes. The usual process of returning equipment was completed.

Meanwhile, much was transpiring in the rest of the world. It had not taken long for the severity of "the most colossal scandal leak in history" to dawn on those within the ranks of the clergy. Fear had chased down the guilty like a bloodhound. The awfulness of Moses' promise had been realized too late: "Be sure your sin will find you out." Like an otherworldly, ravenous beast had been loosed upon them, the predators became the prey, the hunters became the hunted.

Throughout history, the system of the Catholic Church had protected abusers either from discovery or from consequence. Initially, there was a sense of expectation that this would happen again. But the storm that had come upon them was not blowing over. Too many people were coming forward and pointing to names on the lists. Too many people outside the church in positions of power were unable or unwilling to help diffuse the scandal because of the connection of their own crimes which, if they were not outright listed by name, could be connected to them with minimal investigation. In short, no one wanted to provide cover for the harlot with whom they had all enjoyed so much for so long. She was cast out to fend for herself.

What happened next became known popularly as "suicide weekend." An astonishing number of priests and leaders decided that they indeed did not want to face their accusers in a court of law and took the coward's way out.

And most of them were legitimately classified as suicides. No small number of priests whose names were on "the rolls of the damned," as it came to be called, were visited by former parishioners long forgotten but whose scarred memories would never forget them. When word of possible vigilante justice began to spread, those on the list found that they were no longer safe even to walk down the street. Some attempted to flee but were caught. Most turned themselves in, hoping to secure a reduced sentence.

Nicola had read an article which stated that one local priest had committed suicide in a most unusual manner. A body had been found in a local lake, partially submerged. When the police investigated, they found that the corpse was attached to a heavy piece of marble by a stout rope. Upon extraction of the body, the object was discovered to be a statuette. Even more bizarre was that the statuette depicted a man in the process of drowning with a millstone tied to his neck. The priest had seen in the statue a suggestion or motivation for his own demise. Written in red permanent marker on the back of the statuette were the words, "I'm sorry. God be merciful to me a sinner." Thus passed from this life Rodolfo Antonio Donati, formerly a parish priest, whose name was also included on the rolls of the damned.

It had been a very messy time. The anger was nowhere near subsiding. Whole segments of investigative operations were ramping up in country after country. Banking records were being subpoenaed. The Pope himself could not leave Vatican City for fear of being apprehended and either questioned or even possibly imprisoned based on the level of knowledge he was presumed to have on much of the goings on. It would take years to unravel the tangled web of corruption.

Two weeks ago, Nicola had driven Tina to a convent in the southern tip of the country. She was in no state to drive herself. For the previous several weeks, she had endured the knowledge of her sister's existence without being able to act on that knowledge while the operation was wound down.

Father Donati had spared his own life that day by telling Nicola that for some reason, after he was finished with her, he could not bring himself to kill the little girl in the yellow coat. Inexplicably, he had drugged her and hidden her until he could secure his own release with the local police. His connections had enabled him to walk free. Twice he determined to get rid of her, but each time was kept back from it. In the end, he had changed her clothing, put a scarf over her head and driven her to the South of Italy, where he knew the Mother Superior of a convent. On the way, he had drilled into the young child that he knew where her sister and parents lived. If she ever told anyone what had happened, he would kill her sister and parents in the most awful of ways.

The frightened child had been left in the care of the convent whose leaders were told that she was suddenly orphaned. For years, Davina had lived the life of a ward, a novitiate and then eventually a nun. Her memory had repressed much of what had happened to her. But she always knew that she had a family somewhere. She was simply too afraid that speaking out would bring them harm.

On the day that they arrived, Nicola had introduced himself with his official identification and asked if there were a nun by the name of Davina. He was not sure of what her last name would be. (Many orphans were known only by their first name.) The current Mother Superior said that there was a nun by that name. Nicola asked for a private interview room, whereupon the Mother Superior showed them to a secluded meeting room in the office complex and left to fetch the nun.

A few minutes later, a timid knock sounded on the door, and it opened to reveal a young woman with a pleasant expression but sad eyes. She looked at Nicola first and then to Tina. When their eyes locked on one another, the back of Tina's hand flew to her mouth as she gasped, "Davina." Hearing her name and Tina's voice, Davina swooned and would have collapsed had Nicola not hastened to catch her.

When she revived again, Davina reached out a trembling hand and placed it upon Tina's cheek. "Sister?" she asked. "You didn't forget me? You found me?"

There was an effusion of tears as they fell into each other's arms. For Nicola, it was too sacred a moment to intrude upon any longer. As he left the room, he looked back for just one more moment. Tina's heart was breaking into many, many pieces. Rather, the granite casing around it was breaking. The tune of a hymn came to his mind, and he began humming it as he ever so quietly closed the door.

Later, Tina had the joy of reuniting Davina with her parents. She was staying with them at the moment. The bogeyman of her nightmares was dead. Freedom from that fear was sweet, but it was still very new and fragile.

Now, here at the sea, as he looked over at Tina's face, partially obscured by a hat, Nicola found himself humming the tune again. He began to softly sing the words.

Almighty Father, who dost give
The gift of life to all who live,
Look down on all earth's sin and strife,
And lift us to a nobler life.

He paused. Tina spoke softly to him, "That's beautiful, Nicola. Please don't stop."

He began to sing again.

> Lift up our hearts, O King of kings,
> To brighter hopes and kindlier things;
> To visions of a larger good,
> And holier dreams of brotherhood.
>
> Thy world is weary of its pain;
> Of selfish greed and fruitless gain;
> Of tarnished honor, falsely strong,
> And all its ancient deeds of wrong.
>
> Hear Thou the prayer Thy servants pray,
> Uprising from all lands today,
> And o'er the vanquished powers of sin,
> O bring Thy great salvation in.

He had watched her as he sang to her. Tina was crying. Nicola sighed a deep sigh.

"God heard your prayer, you know, the one you prayed that day."

"I know," Tina said between sniffles. "I've been so angry. And all along God had answered that prayer. I don't know why. Not everyone gets to see their sister again like I have."

"No. No, they don't."

"Nicola?"

"Yes, Tina."

"How did you know he was the one? When did you find out?"

"I began looking for him after you told me the story seven years ago. I found him two years later as we began planning the operation."

"So you've known all this time?

"Yes."

"Why didn't you tell me earlier?"

"Because the whole corrupt system had to be burned down in order to catch him. If you or I or anyone else had tried to move on him any earlier, he would have been protected just like before, and you would have lost your chance."

Tina was silent. She knew he was right.

"Did he just happen to be the one priest who was involved in this project to produce fake antiquities?"

"No." Nicola paused. "There were several others around the country. After we planted the suggestion, the Vatican had several choices in who to use. Donati was actually lower on the list. At my suggestion, our contact bumped his name up the list."

"So you picked him because of what I had told you about the man who had taken Davina?"

"Yes. I wanted you to have justice. But in the end, it was God who offered you a second chance at life."

They were silent for a spell. The wind blew across Nicola's face. He closed his eyes and savored the breeze. Here there was no subterfuge. For this moment in time, they were tasting a small portion of Eden. Finally, Tina spoke again.

"Nicola?"

He looked down at her again. He could see just under the edge of her hat. Her eyes were closed.

"Yes, Tina?"

"Why did you do all of that for me?"

"Because I love you, Tina."

Tina's chest rose and fell as she breathed a sigh. A smile formed on her lips.

"I thought so," she said.

Nicola smiled and closed his eyes again.

Epilogue

Coastal Italy

The Don sat in his leather club chair, calmly enjoying the view out the window of his villa overlooking the sea. In one hand he held a hand-rolled cigar. In the other, he held a carnation.

Ever since he had taken over the organization, he had received at least one phone call per year from a man with a refined accent and cultured voice. The first time he called, the Don had been resistant to the idea of listening to the man's suggestions about how to conduct his business. Within a week's time, an exquisitely carved dagger had been placed on his desk. Past thorns, dogs, guards and cameras it had appeared. No one knew how it got there. All the recordings had nothing. The man called back a day later. Was the Don willing to listen?

Every year since, he would enter his study at some point and find upon his desk a single red carnation. Whether or not the man who called him cared about flowers, the Don knew what a red flower meant. It meant life. It meant he had pleased someone. Last year, on the heels of Aldo's apparent betrayal, the carnation had been pink.

This morning, he had entered the room to find a single white carnation on the center of his desk. As he reflected on the past years, he thought about the fact that the man with the cultured voice had never asked for money. Apparently, he had no need of it. Nor had he asked for a piece of the action. What was apparently most important was that the Don's organization ensured that certain tasks were handled. The mere fact of their ability to produce the desired results was helping the man's own organization at a higher level.

The biggest way the Don had failed over the past year was in the complete destruction of the doll business. First, Aldo had been taken out. Then Giacobbe, once seen as a future leader in training, was rotting in jail. There were no more shipments scheduled because there was no one alive or free who was capable of handling them.

Narcotics? They had barely been touched. But he was caught in a war between those who wanted to buy and sell children and those who wanted to save them. Maybe he should have just stuck with the drugs. What could they possibly want with so many kids anyway?

The door to his study opened just wide enough for Antonio to peer around the iron-banded wooden frame. "He's here, sir," he announced.

The Don glanced across the room to Antonio's face. "Show him in," he said.

The door opened wider as Antonio allowed a man with Slavic features and pockmarked skin to enter. He strode across the room and shook the Don's hand heartily.

"Is good to see you again," he said in a heavy accent.

"You have news?"

"Yes. We looked at everything. All the computers we checked are compromised. The laptop and phone you gave me from your problem one year ago, they have what is called a Trojan horse. You're familiar with the story, I am sure."

The Don nodded.

"You say that your man bought the software in Sophia. We are not so sure about that."

"Why do you say that?" asked the Don.

"This software, is very good. It looks like the command and control software you described. But really, it is filled with backdoors."

"Couldn't he have just purchased bad software?"

"No, we do not think so. This software has a signature, as they say, which is similar to other programs we have seen developed by Western governments. And this hacker group you say he bought it from, they do not exist."

"What do you mean? I sent men to verify the story."

"There is no one there, my friend. Believe me, we know the hackers in Sophia. The good ones were trained by us. Most of them still do work for us. No one knows of your mystery woman selling such software."

So Aldo had been set up. They had all been set up. The Don thought of one more question.

"This software on Aldo's laptop and phone, what does that mean?"

"It means that someone was privy to all of his communications for two, maybe three years. Everyone he contacted, their phones are probably all tapped. The network of people he spoke with are probably all under surveillance. Probably Interpol."

"Thank you for coming," said the Don.

"We had discussed a fee," said the man.

"It will be paid per the usual method."

"Thank you. Always a pleasure to do business with you," said the man as he got up from the chair and walked to the door.

Antonio opened it for him and closed it behind them both as he escorted the man back to his vehicle.

The Don took another puff from his cigar. Aldo had sworn on his mother's grave that he was loyal. He may have been loyal, but someone was smarter than all of them. It had cost Aldo his life.

He looked at the white flower in his hand and raised it to his nostrils. He drew in a deep breath and exhaled. All carnations normally smelled the same to him regardless of color. This one smelled too much like death.

Acknowledgments

A book such as this does not happen overnight. First, I would like to thank my wife and family for their patience as I spent time researching and writing the manuscript.

To my editor, David Thompson, I greatly appreciate your expertise and the excellence you demonstrated in the many corrections and comments you made on the original manuscript. You made me recognize several of my own shortcomings in the manuscript, and you also encouraged me by highlighting some of my successes throughout the story. Any remaining errors are my own.

If you were appalled by the plight of the Chinese Uighur girls who were trafficked in this book, I encourage you to begin your own research on the topic of global human trafficking or the persecution at the hands of the Chinese Communist Party of both Muslim and Christian religious adherents. Yes, traffickers do use shipping containers and many other methods to move human beings around the globe in a modern-day slavery system. It is estimated that eight million children go missing each year worldwide. Eight million. Ask yourself who pays for them and why they buy children.

To the countless men and women and even the boys and girls who care enough about their communities to expose injustice and bring to light the dark and hidden secrets of the corrupt people in the media, government, industry, education or the towers of religion, I salute you and applaud you. Please, do stay safe.

Finally, I want to express my gratitude to my Creator and best Friend, Jesus Christ. The fact that I am getting to write books is a lifelong dream He has fulfilled. Some of the weird, freaky or supernatural events described in this book come from the realm of happenings I have either experienced personally or have heard about in numerous stories from friends through the years. I hope this book makes thinking about and believing in God more plausible to you.

Comments

Did you enjoy this book? If so, we would really enjoy hearing from you. To share a comment on this book or a story about how it helped you, send us a note at:

colossusbook@walkwithgod.com

Please visit us on the Internet at https://thompsonpublishers.com where you can find more resources.

Errata

A list of corrected errata is maintained at:

https://www.thompsonpublishers.com/colossusbook

The publisher requests that any additional errata be sent via the form on that page.

Made in the USA
Las Vegas, NV
29 November 2020